For my husband, Corey —
Who accepts my scars and bears my burdens.
With a gratitude beyond words for believing in my dreams.
I love you.

Pronunciations

Character Names

- NATYLIA — *Nat-ill-ee-uh*
- CAMION — *Cam-ee-on*
- MERYN — *Mare-in*
- PALINA — *Puh-leen-uh*
- AUDRI — *Aw-dree*
- PHELIX — *Fee-licks*
- DEVLYN — *Dev-lin*
- WULFRIC — *Wool-frick*
- VALERIA — *Va-lair-ee-uh*
- CYRUS — *Sigh-russ*
- RAUL — *Ra-ool*
- ANDIMIR — *And-uh-meer*
- AILUROS — *Eye-lur-ose*
- CALLITHYIA — *Cuh-lith-ee-uh*
- SYLVR — *Silver*
- HELYNA — *Hel-een-uh*
- FETIAN — *Fet-ee-in*
- MARIUS — *Mar-ee-us*
- KALÏA — *Call-ee-uh*
- SÓLAYA — *So-lay-uh*

Elven Names

- Vaalyjyn Ayamere Herenyur (Jyn) — *Vall-uh-jin Aye-uh-meer Her-en-yur*
- Myrdin — *Meer-din*
- Lytheria — *Lith-air-ee-uh*
- Eárynspieir Tikari Myriani (Eáryn) — *A-ryn-spire Tik-are-ee Meer-e-ah-nee*
- Izoryian Darcassyn Esteilar — *Is-or-ee-an Dar-cass-in Es-teal-ar*
- Afemriel — *Uh-fem-ree-uhl*
- Faeryndûil (Faeryn) — *Fae-rin-doo-ill*
- Luthaís — *Loo-th-eye*
- Myriil — *Meer-ill*
- Pháendar — *Fae-en-dar*
- Rymäthil — *Rim-uh-th-ill*
- Saélihn — *Say-lin*
- Andáerhyn (Rhyn) — *An-day-rin*
- Duröthyn — *Dur-oh-th-in*
- Hárivä — *Hay-riv-uh*

Race & Creature Names

- Numyra — *New-meer-uh*
- Skyva — *Sk-iv-uh*
- Zylarra — *Zil-are-uh*
- Nyoka — *Knee-oh-kuh*
- Kotsani — *Coats-on-ee*
- Cavia — *Caw-vee-uh*
- Ercine — *Er-sign*
- Marawolves — *Mar-uh-wolves*
- Nereid — *Nee-ree-uh-d*

Location Names

- ARAENNA — *Are-a-nuh*
- THRAIS — *Th-race*
- WYDUS — *Why-dus*
- KALUM — *Cal-um*
- FALMAR — *Fall-mar*
- HEXRYN — *Hex-rin*
- SAHRI DESERT — *Saw-ri Desert*
- EMBERLYN FOREST — *Ember-lin Forest*
- EYTHERA — *Ith-er-uh*
- PHERYN LAKE — *Fair-in Lake*
- LAKE MYRIA — *Lake Meer-ee-uh*
- MORLAND — *Moor-land*
- VITIC — *Vit-ick*
- MT. CERBIUS — *Mount Serb-ee-us*
- BORLAN SEA — *Bore-lyn Sea*
- COROTHEAN BAY — *Core-o-the-an Bay*
- DALBRAN — *Doll-bran*
- EMERYN MARSH — *Em-er-in Marsh*
- SERYN — *Sare-in*
- ARNETH — *Are-nith*
- EMERA — *Em-air-uh*
- LYTALIAN — *Lit-all-ee-an*
- MENDLYN — *Mend-lyn*
- EVENLEA — *Evan-lee*
- SAPHIR LAKE — *Saf-ear Lake*
- EDRA — *Ed-ra*
- TWILOSE FOREST — *Tw-eye-low-se Forest*
- AREN MINES — *Air-in Mines*

Glossary of Titans

First and Second Generations

- NAHARA — *Nuh-har-uh*
  Leader of the Ancients
  Primary magic: Fire

- VALDIS — *Vall-dee-s*
  Ancient of the Nether
  Primary magic: Darkness/Shadow
  Father of Thanatos

- DRAVEN — *Dray-vin*
  Ancient of Chaos
  Primary magic: Lightning
  Mother of Thanatos

- ALVAR — *All-var*
  Ancient of Guardianship
  Primary magic: Fire

- USHRIYA — *You-sh-ree-uh*
  Ancient of Luck
  Primary magic: Fortune Manipulation
  Mother of Cybele

- JURIS — *Jur-es*
Ancient of Earth
Primary magic: Earth
Father of Cybele

- MARINUS — *Mare-in-us*
Ancient of Water and Coastal Weather
Primary magic: Water
Father of Eurybia

- CELESTYNA — *Sil-es-tee-nuh*
Ancient of Sun, Moon, and Seasons
Primary magic: Weathers
Mother of Eurybia

- AURIAL — *Aw-ree-ul*
Ancient of Air
Primary magic: Light and Air
Mother of Boreas

- CARU — *Car-oo*
Ancient of Love
Primary magic: Emotional Manipulation
Father of Boreas

- BERIT — *Bear-et*
Ancient of Prophecy
Primary magic: Prophetic

Third Generation Titans

(Third Generation Titans are considered children, and as such the humans do not worship them as Ancient ones.)

- EURYBIA — *Yew-rib-ee-uh*
Primary element: Water
Daughter of Marinus and Celestyna

- CYBELE — *Sib-uh-lee*
Primary element: Earth
Daughter of Juris and Ushriya

- BOREAS — *Bor-ee-us*
Primary element: Light
Son of Aurial and Caru

- THANATOS — *Th-an-at-ose*
Primary element: Disease
Son of Valdis and Draven

Chapter 1

"Hello, Natylia."

His words echoed in my mind. Over and over. They were almost as painful as the betrayal itself.

My eyes fell to the stone floor beneath me, to a scrap of blanket left only to taunt me. Any hope I held of escape or release dwindled with each passing minute, and the longer I was trapped, the more I realized how deep the hurt truly ran.

Drask.

King of Wydus, father of Prince Lucian, and a man I had once considered a second father.

Now I couldn't even look into those yellow-flecked hazel eyes without the sting of old memories rising to the surface. My captor was not the man I had known.

I tugged at the thick shackles tight around my wrists. Yanked on the chains that wouldn't relent even a little. My magic didn't respond, beyond the slight warmth of the gryphon pendant at my throat—a gift, from the Elf, Luthaís, when we visited the Elven city of Eythera. The green goldstone necklace frustrated Drask to no end; no magic could remove the cord, no other hands or blades. Only I could loosen the knot.

Not that the pendant was any help here. The charm was meant to act as a damper on my powers so I didn't accidentally spill all my life essence into a spell, as my arcane abilities could require. The little gryphon was supposed to stop me.

But I couldn't seem to access my abilities, and I wondered if there was a spell or curse on these chains or in this room to prevent me from using my powers. Drask might have wanted a failsafe: either so I couldn't escape or in case I decided to end everything.

I had considered both.

Drask wouldn't confirm if he had my friends, wouldn't tell me if any of them were alive. Instead, I got a sly smirk, a wink, an assurance that if I used my magic—to his benefit—I could rejoin them. One simple act. A little magic.

All I had to do was combine the Imber, Tellus, and Ventus Scepters. He wanted me to form the Stave of Thanatos and release the final Titan, the Stave's namesake, to join his siblings under the leadership of Valdis—the second most powerful Titan to have ever lived. All to destroy humankind.

Potentially all Araenna.

Of course, he needed the magic in my blood to do this. Myrdin's magic, the Elf who helped fuse the Scepters into a Stave in the first place. I didn't want to help Drask, and if he was going to kill my friends regardless, well . . . why fight him at all?

Giving up seemed easier, if there was no one left waiting.

Despite the thoughts that filled my mind, I didn't relent. Not when there was a slim chance that Jyn and Andimir had escaped into the forest and, if they had, the Titan, Boreas, and the Vampyr, Valeria, hadn't managed to stop them. Valeria was now grieving the death of her brother, Cyrus. I hoped the loss would slow her down, as cold as the words sounded. I resisted Drask on the belief that Meryn was safely in Thrais, far from the danger I now sat in, and that my sister might yet live.

On those hopes alone, I withheld my powers.

The door to my cell creaked open and Cybele—the earth Titan previously locked away by the Tellus Scepter—strolled in, a wicked smile spread across her face. She was in the same style of clothing she wore everyday: brown leather, the bottoms cut too high, and the top a sharp vee over her exposed stomach. Bits of metal curved along the edges, more of an accent than a guard. Overconfident, if I had ever seen it. She prowled closer, my eyes drawn to the whip hooked at her waist. My jaw clenched. So today was to be one of *those* days.

"You look tired," Cybele crooned. She leaned close. Too close. The scent of leather flooded my nose, blended with the flowers woven into her long, mahogany colored hair. "I hope you don't black out too early. I'd have to find another toy to play with."

"If you touch anyone I've even met in *passing*, I will slit your throat the moment I'm free," I snarled.

The Titan grinned, an eyebrow lifting in amusement. "Let's get you situated. I can't very well do my work properly like this."

I lashed out at her as much as I could; my feet and hands were heavy from the chains and shackles, and she nimbly slipped around my attacks, clicking her tongue.

"Seems you still have a touch too much fight left." She shrugged. "I know how to fix that."

Her grin returned. She unfastened the chains on my feet, then my hands and, with such swift movements, I nearly fell. Her calloused fingers gripped my chin before my knees hit the floor. I fought to land a blow on her, but she merely held me at arm's length. She knew I didn't have the strength to truly resist.

"Why must you always be so difficult about this?"

I didn't answer. Cybele didn't care. She had already set to work, nimbly tightening my constraints to new hooks in the center of the room, and so tightly fastened, all I could do was stand. Even turning to frown at her was painful. She twisted the bolts on my cuffs, as if to ensure they were secure. But delight danced in her eyes as the cold steel bit into my skin and crimson trickled down my hands. Cybele had instructions not to kill me; I had heard Drask give the order.

Torture wasn't part of their deal.

"Now then." Cybele stepped in front of me, tugging the whip free of her belt. "Drask is busy today. If you agree to use your magic on the Scepters, I'll go get him." She leaned in close, her breath a soft whisper over my cheek. "But since I doubt that will happen, I think I'm going to enjoy myself instead."

I gritted my teeth and stared at the wall in front of me, trying to ignore her entirely. Leather brushed stone as she dragged the whip across the ground. Then she waited. I knew the routine. Adrenaline spiked into my veins, and I also knew she sensed it. A trained hunter, playing with her kill instead of offering a clean death.

though, because she didn't deserve to see how deeply my suffering ran. Cybele's expression filled with loathing at the sight. Then she slammed me against the wall for good measure before stalking from the room. The door banged shut; the grating sound echoed off the stone walls and screeched in my ears.

I took the chance to pray then, whispering pleading words for my family to stay safe, alive. I didn't know who I was praying to. Knowing that one of my closest friends was Nahara made the idea of begging her for aid seem . . . graceless. But I still said the words. Habit, maybe.

Over and over I prayed, without fail. An echo in my mind, a plea drowned in the darkness.

Please let them be alive. Let them be safe.

Some days I offered up prayers for rescue.

Or to be executed.

How my story ended didn't really matter.

Footsteps sounded down the stone hallway, echoing around whatever kind of Nether-cursed dungeon I was trapped in. We weren't anywhere I had seen before, and there was only one prison I could imagine to be this cold—one high in the north.

Silence fell outside my door. A click of the lock, a soft wooden groan, and hazel eyes met mine. They held an icy disregard that I was still unused to seeing. For a moment he simply stood, watching me, Cybele creeping toward my cell in his shadow. Then Drask turned and latched the door shut, closing out the Titan behind him, as well as the stone wall that was all I knew of the building beyond this room.

I was surrounded by stone. Cold, endless, unfeeling stone.

Drask raked his fingers through his chestnut brown hair, the match to his son's, but in small piles of curls. His gaze slipped over my body: the thin clothing, the bloodstains, my frail, unstable form. I wasn't sure how long I had been in this cell, but even I could see the effects his meager rations were having—when I received them. Letting Cybele visit wasn't helping anything either.

"Natylia," he said, his voice dripping with the honeyed tones he used when proposing business. "You could put an end to all of this. You could go free, instead of letting Cybele torment you every day."

"Long enough to fuel the Stave and die trying, you mean."

The corners of his mouth tilted down at the bite in my voice. "Is that any way to treat your elder?"

"Given the circumstances, yes."

My captor sighed, steepling his fingers together. "Seems that Sahrian you insist on dragging around has worn off on you."

Fury blazed through me at that, at the dirty Elven slur I knew would set Jyn's blood boiling. A twitch of Drask's lips and my anger fizzled out. He knew I desperately wanted news of Jyn—and he used the knowledge against me as often as he could. I bit my tongue.

Drask paced the room, inching closer to me with every pass.

"Nothing to say, *Natylia?*" he emphasized my name, the disrespect clear in his dismissal of my title. He was impatient today.

"Nothing," I muttered.

"Come now," he cooed, the sound vile in my ears. "Are our kingdoms not allies? Will Thrais not aid Wydus, in our time of . . . *need?*"

Those gold-flecked eyes crinkled at the corners, glittering with amusement. I was momentarily angry with myself, that I had ever considered this man family. I had cared for him once. And now . . .

Now he could burn.

He was meticulous in concealing my presence here, wherever "here" was. I had asked after his wife, Kathryn, as well as Lucian, but he said they were completely unaware of my presence. They had been dragged into his ruse and followed his lead as he publicly feigned concern while planting stories of how my group was spotted in the far south. Kalum was important in this, because he needed to say I was spurning the help of Wydus in light of Lucian's inappropriate behavior.

Or so he told me as he circled my cell in the days prior.

Drask could be lying, of course. Lucian could know and simply not care after how I had treated him last. Deep in my soul, I wanted to believe he cared for me more than that. His heart still held kindness; I saw it in his hesitation and the way he seemed genuinely worried when I vanished.

But then, look who his father is.

A hum fell from Drask's lips at my silence. His frown deepened. "Shall I assume your answer remains no, then?" I pressed my lips together, staring at the wall behind him. He shrugged. "Well, thankfully I had a feeling you'd continue to resist. I made some arrangements—brought you a new neighbor. Let's start with a small taste. Then you can decide how we'll proceed."

He strolled to the door. Then, as if I would change my mind, he glanced in my direction. When I didn't move, he lifted a shoulder and tugged open the door. "Have things your way."

"Cybele," he called down the hall, "could you bring our friend down here? Do be gentle, we need him in one piece. For the moment."

My gut twisted, the thunder of my heartbeat painful in my ears.

Breathing was impossible.

I think I stopped entirely when Cybele entered the room, throwing their prisoner to the floor.

And when those blue and green eyes met mine, my heart clenched, shattered, crumbled. An invisible fist squeezed down on my chest—harder, tighter—and my eyes burned with tears that wouldn't fall.

"Let him go," I growled in a voice that was barely more than a rasp.

Drask spun, expression gleeful. My stomach churned at the sight, sickened by the joy he took in causing me pain.

"Is something wrong, Natylia?" He grinned. "What? You didn't think I could possibly dispose of such a useful prisoner so quickly?"

Cybele landed a hard blow to Camion's ribs. He winced, silent behind the gag tied around his mouth. He was thin . . . so thin. A blue-black bruise circled his right eye and a slashing cut trailed down his left cheek. His skin was marred by evidence of Cybele's torture; for fun, I realized, or simply to parade him in front of me like a wild, prized animal they had caught. Camion met my worried stare. I held it, willing him without words to know all the things I wanted to say.

"Release him," I demanded between gritted teeth.

Drask chuckled at the crack in my voice. "I don't think so."

"Why? Why him? Because I scorned Lucian for him?"

"Marrying Lucian would have made all of this much easier.

I could have siphoned your magic over time, or feigned interest in training you." Drask paused, but I refused to look away from the bald fear in Camion's eyes. Cybele knelt beside him, twirling a dagger, and Camion's expression faded into blank indifference. Drask circled between the three of us, then continued. "I have no mind for petty dramatics, Natylia. If I had been given a choice between your blacksmith and the Sahrian, I would have picked the Sahrian, but well . . . Unfortunately for them both, this one has an ingredient I need. Thankfully, my pathetic excuse for a son has no clue you two are down here. The last thing I need is for that sorry spawn of mine to play hero."

I tried to keep the confusion from my face. What did Camion have that Drask might want? Fear was a slithering presence that curled around my chest. If Camion was in any way a component to freeing the Titans, Drask wasn't going to spare him.

Still. I had to try.

"Let him go." I broke Camion's stare long enough to meet Drask's eyes. "Please," I whispered.

Everyone in that room heard the desperation in that final word. Groveling for Camion's life was easy. I had long ago accepted that magic and sacrifices were my destiny. I would give anything. Everything.

Short of using my magic . . .

Drask strolled closer, until his nose was mere inches from my own.

Chains rattled throughout the room as Camion thrashed against Cybele's hold. She pressed the point of her blade into his throat and he stilled.

Drask grinned. His breath brushed over my face, but I refused to break his hard stare. "Understand this, Natylia. I need something from you. I daresay you now understand that you need something from me. Use your magic and you both go free." He smirked, tilting his head. "Maybe you could even manage to stop us from wiping out your pathetic race. Doubtful, but you certainly can't do anything from in here."

Cybele cackled with glee, her blade drawing beads of blood from Camion's neck.

"You could at least spare him from Cybele's . . . fun." Drask shrugged. "Cybele, let's see if your friend has anything of interest to say."

She jerked the gag away from Camion's mouth and he scanned my face, my body, as he said, "Don't you quit fighting. Don't you stop. And don't you dare use your magic. You—"

Cybele jammed the gag back into his mouth with a frown. His jaw flexed but I nodded sharply.

"Well then. Seems he's as dull as I imagined he would be." Drask sighed. "Take him away."

No, no, no . . .

I didn't recognize the words coming from my lips. Offers, pleas—maybe both. Drask paid them no mind. They weren't what he wanted to hear. But I kept trying.

Cybele dragged Camion from the room, even as he fought, even as he cast another look my way. The crumbled pieces of my heart scattered to the wind.

Drask spun on his heel and was halfway across the room before I said, "Answer a question for me." His eyebrow raised, amused this time, but he gestured me on. "How long have you been parading around as a friend to my family, with plans to betray us? What will helping the Titans do for you?"

"That's two questions, little queen." Drask drew a thumb across his chin, then said. "But I'll humor you." He crossed his arms over his chest. "There wasn't a moment I didn't know I was going to betray you all, not as long as you've lived. And as to your second question . . . everything."

"Don't you already *have* everything?" I snapped, anger rising again. Torture, hunger, exhaustion . . . and that look on Camion's face, that fear. I couldn't seem to stop myself as I blurted, "You have an incredible family, a beautiful home, what more could you want? What could Valdis possibly have offered you?"

Drask's grin spread wide then. He moved closer again, brushing a piece of hair from my face. "Oh, you naive little girl. My family, my only true family, is buried because of those filthy Sahrians and their stupid human allies." His breath was warm against my cheek when he spoke again. This time I flinched, rattling my chains as I tried to back away from the malice in his smile.

"I *am* Valdis."

Chapter 2

Camion's cries of pain jarred me awake every time I closed my eyes. I couldn't determine if the sounds were real, or echoes that played in my dreams.

Cybele's visits to me had ceased, and I hated that her attention had shifted to Camion. Drask had been using him against me for at least a week—I only knew because he visited once a day, what I guessed to be around morning, and then not again until the next day.

The same request: use my magic, end Camion's suffering.

When I refused, Camion paid.

Again.

And again.

I begged Drask, every morning, to let me see Camion again. Only for a minute. He always replied that I could see him as long as I liked—if I used my magic.

Images clogged my mind. I hadn't heard the whip yet, but there were other ways.

Cybele favored knives and flame and that nasty axe she carried on her hip. She threatened other methods too, worse methods that I hadn't fallen victim to. Yet. Maybe Drask worried they were too much for his "investment." But he didn't care if Camion lived. And the thought of that beautiful man, that bright, brilliant soul, being marred by such horrors . . . Camion had lived through so much already. The thought that he suffered even more because of me, because of my resistance, threatened to rip apart the chasms cracking to life under my skin—no matter what he had said to me last.

What were my last words to him? I couldn't even remember.

They should have been, "I love you." I should have opened my mouth when he was right there, in front of me, maybe for the last time.

The weight of my mistakes was a heavy burden.

I tried to shut off the emotions, to ignore them, and pretend them away. Camion would be disappointed if I broke—I knew he would. But grief and fear sank dark claws into my mind, ripping me open, the gaping wound exposing my heart so keenly I suspected Drask only had to reach out to steal it away.

And he could, I knew. He had my heart in chains and every second that ticked past was an eternity that pounded in my ears.

Hunger pains gnawed at me. Lack of sleep swirled my thoughts, made me question details. Reality became blurred. I managed the daily offering of water when the liquid was poured unceremoniously down my throat.

But listening to Camion's cries, his pain, for hours on end? I would be driven to madness like this.

Every day Cybele broke him a little faster. I knew what Camion could endure, what he had endured most of his life. Whatever was breaking him had to be truly horrendous.

I had never felt more helpless and weak.

Ending Araenna for the two of us was tempting, but it wasn't a reasonable option. If he endured, so could I.

In the meantime, I would try to form a plan for escape.

But his cries grew weaker. I found myself wishing he would die. The thought was morbid, and I hated myself a bit more each time the words crossed my mind. Not because I truly wanted such a thing. Losing him would shatter the piece of myself he had stolen away. His loss would carve out a chunk of my soul. But he was suffering and, even though I loved him, death would be kinder.

Because I loved him, death would be kinder.

Staring down at my thinning frame, at the bumps of bone pushing at my pale skin, I thought the same for myself. Weeks had to have passed.

If he died, I wouldn't be far behind. We could find each other again in the next life.

Valdis strolled into the room, interrupting my thoughts. Intention was clear on his face, his hands clasped behind his back. His clothing was splattered, and I tried not to stare at the dark stains for too long. He stepped closer, close enough that I could smell the cedar and snow on him—the blood.

"Feeling cooperative today, Natylia?"

I met his eyes unflinchingly. Even if I had wanted to argue with him, I didn't have the energy. He shrugged, as if expecting as much.

"Well. You've held out remarkably well, but since you don't

seem to care enough about Camion himself . . ." He paused for the words to sink into my skin. I kept my face neutral, even as fury raged beneath the surface. He smiled. "I guess we'll have to *encourage* you a bit more."

He pulled his hands from behind his back.

My heartbeat leaped into a frenzy.

His fingers were tight around the grip of a cat o' nine tails. Nine thin, vicious thongs dangled from the whip. Bile rose in my throat. He twisted the leather until it groaned and my skin recoiled in a shuddering spasm. I swallowed, acid burning all the way down. Then he spoke again.

"Oh no, Natylia, this isn't for you." He turned on his heel and my blood froze.

"Don't. Please don't. Not to him," I begged, my voice barely more than a dry bark. They had to have seen the scars on his back. Instead of feeling a shred of pity, they were going to use his past against *me*. This was wrong. So wrong. "Please. Hasn't he had enough?"

Valdis smiled, looping the whip around his hand. "You're still able to resist helping me, correct?" He paused, waited. But he knew I wouldn't answer, so he said, "Then no, he hasn't had enough."

Whips . . .

I couldn't submit him to whips. Not knowing the nightmares he still suffered. A warm weight pressed down on my chest, the gryphon charm heating slowly. My stomach lurched. A painful knot rose in my throat. Valdis's smile grew as he scanned my face, as he read the rage and sadness there.

"I'll take them," I said. "Please. I'll take the lashings in his place."

Valdis leaned against the door frame, as though he might humor me, then said, "That's too easy. You'll bear the pain, as you've done before, and resist helping me yet again. I need your magic. Torturing your man seems to be an easy way to accomplish this."

My shackles trembled with my arms, small jangles that shivered through the chains.

"Last chance."

"*Please*," I croaked.

He laughed.

Laughed—raucously and full of amusement. Then he was gone.

He didn't close the door behind him. Quiet conversation reached my ears, then a delighted female squirm. I couldn't breathe.

A crack shattered the silence.

And, with Camion's anguished cry, I heaved all the bile in my stomach onto that wretched scrap of blanket.

***

I jolted awake. Across the cell, the door sat open. The flicker of torches casted dancing figures across the dark stone. Night, then. I didn't find comfort in the fact.

Cybele had tortured him for hours. I had listened, helpless, crying tears that squeezed themselves from my eyes. His pain wasn't even the worst part. No. Worse was knowing that if he forced Camion to endure another day, I might not survive. I might be willing . . . I would . . .

Use your magic.

No.

He had fallen silent before I passed out from exhaustion. I didn't have much energy left to begin with and expending what I had on grief wasn't going to help anyone.

Not that I could help Camion.

Unless . . .

My head throbbed. *Enough.* Wallowing in self-pity was draining and counterproductive. I had been doing enough of that lately. I needed a real plan.

The pendant at my neck warmed. Luthaís had warned me, when she gave me the charm, that if I didn't use my magic there were risks. When my emotions spiked, the green goldstone would heat, then cool while gathering my magic inside.

Maybe the charm would burst and kill me.

Stop it.

I tested my powers, pushed toward the cuffs around my wrists. Nothing. I wasn't sure why I had expected anything different. Closing my eyes, I focused inward, pulling from the deep well of power that curled in my blood. I then tugged the glittering strands upward, toward my fingertips, all the way from my toes. But though my magic twisted through my veins easily enough, nothing happened. No warmth, no sparkling hope.

My head fell against the stone wall behind me, the rough peaks sharp against my scalp. Without magic, I was no one. "Queen" was a passable title and held no value here. The Titans didn't regard me as any kind of ruler.

Even Drask—Valdis—didn't respect me as such.

Chains rattled quietly down the hallway. I stood straighter.

Listened.

"Camion?" I called out. My throat was raw, the hoarse yell barely more than a raised voice. No response. Wind whistled sharply around me. A chill shivered all the way up my spine.

I didn't know what I had expected. I hadn't realized I had expected anything at all, until my heart fell into my stomach. If he heard me, he might not be able to respond. I slumped against the chains again.

Valdis had left the door open to lure me out and I had been baited.

Hook, line, and sinker.

Falling into a pit of darkness and allowing the quiet to envelope the feelings that threatened to swallow me whole would be easier than trying to unravel a way out of this mess. I would be safe in that little corner of my mind. Hope didn't exist in my darkness.

But . . .

If Camion were to have a chance—if *I* were to have a chance—I needed to let those emotions in. To face them and conquer them.

I needed my magic.

I spent a few minutes trying to dredge up my powers from wherever they had been hiding since arriving here. Early on, before I realized how truly unresponsive my powers were, I had spent days trying to pull forth my magic. But after so many days, I had given up . . . my life force was now at an all-time low. And I couldn't feed my powers on wishful thinking alone.

If giving my life would save Camion, though . . . It might already be too late. I tried not to think about that. Eyes closed, I focused on the pendant. Much of my magic swirled in there, heavy, laden, ready to be used. If I could get access to even a drop, I knew I could push part of myself down the hallway, as I had done in the Silverglass Forest when I needed to spy on the Cloaked Shadows. If I was able to see Camion, I could determine what condition he was in.

My breathing grew shallow. I didn't want to see what they had done, but I needed to. If he was too far gone, if I couldn't get him out of here, I needed to know. I had to form a plan, and whether I included him depended on how much I believed he could survive.

I wasn't going to use my powers for Valdis. But I would use them to escape this nightmare. I would use them for *us*. One way or another.

Shadows of despair curled around my mind, even as the pendant sat warm against my throat. The stone didn't cool, even when I released my hold on the threads of magic I couldn't find. Heat was welcome against the cold, but I didn't understand why the charm remained warm. Maybe the pendant knew I was dying. Maybe the enchantment intended to prevent magical burnout now blocked me from using my powers. I couldn't be sure, and I couldn't seem to make the stone respond.

Drask returned in the morning, his usual taunts and grotesquely small offering of water even more unbearable. He didn't seem to notice the warmth of the pendant as he held the glass to my lips. Nor did he seem any the wiser that I had spent the entire night trying to summon enough magic to break whatever enchantment or artifact held me in place.

When he turned on his heel and left, I started again. Pulling, digging. I tried to ignore the sounds from down the hall.

The crack of the whip, the celebratory sounds of Cybele enjoying every lash. My stone pendant heated so much I could no longer touch it and had to lean against my chains to move the stone off my skin. Hours passed, the sounds still echoing around the halls, louder through my open door. Still I tried to tune them out and focus only on magic.

When night deepened the shadows, and the torches were re-lit, silence fell. Almost an entire day of various forms of torture passed, and Cybele had finally taken a break. I felt like a monster. Like my own hands had administered the blows.

Then, through the quiet, there was a cry of pain—an agony not so different from the days before—followed by a sob. A choked, broken sound.

He had finally broken . . .

I could have stopped this. I could have saved him.

Pain lanced through my chest. My world splintered alongside his cries, obliterated into little pieces.

I should have saved him.

This wasn't my fault.

My mind grew quiet and I listened. He was in pain, worse pain than he had been when he looked at me with fear in his eyes. Raw, open fear. My limbs shook with the rage that coursed through me.

Enough.

I exploded.

Around me, the walls of the prison started to tremble. Jagged chunks began to cascade to the floor, bouncing harmlessly away. The gryphon glowed brighter, golden sparkling magic circling the stone—until the charm cracked.

Half fell to the floor, skittering away, but the half at my throat filled the room with magic, with blue and purple sparkles that coiled around my chains. I tugged on my restraints, gritting my teeth at the effort. The shackles burst into pieces and I choked back a bitter, angry laugh. Pain ripped up my left side, a scar I had nearly forgotten about, a token of my sacrifice in the Emeryn Marshes. A token that inflamed every time I used my magic.

I collapsed to the floor, limbs shaking. Shouts rang out from down the hallway, but I didn't give myself the chance to catch my breath. I leapt to my bare feet. My head spun but I stumbled forward over the shaking, uneven floor. The prison tilted and dropped. My magic swirled around me, and everywhere the blue and purple touched uncontrollable destruction spread. Walls crumbled. Biting cold slithered between the cracked stone, nipping at my exposed skin.

Every step was an effort, the muscles in my legs weak and uncoordinated, the stone floor cold on the soles of my feet. I gripped the walls for support, but my arms were barely stronger.

Still, I moved. If I stopped, I might not go again, and I needed to try. To push, to move into what might be the only window of freedom I had. My feet tripped awkwardly over the rubble. I threw my hand out and grabbed the wooden door, smooth and cool beneath my palm. As the hinges whined in protest, I shoved past, leveraging my unsteady weight against the door frame.

Pebbles rained into the hallway as the prison shuddered. I couldn't see the other end, the farthest torches now dark. A glint of metal caught my eye. I crept closer, jaw falling wide in disbelief.

The Scepters hung on the wall in silver brackets, locked in

tightly by the chains woven around them. He left them so casually? So unguarded?

Drask's mistake.

No.

My mistake.

As my magic coursed through the walls of the prison, purple and blue sparkles danced along every surface without regard to their destination—without discriminating against the Scepters chained to the stone now covered in the shimmers of my arcane magic. *Myrdin's* arcane magic.

He must have known that eventually I would try to escape . . . or maybe he knew more about the Elven pendants than he let on. Maybe he had simply bided his time. Whatever the case, I needed to get the Scepters away from him.

I reached for one, zapped by the chain immediately. I focused my magic into the links but the blue and purple rebounded. Then I looked closer. Each tiny piece of chain had engravings on it. Enchanted, not unguarded. I didn't have any idea what kind either, and I frowned.

"Don't move!"

I spun, eyeing the guards slowly closing in from the farthest end of the hall. I tried once more to grab the chain and failed. Each of the Scepter's stones began to glow with vigor, dancing to life beneath my magic, and the guard's eyes turned toward the glittering Scepters.

My palm lifted and I struck, sending all three men backwards, down, down, through the hallway and out the door there. A flick of my wrist slammed the door shut behind them.

The walls groaned and shook. My fingers trembled near the

chains, but I had to leave them. My only hope was to free Camion, and I needed to focus on that. Afterward, I would do whatever was necessary to ensure the prison collapsed and buried those Scepters alongside.

My heartbeat was a thunderous rhythm in my ears as I moved down the hall, closer to the nearest room. Five steps away. Four. I could smell the tang of iron, of blood, before I was two steps away.

His door was locked: a thin, sliding bit of metal that was so useless I could almost weep. Heavy chains and padlocks hung from the old wood, but Valdis was so certain Camion was unable to escape, he hadn't bothered with more. A chill raced the length of my spine. I threw open the door.

And fell to my knees.

The scene before me was more horrific than my mother's murder had been. Every wall was splattered with dried blood, the floor a splotchy blanket of dark crimson. A narrow channel circled a raised platform, a shallow moat of red fed by . . .

I almost couldn't bear to look.

Camion lay slumped on the ground, skin pale, heavy cuffs around his ankles and biting into the skin above his elbows. His shirt was gone, the pants he wore torn and stained with blood. Fresh lash marks covered his back. Cuts and burns lined his arms, some familiar, some dark and blotchy. He wasn't conscious, but his chest moved quickly in short, jagged breaths. His hand twitched, and the slight movement caught my eye.

Then I saw his wrist and the shallow slash draining slowly onto the floor.

I leaned against a wall, heaving until my stomach ached, until my eyes burned with tears they still couldn't cry. More shouting sounded down the hall and I moved, scrabbling on hands and knees over slick stone. I pressed my fingertips into the crook of his elbow, waiting until I felt his thundering heartbeat. His skin was clammy beneath my hands.

"Cam," I whispered, squeezing gently. The voices grew louder. Panic gripped my chest, but there was nothing, no answer. I couldn't move the chains. My magic wouldn't respond, drained to what the last half of the pendant would allow. I couldn't find so much as a tendril that wasn't already circling the room, and if I pushed too far, I would only strand us both.

I looked at him again, at the blood, sweat, and grime matted in his hair. His breathing worried me. Softly, I flipped his other wrist over and found a matching cut. They had drained him . . . drained him into that morbid, shallow moat circling us on all sides. An invisible fist clenched my heart. He would die if I didn't figure out what to do *now*. But he was in no shape to escape a collapsing building either. And I couldn't carry him.

"Camion, please," I pleaded, voice cracking. I knew the words were wasted effort but the panic building in my chest told me I had to try. Footsteps neared the door. I knew their rhythm far too well by now—Valdis. "Please, wake up."

Nothing. I needed a plan. I needed magic.

I needed *help*.

Those steps stopped. A soft chuckle reached my ears.

"Oh, Natylia," Valdis said. Then he was there, standing in the door frame, a smirk spread across his face. He clicked his tongue. "What have you done?"

Fear paralyzed me. I didn't know what to say, or do, or how

to keep him away from Camion. I couldn't save either of us, if he attacked. But he read the terror in my eyes and *laughed*.

"Are you trying to destroy yourself, or my prison?" A light sparkled in those eyes. "Or maybe you're simply trying to destroy the Scepters?"

He turned away. The rattle of chains echoed in the hall, the crashing sound of stone growing louder as the building shook beneath me. Valdis returned and waved the Scepters cheerfully.

"Don't worry, they're fine. And I dare say I got what I needed from this one as well." His grin grew as he drew a vial from his pocket. I shifted to the side, trying to conceal Camion from his view.

"Stay away from him," I spat, the fury in my voice barely more than a growl.

"Oh, I will," he purred. He leaned down to scoop blood into the clear glass, then stoppered it carefully before spinning on his heel. "Die quickly, would you? I have a funeral to plan."

My hands shook with anger, dancing with sparkling magic that circled my fist as though called to its master. Before I could consider the implications, I released the power, loosening the sparkling energy toward Valdis. Pain exploded through me; the scar at my ribs ignited with fury.

Stone quaked and clattered to the ground. The hallway began to collapse. Valdis had the sense to look concerned before the door frame gave way, becoming a pile of rubble that blocked the Titan from view. I hoped he was buried—and dead.

Camion's chains came loose at the ends as the long bolts holding them shook free by the trembling building. The floor cracked around us. I paused long enough to rip long strips from the bottom of my ragged dress and tightly wrap each of Camion's wrists.

But as the prison fell around us, I knew I didn't have the power to get us out. There were no exits from this room. No windows.

So, I curled up next to Camion and let the few tears I could manage slide free. I succumbed to the ache of using my magic and pressed all the warmth I had against Camion's chilled form.

"I love you," I whispered, clasping his hands between mine. Then I threw what power I could find into healing him, using every last drop of my magic until pain burned up my side and the world fell dark.

Until I failed, and let the world fall apart at the seams.

Chapter 3

A soft, cold kiss brushed over my nose.

No. Not a kiss.

Snowflakes.

I blinked hard, shaking away the crystalline forms that clung to my lashes. A solid weight pressed on my chest. Not heavy, not crushing. A distant caw shattered the silence. I reached out, trying to find Camion's hand. My palm met rough wool.

I shot upright. My head spun at the motion and I closed my eyes. Pain exploded across my back, a lightning pattern as the wounds there pulled and strained. Swallowing hard, I pressed my fingers into my temples to try to ease the nausea rolling over me in waves.

"Easy. Careful now," a voice said from nearby. "I barely managed to get you both out."

His voice was familiar, but I couldn't decide why the sound immediately set me on edge. I took another deep, steadying breath. Opened my eyes. Snow glared bright in my vision. I closed them again, blinking steadily until looking around was no longer painful.

Freshly fallen flakes lingered on my skin and across the blood-stained rags that were the flimsy dress I had been wearing for weeks. I glanced down at the cloak I sat on, one tossed haphazardly over a heavy blanket of snow. My fingers curled around the coarse fabric, confusion clouding my thoughts.

"It's the best I could do quickly. I can't linger much longer," the man said.

Recognition slammed into place and I spun. Stars scattered across my vision, but still I scrambled backward, palms sinking into the cold snow. My eyes shot to all sides, to the trees that surrounded us. I locked onto daisy-yellow eyes and my stomach lurched.

"Lucian." I tried to make my voice brave. The words fell flat instead, barely more than a croak against the chill wind and groaning trees.

He held up his hands in surrender. "I don't know the details. Guards went running from the palace and I followed. Most of the prison has collapsed . . . But I managed to find the two of you, barely alive in a pile of rubble. I did what I could."

Two of—I looked down, to the blanket-wrapped form that trembled at Lucian's knees, then I crawled the distance between us. My bare calves sank into the snow. I reached for Camion, but Lucian caught my wrist.

"He's in bad shape, Natylia. I may not care much for him, but he didn't deserve—" His words caught. He released me, gesturing at Camion. "I have so many questions, and I know this isn't the right time, but I have to know . . ." I looked up at the pause.

Waited. His throat bobbed, and he dropped my gaze. "Was my father involved in this?"

I wanted to say yes but the word stuck in my throat, reigniting an angry place in my heart. Without thought, I lifted my hands to Camion in front of me, gripping him for reassurance. He shook beneath my grasp and a fresh wave of pain lanced my heart.

A lock of chestnut hair had fallen onto Lucian's forehead. He met my eyes again and waited until I gave him a short nod to continue. "I bandaged as many wounds as I could and tried to prioritize the worst of them."

"I tried to help." My throat burned at the effort. My fingers tightened instinctively.

"I don't have water, but there's a cave nearby. If I can get you both to it, we can make a fire." He waited to see if I would respond before he said, "You might have saved his life with those wrist bindings. I can't be sure, he's not . . ." Another pause. "Father's been absent from the palace so much lately. Every time Mother or I asked, he said he was interrogating a prisoner. Because this prisoner had leads on you . . ." Lucian's voice was thick, and for the first time in a long time I saw the boy who cared instead of the jealous, entitled prince he had grown into.

"Thank you," I said after a moment. "For trying, at least."

"Mother will probably come looking for me, if I don't return soon. Given that I don't know what she knows, I don't want to lead her to you. I'll help you get to the cave, then I'll come back after nightfall. I can get you two away from here. But you have to get him real help, Natylia, and fast. We bought him time, but he's lost a lot of blood. I don't think his shivering is all from the cold."

I winced at the thought, but my own skin was freezing and the cloak I had been sitting on had grown damp. I had no means to help Camion like this. Panic rose in my chest, but I fought the emotion down, refusing to let it consume me.

"I can't believe Father—" A muscle ticked in his jaw and he cleared his throat. "The cave isn't far from here. The inside is dry, and we cleared out the beasts that lived there a while ago. When I come back, I'll try to bring more blankets, and some tonic."

Dry shelter was a solid start. If the cave was deep enough, I could build a fire easily; I could make a plan. The smoke was a risk but, as Camion shivered, I didn't see much choice.

I nodded my head. "How did you find us exactly?"

"Picking through the rubble. You have some kind of luck. Only three cells are left standing, mostly. I had to sneak you out before the guards circled in. A second trip for him, plus a pause to grab a blanket, almost got me caught." He paused. "I still haven't found my father, but I knew there was still time for you two. Or at least, I thought—"

"Let's get to this cave." I murmured, clambering awkwardly to my feet. I teetered, and gripped the bark of a tree to steady myself. A blast of frozen air bit into my exposed skin, tossing the edges of my thin, shredded dress.

Lucian frowned. "I can help you first."

"No. Help him." Even I heard the desperation in my voice.

He didn't hesitate, scooping Camion's limp form against his chest. I picked the cloak up off the snow, noting that Lucian lacked one of his own. I slung the garment around my shoulders, pulling the rough fabric tight as I followed, my eyes locked onto the man I loved. We had come farther than I anticipated. Camion couldn't die now. I wouldn't accept it. But I didn't know how to help him either, not with Drask—Valdis—on the warpath.

If the Titan survived.

I spared a glance over my shoulder. The prison was a fair distance away, no more than a pile of broken stone. Again, I found myself praying. To every Ancient, or deity, that might answer. Anyone.

Please. Let Valdis be dead, and the Scepters along with him.

A human would have died, I was certain. Camion and I *should* have died; I wasn't entirely sure how we had survived. My magic? But my untrained abilities were no match for a Titan, and a first generation Titan, one of the two strongest to ever have lived.

I choked on the thought, nearly tumbling into the snow. My feet were still unsteady, my limbs still weak from hunger and atrophy. I had to be careful. But my mind wouldn't stop, even as I tried to make my thoughts home in on each step I took.

Wydus was our closest option for help, but Lucian's home was no option at all; even he seemed to know it. Mentally, I scanned the map of the northern kingdoms. Wydus ruled over their own kingdom, alongside the cities of Vitic and Morland. Camion's face should be unrecognizable enough to find a healer. But there remained a small chance that, if we made our way to one of the two cities, we would be betrayed. Falmar was a safer option, and closer to Thrais, but equally far away from our current position—days travel at the peak of health, several more in our condition. I wasn't sure Camion even had so many days left, if we didn't get him help.

If the Council were still alive, I would travel to their manor in

Edra without a thought. But we could make faster time by traveling downriver from here, and our path would be unhindered by beasts and harder to track by most anything else. My thoughts raced. Camion wouldn't survive many of our options, and a hole was already beginning to form in my chest.

I refused to let him go so easily.

"Who holds Edra?" I asked.

Lucian paused, turning toward me and, after a moment, understanding dawned on his face. "Father had the place cleared but no one has been there for weeks. Not since the Council's deaths were made public. I wouldn't linger, but we might be able to use the manor temporarily. For supplies, if nothing else."

"We?" My eyebrow lifted.

"I said I'd help you."

"I didn't expect you to leave with us."

Lucian ducked under a branch, straightening as he said, "No, I know. But you two aren't in any condition to defend yourselves and I'm fairly concerned you're going to fall over at any moment."

"Thank you," I said softly. I didn't know what to think of the change. He certainly sensed the confusion, lifting a shoulder in response.

"Can you get us a boat?" My gaze dropped back to Camion. "Help me get him to the docks?"

For several long seconds, Lucian didn't answer. I thought, for a minute, that he might not. That his distaste for Camion might outweigh this burst of good conscience. Then he said, "I should be able to. But what if he—"

"I'll stabilize him." I interjected. I didn't want to hear the words he was about to say. "Somehow."

He didn't ask, merely turned and began trudging again through the snow. My feet ached with the cold, but I could warm them soon. I tugged at my magic, seeking any traces. Small glimmers of warmth brushed where I called, and I sent them down, into my toes and heels. They helped, but the caresses of heat vanished too soon, my side aching at the small magic use. I wondered vaguely if I would even be alive, if the pain from my side hadn't caused me to black out. The wound was a nuisance, but for once I considered the reminder a blessing in disguise. Only dregs of magic remained, though, and I wasn't sure if they would be enough to heal Camion. Especially when I felt as though I could sleep for an eternity. If I did that, Valdis would find us for sure, if not Valeria or another Titan. I couldn't let all of this effort go to waste.

Thinking of the remaining Shadow jarred me. "Where is Valeria?"

"The Cloaked Shadow?"

"Yes."

"She visited the palace a bit over a fortnight ago, but I heard a rumor she went south. And a whisper about the Elves . . ." Lucian hesitated. "But I heard this from Father and I'm not so sure how much truth he's given me lately."

More than a fortnight? We had been here . . . I took a deep breath, quelling the trembling fear that rose in my chest. As long as the Scepters were here, uncombined, there was still time. To . . .

To raise an army.

Anything.

I was trying to convince myself, but I had no real hope to

make me believe. And I still needed to tell Lucian who his father truly was.

"Have you heard any word of my sister?" Lucian shook his head, so I tried again. "Jyn? Meryn? Andimir?"

He shot a confused look over his shoulder. "No, not a word. My father has started some apparently false rumors about your whereabouts . . . to waylay panic. But I haven't heard anything about the others."

"Fine." I stared at the back of his head, at the snowflakes that clung and then faded. "Help us get out of here and I'll tell you everything I can. Everything I know."

"Deal. Though, I would have helped you regardless."

"I know."

His head dipped in acknowledgment, then jerked forward. "The cave."

A dark shadow sat ahead of us, tucked behind snow-laden trees. The top of the cave was only about my height, so Lucian had to duck to pass through. A branch cracked off to my right. I paused. Wind rustled through the trees, shaking snow to the forest floor. I didn't want to be out here alone, unarmed. I ducked into the cave. The ground tipped downward and my pulse jumped, racing to life as I struggled to catch my footing. I tested each step with my toes and rough stones pressed into my numb feet. After a hundred or so steps, a faint glow met my eyes. Bioluminescent plants began to litter the floor, to peek out of the walls. They reminded me of the ones we had seen in Emeryn Marsh, but these were paler. Smaller. I still welcomed their rainbow of light against the harsh darkness.

Lucian busied with settling Camion onto the ground. I itched to race to Camion, but I hesitated, wary, waiting for the other shoe to drop. Waiting for the sound I had heard in the forest to materialize and follow us inside.

Instead, Lucian stepped closer, pressing a flint and striker into my palm. Then he held out a dagger. "I'll be back after dark, and I'll find us a boat. I will get you two to Edra, but after that—"

"You've risked a lot helping us this far," I said quietly. "I won't forget."

His eyes dipped, then he said, "I'm sorry. For how I've behaved. And I'm sorry this happened, to both of you. Can you tend your own wounds at all? I would have helped you more, but I didn't have much to work with."

"My wounds aren't quite as fresh as his," I murmured. "I'm glad you helped him. Thank you."

Lucian nodded. "I'll bring water when I return, and food. Get him warm. The cold is making everything much worse." He paused. "I have to wait until the palace settles for the night, but as soon as I can leave without drawing attention, I will. I promise."

"Thank you."

He hesitated, like he was going to say more. But he didn't, moving past me to climb out of the cave and into the darkness. As soon as he was gone, I adjusted Camion until he was laid out on his stomach. Metal cuffs still clung to his arms and ankles, the remaining chain links marred with the indents of hurried blows. Each rise and fall of his chest sent a wave of relief through me, even though his breaths were ragged and uneven.

After pulling off my haphazard bandages, I made another attempt at healing his wrists. The magic I used on him in the prison had knitted the slashes together roughly—they still leaked, not totally sealed off, but Lucian was right. If he lived—*when* he lived—that little healing would be the reason why. Even if Lucian thought the bindings were to thank. I pulled up my magic, letting the blue and purple sparkles glitter from my fingertips to dance across Camion's skin. The cuts knitted together, slowly. So slowly. I didn't have enough strength for this yet, and the searing pain up my left side was a grueling reminder.

If I pressed harder, I would black out. And I needed to build a fire. I withdrew my power, then draped my cloak gently over Camion's back. His wounds there were unbearably fresh, new lines on top of lines that matched the marks he had already worn. My heart ached.

Fire. I need to build a fire.

His wounds could wait until I returned. If I didn't get him warm, our effort would all be wasted anyway, and he deserved more than that much. I plucked some of the bioluminescent plants, but they barely held a flame. A proper fire needed branches, and to get branches . . . I swallowed. Camion would be alone, unguarded.

Won't matter, if you don't get him warm.

I glanced at him again, at the way his body trembled and shook. Guilt swept over me once more and I piled more glowing leaves together. My fingers were unsteady as I struck the flint and striker together, waiting until a tiny fire flickered to life to creep back toward the mouth of the cave.

What I could see of the sky was grey and filled with soft puffs of white. I winced at the falling snow, almost regretting that I hadn't grabbed the cloak. Damp or no, Camion needed the heat more than I did right now. Every few moments I pulled up small bursts of magic, heating my skin for seconds at a time.

That didn't stop the sharp wind from tearing at my skin. I tried to listen over the sound of groaning trees and stumbled hesitantly out before darting to the nearest tree trunk. If anyone wanted to find me, I was sure they would. But if Camion needed a fire, a fire he would get, and I knew only one sure way to get that. So, I dug my fingers into the snow to pick out sticks, watching each hand transition from pink to deep red as the minutes passed. The bundle in the crook of my arm grew.

When I couldn't possibly carry any more, I returned to the cave. I built the fire up, hoping that the leaves would light the damp branches. My patience waned quickly after the first several failures, but finally the leaves caught enough to ignite a decent fire. Soft heat washed over me. Relief melted quickly into exhaustion.

I moved Camion closer to the flames and knelt beside him. He didn't stop shaking. His skin was still cool to the touch, his breaths still harsh and short. My heart clenched. I didn't know much about medicine, and my healing methods were remedial at best. Camion had lost so much blood . . .

He shifted, the first movement I had seen from him yet. I stroked his hair gently, almost too nervous to touch him. Irrational guilt was trying to convince me that this was my fault. That his wounds, his unconscious state . . .

You could have stopped this.

My fingers froze. I withdrew them and he moved again, only slightly.

"Camion?" I murmured. I wasn't surprised when I was met with silence. My gaze fell to the cloak draped across his back.

The fabric was clean, and though I could melt snow between my hands to clean his wounds, I wondered if the cold would do him more harm than good, not even accounting for the fact that my hands weren't the cleanest at the moment . . . I didn't want to risk infection. I tucked the cloak's edges under him, hoping that would be enough and he would warm up.

Then I held my hands above him, trying to pull up more magic. The pain was immediate, but I tried to push past, to heal him just a little bit more.

Shuffling sounds shook the glowing leaves nearby. I froze. My magic disappeared in a blink; my fingers curled around the dagger's hilt. Lucian had said they cleared the cave, but there was no telling what had moved in since. Another soft sound had my fingers tightening around the dagger. I blinked steadily, ignoring the wave of exhaustion threatening to pull me down.

A tiny, heart shaped face popped from the foliage, a bloodied animal gripped between its sharp teeth. I tilted my head to the side, confused, as a lithe silver body followed, a fluffy tail flicking behind. The Zylarra, from Emeryn Marsh, the one Izoryian had said was following us. She trailed us all the way here?

She waited?

"Why are you still here?" I asked gently. "Don't you want to go home?"

Dark eyes met mine, pointed ears turning as though she didn't quite hear the question. She moved closer, timidly, glancing toward Camion. Then she nudged the bloody rabbit closer. Whined. I frowned, further confused.

"Thank you, friend, but I don't think he can eat this right now."

The Zylarra insisted, nudging the meat closer. I stared at the puddle forming in the dirt. Meryn's words echoed fresh in my mind.

. . . a small animal would be acceptable. More often than not, a little blood will do the trick to activate the necessary magic . . .

"Oh," I whispered. "Oh, you brought me more magic? Thank you, little friend."

Her small silver ears flicked. She looked at Camion again. I took the hint, pressing my fingers reluctantly against the small animal. The flesh was still soft and warm under my touch. I winced, then focused, breathing in slowly. Lingering traces of life energy brushed against me, golden like that of the Elves, but weaker. A feather-light caress instead of a force of magic. I pulled what I could from the little corpse, enough to completely close Camion's wrists and a bit more. As I worked, the Zylarra laid down beside him, curling into his side, as careful and aware of his wounds as I was.

Exhaustion tugged at my eyes again.

If I slept, would he . . .

My eyes burned at the thought. I bit into my lip, closing my eyes when the copper tang of blood filled my mouth. His body shook; he was still unresponsive. If he passed in his sleep, it might be a kindness. But he was alive, and breathing, and I was willing to keep fighting for him as long as that held true. I refused to believe these might be my last moments with him, didn't want to confront the feelings those fears lit up.

Instead, I curled up beside him, trying to avoid agitating either of our wounds, but to also share body heat. I fought sleep, for several minutes, before I realized the only way either of us would survive was if I regained more of my magic. The thought carried me into sleep.

Chapter 4

Soft shuffles interrupted my sleep, followed by muttered curses. I shot upright, my vision swimming and fingers locked tightly around the hilt of the dagger Lucian had given me.

"Easy, Natylia. You're safe."

I scanned the cave. The Zylarra had fled, probably when the prince arrived. I met Lucian's yellow eyes over the faint glow of dying embers. He lifted his hands, two large satchels tight in his grip. "I have bandages and yarrow. I wasn't really sure what I needed, but I had to move fast, so . . ."

"They'll help," I said, nodding wearily. I knew we needed to move, but I wanted to curl up and sleep. My head dipped.

Lucian cleared his throat. "We have to go. As soon as I get both of you bandaged. If we don't, he won't survive."

His words were all the fire I needed. I rolled up to my knees, gently removing the blood-dappled cloak from Camion's back. Lucian passed me the supplies, but his eyes weren't on my hands as I cleaned the lash-marks.

"You didn't do anything for yourself," he said softly.

"How would I have?"

"Magic?"

I hesitated, glancing up. "How . . . how did you know—"

"I guessed," he admitted. "At first, I was fairly confused when his wrists were mostly healed under your bandaging. But then I remembered you saying your mother had magic. Nothing else made sense."

"Ah." I didn't know what else to say. Lucian knowing I had magic might complicate things. But when he waited expectantly, I added, "I can't afford to waste the magic on myself."

"Your life isn't a waste."

"I'm not dying," I clarified. As soon as the words left my lips, I froze. Then I hurried my pace, pushing my fear aside. *No.* Camion wasn't dying. I wouldn't let myself start thinking like that and I certainly wasn't going to let the prince, either.

"Can I at least take a look?" Lucian asked.

"We can worry about my wounds in Edra." I motioned for him to help Camion up, so I could wrap his chest and stomach. "Most of my injuries are scabbed over anyway."

"Most." Lucian's gaze fell to my wrists, where the shackle had torn into my skin. The raw marks glistened in the dim firelight.

"I'm fine," I grumbled.

My hands moved steadily, looping the soft cotton around Camion's chest, up around his shoulders, around and around until his wounds were as tightly bound as I dared. His head lolled onto his shoulder, his skin still cool beneath my fingers. In my mind, I knew he was more stable than he had been yesterday. I could feel his pulse, still too quick but more normal than before.

But I couldn't shake the fear that he was on the precipice of death, and my own heart thundered riotously against the idea. When I finished wrapping him, Lucian helped me slip a shirt over Camion's head, one of Lucian's own.

"Thank you."

The prince shrugged, digging into one of the satchels before he shoved a waterskin into my hands. "I didn't forget. I have food, too, though not much. Enough to get some weight in your stomach." His eyes turned to Camion. "If you can get him conscious, he needs to drink. And eat. He needs to start rebuilding the lost blood."

"I know."

I was secretly trying to steel my mind to the idea that he might not wake up.

Unacceptable.

My fingers fumbled over the waterskin cap. Lucian lowered Camion back to the ground, settling him gently before he packed up the excess bandages. I lifted the mouthpiece to my lips.

As soon as the cold water hit my tongue, words echoed through my mind.

"Easy, slow down . . . nothing will stay . . ."

Jyn.

He can't be dead, he can't be dead . . .

The sudden, painful ache that blossomed in my chest winded me. I gasped for air, the waterskin dropping to the dirt. Lucian jumped over Camion, grabbing the waterskin before all the liquid leaked out.

"Natylia?"

He reached for my arm, but I backed away, my bare legs brushing by the softly glowing plants around us. My eyes burned, though only a few tears managed to squeeze free. I swiped them away, backing up once more at Lucian's extended hand. My teeth pressed into my lip, against the wound that throbbed there, and I tasted metal. Lucian made to withdraw and I reached out, impulsively gripping his wrist before he could fully retreat.

"Tell me you haven't heard anything about Jyn. Please."

He stared, bewildered, at my trembling lips and watering eyes, then shook his head. "No. I promise you. Not a word."

His reassurance was no comfort to the tightness in my chest. Instead of trying to explain, I forced a breath and said, "We should go."

"I need to know what happened to you."

"We need to get to the docks," I said firmly.

"Please?"

Air returned to my lungs. Concern softened his voice, but Lucian had blown so hot and cold the last few months, I wasn't sure I trusted him. He had helped us this far, though. If he got us to Edra, I could fill him in. Completely.

"We had a deal. You still have to get us out of here."

"Nat, my dad locked you in our prison and lied about you for months. I need to know *something*."

I closed my eyes, taking a long slow breath before I said, "Your father wanted my magic. But please. I'll tell you more as soon as I can."

Lucian nodded reluctantly, and I saw the wheels turning in his mind, processing the small bit of information I had offered. He didn't press, though, when he saw my eyes locked on Camion.

"You're right. Okay. Let's go to Edra."

I waved my ascent, but as he moved toward Camion I reached out, brushing my fingers to Lucian's arm. When he turned, brow furrowed, I asked, "Won't your mother at least notice you missing?"

Lucian dropped my gaze. "No, probably not. She hasn't been the same since your mother—" He broke off, shifting uncomfortably. "Don't worry. She won't notice. I thought she might have searched for me earlier, but she didn't even notice I was gone."

A bitter tone tainted that last sentence. Before I could ask more, he turned away, slinging the bags over his shoulder.

"I can carry those."

"You need to save your strength." He shifted a bag around to his chest, tugging most of the contents free. "Besides. These will lighten my load."

Lucian held out a smile pile of dark lumps. It took me an embarrassingly long moment to realize they were clothing. Leathers, from the looks. I pulled them from his hands, then looked back up to see him holding out a pair of boots too.

"They might be a little large. I took them from my mother's things. Fairly, I don't think she's worn them since I was born. But they'll be warmer, at least."

"I . . . don't know what to say," I admitted.

A ghost of a smile crossed his expression then faded. "I thought I knew a lot about the world. Seems I've only seen a very sheltered part." A soft rustle from the plants nearby made him pause, but I saw no sign of the Zylarra I assumed was still hiding within. He gestured to the leathers. "Put them on. I'll meet you outside."

I draped the cloak over Camion again, lending him the extra heat. Lucian stamped out the last embers from the fire. My eyes took a few moments to adjust to the lower plant light but, when Lucian was out of eyesight, I slipped into the soft, fur-lined leathers. They were slightly too long, but I wouldn't have complained if they fit worse; they were warm, and unexpected, and more appreciated than I knew how to express to Lucian. And as I tied my feet into the equally comfortable boots, I wondered if the prince really had changed.

Maybe all he needed was to see the reality of what I had been dealing with, instead of us simply telling him.

At the least, I owed him explanations. I would tell him what I could as soon as I thought we were safe enough. Edra or no.

Despite his kindness, I couldn't help but wonder if he was leading me into a trap—straight back to his father. That would be the end for me and Camion. But Lucian had left his dagger with me, and when I reached the cave entrance, he was patiently waiting, even under the heavy weight he bore. My distrust faltered. The expression on his face . . . he looked like the Lucian I remembered making daisy crowns for.

Cold snow bit into my toes. I closed my eyes and pressed on. We couldn't save Camion standing here, and if he were all that I had left in this world, then I was going to fight until there was truly nothing remaining.

I had already gone so long with no news of my family, good or bad . . .

They're fine.

Maybe.

They're dead.

I resisted the urge to thread my fingers into my hair and pull. Instead I followed Lucian, trying not to think about anything but the groaning tree and fluttering snowflakes. The docks weren't too far; the prison was tucked into the forests north of Wydus. But as long as we followed the trees southwest, we would hit the river. Behind the palace, and across the river, there were three docks, ones I remembered well from childhood. I hoped Lucian had already secured a boat—I also remembered the minutes we would need to undock and push into the water.

We didn't have minutes.

Our steps were tired and heavy, silence thick between us, with nothing but trees pressing in on either side. Lucian's breaths were large plumes of white in front of his mouth. Despite the warm leathers, I was shivering by the time we reached the tree-line, my hands hues of red and pink from the cold. If Camion hadn't been held tightly to Lucian's chest, I might have insisted the prince offer him more body heat; as it was, I wasn't sure there would be enough. But I hoped.

That was all I had left. A tiny kernel of hope.

A group of palace guards forced us to crouch in the shadows, barely breathing. Lucian seemed to relish the break, resting himself against a tree that he leaned around to peer out. A guard paused, staring a suspiciously long time at the trees we hid behind before moving on. Thankfully, no alert was yelled when we bolted onward.

Several more minutes passed, tense minutes spent on open terrain. Lucian walked in front of me, a barrier in case any of the guards were around.

"I tried to send them away," he whispered, "but I'm not sure if they listened."

I only nodded.

Too many heartbeats passed before the sound of sloshing water met my ears. Relief coursed through me like the river we were clambering toward. Lucian glanced around, narrowing his eyes on the small boathouse that sat on the palace's side of the water. Nothing. The three docks were empty, as he had requested, and not a soul moved in the boathouse.

"I can row. Reserve your strength and eat, please?" Lucian asked as he laid Camion along the bottom of a wooden boat. He waited until I was settled, with Camion's head and shoulders nestled between my crossed legs, to pass me a bag of food and two waterskins. "Edra should be well stocked. Father didn't remove anything. You might even find healing supplies."

I didn't mention that as soon as my magic was ready, I was going to drain myself again. Instead, I waited until Lucian was perched on a bench, his hands gripped around the oars, to say, "I'll repay you for this. I don't know how. But I will."

"You know I didn't do this for payment, or repayment." Lucian pushed our boat away from the dock, tossing the rope into the water beside us. "I may not have expressed myself well, but I really have always cared about you."

Instead of responding, I nodded once more while digging into the satchel Lucian had given me. I bit into the pear I pulled free, closing my eyes in gratitude as the sweet flavor burst to life in my mouth. The scraps of bread Valdis called rations were nothing to this pear; I wanted to devour the fruit as much as I wanted to savor every bite. I knew better, though. My stomach warned me, groaning angrily at the weight of food. *Slow and steady.*

Lucian's gaze was on me when I opened my eyes again. But there was no joy there, only sadness. "You've had a terrible moon cycle." It wasn't a question.

I glanced away, scanning the banks around us. Beyond glittering snow and the distant shadows of trees, there was nothing: no guards, no sounds breaking the nighttime stillness. I took a deep breath.

"All right. Let me start from the beginning."

And I did, my fingers running slow trails through Camion's hair as I spoke. My voice was little more than a soft murmur as I filled in the details, starting from the moment we were ambushed by Boreas and the Cloaked Shadows in Light's Pass to the wound on Andimir's chest and the dagger that bit into Jyn's shoulder. Lucian winced at the latter two, a small hint of glee flickering over his face when I described Cyrus's death and Valeria's rage.

"I never liked them," he admitted softly, then gestured for me to continue.

But my words faltered when I started to speak of the prison. Of his father. The memories were still too fresh, and some small part of me wondered if my stories were to be the nails that sealed my own fate. Lucian could still betray us.

He fell quiet when I stopped talking and waited.

The half of me that wanted to believe he was truly here to help smiled at that, at the fact that he didn't press. That he understood how I might be feeling.

But as I threw the pear core away, watching it softly plop into the river, I realized there was one part of the prison I *had* to tell Lucian about.

"I may not be able to tell you the whole story right now. I'm sure you can glean some of it. I told you that your father wants my magic," I said. Lucian nodded. "Lucian . . . he's a Titan. No, he's not simply a Titan, he's *the* Titan, Valdis to be specific. And he's the one trying to unite the Scepters I've been searching for."

Lucian's jaw flexed. Then he blinked, slowly, as his throat bobbed. "Valdis. The Ancient of the Nether?"

"Yes. He's your father."

"And Drask?"

"A cover, so that he could live among humans while he hunted the Scepters down." I frowned. "His goal all this time has been to bring Thanatos back."

"Thanatos . . . isn't he the son of Valdis?"

"Yes."

"And that makes him my . . . brother?" Lucian's eyes were zipping side to side, as though he didn't know how to process the words I was saying.

"Half-brother, but yes. I'm sorry," I offered softly. "I know this can't be easy."

"No," he admitted, "it's not. I can't quite wrap my head around this. I've been raised by a man who isn't a man at all, but a Titan?"

"Yes."

Lucian's arms stilled. The boat slowed to the river's current instead of his strokes. His eyes were locked on the spot where I knew, in the distance, the palace lay.

"When you found out you had magic, how did you feel?"

The question surprised me. I considered. "Confused. Uncertain. I didn't know what I was doing with my powers. Still don't, if I'm being honest." I took a long drink from the waterskin, then said, "But I have more control now. I can see the bright sides of magic."

"You're not half-Titan though," he murmured darkly.

"No, I'm not. But does knowing really change anything for you?"

"What if I . . . What if I'm like them? Mean, evil, demented, and I can't stop myself because it's in my blood?"

"Evil isn't a blood type. You're evil or you're not. If you're clever, you can change your path no matter which way it's pointed. And for what it's worth, I don't see you as evil, Lucian." I paused. "How do you see yourself?"

"Confused," he whispered. His fists tightened around the oars and he began to move the boat again. "I'm sorry my father . . . Valdis . . ." He hesitated. "I'll be honest, I don't know if I want to call this man my father. But regardless. I'm sorry for what he's done to you. Both of you."

"I know you are."

"How long have you known what I am?"

"Not long. I only learned after we were—" My tongue tripped on the words.

Lucian frowned, understanding. "In the prison, got it."

"I'm not entirely sure how long ago that was."

"I'm not positive either," he admitted, "Last I saw you was at least a moon cycle ago."

I didn't respond; I didn't know what to say. Weeks of my life were gone and I wasn't even sure how many.

"Does this mean I have powers, too?" His question interrupted my thoughts.

"You'd have to tell me."

He stared at his fingers, as though willing them to do magic.

I could almost laugh, if the emotion wasn't a spot of hollow emptiness in my chest. Instead, I said, "If you do have powers, they'll come naturally. Like so."

I laid my fingertips to Camion's temples and exhaled slowly. Fear shivered through my veins, even as I let my magic pour out, even as I saw his skin knitting together with my own eyes. His breathing was a bit more even, but he was still cold to the touch. I didn't know if I was helping him or losing him. And the dregs of magic pulling at my energy weren't enough to heal the marks entirely. What if I was only healing him superficially?

Meryn might be able to heal his scars.

Meryn.

Spirits, I had never missed my friends so much in my life.

Nor had I imagined the sharp loneliness from the lack of Jyn's constant, steady presence. Or how little I appreciated his company until he was gone. Now I longed for nothing more than for Jyn to come flying out of nowhere and hug me until the ache in my chest faded.

But there was no Jyn.

Maybe no Jyn at all . . .

A choked sob broke free of my throat, and I felt a warm weight press down on my hand. Startled, I jumped, and lifted my eyes from Camion's chest, where I had been staring without seeing. Lucian's brow furrowed.

"I want to ask if you're all right, but I know the answer," he said softly.

I lifted my hands from Camion's face, my fingers twisting together on my lap. "I don't know how to . . ."

"How to?"

"To go on. Without—" I couldn't bring myself to speak any of those fears aloud.

Lucian's head dropped for a moment, the only sound the soft sloshes of water against his oars. Then he sighed. "I don't want to give you false hope. Because I truly don't know what my father is capable of, especially now, and I don't know who he employs. But you're not alone."

"I know." I looked to Camion when I said the words, but I was doubting. I could feel him slipping and it hurt—it hurt *so* badly.

"Maybe you should rest?"

I didn't have the strength to argue, so I muttered an agreement. Lucian offered me another satchel, one filled with spare clothing of his own. Without questioning why he had brought the extra, I shoved the bag under my back, then leaned my head on the second bench and ignored the ache in my side. My finger slipped into Camion's hair, running familiar patterns. Because I missed him. Because I needed him, even if he didn't know I was there. And as I ran my thumb across his cheek, as I listened to the soft, constant rustle of underbrush in the trees that I knew had to be the pursuing Zylarra, I counted the stars and hoped the universe couldn't truly be so unkind.

Chapter 5

Bright morning sun woke me after we were well into Lake Myria. My heartbeat leaped into a frenzy at the idea of crossing open water and I sat up straighter, trying to ignore the pain that zipped across my back as I stretched my healing wounds. My neck ached from the awkward angle I had slept at. I rubbed my fingertips into the muscles, kneading the tension free as I checked Camion's pulse. Still too fast, but more regular. His skin was warmer beneath my hand. I almost didn't dare hope.

You did this to him.

I didn't. In my heart, I knew I didn't.

But when I looked at his wounds, when he didn't wake easily, I couldn't shake the guilt. I had uprooted his life, dragged him into my messes. And I knew if he were awake, he would say he made his own choices . . . but I couldn't help feeling responsible for him. I sighed.

"He moved a couple times. Hasn't woken though. I'm glad

you slept."

I nodded my head sleepily at Lucian, reaching for a water-skin. "You should do the same."

"Soon," he said. "If we cross the lake quickly, we should arrive at Edra by nightfall."

"When did you sleep last?" Dark rings lined his glassy yellow eyes.

"Irrelevant," he murmured. Before I could reply he held up a hand, pushing hard on the oars to steer us toward the southern bank.

"What?"

His brow pinched. "Soldiers. Likely my father's men."

I pulled my legs from under Camion, slowly, careful not to rock the boat too much. Then I slid lower into the boat. A raven cawed from across the lake and Lucian's eyes turned at the sound. I lifted myself a fraction of an inch, enough to see over the edge, curious if the sound was truly familiar or if I was imagining it.

Silver glinted in the sunlight and drew my eye. A party of soldiers decked in full armor traveled across the nearing shore, moving not west toward Edra but east, toward Wydus. Their pace was slow, their gear minimal. They joked as they walked, their loose postures and laughter clear even from our distance. If they were patrolling, they weren't observant. Maybe they were returning from a mission empty handed. The thought brought me small joy, until I considered what kind of mission they might have been sent on. Annalea's face appeared in my mind, her sapphire-flecked lavender eyes wide and bright. The ache in my chest grew stronger. A low throb pounded at my temples. I dipped low again, sighing.

I miss my family.

Our boat jerked as Lucian navigated us carefully along the shoreline, watching the soldiers as he tucked us beneath a cascade of willow branches. As soon as we were hidden from view, I sat up.

"I'm going to scale the bank, see if I can overhear their orders," Lucian said quietly, his eyes on the soldiers. "If they do catch me, they shouldn't give me any trouble alone." He ran a hand through his hair, the chestnut locks glinting in the dappled sunlight. "If I haven't returned soon, take the boat and go. I'll catch up to you if I need to, but you two can't be recaptured. You . . ."

"Won't survive if we are," I finished for him. "I know. I'll be cautious."

Lucian's mouth opened, as though he would offer some condolence or final warning, then snapped shut. He dipped his head, then whispered, "I'll be back."

He leapt onto the shore and vanished into the willow branches. I held my breath, listening, waiting for the sounds of footsteps, voices . . . betrayal. I was waiting for the latter most of all. My hands tightly gripped the oar handles. Logically, the prince wouldn't bring us this far only to betray us. Reason said that if that were his plan, he would have taken us to the palace as we passed—neither Camion nor myself were in any kind of condition to resist.

My tense muscles refused to listen though. A soft caress brushed my leg. I jumped and glanced down. Camion's fingers were stretched out, reaching for me. My eyes widened and I scanned his barely moving form, then looked back to where I had last seen the soldiers. A soft groan left his lips. I froze. Panic leapt into my chest. If they heard him—

I glanced between the slowly waking Camion and the glints of armor that peeped through the willow branches. My heart thundered riotously against my ribs, my breath stuck in my throat.

A minute passed. Then two.

Grass rustled near the boat, but otherwise, I heard nothing. No approaching soldiers. No Lucian.

"Tyli—" Camion's voice was barely a whispered breath.

I tucked the oars into the boat, then leaned close. My mind was flooded with the sounds of his pain and, for a moment, I froze, uncertain of what to do. But he shifted slightly and I was able to move, crossing my legs to rest his head in my lap.

"How are you feeling?" I whispered.

His breath caught, the softest sound. A crease deepened along his brow.

I brushed a finger along the lines, withdrawing my hand when I noticed the tears that slid down his cheeks, even as they remained closed. I leaned closer to his ear, keeping my voice low as I said, "Are you in a lot of pain?"

He jerked his head, the smallest no. The motion seemed to pull a lot from him, though, and I reached for one of the waterskins.

"Can you drink? Even a little? You lost so much—" I couldn't make the words fall from my tongue. Camion's head lifted a fraction of an inch and I reached to help him, lifting the waterskin to his lips with my other hand. His throat bobbed as he drank, but he still didn't open his eyes.

"We're free, you know," I murmured to him. He stilled and I

went on. "You should rest. But I thought you should know. We're free, my love. We're free."

His eyes cracked open then, the smallest bit. Slivers of bright blue and green shone up at me for half a second before he closed them again, wincing.

"My head," he groaned.

"Shhh," I soothed, shooting an uneasy glance at the soldiers. They were still oblivious, thankfully. "I thought you said you weren't in much pain?"

When he didn't answer, I gripped his arm, offering small bursts of magic that might help ease the headache. My scar screamed to life almost instantly, then a wave of stars glittered across my vision. I released my hold, covering my eyes, panting softly. Camion stilled again.

"You've been . . . overexerting yourself," he murmured.

I didn't have to confirm. He knew without words. Still, I whispered, "I won't give up on you so easily."

Camion blew out a slow breath, his hands lifting on trembling arms to run through his hair. "I need . . . I'm so . . . tired."

"Rest then," I murmured, brushing my fingers over his arm. "I'll get us to safety."

He caught my hand and lightly squeezed before his other arm fell over his eyes. And even though he was deeply asleep before I could count to five, he had woken. He had drunk water. I might be exhausted and ringing with guilt, but my magic may have saved him.

I saved him.

Maybe. I couldn't be sure. What if he didn't wake again?

My thoughts were turmoil.

I sighed, casting a look across the water; no silver caught my eye. The soldiers were gone, or at least well past my vision. A soft caw broke the chittering birdsong around us and I glanced up, only to see black wings dart away before I could get a closer look.

"They're gone."

Lucian's voice startled me and I loosed a string of swears under my breath. He grinned.

"I didn't pick up much from their conversation though. Nothing useful, for sure." I studied those yellow eyes now narrowed on me. "You all right?"

"He woke up for a minute," I said, gesturing at Camion.

Lucian's expression softened. "Did he say anything?"

"Not much. That his head ached. Though, as dehydrated as he is . . ."

"A headache is to be expected," Lucian agreed. He lifted the oars, dipping them in the water.

"He drank some water. Not enough."

"He'll be okay, Natylia."

I nodded my head. If I told him what I really thought, Lucian would argue. To reassure me, I knew, but words wouldn't help.

Only time.

***

By nightfall, I could see the outline of Edra in the moonlight.

Once, the massive manor had been home to the Council, the group responsible for monitoring the three kingdoms and ensuring a balance of power between them—until they had all been murdered, violently. We had suspected Wulfric was responsible for the slaughter, especially when he had vanished quickly after but, with Valdis's identity revealed, I was no longer certain.

The manor was shrouded in darkness, not so much as a guard's lantern flickering in the night. Lucian did say the place had been abandoned. Maybe Valdis assumed no one would come here now. He certainly hadn't thought Camion and I would escape. Then again, as Lucian's profile caught in the moonlight, his eyes focused ahead, I hadn't thought we would be free either. If not for Lucian's own betrayal, we wouldn't be.

"Climb up onto the dock," the prince said, as he grabbed onto a piling. "I'll have you tie off the boat first. We'll get Camion out after. If you can brace him, we should be able to lift him up and then I can carry him the rest of the way."

I took a steadying breath, then carefully pulled myself up onto the wooden boards. The effort left my arms trembling, but I caught the rope from Lucian and wrapped it around a piling. As I tried to tie the knot, an end dropped into the water and splashed loudly. I winced, locking eyes with the prince. We listened with bated breaths. Footsteps sounded behind me. I twisted where I sat to reach for the dagger Lucian had given me, only to realize I had left my blade on the boat.

"Need some help?" The sound splintered something inside me. I shot to my feet, wobbling unsteadily. A hand gently gripped my arm. "I'll take that as a yes."

Green eyes met mine. I scanned his face, the soft smile that skewed his blond-flecked goatee, and tears fell freely down my cheeks. Andimir grasped my other arm, holding me steady until I wrenched free and flung my arms around his neck, ignoring my protesting wounds to hug him tightly. I couldn't let him go. I wasn't certain he was real, even as the scents of sea and roses and tobacco washed over me.

"Nat? Nat, hey, I'm here. I'm real," he said softly, as his warm arms squeezed me closer. I must have vocalized the latter concern. Heat rose to my cheeks.

"You're okay?" I stepped back to wipe at my face.

He tugged at the buttons of his shirt and revealed the jagged scar that ran down his chest. "As well as I can be."

"And Jyn?" Andimir frowned, his gaze dropping to the toe of his boots. He glanced behind me, toward Lucian who had climbed onto the dock, and cleared his throat. My stomach twisted. "Andimir. Where is Jyn?"

"In Eythera, last I knew," he said finally, still refusing to meet my eyes. "Nat . . . Jyn . . ."

"Don't you dare," I whispered. "Don't say it."

"Nat . . ."

I shook my head as Andimir's mouth opened, then shut. He met my eyes, finally. When he spoke again, I almost missed what he said over the thunder of my own heartbeat.

"He died, Natylia. I'm so sorry. He died in my arms. I . . ." His voice was thick, his eyes glittering. "I tried. I tried so hard. I took him to Hexryn, but the healers could only prolong the inevitable. I wasn't fast enough. I'm so sorry."

"You're lying. How are you even here?"

"Nat you know I wouldn't—" He reached out for me, but I backed away. When my arm bumped Lucian's, I moved from him too, cornering myself at the end of the dock. "I can explain more inside. Please, Nat. Trust me."

"You're lying." My voice wavered. "He's not dead and you're lying."

"He asked me . . . he asked me to give you these."

"Stop," I whispered. My eyes burned.

Andimir took a step closer, unfastening something from his belt. I looked down at what he held out, and my heart plummeted into my stomach.

Jyn's daggers. Tucked safely in their sheath, but they were unmistakable: custom Elven blades, a gift from Queen Audri and King Phelix of Kalum.

The dock flew up to meet me. Wood bit into my knees. Andimir passed the daggers to Lucian with a pointed glare, then lifted me gently, pulling me to him. Pain like I had never known lanced through my chest, but I couldn't find my tears. I was frozen in place, unable to move, unable to breathe.

"Izoryian took him. He—" A tremor ran through Andimir's body.

"You didn't bring him back?" I rasped. "So, I could . . . my family . . ."

"I couldn't. Fetian returned. Audri sent word. Eurybia . . ." I stiffened at the water Titan's name and Andimir's grip tightened. "Eurybia took out another of my fleet. A runner this time, making a trip south to bring Lytalian food and medical supplies. At least a dozen of my people are gone."

"I'm sorry," I offered. I meant the words, but my heart wasn't behind them. A world without Jyn . . .

"Audri said more." Andimir pulled away. My gaze slipped to Lucian, nervously clutching Jyn's daggers, then back to Andimir. His eyes were damp, but the corner of his mouth tilted in a small smile. "Annalea is alive. Audri didn't send details, but she knows she's alive and she's trying to make contact. Your sister is *alive*."

My conflicted emotions threatened to barrel over me. Joy at the news of my sister, unrestrained joy that I hadn't dared dream I would feel again . . . straining against the heavy, painful weight that Jyn was . . .

Jyn . . .

"Where's Camion?" Andimir asked, brow pinching as he really took in Lucian's form. He side-stepped, putting himself a bit more between me and the prince. "And what is *he* doing here?"

My mouth opened and closed. Words were hard—processing them, speaking them.

Lucian noticed my struggle and stepped forward. "Camion is in the boat. He's not doing well, but he's more stable than he was when I found them."

"He found you?" Andimir studied my face until I nodded, then looked back to the prince. "You rescued them?"

"Lucian saved our lives," I interjected, glancing around. We had been on the open dock too long and I wanted to continue processing inside. "We should get Camion. After he's settled, we'll talk some more."

Andimir released his grip on my arm. He took Jyn's daggers from the prince, holding them out to me. I took the sheath, nauseous at the wrongness of this whole situation. But I held them to my chest as Andimir jerked his head at Lucian, who followed without question. The two of them managed to carefully pull Camion from the boat, then Andimir carried him while Lucian shouldered the satchels. I followed them up an overgrown path, to stone stairs that rose over massive, untended gardens. An eerie, haunted feeling sent goosebumps sprawling across my skin. My brow furrowed at the sight.

With the Council's death, their home had been abandoned—and after Drask's searches, it must have remained so. The empty dark felt as though there was no intent to ever establish a new Council. Not that the matter had even been officially discussed, but there was an arrogance behind Drask letting this place crumble. A certainty in his success. The thought made me angry.

My fingers knotted in the coarse fabric of the cloak surrounding me. I pulled it closer, tighter, my footsteps lagging behind the others. They waited until I caught up. Andimir eyed my sluggish steps.

"Have you slept?" I shook my head, and he frowned. "And Camion—"

"Inside," I murmured, shaking the doorknob. Locked.

The curve of Andimir's lips deepened. "Help me out? Inside pocket of my jacket, there's a key. I've been here a couple days already."

I hesitated a moment, brows scrunching in confusion. But, instead of commenting, I reached into his pocket and pulled out the antiqued key. The lock released with a soft click and the door swung open to near darkness. On instinct we all paused to listen, but no sounds met our ears.

Only silence.

We exchanged glances, then Andimir jerked his chin toward a staircase set in the far corner. Each step of his and Lucian's heavy boots disturbed the thin layer of dust lining the floor, which rose and settled again as they passed. Vague forms stood in ominous shadows—covered furniture that was both threatening and unfamiliar, and barely lit by the few candles in sconces along the wall.

Jyn would have checked every corner, every inch of the house before we left the main room. Jyn would have—

Jyn would—

I stopped halfway up the staircase and dropped to my knees. I curled over the steps, burying my face in my hands. Sobs shook through me, agony that wailed through the silence around us. Andimir and Lucian's footsteps trailed away, then one set hurried back.

When Andimir scooped me into his arms and held me against his chest, I fell into him and sobbed. I cried until there wasn't a tear left in my tired, worn-down body. I cried over things that had nothing to do with Jyn, and everything to do with Jyn. Even the ache of my wounds didn't shatter my grief. Movement stilled my downward spiral. Andimir was shaking with anguish of his own, and my sorrow renewed as my hold on him tightened.

How could I face all that was yet to come without Jyn?

Chapter 6

I must have slept. Exhaustion might have claimed me, I wasn't sure. Bright, midday sun streamed in through the windows. White lace curtains draped the bed I was sprawled in, too translucent to keep out the light, and the cream-colored blankets that had covered me were now shoved into a wad at my feet.

Andimir flipped the sheets, I remembered, and he had forced me to swallow some broth. My mind was still fogged. Andimir must have tucked me into bed too; I still wore the warm leathers Lucian had given me. The leather had pressed into my skin, leaving small aching spots across my body as I stretched out. My wounds burned at the movement. I released a heavy sigh.

In less than a year, my life had been completely flipped upside down. My mother was brutally murdered, and I had needed to shove that grief aside to learn about the Scepters and Titans. I had failed, time and again, to accomplish anything to stop their return. I lost my seventeen-year-old sister. We had been thrown to the depths by Eurybia, fought, lost, and were captured by Boreas. Camion and I had been tortured by Cybele and Valdis, physically and mentally. Emotionally.

I lost Jyn. I lost my best friend, the person I trusted most in the world.

Most people in my position would have cut their losses by now. Gone into hiding until the worst past. Spirits, I had wanted to more than once.

But so much good had happened in the last year too. I conquered fears I hadn't known I had. My closest friends fell but also grew. Meryn was one of the most powerful people in all three kingdoms—one of the most powerful people to have ever existed. An old love had returned and instead of being the terrible burden I feared he would be, Andimir had again become one of my dearest friends.

And, on top of all that, I knew deep in my stomach that if we came out of all this alive, I wanted to marry the man who slept only a room away. A year ago, I had truly considered the idea impossible.

Anything could happen in a few short months.

I had debated staying with Camion through the night, but I knew the need to watch him—to make sure he was still breathing, to check his pulse—would keep me awake. Andimir had promised to let me know if Camion woke. I believed him.

My eyes slid to the door and I realized, with a pang, I was waiting for Jyn to storm into the room. To demand I get up. Time to go, time to dress, time to stop wasting the day. Time to do something.

Anything.

Instead my gaze slid to the bedside table—and Jyn's daggers waiting there.

Spirits, I would give anything for him to be here.

I would give anything for him to be *alive*.

Tears trekked paths down my cheeks and my stomach twisted. I buried my face in the velvet pillows and let my misery flood through me, simmering into the grief that flooded my mind. Losing Jyn . . .

I hadn't felt such pure, raw pain since I lost my father. Jyn was family, in every sense of the word, but also my best friend. My closest confidante. The time we had been apart after Boreas and the Shadows attacked was the longest I had been without him since I was ten.

In the back of my mind, I knew I still had family. Camion, Andimir, Meryn, Annalea—when I found her.

But the pain that tore at my chest, that ripped from my throat in an anguished cry, was one I didn't know how to bear. I curled into a ball, as small as I could go without upsetting the wounds on my back, and sobbed until my eyes burned. Andimir wouldn't lie about this. I knew he wouldn't, even as much as I wanted to deny it. And I didn't know how to process the loss.

A piece of my soul had been brutally torn out.

"He didn't want to leave you. Not for one minute."

Andimir's voice came from near the door. I knew he wasn't talking about physically leaving me either, in the forest when I had ordered Jyn away.

"Then why did he?" I wailed.

Weight pressed on the bed near my head. Andimir laid a hand on my shoulder, but I recoiled. He withdrew. If I couldn't feel the world, I didn't have to believe the words were real. Right?

"The poison moved too fast." His voice cracked. "I barely got him to Eythera. You did the right thing, sending him away."

"He should be buried with family," I sobbed.

"Maybe he still can be," Andimir murmured. He paused before he added, "Valeria was there. In Eythera. Well, outside I mean. Waiting."

"She what?" I sat up, wiping at my face. "She knew you'd go there?"

"Assumed, more like. Or tracked us. I'm not sure. But she couldn't find the Elves. Not until Andáerhyn and Izoryian came out for Jyn."

"The Lord of the Elves himself came out for him?" I sniffled, but the thought was a comfort.

Andimir nodded. "Indeed. But Andáerhyn was there first. I've never seen an Elf so angry, and that's saying a lot. He went straight for Valeria."

"She didn't—"

"No, she wasn't able to hurt them. Nor her companion." I looked up at him expectantly, too tired to puzzle out his words. Andimir's eyes were locked onto his lap, sadness in the lines of his face. But he said, "Boreas. They were together. I'm not entirely sure why. But Andáerhyn and I kept them off Izoryian long enough that he could take Jyn underground."

For a moment I wondered why the Titan of light had partnered with the Vampyr. Then my thoughts snagged on Andimir's words.

"You left him there? Alone?" I asked, suddenly angry.

"No. I told you. Fetian returned and I raced north. Andáerhyn barely got me away from them. He said he would send word as soon as he had a clearer idea of what was going to happen with Jyn. I don't know what that means, Natylia. I'm sorry."

"And you're sure—"

"Natylia please," Andimir groaned, burying his face in his hands. His throat bobbed, and even as tears welled in my eyes, they spilled over from his. I kept forgetting he was mourning too, that Jyn had died in his arms as he raced to save him.

I swallowed the knot that jumped into my throat and, for the second time in less than a day, I wrapped my arms around his neck and hugged him tightly. For a moment he froze, surprised. But then he was crying, silently, into my shoulder.

"I tried, Natylia," he said finally, withdrawing and dragging his sleeve across his cheeks. "I tried to save him."

"Don't blame yourself," I murmured, reaching for his hand. I squeezed softly, then added, "I know you did what you could. Forgive me? I'm so . . . I'm so lost."

"I know. You know I'll do what I can to help you."

"And I you," I said, meeting his eyes. His lips tilted in the faintest smile. "How's Camion?"

"Better. Lucian is sitting with him at the moment. Which is . . . weird," Andimir said, brows pinching even as his shoulders relaxed. "His skin has warmed up, at least. Your magic saved his life. He'll need water, food, and rest, but I truly think he'll be fine. Plus, I haven't seen any sign of infection and most of his wounds were at least sealed."

"You haven't seen any sign of infection *yet*."

Andimir stared at me, unblinking, for a long moment, lips curving into a deep frown. "You've given up on him."

I met his eyes, mouth slipping open. "I haven't. I would never." I paused, then admitted, "But I had accepted our deaths. His and mine. You didn't see . . . hear . . ."

"I can see enough," Andimir said quietly. "I don't need more, unless you want to talk. But we should tend to your wounds now."

My tongue was cotton in my mouth, but I managed, "I don't know. If I—"

I studied the cuff marks on my wrist, peeking out from the skewed leathers on my forearms. They were raw and painful, but I pulled my sleeves down to cover them.

Andimir put a hand on my arm, squeezing gently. "We can talk when you're ready. You have to take care of those wounds though."

"So, why *are* you here?" I asked, slipping free of his grip. At the hurt on his face, I shook my head. "No, sorry, I didn't mean that. I meant, I'm grateful, truly, but your timing was convenient."

"Fetian." He shrugged. "I sent him to look for you while I patrolled the northern coast. He returned this morning and led me to the river. I assumed that if nothing else, you would at least pass by Edra."

"He was watching me the rest of the day?"

"Yes. In case you changed course."

"Thank you. For looking."

"I wouldn't have stopped."

I nodded slowly. "We should check on Camion."

"No, we should tend your wounds. Then you need rest."

He was right but, with everything else on my mind, I couldn't simply sit in a room and wait to heal.

"Let me heal him some more. Then you can see to my wounds

and I'll lay down again."

Andimir scanned my face, then sighed, pulling his locs over his shoulders. "Fine. I've searched the house three times and found no sign of anyone. The pantries are stocked for months."

"We won't be here for months."

"No, but we could refresh our rations."

I had to agree. "Water?"

"There's a pump that runs to a spring nearby."

"Did you sleep at all?"

Andimir looked away then. "Not much," he admitted after a moment, tugging at his goatee. "I needed to make sure you two were looked after. And I'm still not sure about Lucian."

"Give him a chance. His story isn't mine to tell. But for now, know that I think he's trustworthy. Or trustworthy enough. He risked a lot getting us out." I paused, studying the dark circles under Andimir's eyes. "You need to make sure you're looked after too."

His eyes met mine for a fraction of a second before they fell again. "You made sure I'm alive. The least I can do is lose a little sleep."

"Still. We need everyone at their best."

"Did you see the Scepters, then?"

I winced but inclined my head. "And they've been magically charged."

"What? How?"

"Me. I . . ."

He scanned my face, nodding sharply. "Later. What now, though? I imagine we can't stop them."

"No. Now we have to find allies. Try to build an army."

"Who?"

"I don't know."

Andimir sighed. "We'll figure this out. Together. If you think I'm letting you or Camion out of my sight again, you're both crazy."

"I don't know how we're going to fight Thanatos."

"Titan of death? No big deal." My eyes widened, and he gently smiled, adding, "We'll find a way. It's not like you to give up."

He wasn't wrong but giving up felt . . . easier. Andimir understood.

"You're tired, that's all," he continued. "Don't quit on me now."

I squeezed his hand gratefully. Andimir didn't say more, climbing to his feet instead, and then offered me his hand. I swayed slightly, my legs unsteady again. Next to Andimir's hand, the lines of bone in my own fingers were sharp and unnatural. Too thin. Too weak.

How am I supposed to save a kingdom like this? A world?

"You need food. Drink. And rest," Andimir repeated, as if reading my thoughts. I pulled my hand away, crossing my arms tight across my chest. He frowned again. "And fresh clothing. At least agree to those, and a bath. I'll even draw the water."

I patted the top of my head, the matted, blood-caked mess that was my hair. Agreeing wasn't much effort. A bath felt so unimportant, but the thought of being clean lifted some strange, small weight from my shoulders.

The manor was bright with daylight now. I paused outside the doorway. Rarely was anyone invited to Edra unless the Council wanted them there. Edra was meant to be a haven for Council members, if they wanted to use it. Many did. The seclusion kept the Council away from political temptation, and with so many powerful beings in one place, not many would have dared take them on.

Which is what made their deaths that much more terrifying.

Looking around, I couldn't even imagine the Council here. The manor was built of stacked stone and raw wood, bound together in ways that made the home feel beautiful and wild. I inched closer to the railing across from me, brushing my fingers over the branches that grew in tangled messes over the balustrade, from a tree whose roots were buried deep beneath the hardwood floors below. Every inch of honey-toned wood shone, even under the thin layer of dust. Tinkling water caught my ear and I tilted my head to listen.

"There's a fountain under the stairs," Andimir said, stepping up beside me. He leaned against the twisted railing. "And I think you'll enjoy the bathing room."

My brows pulled together and he smiled, a small expression that didn't brighten his face as it usually did. A string tugged at my heart, the one that knew he too was bleeding over the loss of Jyn. But I pushed the thought aside, done with my scrutiny for the moment.

"Guess I should get to healing."

Chapter 7

Camion lay sprawled across the bed, soft snores breaking the quiet. His torso was bound with white linens. I studied him cautiously; he looked thin. Frail. Starved, like myself. The line of his jaw was sharper, his cheekbones more prominent, and dark circles curved under his eyes. A wave of emotions tumbled over me, the urge and desire to protect him at the forefront, and I almost crumbled all over again. So much of his current state was my fault.

Lucian had left Camion's side to attempt some sleep of his own. I lost track of the minutes as I leaned against the post at the foot of the bed, waiting for Andimir to return and report Camion's injuries. He almost looked peaceful in sleep, even despite the pain he must be in. His sandy-blond hair was longer and splayed across the pillow around him. His chest rose and fell in uneven waves. Broken ribs, maybe. I would need to tend to those first. They would heal faster on their own should my magic run out before I finished.

"I sent Fetian to Audri," Andimir said from the doorway. I jumped at the sound and he winced apologetically. "I wanted to see if she had any further updates about your sister, but I tried to update her on all of us as well." When my eyes narrowed, he added, "Vaguely. No names, no titles. No locations. I'm not even sure she'll understand half of it."

"And Meryn?"

"I've heard nothing about her, so I assume she's safe and keeping to the shadows. I can send Fetian to Thrais, if he returns before we leave. I haven't wanted to risk her being caught receiving messages by raven, if she decided to show her face in Thrais but . . ."

"Wise," I admitted. "As an extra precaution, let's send him to Sylvr. She can make sure Meryn gets the message."

He nodded and I returned my attention to Camion. Inhaling deeply, I sat on the bed beside him. His left hand was wrapped securely. Other bandages were scattered up his arms and down his legs.

"His left hand was shattered," Andimir murmured beside me. "I don't know why they left his sword hand intact, but the first two fingers were broken."

"I don't want to think about the implications," I said under my breath.

"A few of his ribs were broken. I'm sure there are more fractures that I haven't found yet. Despite your healing, there's still a fair amount of swelling." Andimir paused. "The lacerations were by far the worst of his injuries. I won't detail. But if you can finish healing his back, and fix some of his bones, he'll be much better off than he is now."

"I'll focus on the worst of his wounds."

"Would you like to use some of my . . . blood?" Andimir winced.

I shook my head. "We need you unwounded and at full strength, in case anything happens. I can handle this for now. But I appreciate the offer."

"If you need help, the offer stands."

I nodded slowly, brushing my fingertips along the bandages on Camion's torso, nudging up an edge so I could make direct contact with his skin. Closing my eyes, I pulled in a long breath, then exhaled, focusing myself. My magic responded sluggishly. I had to dig far into the depths where it hid, the tendril of power still barely present after my exertions in Wydus. My scar began to ache, dully at first, sharper the farther I delved. I waited until the magic warmed my arms and hands before I opened my eyes to watch as sparkling blue and purple slowly coursed over Camion's chest. When I had done what I could for his ribs, I closed my eyes again, focusing on directing the remnants of my magic through his back. Lacerations covered the expanse of his skin, dark marks that pulled my powers and drew them in, healing each wound before my eyes.

But my magic began to fade. My scar throbbed and burned as I pushed myself, trying to force his wounds closed. I steadied myself and demanded more of my powers, dragging the magic forward. Beads of sweat dotted my forehead, then trailed down my cheeks.

Andimir spoke, his voice sharp with warning.

Still I kept going.

I refused to stop until every wound on his back was at least closed, and many healed throughout, even though the strain on my magic was tangible. The scars wouldn't be pretty, and they would be relatively fragile. Camion could rip them open again, would if he did anything too strenuous. But the injuries weren't as likely to become infected and, next to the wounds I had healed before, he already looked more . . . whole. He would heal faster now. That was progress, at least. Even if my mind yelled at me, insisting that I hadn't managed much.

I withdrew my fingers, panting quietly. Andimir knelt on the floor beside me, his hands poised to catch me if I fell. Nausea swirled through my stomach, the pain still burning up my left side.

"I couldn't heal them all."

"But you did what you could. You helped him," Andimir said. I knew he was trying to assuage the guilt in my voice. "Do you want to sit here while I draw you a bath? Then I can help you downstairs?"

He gestured at my torso and, for a moment, I thought he meant the bandages. Then I realized that the leathers I wore were soaked through with perspiration. A bead fell from my forehead, trailing down my chest. I brushed my fingers across my sweat-slicked hair and recoiled.

"That's never happened before," I murmured, transfixed as a droplet landed on the back of my hand.

"You don't have the life force to be sharing right now," Andimir said quietly. "Let's get you another bath. I can bandage you, then you need to eat."

"Thank you."

Without another word, he dipped his head and vanished

from the room. The sound of his quickly fading bootsteps thudded throughout the house moments later. I scooted backward, leaning against a bedpost, my eyes trained on Camion's chest. Rising and falling. A reassuring sight, his breath not quite as uneven as before. I loosed a long sigh, wrapping my arms tightly around myself. Sleep sounded nice.

Camion groaned and I stilled. He didn't wake, but his hands balled into fists as much as they could around the bandages. I clambered to my feet, scanning the room for the supplies Andimir and Lucian had used to bandage him the night before. A pile of linen sat on a table, alongside bundles of herbs and a pitcher of water. I nudged a few sprigs aside, hoping I would recognize one that might give Camion some relief, but nothing drew my eye. Most of the options were unfamiliar: roots and leaves I had only seen illustrations of or that I had never seen at all.

"He took a bit of ginger water this morning, but I can't say that it helped." I jumped at Andimir's voice, and nearly lost my balance before he crossed the room and gripped my arm. His brow wrinkled. "Come on. Bath, food, rest. Let's go."

I didn't argue.

✳✳✳

Edra's bathing chamber was a wide, open room at the far end of the first floor, walled in by the same stone used throughout the house. But these were raw, jagged, like they had carved the room in a hurry. Around the massive, spring-fed pool of water were smooth wooden floors that were lined and accented with marble.

While the heated water soothed my aching muscles, the quiet

house sent my thoughts racing as painfully as the water over the lash marks across my skin. I gritted my teeth and sank deeper in. I wasn't going to complain. My bones were intact. I was tired and weak, magically drained and covered in lacerations—but I could move, walk, bathe. As long as Camion could do none of those things, I wouldn't utter a sound about my own discomforts.

But I scrubbed my uninjured skin raw with a rough bar of soap that smelled of cookies and picked at the knots in my hair until my arms shook with the effort. No amount of bathing seemed to make me feel clean.

Camion took the brunt of the punishments.

A set of mental claws raked toxins through my blood, reminding me over and over how much he suffered. I felt guilty when I looked at him, when I touched him, when I longed to see those blue and green eyes peering up at me.

I felt guiltiest when I thought about hiding in his arms until the world collapsed around us.

But I hadn't done those horrible things to him. I knew I hadn't. Still, I couldn't seem to believe that I wasn't responsible. That I might as well have personally administered every single lashing.

So many lashings . . .

I submerged my head, holding my breath until a low throb pressed at my temples and my lungs began to burn. When I broke the surface, I pulled myself up the marble steps and wrapped a robe around my shoulders, securely tying the waist before I called for Andimir.

My voice barely carried across the room. I wasn't sure how he heard me, but he did. He had managed to find an assortment of clothing around the house while I bathed. I tried not to think about whose they were, whose they might have been. Why the manor was so dark and empty.

The loose-fitted shirt and breeches were welcome changes from the thin cotton gown, or even the leathers Lucian had lent me before. They were warm, but comfortable. Even though Andimir had lit several fireplaces, the house was only now beginning to heat up.

More trees vined throughout the manor, supporting cabinets and bearing sinks, even climbing the tall mantles of most of the fireplaces. The mix of branch and stone, wild and carefully placed, was soothing somehow. And with sporadic fountains filling the home with the soft lyrics of tumbling water, I could understand why the Council would have wanted to hide away here.

I wanted to hide away here.

Andimir led the way to a small kitchen, jerking his head toward where Lucian stood in a corner stirring a black pot that hung over a small fire.

"The prince is making you more of that bone broth you had last night." Andimir gestured to a small wooden table that seemed grown into the adjoining wall. Its long legs were roots that tangled beneath and into the stone floor. "You need more in you than a few spoonfuls."

"I ate a pear on the way here," I protested.

Andimir pulled out a chair, staring pointedly until I sat. When I did, he leaned closer, a sly smile on his face. "And you're going to tell me that eating after so long didn't bother your stomach even a little? Make you want more?"

"I didn't say that."

His grin grew and he spun away, snatching up a bowl. Lucian took it from him, ladling soup until the broth lapped at the edges, then slid the dish across the table toward me. Andimir shoved a spoon alongside. Green eyes locked onto mine. Both men waited while I filled my spoon, then slowly sipped at the broth.

"Better?" I asked, raising my brow. I shot a glance at Lucian. "This is actually pretty good. Since when do you know how to cook?"

The prince offered a half smile. "My mother taught me. Only over the last year or so, though, and I don't know how to make much. But Andimir asked if I would make lunch, and here we are."

Andimir nodded and turned, but Lucian had already moved. He pushed a bowl into Andimir's hands before he dropped into the seat between us. Andimir eyed his stew warily, pushing potatoes and meat around. Instead of eating, he turned his attention to Lucian and asked, "Why *are* you here?"

Lucian paused his eating and focused his attention onto me. I looked away, feigning interest in the broth in front of me. He sighed. "I could ask the same of you."

"True." Andimir lifted a shoulder in a slight shrug.

"Natylia hasn't told you anything?"

"I haven't really asked."

The barb hit a mark. Lucian cleared his throat uncomfortably. "Right. Well. I don't know all the details about Natylia's side, but I know what I saw when I pulled them out of that prison."

Andimir stiffened beside me. "You pulled them out?" His eyes narrowed on me. "You were in Wydus's prison?"

"Yes," I murmured. "To both of your questions. I told you he saved us."

"Why did you stay here then, after Natylia was with me again?" Andimir's attention was fully on the prince now.

Lucian sighed. "I'm not sure where else to go. Before I left, I told my mother I was going to travel, see if I could find Natylia. She barely said a word. And my father . . . my father . . ."

"Your father would have you hunted for your betrayal," I whispered. Andimir's brow furrowed.

The prince nodded. "You're stuck with me. For the time being."

"You saved Camion?"

"I'm not a monster."

"Tell me, then," Andimir said. "What happened in your kingdom?"

"I don't know the details, Andimir," Lucian said softly. "But what I can tell you is that I found Camion and Natylia laying near dead in a pile of rubble and snow."

Andimir's hand balled into a fist, his jaw clenched. I rested a calming hand on his arm. He studied my fingers, wrapped around his sleeve, and his expression softened. The muscles in his arm relaxed.

"He saved us," I whispered. "Regardless of what we've been through, Lucian saved us. Don't forget that."

"What happened?" Andimir's voice was too rough. "Why were they in *your* prison?"

Lucian frowned and studied his bowl of stew. "My father had them."

Confusion flickered over Andimir's face. The worry lines softened. His shoulders loosened. "Your father?"

"Look, I'm officially a traitor to my own kingdom, what more do you want from me?" The prince snapped. "My father has been telling everyone for months that Natylia was missing, and he was spending every minute looking for her. And in between all of that, he forgot to mention that he had her locked away in a prison cell."

"But *why?*" Andimir growled.

"Ask her." Lucian dropped his spoon into his bowl with a clatter, lifting a hand in my direction. "I find one of the people who matter most to me in this world nearly dead, and now the other is drilling me with questions I don't have answers to. Maybe I should leave."

Andimir's expression fell. "Lucian . . ."

The prince stood, rocking back his chair. "I'm sorry. I need a minute. Maybe you should ask Natylia why I'm a half-Titan. No, better yet, don't bother, I'll tell you. My father is Valdis. *The* Valdis. The Titan. And I have no idea what to do with that information, but I know that he wants us all dead, including me, and that he spent the last moon cycle torturing the queen of an allied kingdom. Do with that what you will."

Lucian spun on his heel and stormed out of the room. Andimir turned his eyes toward me, a deep crease between his brows. I laid my spoon beside my bowl, the broth now a lead weight in my stomach. A lump rose in my throat. I wasn't ready to talk about the more elicit details—not with anyone—but I would give him what I could.

"Lucian is right. His father is a Titan. Drask is Valdis."

"Wydus betrayed us, then?"

I nodded. "Very much so. Drask had been pushing for my

marriage to Lucian for so long, and for all the wrong reasons. He didn't care about Lucian's happiness, or my own. He wanted my power. And he got it. He has all three Scepters and they're all fully charged to save Thanatos."

Andimir murmured a string of swears. His gaze flitted to the doorway where the prince had left. "I should apologize."

"Not a bad idea."

"You weren't supposed to agree," he said, flashing me a grin.

"He saved our lives, found out he's half-Titan, and betrayed everything he's ever known for us. We don't have to trust him. But we should give him a chance."

Silence fell between us and, for a long moment, I didn't think Andimir would say anything more.

"Keep eating," Andimir said, scanning my face. "That's more important than all of this. I'll talk to Lucian later. I promise."

I nodded, trying to restrain the tears that filled my eyes. Andimir moved closer, pressing into my side, silent as he focused on his stew. He didn't need to speak. I understood the gesture, the quiet comfort he was offering. The tears spilled at that, at how willing he was to step up to fill Jyn's shoes when he didn't have to, when he was grieving on his own as well.

"Hey," he said. I tried to meet his kind gaze. "Food now. We'll talk about the rest when you're ready, remember? No pressure."

I gripped the spoon, but eating was a task. A conversation would happen soon, and I didn't know if I wanted Lucian to divulge all he had seen.

If I were being honest, I didn't want Andimir to see me the same way I saw myself.

Weak.

Chapter 8

Glittering water spread across the horizon, shimmering beneath the setting sun. Reds and oranges twisted together behind cotton clouds. The back of the manor was wrapped with a porch that opened to a small lawn—which then dropped off a sheer cliff face to the ocean below. I inhaled, slowly. The flowers in the surrounding gardens blended with the briny sea air and filled my senses.

My back was pressed against a stairway banister, Andimir on the stair above me. Honey-kissed wine swirled in the glasses in our hands, our eyes on the view. Nearly a fortnight had passed since he sent Fetian to Audri, and we were reluctant to move on until we had some idea of what was going on in the south.

"He'll be back soon," Andimir said.

I looked up to find his eyes on my face and sighed. "I know. I'm more worried about what happens when he returns. What if Camion doesn't wake up?"

"He'll be okay. He's doing better every day."

Camion hadn't woken, not coherently, since the boat. Andimir was able to get water in him a few times a day. Once a day he even managed small portions of softer food. Mashed fruits or vegetables, mostly. Andimir cared for us both, in the way of one who carried a guilt he shouldn't bear—a feeling I was all too familiar with. But until Camion could support himself completely, eat true meals, the nutrients were only sustaining his life. I wasn't even sure they were doing that.

"I still regret wasting my magic."

Andimir frowned. "Healing yourself isn't 'wasting your magic,' Natylia. We knew this would take a while. You've reset bones, healed skin, fixed wounds I couldn't even begin to see. Give yourself some credit."

I nodded, but the words felt hollow. Every day I grew stronger—and every day I wasn't sure the same could be said for Camion. He hadn't put on weight like I had. He slept endlessly. I was worried, not only for the wounds and fractures and breaks I hadn't quite finished healing, but for his mind. For the things he had endured and was still trapped with.

The guilt that lay on my shoulders was heavy, and when I thought of those Scepters, sparkling with magic, my heart felt like a rock in my chest. Valdis won, in the end. He had my magic.

He had probably already reforged the Stave.

I didn't say any of that to Andimir. Instead, I voiced another fear, one that crossed my mind frequently enough that I was beginning to feel paranoid. "I don't know why Valeria hasn't found us yet."

Andimir shifted uneasily, but admitted, "The thought has crossed my mind. Any reason she's on yours?"

"I think about her most when the world feels too still. Subconsciously, I think I'm waiting for her to arrive."

Before Andimir could reply, bootsteps thudded across the porch boards. "Mind if I join you two?"

I waved at the steps. Lucian dropped to the same stair I perched on, leaning against the opposite banister, but the small jug he carried held a much stronger drink than our wine.

"How are you holding up?" I said.

"As well as I can be. Better than you and Camion, so I have no complaints."

I appreciated the sentiment, even if I couldn't quite vocalize the words yet. He at least looked more rested, even despite spending days trying to help in any way that he could. I could tell his past weighed on him. It made sense that he now wanted to do penance for his missteps. I was willing to let him try, especially when he had left before dawn more than once only to return with fresh meat or fish.

But, some nights, his yellow eyes would catch the light and I would recoil. His face always fell when it happened. I knew he wasn't his father. But a flicker of those yellow eyes sent me back.

We drifted into an easy silence, sipping our drinks, watching the sky darken and the stars began to sparkle in the setting sun's wake. After Andimir had apologized to Lucian, the three of us had spent many nights like this—soaking in the small moments where we had them. Listening for anything amiss: signs of danger, or Camion waking, whichever came first. Mostly we were quiet, reminiscing about the last few months. Mourning. I was grateful for the peace. The stillness let my mind release the frustration and guilt and loss that I felt, the uselessness. When my mind was too heavy, the world would stop to listen. There was healing to be found in silence.

As the thought crossed my mind, a caw broke the near silence, soft at first. Then another followed, a bit louder. Andimir sat up straighter.

I caught his eye. "Fetian's back?"

"Guess so."

Lucian stood, leaving his jug abandoned next to our wine glasses. Andimir offered me his arm and I accepted, leaning into his shoulder. I was getting stronger; I could feel the change in my mind, my alertness. The fog was clearing. I didn't shake when I walked. But the spasms were still unpredictable, so I accepted the support offered to me.

Fetian sat on a stone statue off the main path to the manor, an impatient expression on his face and his claw locked tightly around a glass vial. A slip of parchment was tied to his leg. Andimir took them both, offering the raven a tiny strip of dried meat that he procured from spirits only knew where. Fetian cawed his appreciation and Andimir guided me back inside, motioning for Lucian to follow. His eyes never left the parchment.

"Audri was vague, no surprise," he said as he led us into one of the studies. He helped me down to a pile of red velvet cushions near the fireplace, then flopped himself onto a stiff-backed chair, throwing his legs over the arm. Lucian followed, returning our drinks to us before dropping into the match to Andimir's chair.

"Now that we're situated," Andimir continued, "Audri says they're preparing to move their armies north without attracting too much attention." He studied me for a moment. I lifted a brow at the appraisal. "We need to move for Thrais soon. Maybe a few more days, tops."

I winced. "So, we'll be here for half a moon cycle? That seems like such a long time to do nothing."

"Healing isn't the same as doing nothing," Andimir chided. "I'm pretty sure you can't fight a Titan when a strong breeze could knock you over."

I narrowed my eyes on him, but Lucian intervened, pointing to the bottle. "What's that?"

"This"—Andimir shook the vial between his fingers—"is for Camion. She didn't explain though."

Sitting straighter, I said, "What do you mean she didn't explain?"

"I mean the letter says, 'have him drink this' and, since the letter is addressed to me, and I didn't mention the prince . . ."

Lucian didn't comment, but a flicker of appreciation passed over his face.

"What did you tell her about him?"

"I said something along the lines of . . . our friend is malnourished and weak and has been put through his paces in ways too heinous to describe."

My throat grew thick. I struggled to swallow, failed, but managed, "What do you think she sent?"

Andimir shrugged. "I don't know. Are you willing to try this?"

"I'm willing to try anything," I admitted quietly. "He can't continue like this. If not for my magic . . ."

"I know." Green eyes met mine once more. "We'll save him. When he's back on his feet, or at least awake, we'll make for Thrais. I'll defend you both to the death, if I have to."

"If we're spotted," Lucian murmured, "we won't be given a choice."

Andimir frowned, holding up the tiny vial and eyeing the teal liquid within. "I hope this works."

***

Camion spluttered as soon as the liquid hit the back of his throat. Andimir lifted him, holding him upright until he calmed enough to drain the remaining tincture. Lucian stood a step behind me as I watched with bated breath, staring at Camion as though the medicine would be a cure-all, as though he would immediately spring back to his old self—full of life and color and love.

But when Camion fell into a restless sleep, and Andimir laid him back down, I realized how selfish the thought was. As though I was expecting him to do what I couldn't, even with magic. I wanted the comfort and reassurance of the man I loved, but he needed me right now.

Still, I had let my hopes climb and, with those dashed, I excused myself, hurrying down the hall and crawling into the bed I had unintentionally claimed as my own. I couldn't even bring myself to sleep beside Camion yet, or to visit him outside our healing sessions, too ashamed, too guilty. My magic had helped, but the mind . . . the mind is a tricky thing, not to be toyed with. No number of apologies felt adequate for what he had suffered.

If I were being totally honest, I missed him. More than I ever could have imagined possible. I missed his steadfast presence, the reassuring warmth of his hand in mine, the silence he offered when the world was too heavy. I missed my other half.

I wasn't sure when I fell asleep.

Early morning light filtered through my window and I stared absently at the swirling particles of dust, for what was surely hours before I finally relented to the restless feeling. I had grown used to a routine of eating and healing and eating and bathing . . . but my steps were sluggish, slow with the heavy weight on my shoulders. I tested each limb as I yawned, the same way I did each morning, biting back my complaints as every muscle stretched and groaned in protest. The heels of my feet hit the cool floor before I looked toward the doorway.

Everything inside of me stopped. My breath. My heart.

My hands flew to my mouth.

Camion.

He leaned against the door frame and watched me, only the barest whisper of a smile on his face. His eyes though . . .

Where I was used to seeing light and love and hope, his eyes were dull. Pained. His arms were crossed over his chest. I remained frozen, examining each tremble of his muscles, each steady lift of his chest. And when I finished, as much as I wanted to run to him, hug him, kiss him . . .

I had put a distance between us that I didn't know how to cross. The scars that climbed his shoulders and littered his arms were my fault.

You should have used your magic.

I know.

But I hadn't and now . . .

Now I didn't know how to approach him.

Camion's silence didn't help. He studied me as though unsure of what to make of me and peered at the new scars that lined my own skin—the ones he could see.

Finally, after what felt like minutes, he drew a shallow breath and said, "I love you."

His voice was raw and dry and strained. A new wave of hesitation washed over me, but I took a step closer anyway. Then another, and another, until my arms were wrapped loosely around his waist. His own arms tightened around me and his breath warmed my head when he pressed his lips to my hair.

"I told myself, if I could see you again"—Camion coughed lightly—"I wanted to tell you, one more time."

"I love you, too," I murmured, rising to my toes so I could press my forehead against his.

He swayed lightly, loosening an arm to steady himself. My brow furrowed. He twisted, gingerly leaning his back against the door frame, then lifted my chin with a finger.

"You didn't do this to me."

The words echoed in my ears.

My pulse thundered louder.

I couldn't meet his eyes.

An invisible fist squeezed my heart. I retreated a step and wrapped my arms around myself.

You did this to him.

"Tyli."

Apologies streamed from my lips before I could stop them. Words. I wasn't sure half of them made much sense. Apologies and grief, problems he didn't deserve laid at his feet so baldly. In my remorse I spewed more words than I had in day, than I had in at least a month, still skirting widely around everything that had been done to me at Valdis's hands.

Camion reached for my arm, but he froze before he touched me. "Tyli. What was that last thing?"

My jaw snapped shut and I racked my mind. "I don't . . . remember."

"About Jyn. What did you say about Jyn?"

The tears welled in my eyes. Before I could repeat the words, Andimir appeared and laid a hand on Camion's arm. "Camion! Welcome back to the land of the coherent. Let's get you some food, then we can talk some more. Get you up to speed. Nat, are you hungry?"

I nodded, even as Camion's brows drew together. He didn't say anything though, offering me his hand as Andimir waved for us to follow him down the stairs.

But instead of following, I looped my fingers through Camion's, my eyes welling with tears, and blurted, "I missed you."

His expression softened. Then he pulled me against him, slowly, as though the movement pained him. But his hold remained tight. "I missed you every damned second," he whispered in my ear. "Even in my dreams."

"All right, I guess you'll meet me down here," Andimir called up the stairs.

I sighed, even as I stepped away from Camion, even as the corner of his mouth curved up ever so slightly. Andimir led us into a study where Lucian already lounged, a book sprawled open on his lap. He leaped to his feet when we entered, and Camion's expression went from cautious joy to fully guarded. Recovering or no, he side-stepped in front of me, those blue and green eyes steady on the prince.

"I'm not here for the reasons you think I am," Lucian started.

"Easy, Cam," Andimir interjected. "The prince is the reason you two are walking."

Questions burned in Camion's eyes. A muscled flicked in his jaw. I nodded, squeezing his hand. "It's true. If not for Lucian, we would have died in that prison."

"You did . . . mention that," Camion recalled slowly, his shoulders relaxing a bit.

I led him to a wide, soft-cushioned chair big enough for two people and settled him before moving for my pile of cushions. He grabbed my wrist and, as much as my mind screamed that I was unworthy, I pushed it off, accepting his offer and climbing into his lap.

"What she said—" Camion started. I winced and his grip tightened, his eyes on my face.

Andimir shook his head. "Food first."

And then he vanished into the kitchen.

Camion's attention snapped to the prince, who sat uneasily at the edge of his chair. "I have you to thank that Tyli's alive?"

"I suppose so."

"Why the change of heart?"

"I didn't have a change of heart." Lucian sighed. "Look. I've made some huge mistakes the last couple of years, the biggest of which was listening to my father and assuming I could take whatever I wanted. Whomever I wanted. But then I saw what my father did to you two. And I realized that, for all his talk of taking over the world, he really meant hurting the people I cared about. Regardless of our past, I wasn't about to let him kill you two, if I could help it."

Camion studied him for a long moment before he nodded. "And now?"

"And now I'm trying to figure out what being a half-Titan means."

"You're—" Camion considered. "That makes sense. Do you have any abilities?"

"None that I've seen. None that Natylia can detect, though she hasn't had much practice with Titans, to be fair."

"And your father?"

"Doesn't know I'm here. Nor my mother. And, disappointingly, neither have come looking for me."

"Maybe they're being thorough," I offered softly.

Lucian gave a small smile but shook his head. "I think they're both too caught up in their own problems to even notice I'm gone."

"Two bottles of wine for Lucian, understood," Andimir said with a grin. His left arm was looped tightly around several glass bottles, his right balancing a large platter. I jumped to my feet to help, pulling bottles free as he sat the platter atop a rectangular table that ran between us and the fireplace. Once all the bottles were lined up on the floor, I clambered back into Camion's lap. He leaned his head against my back, taking a deep breath, trying to conceal how exhausted he really was. Maybe this was too much for him so soon.

"Only one bottle, thanks," Lucian said, his smile genuine now. "I don't much care for the stuff anymore. And one certainly isn't enough to addle the senses."

"Aye," Andimir said, tipping a brown bottle to his lips, one I suspected was full of rum.

"Is it true?" Camion asked, lifting his head to focus on Andimir. "What she said about Jyn, is it true?"

"Yeah," Andimir admitted quietly. Pain flickered through his eyes, his voice wavering as he said, "Jyn is . . . Jyn is gone."

I gritted my teeth, focusing hard on the floorboards. I desperately tried not to hear the words or focus on the daggers still resting on the table upstairs. Camion's arms tightened significantly.

"I should have been there," he murmured. "I'm so sorry, Tyli."

"You've been through enough, my friend," Andimir said. "We're honestly more glad that you're awake than worried about what you've missed."

"What he said." I twisted and buried my face into Camion's shoulder, taking a few seconds to savor that he was here and awake and mine. I missed him so much.

"How are you feeling?" Lucian asked.

"Like I was killed and brought back. A few times. For sport." I stiffened and Camion whispered an apology for my ears.

Andimir replied swiftly, "They nearly did. How's your . . . how's your mind?"

"Not pleasant." Camion had never liked talking about his demons. Then he added, "I'll be fine."

"Get some of this food into your stomach," Andimir said, "then you need more rest."

Camion quirked a half-smile. "And a bath."

"Aye." Andimir laughed.

We managed to get Camion to eat almost a full meal before he followed Andimir to the bathing room with promises that he would be quick. I didn't mind. I remembered how much I appreciated my first real bath after everything: the silence and the heat of the water.

With him gone, I curled up on the wide chair and yanked a blanket over my shoulders, then stared absently into the flames in front of me. I felt Lucian watching me and glanced up. His face was open, with a kind of sincerity I hadn't seen in such a long time.

He picked up his book, waving the volume in the air. "I'm going back to this . . . do you want me to read to you?"

"Yes, please," I murmured.

And he did. He read the story of a pair of twins who were aligned with the sun and moon, and he was almost to the end when the story faded away and I let the weight of exhaustion press me back into sleep.

Chapter 9

"**S**top thinking about your bow and focus on using your blade," Andimir chided.

I peered up from the dagger clenched in my hand and lifted an eyebrow. "How did you know?"

"You keep giving the dagger dirty looks." Andimir snickered. "And every time we pass the bows, you've given them looks Camion should be jealous of."

Heat spread up my neck. I was suddenly grateful Camion was in the manor. "I do not."

Andimir gave me a knowing look. But he gestured to the dagger again and waved an impatient hand.

I wasn't fast, and the combat felt foreign; I could use blades, and I could use fists, but I had never really worked with such a small, close-ranged weapon. Andimir had a strong advantage thankfully, because the daggers were sharp and my motions were clumsy. He easily parried attacks that should have hit their mark. I couldn't help feeling like a toddler learning to walk. I wasn't even sure why he wanted me to learn to use them; if he thought I was going to use Jyn's daggers, he had another thing coming.

Andimir slipped past my guard, landing a harder-than-intended strike on my arm. I rubbed at the sore spot, groaning. "I'm no good at this. Give me a sword."

"Nope. Again."

"I'm not strong enough or fast enough or good enough," I snapped. Andimir's eyebrow lifted and I sighed. "I'm sorry. I'm . . . I'm sorry."

He didn't answer, pulling me into a hug instead. I rested my forehead on his chest, murmuring another apology. When the anger that brewed at my failures calmed a bit, I stepped away and rotated my wrists to signal another round.

"You know, you've been through a lot," Lucian offered from the porch, where he had reclined on the stairs to watch us. "You can't be expected to pick any blade right back up. Andimir and I can compensate for you and Camion until you're feeling stronger."

"That's the problem." I released a growl as my head fell back onto my shoulders and my arms slumped at my sides. "I *am* feeling stronger."

"And you are," Andimir soothed. He hesitated, then added, "But putting on a few pounds and ignoring your demons? That's not healing."

"Then what is?"

"Accepting that what happened to you, to Camion, wasn't your fault. Forgiving yourself. Moving on."

I huffed. "What would you know about that?"

Andimir's small smile was sad. "A lot, actually. And I can tell

-108-

you that holding onto your past, your demons? It's not hurting them. It's hurting you."

My eyes fell to the blade. I sighed. Andimir was right. I simply wasn't in a place where I could move past the horrors—yet. Plus, Audri's concoction had Camion up and moving. Eating. That was progress. My mouth opened and shut, then I nodded. "You're right."

He gently squeezed my arm. "Don't forget you haven't even been free a full moon cycle. Healing takes time, and you've come so far already. Give yourself credit for that."

I patted his hand and yelled a thanks to Lucian, who was back to sipping at that jug he seemed to have glued to his hands.

Andimir was right. I didn't think I would ever be the same. And I couldn't decide if that was a good thing.

"All right, smart one," I said, rotating my neck. "Let's go again."

***

I jolted upright, breathing heavily. My fingers clutched at my nightshirt while I scanned the room frantically. I waited for Jyn to burst in and tell me everything was all right. And when he didn't, pain split through my chest and cut off my air.

Then I heard the sound again, the one that had awoken me—a loud bang from downstairs. I crept to the top of the stairs, my fist clenched around the hilt of the dagger Lucian had given me. The one I now kept hidden beside my bed at night.

A floorboard groaned behind me and I spun, grateful when I locked eyes with Camion. He lifted a finger to his lips, creeping up beside me. He reached for my arm and I restrained the wince that urged me to pull away. His fingers brushed over my skin . . . a reassurance.

You don't deserve him.

I clenched my teeth, trying to ignore that persistent thought. Camion seemed steadier on his feet as he followed, a relief since we needed to be quiet. Doors on the far end of the hall opened. Closest to us was a yawning Lucian, who held a sword, and Andimir, who rubbed at his eyes warily. When Andimir processed our positions around him, he crouched in a shadow and tilted his head to listen.

Footsteps echoed across the foyer. A beat of silence passed, then, "Hello?"

That voice was familiar. One from a distant time, a memory that I had pushed far, far down in the trauma of the last couple months. But now here it was, dredged up, fresh in my thoughts.

"Wulfric," I growled under my breath.

Before Camion could stop me, I lithely slunk down the stairs, straightening to my full height on the landing below.

"What in the Nether are you doing here?" I demanded. The thud of boots met my ears. Andimir raced down the stairs behind me, Lucian and Camion on his heels.

Wulfric cowered. The grey streaks of his temples had spread, glittering throughout the rest of his black hair. He looked thin, gaunt, deep circles under his eyes. His clothes sat too loosely, his eyes wide with fear.

He was the last remaining member of the Council. The man who had pledged us help and then vanished when his colleagues were found brutally murdered.

Anger writhed in my gut.

"Don't hurt me," he pleaded, hands held up near his face. My anger faltered. "I didn't do what they said I did. I didn't hurt them."

"How can we prove that?" Andimir asked, stepping up beside me.

Camion and Lucian lurked in the shadows of the stairs, waiting. I doubted we would need them though; Wulfric had paled three shades lighter when Andimir showed himself. And, deep in my gut, I knew the older man was telling the truth.

"You can't," Wulfric admitted. "You can't because I have no proof for you. But I'm telling you. I didn't kill the Council. I couldn't have. I was in Thrais."

I studied him, met eyes that didn't seem to hold any lie. And I didn't understand. He was terrorized, uncertain.

"Where did you go, then?" Andimir asked. "When they couldn't find you?"

I reached out, putting a hand on Andimir's arm. "I believe you," I said to Wulfric. "But I am still curious. What happened to you?"

"I received word of an informant in Thrais. I left to investigate and went to Falmar." Wulfric stared wide-eyed at me for a long moment, his expression calming a bit. "I didn't betray you, Your Highness. I would never. I meant what I said before—I only ever wanted to help you."

Andimir caught my eye and lifted a shoulder.

Wulfric noticed the gesture and raised a brow. His lips curved into a deep frown.

"Your Highness . . . where is Jyn?"

The hand holding Lucian's dagger fell to my side, and the blade clattered to the floor. Andimir's focus locked onto Wulfric with an intensity that reminded me of Jyn. My chest ached. Lucian and Camion pulled themselves from the shadows, the latter pressing into my side. Wulfric shook his head.

"I'm no threat to her, boys, that was merely observation. I won't hurt your queen." He studied Lucian, questions flooding into his eyes, then back to me. "If he's lost to you, I'm sorry."

Camion's arm looped around my shoulders.

I need to push him off, let him go. Let him heal.

I wavered only a moment before I shoved the voice aside and curled into Camion's warmth. The steady rhythm of his heartbeat reassured me. I deserved to be here, in his arms. I certainly wanted to be.

And I hoped more than anything that soon I could look at him without seeing all the pain I had wrought. I wondered, when his grip tightened around me, if he knew what I was thinking. How I felt.

With a sigh, I pressed, "So, what happened to you?"

"I went to Falmar, as I said. Turns out my timing was better than anticipated. I got word from a contact near Thrais to stay hidden. Leaving when I had apparently put me a few steps ahead." Wulfric sighed. "I've been on the move since. Nowhere is safe. Not for long."

"Did you find the informant?"

"No," Wulfric admitted. "I could never get enough evidence to prove anything definitively. Though, I suspect Valdis is involved."

"He is," I murmured.

"Who were you running from, if you never found the informant?" Camion asked.

"Everyone. Anyone. There's a bounty on my head that makes the ones on yours look like a pittance."

"But why? Why do you hold so much value to Valdis?"

"I don't, once I'm dead." Wulfric looked between the four of us. He took in the thick tension between us, the missing people, the scars that littered Camion's and my skin. He stood a little straighter and smoothed the lines of his shirt nervously before he asked, "What happened to you four?"

"You'll forgive me if I'm not eager to share our stories right now," I said.

"Of course, Your Highness."

Andimir crossed his arms over his chest. "What are you doing here? Now, especially?"

"I thought Edra might be safe, having been abandoned for so long," Wulfric admitted. "My sincerest apologies for waking you . . . This is certainly the last place I expected to find you lot."

"I can't decide what to do with you now that you have," Andimir said, eyeing him.

"Your Highness, I mean you no harm, truly. I've been running for so long . . . All I need is a place to sleep, some food . . ."

I glanced around. When the other three inclined their heads, I said, "Fine. You can stay. But you never saw us."

Wulfric swept into a deep bow. "I am grateful. And Your Majesty will find that I have no weapons on my person. I was not so fortunate to take much coin when I fled either."

True to his word, Wulfric didn't have so much as the pipe I had known him to carry like an extra limb. Andimir and I extended the watch schedule, and Lucian offered to take first rotation. Camion retreated upstairs when his limbs began to tremble with exertion, not wanting to reveal the depth of his condition to Wulfric. I couldn't decide if we could trust the man but, if nothing else, he wasn't a threat at present.

After he had been settled into a spare room, a secluded one a fair distance down the hall, Lucian set up his watch post. He leaned back in a chair, tossing his feet onto the stair rail before I said goodnight.

I closed the door behind me. For my own sanity, I flicked the lock shut, then wondered if Camion had done the same. Taking several deep, calming breaths, I ran my fingers through my hair and moved for the bed.

But a soft sound caught my ear and I paused to listen. Minutes passed before I realized what I was hearing, what the repetitive shuffle was—pacing. I moved closer to the wall between my room and Camion's. His footsteps were steady, consistent. Back and forth, back and forth.

I pressed my palm to the wall, debating what I should do. Camion might need time to think. To heal by himself. If I went over to check on him, would I be overstepping? I couldn't decipher the feelings relentlessly stirring inside me. Was it the same, constant voice of guilt, pushing me away from him? Or a voice of reason, encouraging me to do what was best for the man I loved?

Unable to decide, I withdrew my hand, sighing heavily. Tomorrow I would check on him; tonight, I would give him space to process. Pacing was normal. Human. And I remembered how much I had valued uninterrupted silence after we had escaped.

I climbed into my bed and sank into the soft mattress before rolling myself in the plush blankets. My eyelids instantly grew heavy. I was almost asleep when a new sound caught my ear and my eyes flew open.

A scream?

Muffled, though, like the sound was being filtered through a pillow. My heartbeat pounded in my ears and I sat up. Listened. For a beat, the house fell silent. Then the sound of sobs picked up, muffled again. My chest tightened.

Camion.

I leapt to my feet, moving for the door without a second's hesitation. Andimir stepped into the hallway from his own room as I came out, but I shook my head at him.

"I've got him," I mouthed.

He nodded, uncertain, but watched as I knocked at Camion's door. No response. The choked sobs didn't even pause, shredding my heart. I tested the doorknob. He hadn't locked it.

"Camion?" I kept my voice soft, peeking in through a small crack.

No answer, but the sounds fell off. I opened the door wider. His room wasn't brightly lit, only a few candles across one of the shelves. The blankets were strewn unevenly across the bed, draping onto the floor. I cast a glance over my shoulder, at Andimir hesitant in the hallway, and closed the door behind me.

"Camion?" I repeated.

At first, I didn't see him.

He was balled in on himself, curled on the floor, his back to me, his hands laced into his hair. His body shook with the sobs that still trembled through him.

I took a step forward and he groaned softly, his fingers tugging on silky blond strands.

The air caught in my lungs and I clenched my jaw. Guilt tried to gnaw its way into my mind, but I aggressively shoved the feelings away.

Not now. Not when he needed me.

I dropped to the ground beside Camion and placed my hand on his back. He recoiled from the touch, shifting away, and I flinched. But I understood. So, I took a deep breath and tried again.

"I love you. What do you need from me?"

Camion stilled, his soft breaths rapid. Then he shuddered.

"I want—" His voice was raw, raspy. I had never heard Camion so broken, and the sound brought tears to my eyes. His fingers tightened around his scalp, pulling, clawing. "I want this to stop."

"Want what to stop, exactly, my love?"

"The voices, the memories, the pictures, the pain," he spit out quickly, breaking off into another harsh sob. "I can't get them out of my head, I can't stop reliving . . ."

Camion groaned again, louder this time. He freed a hand from his hair, balling it into a fist that he slammed into the floorboards. "I can't do this." His voice was low, raw. "*I can't do this*."

"Can't do what?"

I knew what he was going to say. Before the words left his mouth, my tears were already spilling over.

"I can't live like this."

A lead weight dropped into my stomach. I hesitated for a moment, unsure of what to do or say. His fist hit the floor once more and flecks of blood flew from his knuckles.

And I moved into action.

Instinct took over.

I gripped Camion's wrists, pulling up a blossom of magic that healed his split knuckles. Then I pulled him to me, not relenting when he resisted. Because this was Camion. Because this was the man I loved and I wasn't going to let him suffer through this alone or give up on himself so easily.

Because his heart was good and pure and kind and the world needed more of that right now.

"They tried to destroy you," I whispered. "They tried to destroy you and I'll be damned if they succeed."

"They did destroy me, Natylia, that's what I'm saying," he choked out.

But he lifted his head. I took in his red-rimmed eyes, swollen and bloodshot, and his cheeks stained with tears. Despite all of that, he was still the most handsome man I had ever laid eyes on. The most beautiful man, in ways that went far deeper than skin.

I pulled him toward me again. And I kept pulling until he at last relented, curling up against me to bury his face into my shoulder.

"They didn't destroy you. They broke you. But you know what? If a sword breaks, you don't throw the blade away and call it quits. You take the time to reforge, to salvage all the shattered pieces and make them strong again. Why would you be any different?"

Camion didn't answer, but his arms tightened around me. I went on, stroking his soft hair as I spoke. "It's easy to let the darkness in. To let the dark fog creep into the corners of your mind and push out all your hope. But you've never let me forget, so I won't let you. Darkness doesn't kill hope, it drowns the light. And I'm not going to let Valdis extinguish the brightest light I've ever known."

"How can you stand to look at me? How can you see my scars without being reminded?" he murmured. My shoulder was damp. I pressed a kiss against his hair.

"I can't. I'm reminded every single day. And that guilt is why I've kept you at arm's length so much since you woke up, and why I've been keeping a separate room. I can only imagine you feel the same looking at me. And seeing you in pain—" I swallowed. "I didn't want to cause you more, and I have, and I'm so sorry. I thought I was handling all this right, but I did everything so wrong. I should have been here. From the moment you woke, without hesitation. Because regardless of all else, I love you. I love you so much. And seeing you hurting like this . . . I don't care what I have to do to help you. I'm here now. I'm here as long as you need me."

"I'll always need you," he whispered.

A lump formed in my throat. "I couldn't bear it if you left me. I feel like I just got you back."

"I won't leave you."

"Promise?"

Camion didn't even hesitate. "I promise." Then he sat up straighter, wiping at his eyes, inhaling deep, calming breaths. "I'm sorry."

"For what?"

"For . . ." He gestured to his room and himself by way of explanation.

"You have nothing to be sorry for. If anything . . ." I hesitated.

I wasn't sure now was the time for my own confession, but guilt nudged at me and the words tumbled out. "If anything, I'm sorry that I led you into all this. I'm responsible, directly or no, that you were hurt. And I'm so sorry."

"Tyli, you didn't do anything to me." Camion cupped my cheeks between his hands. "You were right. He did this to us both. *They* did this to us both. But . . ." His throat bobbed. "But I don't know if I can heal without you this time. No, I don't *want* to heal without you. I need you."

Camion waited then, scanning my face with those beautiful blue and green eyes of his. He sought the answer to a question he hadn't asked, permission he didn't need. His breath fanned warm, soft air over my lips. I leaned closer to claim his. And though he returned the kiss slowly, sweetly, he broke away too soon.

"Stay with me," he whispered. A question and a plea.

I couldn't deny him if I wanted to. And I knew what he was asking: for me to let him back in, to sleep side by side again while we healed and figured out how we fit together now. To start over. We were broken, jagged versions of ourselves. But we were stronger together.

We had always been stronger together.

I curled my fingers around his hands, offering him a gentle smile. "Your bed is a mess."

Camion winced, offering a tiny smile. "Sorry."

"Don't be. I'll fix the sheets. And Cam?" He met my eyes, his brows drawn together. "Next time it's too much, come find me? I promise I won't be so far away."

"I didn't want to be another burden."

"You'll never be another burden. I love you, in darkness and in light."

Chapter 10

"You all right?" Andimir tugged on my arm.

I blinked. Andimir and I had come to the stables to check on Lucian, but the distant ocean waves under the lingering colors of the morning sunrise were hypnotizing. "Yeah. Where's Lucian?"

"Complaining about his new . . . attire." My eyebrow lifted at Andimir's tone and he added, "Well if we're going to have a driver, he has to look the part."

"What did you do?"

"Made some suggestions?" He smiled innocently. Too innocently.

I sighed, glancing at the open space we stood beside. Rippling grass stretched all the way to the cliffside, most of the field looped by thick fencing. "And Camion?"

"Still inside but he'll be out shortly. Have you spotted any of the horses?"

"No, I'm wondering if they wandered too far. Maybe our plan

will fail."

Andimir leaned against the fence, crossing his arms over his chest. "Not like you to give up so easily."

"I haven't been much like myself, lately." I sighed.

"Understandably so."

I wasn't sure what to say. He knew how I felt, and enough of what I had been through. I turned to lean on the fence beside him, but Andimir nudged my arm, jerking his head toward the stable building. When I didn't move, he gripped my elbow.

"Come on, we'll be back before the other two get here."

The heavy wooden doors resisted him for a moment, but Andimir wrenched them open to reveal an old wagon that he and Lucian had spent several days piecing back together. They had done their job well too. It was hard to believe that only days ago it had been a pile of barely recognizable pieces.

Andimir patted the wagon. "Thought you could use a confidence boost. We've made sure Wulfric stayed away from the stables." He paused to point at the satchels and blankets piled in the back. "A couple horses and we'll be out of here."

"Tonight, if all goes to plan," Lucian said, and I jumped. He grimaced apologetically, tugging at the coarse jacket he wore. "Is this really necessary?"

"Absolutely," Andimir said, his face serious in a way that neither Lucian nor I believed. "You have to be professional."

Lucian rolled his eyes, itching at his neck. "Fine. But I'm changing before we go after the horses. Are you sure there even *are* horses?"

I nodded as I dug through the supplies to count rations and weapons. "When we stayed with Audri in Kalum, she mentioned that they had been released to the fields after the Council was found murdered."

"You realize that's a lot of ground to cover?" Lucian frowned.

"Yes," Andimir said, "But there will be four of us. We can split up. Or well, we can and Camion and Natylia can go their own way."

"Still don't trust me to defend myself?"

My heart fluttered at that voice. One man in a million, but this one was mine.

Mine.

I couldn't restrain the joy that bubbled up. Without thinking, I moved. My arms were around his waist before he had even taken two steps into the stables. Andimir chuckled.

But Camion leaned down, whispering into my ear, "I missed you too."

"I'll go change. Give me a few," Lucian said, shooting Camion and I a timid smile as he passed.

I watched him leave the stable, then sighed, resting my head against Camion's chest. "It's so strange having Lucian around again . . . acting human. Acting like a friend."

"He isn't some complete stranger," Andimir said.

"No," I agreed. "But he's acted like one for so long . . ."

Andimir considered. "You're right. And you're also sore because his father hurt you two in ways I can't even imagine." I met his eyes, brow furrowed, but he continued more gently, "He isn't his father. And he's obviously trying to do better. I think everyone deserves that chance."

My thoughts drifted to Valdis. "No. Not everyone. Lucian yes, but beyond that . . ."

"Fine, that's fair." Andimir stared at the door Lucian had left through. "You know, he's as much of a victim of his father as you are. Some time, when you're ready, you two should sit down and have a real conversation about all of it."

"Yeah. You're right." I tilted my head back, looking up at Camion. "What do you make of all this?"

"I think I'm willing to give anyone who wants to do better for themselves a clean slate," he said. "And I also think we need to go find those horses, if we plan to leave at nightfall."

Andimir left for the house. When he returned, Lucian was at his side and weapons were in his hands. He handed Camion a set of daggers, knowing full well he was struggling with swords right now. Then he handed me a bow—I was stronger and more confident with them. Feeling the smooth curve of wood in my hands lit a strange excitement in my chest.

Andimir gestured toward the weapons. "Not for the horses," he chastised, a grin on his face. I shook my head as he added, more seriously, "I want you two to be safe. If you need help, call for us."

I nodded. "We'll call you, if we find anything."

"Wulfric is still in the house," Lucian said. His voice was tinged with exasperation.

With good reason. The Council member did little more than exist as we moved around him, a ghost who wandered the manor without purpose. Since his arrival, he had spent countless hours reading whatever book caught his fancy. Fairytales, folklore. He reread a story about a sai-wielding Elf enough times that we started making wagers on him, and the stack of reference books in the front study was getting ridiculous. But he showed no interest in what we were doing, and we were careful to make sure he didn't overhear anything important.

His thinning frame and the timid way his eyes darted toward any sound told a story more sincere than anything my mind concocted. This was a man haunted. A man who stayed utterly hidden, barred inside the house because he was too afraid to leave. I felt no fear of him.

Maybe I was a little haunted too.

I stumbled and Camion gripped my arm. We had started walking north and, so lost in my thoughts, a tree root nearly took me out.

"Thanks love," I murmured.

The field in front of us was bare though. Not a sign of an animal in sight. Far to the west I saw the silhouette of Lucian, and Andimir to the east, but no horses. My stomach flipped. What if we couldn't find even one horse? Maybe they jumped the fencing. We would completely have to reconfigure our plans.

A rumble rolled across the field. I froze, lifting an arm to stop Camion. With my free hand, I unshouldered my bow and yanked an arrow free. I still didn't see anything, but the ground began to vibrate. Camion looped an arm around my waist, pulling me closer.

"I think we found the horses," I murmured.

A stampede of the massive beasts was running south, their eyes wide, several of the horses squealing in fear. I moved, grabbing Camion's arm, and dragged him after me to get us out of their path. Andimir was already racing toward us; I didn't dare look to see what Lucian was doing. Not with Camion struggling to keep pace. Not with my bow slapping my leg with every stride.

But the horses weren't coming for us. They were running away from something. And not knowing *what* was far more concerning.

"Nat, ready your bow," Andimir yelled.

I spun on my heel, releasing Camion. Then I saw them. Risen, scrabbling from the north and chasing the horses with mouths stained with blood so bright, I could see the red even this far away. The Risen moved along at an unnatural speed. They weren't far behind the horses, their focus entirely locked onto their meal. I wasn't glad to see them. Risen were reanimated corpses that would do whatever their masters bid them—and the only living being we knew of who could revive them was Valdis.

"We have to kill them all," I realized. "If even one of them runs back to Valdis—"

Andimir nodded, shooting a wary glance at Camion. "We'll manage."

Camion looked nervous.

I readied my bow, nocking an arrow. Out of my peripheral, Lucian was completely blocked from view by the charging horses. But the Risen were closer now and I loosed an arrow. The point sank into the arm of one. He turned his attention from the horses. Red eyes locked onto me.

The other Risen paused, assessing the situation. As the distance between them and the horses grew, I realized there were only around a dozen Risen—but there were also only four of us and two weren't in fighting shape. Jyn could have taken them on without a thought.

My breath caught.

Jyn.

Spirits, I missed Jyn.

There was no time for grief. All I could do was make him proud.

So, I nocked another arrow and fired. This time the bolt sank deep into that Risen's chest. As he slumped to the ground the others broke into their frenzy again. I shoved Camion behind me, to great resistance, before I nocked another arrow. Andimir and Lucian ran to meet them, slashing and slicing. I launched arrows until my arms and shoulders ached, until my hands trembled. Every time Camion tried to fight, I held him back. The patience on his face morphed into frustration, then desperation.

I fired another arrow. Then another.

Only four Risen left.

I let Camion go with a wince, even as a weight lifted at the relief on his face. The three men dispatched the remaining Risen within seconds, Camion panting with exertion. He wasn't ready.

"Was that all of them?" I asked, stepping forward. "We have to make sure that was all of them."

"Yeah, we got them all," Lucian panted. He and Andimir were both covered in blood that wasn't their own.

"No," I murmured. "No, we didn't."

One of the Risen had stayed to the back. One who looked too calm, too at ease. Too human and in control of his emotions. And as soon as he noticed that we saw him, he bolted.

I raced after.

Andimir and Camion yelled behind me. Footsteps thudded across the grass, but I ignored them all. I knew I couldn't catch him. I tossed my bow to the grass. I wouldn't hit the shot.

Instead I reached out with my magic, felt for his energy, and paused long enough to throw a barb in his direction. The magic launched out in a spear of purple and blue, slamming into the Risen's back. He dropped to the ground and began to crumble and burn, an inferno that matched the anger ignited in my veins. One misstep and Valdis would have been here. We could have been compromised. Wulfric would have been compromised. And Kathryn had put a reward out for news of Lucian. So much could have gone wrong—

"Breathe, Tyli."

I did. I inhaled slowly, glancing down as I exhaled. My body was covered in shimmering magic, my scar seared with pain. But I had taken the Risen down. I shuddered to think what would happen if Valdis decided Edra was worth investigating again. Or if his lapdog Vampyr caught our scents.

Camion's hand was warm against my back, my bow gripped firmly at his side. I patted his arm gently. "I'm fine. Let's get back."

We burned the bodies, made sure there was nothing left of them for Valdis to reform. Then we spent the better part of the afternoon tending the horses—calming them and treating the few that were wounded. Eventually, the afternoon light began to fade from the property and we needed to leave. Andimir and Lucian circled the perimeter to survey for potential threats one last time, then hitched two of the calmer horses to the fixed-up wagon. Camion and I tucked ourselves into the back, atop blankets and pillows, between the satchels of supplies. We had extra blankets to cover ourselves, if we were stopped. I had tucked an extra satchel of herbs and bandages into my own bag.

The wagon jolted into motion. Despite the jostling ride, I easily tied Jyn's daggers to my waist. The action was foreign, painful, but I couldn't bear the thought of hiding them away in a satchel. His daggers deserved better than that. His memory deserved better than that.

The plan was to stick to the coastline, so our tracks would be washed away as we went along. We hoped that Valdis wouldn't realize Andimir joined us, that a cloaked, hooded wagon driver and his guard would earn no more than a glance from passersby.

Maybe he thought Camion and I had died.

I couldn't decide if that was better—or worse. That would certainly explain why there had been no sign of Valeria or the other Titans. Their extended silence sat uneasily in my stomach, but I was ready to be back in Thrais.

Home.

I was ready to be home.

***

"What you got in the back there, son?"

I jerked awake at the unfamiliar voice, at the sudden stillness of the wagon. The blankets were over my head and the unexpected weight made my breath catch. I shot Camion a concerned glance. He pressed a soothing hand on my stomach, holding a finger to his lips. My heartbeat thundered to life.

"Nothing of concern," I heard Andimir say. "Is there a reason you're hassling travelers?"

"Well I imagine you've heard about Annalea, the missing Princess of Thrais?"

I still didn't recognize the voice. My fingers ran uneasily over the hilt of one of Jyn's daggers, my muscles tensed to spring. Camion's fingertips pressed into my shirt, a silent warning not to do anything reckless.

Andimir cleared his throat. "Of course, what does that have to do with anything?"

"Well, with the queen dead, there's a large reward for anyone who can find the missing princess. We've taken it upon ourselves to collect."

A small chorus of chuckled laughter scattered around us. Lucian or Andimir shifted their weight, causing the wagon to sway. I gripped the dagger more tightly.

"You'll find our wagon lacks a princess," Andimir said smoothly. I didn't miss the slight grin in his tone.

Only he would find humor in this situation.

"I wouldn't mind checking," a new voice said.

A chill washed over my skin, a wave of goosebumps leaping to life. I knew that voice. *Her* voice.

Andimir didn't speak this time, confirming my suspicions. Eurybia, the Titan of water, might recognize his voice. Andimir had always had some favor with her father, the Titan Marinus. He would also be a dead giveaway as to the cargo being concealed. The wagon shook before boots hit the ground nearby.

"If it's all the same, I'd rather keep moving. I'm running behind already." Lucian's voice was steady, authoritative.

Shuffling caught my ears, and I imagined he had removed his hood to reveal his face. I winced. Having him conceal himself under his cloak was a last-minute decision. We had wanted to avoid revealing his location if we could, especially with his mother looking for him, and possibly his father. Or maybe Drask thought Lucian had turned tail and ran. Maybe he didn't care, regardless. That thought sunk Andimir's words about him being a victim several inches deeper.

One person was undaunted by the revelation. She moved slowly, tapping long nails on the side of the wagon as she passed. I wasn't certain she couldn't hear my heart trying to climb out of my throat.

"Prince Lucian." Eurybia's voice was a low purr. "I didn't expect to see you this far south. Is your father aware of your location? Last I knew your family was looking for you."

"Yes, they were looking for me to run this load south. Inconspicuously. Clearly I'm failing at the latter."

"Clearly." Eurybia's nails tapped on the side of the wagon again. "You won't mind if I check, right? Part of my job, protecting the assets, after all."

"Feel free, if rations are so interesting to you." Lucian said. His voice was level.

"Rations, hm?" Eurybia sounded amused.

Lucian reached into the wagon, jerking out a bag. He shuffled with the ties for a moment, then silence fell for a few seconds.

"Rations," he said again.

"Still. I think I'll check for myself."

I reached for Camion's hand, gripping his fingers as tightly as I held onto the dagger. Warmth spread through me, an ache tugging at my side, but all I could think about was the fear pooling in the pit of my stomach. Cool air bit into my skin as the blankets were whisked away and Eurybia stared down at us with icy blue eyes. Iridescent scales ran the length of her cheekbones, shimmering against her midnight complexion and vanishing into the line of her hair.

Terror was ice in my veins, freezing me in place. We were nothing against her.

But a frown curved her lips, her brows drawing together. Camion squeezed my hand and I risked a sideways glance at our hands. Purple and blue magic shimmered over our skin.

Our skin.

I didn't dare breathe.

The water Titan huffed, throwing the blanket haphazardly back into place. "Fine. Why wasn't I told about this movement?"

"I'm not sure," Lucian said calmly. "Ask my father."

"I will."

"Can I be on my way, then?"

Silence. I met Camion's eyes. He jerked his head the smallest fraction. What if . . . What if Lucian was betraying us right now? What if we weren't safe? What if she decided to be more thorough?

One thing was for sure though. Eurybia believed Valdis was alive. Or knew.

Valdis survived.

My heart thundered against my ribs. The air caught in my lungs. My chest rose and fell, more rapidly with each second that passed.

"Tyli," Camion whispered. "Breathe."

Cawing shattered the silence. Frantic, angry cawing. My heart sank. What would Eurybia do to Fetian, if she caught him? I couldn't let Andimir sacrifice his raven. But, with warning bright in Camion's eyes, I hesitated. The thundering beat of my heart pulsed loud in my ears.

"What was that?" Eurybia snapped.

She wasn't as near the wagon anymore, and the cawing had stopped.

"A raven?" Lucian asked. "He didn't seem to like your men."

"I wasn't talking about the bird," the Titan growled. "I was talking about that creature. On the ground. Where did it go?"

"Creature . . . on the ground?" The prince sounded sincerely confused.

"The fox-looking thing," she shrieked angrily.

"The Zylarra," I whispered to Camion, barely releasing a breath.

His brow furrowed before he mouthed, "She's still following us?"

"I guess so," I murmured.

Outside, the sounds had grown into a frenzy of confusion. The angry Titan was raging about an object the Zylarra seemed to have taken from her—a shell or bit of jewelry, I wasn't sure. The wagon shifted to one side, then Lucian spoke again.

"I'll be on my way."

"Get that creature!" Eurybia yelled. But her voice was faint, and clearly not directed at Lucian. Very faint, as though she were giving chase to that poor little legendary animal.

While I was grateful for the distraction, I hoped the Zylarra escaped. Then the cart burst into stumbling motion, pulling us onward.

Chapter 11

Lucian and Andimir pushed the horses harder as we moved onward. With the Titan wandering around, we were even more on edge, if that were possible. Thankfully, my magic and a heady dose of luck saved our skins.

Not excluding the help from the courageous raven and the brave Zylarra.

I was still worried about the latter. Fetian was perched safely on Andimir's shoulder now, and I wondered vaguely what the Zylarra had stolen that had distracted Eurybia so effectively. Either way, word was definitely going to travel to Valdis. We needed to be in Thrais before that happened.

When we had cleared the Titan's line of sight, we shoved the blankets away to help keep watch. None of us rested much for the remainder of the journey. Days passed and my muscles remained knotted tight. I was antsy, too busy peering over the edge of the wagon in search of any sign of the Zylarra we still couldn't see. My erratic behavior kept Camion awake, even though I tried to keep still and quiet so he could sleep. But when I wasn't flitting around the wagon, my eyes behind us, I kept fiddling with one of Jyn's daggers. Flexing my wrist, twisting the point into the wood.

"You're going to dull the point," Camion scolded quietly, a frown curving his lips.

"As long as the blade is still sharp." I cranked the hilt around again, taking strange comfort in the splinters of wood that fell free around the tip.

"The point has uses too. Especially with daggers."

I released a soft sigh and tugged the blade free, picking off the wood shards. The warm weight of Camion's hand pressed down on my leg and I glanced up, noting the soft amusement that shone on his face. He hadn't come so close to a smile, a real smile, since . . . I couldn't remember. The expression on his face warmed my heart, and I offered him a small smile of my own.

"I'll stop hurting the dagger," I said.

His grip tightened a fraction. "Good. If you need to blow off steam, you should pick on someone your own size."

Andimir twisted in his seat at that, a wide grin on his face. "Yeah, like me."

"You're at least a foot taller than my own size," I scoffed.

"Still closer than the dagger." Andimir shrugged.

Lucian laughed quietly. He still didn't fit seamlessly with the rest of us. I knew he could feel the lingering uncertainty, and I also knew he didn't dare to press his luck. But I had to admit, he had handled Eurybia well.

"How are you feeling?" I asked him, bumping his elbow.

"Overwhelmed," Lucian admitted. "I've never come face to face with—"

"Well, technically you have. Every day of your life." Andimir grinned. "I mean. You're also half Titan."

Lucian winced. "Thanks for the reminder."

"Look at the bright side. Maybe you have powers too," Andimir offered.

"I keep waiting to explode or . . . or . . ." Lucian shot a glance over his shoulder. "I don't really know how magic works."

"Meryn and I can help you. Or we can try."

Lucian's eyes softened. A weight lifted from his shoulders right in front of me. "Thank you." He sighed. "We should be in Thrais by morning."

"Only took us a week and a half," I murmured. When Andimir's brow furrowed, I added, "I feel like time is moving so quickly and we're moving so slowly. How are we supposed to stop them, if we can't catch up?"

"We hope they don't get too far ahead," Camion murmured. His eyes were on the road behind us, his fingers still light on my leg. I gathered his hand into mine, squeezing. He turned to me, and said, "We'll have to face them eventually. And when we do? We'll win."

***

We ditched the wagon in the forest west of Thrais and released the horses to find their way home. Then we moved for the city, not bothering to stop for rest; I had long forgotten the last time I didn't feel exhausted. Soul weary.

Our hoods were up, cloaks tightly wrapped around our shoulders as we entered the city. The noon-day sun was still climbing the sky but sounds of life reached my ears: the thrum of an anvil on steel, the casual cluck of chickens, the shouts of patrons as they came and went. The streets felt busier than I had remembered. Had I been gone so long? My heart released at the familiarity of the passing faces but tightened once more when Meryn's shop came into view.

The small stone building, roofed with thatch, sat tucked across the street from the small bakery. I tried not to think about Jyn, and how he would beeline straight for the blueberry muffins if . . .

I focused on Meryn's shop again. We didn't have any lead as to where she might be—this was our best hope. I didn't even know if her shop was still fully open. My fingers were crossed that at least Sylvr was around.

But with each step we took, I hesitated a little more. I wasn't entirely sure why. As much as I wanted to see my friend again, I was worried I would open the door to find she wasn't in Thrais.

Or worse.

My friends hadn't fared so well lately.

I took a deep, steadying breath. Gravel crunched under my boots as I strode forward, ducking between passersby. Most of them paid me no mind, cloaked figures as common now as they had been when we left. Not much seemed to have changed here at all, if I were honest.

As I pushed open the wooden door, dark eyes lifted to mine. Sylvr's eyebrows drew together at the sight of so many hooded figures, but she hastily smoothed her expression, inclining her head.

"Can I help you find anything?" Her voice was welcoming,

but there was an edge I was unused to, a caution.

The corner of my mouth twitched as I reached up, drawing my hood back. "Meryn, perhaps?"

Sylvr's jaw fell open. "Natylia? Is it really you?"

I nodded slowly, glancing over my shoulder as Andimir, Camion, and Lucian removed their hoods as well. My eyes lingered on Camion's face, on the dark circles that had deepened in the past few days. I offered him my hand, my fingers curling around his to offer what comfort I could before I returned my attention to Sylvr.

"Have you seen her? Did she make the trip safely?" I asked.

Sylvr dipped her head, her dark mahogany curls bouncing around her shoulders. She straightened the apron at her waist and propped her broom against a wall before stepping around us to lock the door. Then she jerked her chin toward the back room.

We followed, Andimir grumbling under his breath as we pressed into the tight space, shoulder-to-shoulder. Camion's lip curled into a weak half-smile at Andimir's groaning. Even with his eyes lit with amusement Camion looked as exhausted as I felt. Moreso, even. I squeezed the fingers threaded through mine once more, offering unspoken reassurance that we would rest soon.

If I had my way, we would be in my palace before nightfall. Assuming nothing had happened to Devlyn and he had managed to clear the palace of any potential threats. Still, the thought of my warm, soft bed made my toes curl.

Sylvr eyed Lucian in a way that told me Meryn had filled her in on his behavior. Without asking, she turned to me for an explanation.

"Lucian has gone to great lengths to help us. You can speak freely in front of him. We'll choose what to explain."

"Meryn has been spending her days in the forest. Scoping, listening, gathering supplies. High Priestess Callithyia insisted she stay at the temple while she sorts through everything." Sylvr glanced at the walls warily, as though we were being spied on. "I don't think anyone else has realized she's returned, or who she is. That was our goal, anyway, in keeping her out of town."

"And she's still going by Meryn?" I asked. The question was two part, and Sylvr understood. Lucian's face pulled in confusion.

Sylvr nodded. "She prefers it. And no, she hasn't regained her memories yet. We haven't been able to retrieve her life essence."

"Why not?"

"Honestly . . ." Her eyes flicked nervously to Lucian.

"He's fine," Andimir said quietly.

Lucian bowed his head. "I appreciate the vote of confidence. I'm not here to betray you all. I've learned a lot from the last moon cycle. I was wrong."

I was impressed. The humility he was showing was far more than I had anticipated from him. Maybe a future between our kingdoms was possible. If we made it through all this.

"Fine," Sylvr sighed. "Her life essence is hidden in a . . . complicated place. I'll let Meryn tell you the details. Briefly, we need more people to steal the jewel back because Valdis has patrols scaling most of the main roads. We won't get close without trouble."

"That's unfortunate. We're not in the greatest condition for a fight." I considered the rest of the group. "Well. Tell Meryn to return to the palace this evening. We'll need to speak with her, regardless, and we can start brainstorming a plan. You're welcome too, as always."

Sylvr hesitated, not quite willing to meet my eyes.

I frowned. "What aren't you saying?"

"I don't think returning to your palace is wise, Your Highness."

"Natylia," I corrected gently. "And why not?"

"I'm not—" Sylvr frowned, fidgeting with the pocket of her apron, picking out tiny bits of dried plant that lay in the bottom. "I don't think I should be the one to tell you."

"Tell me what?" I insisted.

"I really don't—"

A pounding sounded from the main room of the shop. Sylvr froze, lifting a finger to her lips as she listened. When the sound continued, she stepped toward the door.

"Stay here and stay quiet," she murmured as she squeezed by. "I'll be back."

Camion pressed the door closed silently behind her. I studied the others—the way Andimir's hand had fallen to the hilt of his sword, the way Lucian and Camion straightened. Sylvr's footsteps faded away. A latch clicked.

"Oh, it's you," we heard her say. "What are you doing here?"

I didn't hear the soft response as the door clicked shut. Then Sylvr said, "Well, you have excellent timing."

Each of the expressions around me matched my own.

Meryn.

My heart leapt with joy.

"If they're both coming in here, it's about to get *real* warm,"

Andimir muttered.

The footsteps picked up again. A soft rap of knuckles on wood broke the quiet, then the door beside us swung open again, bringing a new cloaked figure into the room. Sylvr appraised the situation, smiling before she looked over her shoulder into the shop.

"I'm going to reopen and tend customers."

"If there are any questions on the brief closure, you took a break for lunch," said the hooded figure.

"Yes *mother*," Sylvr snarked, rolling her eyes.

"If you've done the things you've done with me with your mother . . ."

"Ew." Sylvr's face scrunched before she stepped through the door, tossing over her shoulder, "You're disgusting."

"You agreed to marry me."

My eyes burned at the familiar voice. Joy and relief were warm weights in my chest, welcome after all the sadness that had dragged on me for days. Meryn was okay.

Meryn is okay. My sister is alive.

For the moment, I shoved away the tiny voice trying to remind me of Jyn.

Then I focused on Meryn's last words. *Marry?*

When the room was secured behind her, Meryn waved a hand. I waited patiently to ask my questions, while the sounds of Sylvr moving about the shop vanished under the magical sound barrier. Meryn dropped her hood, her hazel eyes locked onto my face. Before I could speak, she was on me, her arms looped around me so tightly, I couldn't hug her back if I had wanted to.

"I missed you." She leaned away but kept me at arm's length, adding, "What happened to you? To all of you? I knew when you weren't in Thrais after a full moon cycle something must have happened, but the tension between you all . . ." Her gaze slid to Lucian. "And this. This is new."

"I—" The joy faded a bit as the overwhelming cascade of memories flooded my mind. I pushed them off. "You're getting married?"

"Yes, I'm getting married." Meryn's cheeks flushed so dark her freckles nearly vanished. "Soon, when all of this is over. I don't know. Don't change the subject."

I pulled her into a crushing hug. "Congratulations."

"Yeah, yeah." She wiggled free, a grin on her face. Her smile faded when she scanned my face. "Now, tell me what happened."

"I don't know where to start."

Meryn crossed her arms over her chest, studying me carefully. I knew she saw the tension there, my unwillingness to hash out the story right now. Then she locked her eyes onto Andimir. "You tell me, then."

"I can't tell you everything," he said. When Meryn frowned at him, he added, "It's not my story to tell. And I don't know much, regardless. I know how they were when I found them. I know that Lucian has gone to great lengths to protect them. That's all."

"Found them? You weren't with them?" Meryn crossed her arms over her chest, copper curls bouncing. "And where is Jyn?"

There was a marked shift in the air at her last question, a weight that the nature witch didn't miss. She looked at each of us in turn before returning her attention to Andimir. "You *need* to tell me what happened."

Andimir told her what he could. He told her about the forest, the Cloaked Shadows, Boreas. He told her about his wound, gesturing to his chest with a frown, opening his shirt to show her the long scar that ran across his pectoral.

Lucian told his part of the story, how he had found us in the rubble and all that had transpired after. He only referred to his father as Valdis and I wondered if the relation was still hard for him to speak out loud.

Camion's grip on my hand tightened as Lucian spoke.

When the prince finished, Andimir wrapped the story up, neatly summarizing the last moon cycle in a few short sentences. Hearing it all again . . . I thought I might be sick.

Andimir gestured to Camion and me. "The rest is their story to tell."

"And I'm guessing neither of you are ready to delve into those details?"

I shook my head before Camion had a chance to respond.

Meryn's gaze flitted between the two of us. "You're both thinner. And the thought of talking about this has both of you tense."

She gestured to our shoulders, which we relaxed in unison, then to our hands. I frowned; I hadn't realized I was squeezing Camion's hand so tightly that my knuckles had turned white. I loosened my grip with an apologetic glance. The fist his free hand had been balled into also relaxed. He didn't even seem to be aware he had been flexing it.

Meryn sighed. "I won't pry. It's clear you don't want to hash this out and, from what I can see . . . well, I don't blame you. Take your time."

"Thank you," I said.

"What if we talk more after I get you all a meal and hot baths?

We can go to the temple. You'll be safe there. Plus, the Priestesses have far more rooms than people."

"Why not my palace?" I watched her face as I asked. The reaction was instant; Meryn's gaze dropped to the floor.

"That's . . . not a good idea."

"Sylvr said as much," Andimir replied. "Why not?"

"With Annalea missing and you gone . . . Devlyn has declared the throne abandoned. As per the treaty agreements your mother and father signed, your nearest allies have taken control of Thrais until an adequate ruler can be named. Drask and Kathryn, specifically."

"What?" I fought to keep my voice calm, even as hot fury blazed through me. "He knows I'm returning, what is he thinking?"

"I don't know, Natylia. But given the fact that you disappeared in the north, and Lucian was the one who found you, I think I can at least put together *who* had you for the last month. Who Valdis really is. Am I right to assume the Kingdom of Wydus has betrayed us?"

"My father is Valdis. You're right," Lucian confirmed. The confession seemed to pain him. "As to the rest, my father betrayed you. I can't speak for my mother. But when I take the throne, Wydus will be as firmly allied with Thrais as it's ever been. More, I guess."

Tears of gratitude filled my eyes. I didn't know what to say. Lucian was being so . . . so good. I was so appreciative of the support, in a time when allies ran thin.

"In that case, I think you know exactly what this means," Meryn said. "Devlyn can no longer be trusted in any capacity.

Not only that, but he's offered your armies to a kingdom that has betrayed you. Seems too strategic a move for me to believe he's still on your side."

Devlyn too?

Devlyn betrayed me? My heart sank. I could truly trust no one.

The confession didn't sit as heavily as I expected it to, though. Maybe I wasn't as surprised by the betrayal anymore. Still. An ache spread through my chest and a wave of exhaustion washed over me.

"So, what do I do?" My voice was barely a whisper and I felt Camion's thumb begin slow circles on the back of my hand. Andimir's hand fell to my shoulder.

"We get your palace back. The hard way," Meryn said. "Thankfully, your guards don't seem to be loyal to Devlyn. Not after he offered control to Wydus. Most of them remember that he was the one to send you away. They see through the lie. But with no Council to plead the case to—"

"Wydus can legally take my armies and execute deserters."

"Exactly," Meryn said.

"Wulfric still lives," Andimir offered quietly. "As the last living member of the Council, he has the authority to fix this."

I groaned. "Yes, and he's currently cowering in Edra with a target on his back almost as large as the ones on ours."

"Shouldn't we be focusing on the Scepters?" Lucian asked warily.

Andimir lifted a confused eyebrow.

"Yes," Meryn agreed. "But we need to reclaim Natylia's soldiers, and if we don't have a base of operations, we're going to have a vulnerable army spread all over the place. We need a safe place to house and feed them. The temple isn't an option for that."

"And I don't exactly trust the temple to be guarded well enough for strategizing our next moves," I added.

Lucian nodded. "Liberate your palace it is."

"Let's worry about this later." Meryn tugged her hood back over her head, tucking her hair out of sight. "How about we get you food and rest?" She took a step forward, then added, "Tomorrow we'll talk about how to steal back your kingdom."

Chapter 12

"Since you hadn't heard about your palace, I assume you haven't had much other news?" Meryn's voice was hushed beneath her hood as we followed her through the cobbled streets and ducked between passersby.

"No, not much."

"Well, thankfully, what I do know is pretty common knowledge now," she said. "Morland and Vitic were evacuated. No one knows much by way of details, but people were dying so the survivors fled."

"And came here?" I glanced around. The small city did seem busier than usual, but not with two towns worth of people.

"Some. The others probably fled north to Wydus, since that's where their ruling bodies are, or maybe to Falmar. A brave few probably went south. I'm not sure." Meryn gestured ahead, to the far end of the path where the Temple of Nahara waited. "Callithyia has been allowing the ones here to shelter with the priestesses. I'm not sure how much longer they'll have room."

Callithyia, the High Priestess of Nahara. I considered Meryn's words. "Are you sure we'll fit then?"

Meryn nodded. "They only use the public quarters. We'll be using the private ones."

"When were the northern cities taken? Conquered?"

"To your second question, I don't know what the purpose was either. But to your first, before the last moon cycle. There were large gaps between the attacks, but it's been quiet lately." She shook her head slightly, lowering her voice to little more than a whisper as she said to me, "I'm suspecting Risen. If I had to guess, Valdis is looking to bolster his armies, so he's sending his minions to secure bodies to create more soldiers. My thinking is that he doesn't care at all about the cities themselves."

I stumbled, the toe of my boot catching on a cluster of weeds in my path. Camion's grip tightened on my hand and he caught my arm before I fell. I offered him an apologetic smile as I jerked my hood more firmly into place. I was starting to think I would trip over air if given the chance. Clumsiness wasn't new to me but lately it was out of hand.

"We saw them," I whispered, steadying myself. "Not all of them. A small group. In Edra."

Andimir's own hood turned and I knew, without seeing, that his eyes had widened. "You think—"

"I think they were going to make sure Edra stayed clear."

"And when they didn't return?" Lucian murmured.

I paused. "I'm willing to guess they're going to be searching Falmar and Thrais really soon."

"We'll be on our guard," Meryn said. "But for now, you all need rest. Or you won't be up for fighting anything, if we need you."

I dipped my head in agreement.

The roadway opened to a field green with soft grass and a large, white building. The Temple of Thrais. The structure was an architectural work of art, with smooth, swirled marble that glittered in the sunlight. There were no adornments outside: no carvings, no tapestries, only the pillars on each side and the wild ivy that grew over them. Stairs scaled the front, carved right into the foundation of the building.

We followed Meryn up, one step at a time, Camion's steps lagging with exhaustion. I waited for him, patiently, refusing to leave even when he nudged me ahead. No matter what I had been through, he had fared worse. For once I needed to take care of him when the world was too heavy. And I was all too glad to do so.

Callithyia waited for us outside the room Meryn indicated as hers, located on a lower level of the temple only accessible through a secret door. The High Priestess dipped to a knee, long black hair spilling onto her bronze-toned cheeks. Meryn waved a frustrated hand, grumbling under her breath.

"Ridiculous," she huffed, then paused. "Well, all right, in then. If we want to talk, I'll need to put up a barrier."

The High Priestess rose, leading the way, the flowy fabric of her white gown dancing around her ankles. I was reminded of my mother, of the gowns she wore, and tried to ignore the pang of memories that rose at the thought.

Meryn slipped the door closed behind us, the sounds from passersby cut off completely with the latch's click. At Meryn's subtle gesture, we removed our hoods and allowed Callithyia to perform her blessings. Her expression was almost reverent as she blessed Meryn. Holy water dripped down Meryn's freckled forehead while soft, murmured prayers left Callithyia's lips.

I didn't move when she came to me. She paused, fingers outstretched in the air, not quite touching me.

"I'm so sorry, Natylia. For all you've endured. For all you will endure." She pressed her fingers to my forehead, whispering softly. But she pulled away abruptly, eyes widening. I narrowed my eyes on her.

"The things that have been done to you—" Her attention slid to Camion. "To both of you. I'm . . . I'm so sorry."

Meryn caught my eyes and nodded toward Callithyia. "She's as human as you are, but she has some abilities. Namely, if she touches someone, she can find their wounds. It's useful for healing, but some wounds . . ."

"Have to heal in their own time," I murmured. I slid a step closer to Camion, looping my hand through his elbow and resting my fingers on his arm. He pressed a kiss to the top of my head. The small gestures only made Meryn frown.

"Are you two going to tell me what actually happened or do I have to strip you down and see for myself?"

"Don't ask them to relive this so soon," Callithyia said, her voice soft but edged with unmistakable warning. Meryn's eyes widened. But the High Priestess focused on Lucian, marking him with the holy water. She paused again, this time to stare into those yellow eyes, and blinked. "What are you?"

Lucian winced. "Half Titan?"

Meryn's jaw dropped, but she quickly recovered herself. "I didn't even consider the implications of Valdis being your father."

She stepped closer and Lucian eyed her warily. "This won't hurt."

She laid her hand on his arm, closing her eyes and inhaling deeply. As she exhaled, goosebumps spread over Lucian's arms. Meryn's eyes popped open. "Oh, there's an aura to you for sure. Whether it's power that you can use or not remains to be seen. Interesting. If you do have any magic, I'd be glad to help coax it out of you." Her smile was too feline to make anyone comfortable.

"When did you get that trick?" Andimir asked, clearing his throat.

Meryn shrugged. "I've always had it, but I was never really aware that the way I experienced the world was different from others. Something about my lingering dormant magic, like a subconscious awareness. I can sense the life essence, large or small, essential or only a whisper. Even the smallest leaf carries energy of its own. Sylvr and Callithyia have been teaching me what they know."

Lucian frowned. "Why those two?"

"Our fates have been tied to Nahara before we were even born," Callithyia offered softly. "We have had her story, her true story, passed to us since we were young."

"Nah—*Nahara?*" Lucian stuttered.

"Oh. You didn't tell him." Meryn smirked. "Guess we all have secrets, huh?"

The prince didn't answer, staring slack jawed at Meryn with an expression that bordered between admiration, awe, and terror. Her grin only grew.

"Answer a question for me," Andimir said. Meryn's eyebrow arched and she lifted her chin, waiting. "Where is your life essence hidden that you haven't retrieved it yet?"

Meryn shook her head, waving at Callithyia. The priestess, whose eyes had returned to studying me and Camion in a way that made me squirm, blinked again.

"Meryn's life essence isn't here," Callithyia finally answered Andimir, though her gaze was still firmly fixed onto me. "Not in Thrais, I mean."

"Life essence?" Lucian finally managed. "None of you specified what that actually is, earlier."

"When a Titan is born, as their organs are forming, a gemstone grows in their chests. Right next to their heart," Sylvr said. "You can't kill a Titan if you don't remove them. But they contain the very essence of the Titan. Memories, some of their powers . . . you could compare them to souls. They're vital to their Titans, and without hers, Meryn isn't able to access her full self."

"Do I have—?" Lucian glanced at his chest.

Sylvr shook her head. "Likely, no. You're still fairly human."

"So, where is Meryn's essence then?" I asked.

"Not far. Starberry Lake."

Andimir groaned. "What is it with you people and hiding things in lakes?"

"You people?" Callithyia asked, lifting a delicate brow. Her lips twitched, but she kept her expression flat as she said. "*I* am as human as you are. And, since you've mentioned it, the gem wasn't technically thrown in the lake. The Elves cloaked her essence as an ordinary rock, stuffed it in a small chest, and then buried that. Near the lake. When the water flooded the banks and the lake expanded, the Elves considered the advantages to the hiding place. Unfortunately, they didn't seem to consider Nahara's need to retrieve her essence . . . or maybe they did, considering they left Sylvr with her."

"Sylvr?"

"That is her story to tell," Meryn said smugly. I rolled my eyes.

"You're telling me we have to find a rock. In a lake." A muscle in Andimir's jaw ticked. Jyn would be proud. My chest felt hollow.

Meryn grinned. "Don't forget it's in a box."

"If Valdis were to find out Nahara was in Thrais, he would destroy the entire city," Callithyia said, stepping closer to the pirate. Her sharp eyes studied him. "Surely you can understand not putting a treasure where it's most expected to be."

His nostrils flared a bit at that, but he jerked his head in acknowledgment. She went on. "Without Sylvr, you won't be able to find the gem anyway. Her bloodline is tied to the stone. To be honest, when she first arrived in Thrais, I wasn't sure she was even the right person; she's so unassuming and quiet, so different from what we know of Nahara's former protectors."

When I frowned, she added, "Don't worry. I have no doubts now."

Meryn tilted her head. "I have none of my Titan memories. But that's another subject we need to discuss because, when I get them back, Valdis will be able to home in on my power, like a beacon lit for his personal navigation."

I slid my hand free of Camion's, rubbing at my temples slowly. Meryn studied me for a long moment. "We can discuss this more tomorrow, Natylia."

"There are free chambers in this hallway," Callithyia said gently. "Nothing extravagant enough to properly host the queen, but—"

I held up a hand. "If there's a bed and clean water, I'll be perfectly fine."

She nodded. "Plenty of both, Your Highness. I'll have the wash basins filled in the rooms you each pick, and I'll send the priestesses with food and wine."

"We would be most grateful," I replied.

"The bathing chamber beneath the temple is vacant for three hours at dawn, while everyone is at morning prayer. If you wish, that might be the best opportunity for privacy."

"Thank you."

We lifted our hoods again and moved to follow Callithyia from the room. Meryn grabbed my and Camion's wrists, tugging us to a stop right before the threshold.

"How are you two? Really?"

"I'll be fine," I murmured.

"And you?" Her gaze rose to Camion's hooded face. He lifted a shoulder, feet shifting uncomfortably. Pain flickered across Meryn's eyes. "Get settled. I'll come see you in a few minutes. I'll do what I can."

I dipped my head, warmth blooming in my chest at the realization that we were together again. We turned, following Callithyia from Meryn's room. Lucian took the room beside Meryn, Andimir the next, and Camion and I accepted the last of this corridor.

The room was better furnished than the High Priestess let on. A large, round cushion took up a third of the room, made of a soft looking fabric and draped with blankets. Plush furs were stacked across the floor as makeshift rugs, and a chest of drawers leaned against the far, white-marbled wall. A small table was tucked into a corner, two chairs on either side, and a basket of fruit perched on top.

"If you need anything more, don't hesitate. Blankets, food . . ." Callithyia hesitated, staring at me. "Your secrets are safe with me." Her eyes slid to Camion. "Yours, as well. I will not tell what I have seen."

"We are truly grateful, Callithyia, thank you," I said, dipping into a curtsy. Camion inclined his head deeply and the High Priestess took her leave.

For the first time in as long as I could remember, I felt something like peace wash over me.

I could only hope the feeling lasted.

Chapter 13

Screaming cut through the silence. At first, I thought it was my own; the sound wasn't so abnormal in my nightmares these days. When I woke with a raw, sore throat, I wasn't convinced of the alternative. But Camion sat upright beside me, eyes alert and full of terror.

"What's happening?" I croaked.

He shook his head, listening intently.

Growls and snarls broke through the screams and I shot Camion a glance.

"We have to go help," I murmured.

I leaped from the bed, scrambling for my leathers. Camion followed and I knew this was going to be a hard test of how ready he was, without even knowing what waited. I slung the bow we had pilfered from Edra over my shoulder, tightening Jyn's daggers around my waist and strapping an extra short sword alongside. The weight pulled at me, but not enough to drag me down. I kept moving, helping Camion with his own leathers, moving faster until a knock thudded at our doors. Camion moved before I could stop him, so I chased after, buckling his sword's sheath on his side after he tugged the blade free.

"Get that thing out of my face," Meryn snapped, though a grin tugged at her lips. The expression faded quickly though, replaced by worry. "We've got work to do."

Andimir and Lucian were stumbling down the hall, equipping weapons of their own as they moved.

"Do you know what's happening?" I asked, catching Meryn's eye.

"Nothing good."

We bolted down the hall and through the secret passage. The main temple was almost deserted, but smears of blood were bright against the pale marble. Chaos flurried outside the main doors, which were thrown wide in what I assumed was a frantic rush to escape. I pulled my bow loose, nocking an arrow before I stepped outside.

Chaos wasn't the right word.

The temple lawn was a frenzy of running bodies and angry, snarling creatures the size of large bears.

"Marawolf," Meryn whispered. I didn't like the edge to her voice.

I drew my arrow back, releasing as one of the massive animals lumbered toward an unguarded priestess. The point sank deep into the creature's eye and it turned, hackles raised.

Before I could move, the Marawolf was on me. Massive paws landed on my chest, sharp claws digging into my collar. I barely managed to avoid slamming my head on the stairs as I fell. I heard movement around me—the men, trying to take down the beast, I assumed. But deep brown eyes were focused on my face and I couldn't spare the glance to be sure. A glob of warm drool splattered on my cheek. I reached up, gripping the arrow's shaft, and ripped it from the Marawolf's eye. The roar the animal released filled my nose with the stench of its rotten breath.

Then the creature turned, swiping angrily for Camion and Andimir as they taunted the animal away. Their swords were out but had no blood on them. Surely, they tried to stab the beast first?

I glanced at the arrow in my hand. Nothing.

Meryn was a whirl of fire on the field, Lucian guarding her back. But he wasn't using his blades on the creatures, no—his focus was on the soldiers.

Soldiers who were decked in the colors of Wydus, a dozen or so, and attacking innocents.

Refugees, and the priestesses who aided them.

My vision burned red.

I pulled my magic up, panting when the animal stuttered and resisted. Pulled until every dreg was summoned to my will, ready to be used. My eyes landed on the Marawolf now attacking Camion and Andimir, at the crimson claw marks that lined Camion's shirt. The beast dove for Andimir and latched onto his forearm.

I shot a ball of magic at the Marawolf.

The blue and purple sparkles were swirled with black, but they landed their hit, right between the Marawolf's shoulder blades. Burning hair and flesh filled the night air. I fought the urge to gag. With an anguished cry, the creature fell before Andimir and Camion with a hard thud.

A magical creature, then. Animated, perhaps, but without blood. I should have followed Meryn's lead and used magic on the beasts earlier. Maybe that was the only way to kill them, and Meryn would be the one to know.

Pain flashed through my body. A different beast sank its fangs into my arm and my magic shuttered to a halt. Reflexively, I reached for the daggers, yanking one free to swiftly stab the Marawolf in the neck. The creature winced, eyes narrowing, but it held tight, jerking me off my feet and yanking me down the temple stairs.

I stopped struggling long enough to loop my arm around my head to protect myself. Vaguely I saw the shadows of Andimir and Camion running after me. As soon as I hit the ground, I reclaimed the dagger, stabbing again, this time into the Marawolf's dark-furred snout. A roar shook the field and the animal moved. Dark claws raked down my side, and I knew my end neared in a whirl of hot breath and sharp teeth.

Then I was free, and the Marawolf that had pinned me became a fireball streaking across the field. I rolled onto my side, panting, and pulled up enough magic to hold the animal in place. Meryn finished the job.

"That's the last of them," she said, her own breathing labored as she dropped to her knees beside me.

"And the soldiers?"

"Mostly dispatched. Camion and Andimir went to help Lucian finish up."

I glanced in their direction. She was right. I hadn't noticed them missing.

But I was suddenly acutely aware of the fiery burn that spread across my torso. I gasped at the pain, at the acidic ache that ate at my arm. My magic became a pit inside me, a dark void that went on and on . . . I felt the loss as keenly as though my powers had been completely stripped from me.

"Venom," Meryn said quietly, examining the wounds. "We have to get you all into the temple and treat these wounds fast. Marawolves secrete venom from their claws, their teeth, and the poisonous barbs on the ends of those bushy tails. But the antidote is common enough."

I struggled to catch my breath against the pain, so intense that I blinked to make sure I wasn't dreaming. In a fog I reached out, gripping Meryn's arm. "Why were they here?"

"Hoping to gather some of the refugees?" She looped my unwounded arm around her shoulders, struggling to hoist me to my feet. "I don't know. Come on."

"But the others—"

"Will be fine, I promise you."

But I squirmed from her grip long enough to grab Jyn's dagger. To this, she didn't protest. Especially when I started toward the temple, my steps slow and steady, even on the stairs. I couldn't resist looking over my shoulder halfway up. Meryn was right; the others were fine. And making their way to the temple too, unsteady with wounds of their own.

Meryn and Lucian seemed to be the only two with no bites from a Marawolf.

I had to admit, I was impressed.

* * *

"Nat, you have to drink the *whole* vial. That bare sip isn't enough to cure your pinkie."

"Whatever is in here is terrible."

Meryn sighed, crossing her arms over her chest. "If you don't drink that potion, you will *die* from Marawolf venom. Is that what you want?"

"No . . ."

"Then drink the vial."

I groaned, staring at the deep green liquid. Whatever was in here tasted like soured milk and mold. Or so I imagined that's what those two would taste like. The texture was even worse, lumpy and slimy . . .

"Andimir and Camion have already drunk theirs. Are you going to let them show you up?"

My eyes narrowed on the two men in my and Camion's room, who rested on a blanket in front of the fire and looked anywhere but where I sat. Lucian was perched on a chair nearby, uneasy enough that he kept opening and closing his mouth like he would reprimand me, but not quite pulling up the nerve to do so.

"I hate you all," I muttered. The liquid slid down my throat like soggy bread, and it was an effort of will to not vomit every drop back up. But I had to admit—within seconds the burning started to dull.

Meryn pressed a hand to my forehead, sighing heavily. "Already warm. You almost waited too long."

"And?"

"And if you don't drink the antidote before the fever breaks, the Marawolf venom *will* kill you. That's how they hunt their prey. Not hard to follow when it drops over a couple miles away."

I winced at that. She lifted her eyebrows, but I was saved from further lecturing when Sylvr pushed open the door.

"Did you find what I needed?" Meryn asked her, spinning away from me to take the basket of supplies in Sylvr's arms. She paused long enough to press a kiss to Sylvr's cheek before she returned, pouring the bandages and medicines on the table.

"Andimir first," Meryn said, "because I'm going to need to strip Nat and Camion down a bit to tend their wounds and you'll all need to clear out first."

Dutifully, Andimir stepped forward, offering his arm. The other wounds he had obtained from the remaining soldiers, nicks and bruises not severe enough to require treatment. But Meryn took her time with his arm, carefully cleaning the bite before she packed the wound with a poultice and bandaged him up. Sylvr stood at Meryn's side the entire time, helping without asking, knowing what her other half needed without words.

When Meryn had finished, and had sent Lucian and Andimir on their way, Sylvr finally asked, "Do you need anything else?"

"No, thank you." Meryn's eyes burned with a light I had never seen when she looked at her partner, and I couldn't help the smile that curved my lips. I knew that feeling, that fire. Camion made me feel that way. Only Camion ever had. So, I wasn't a bit surprised when Meryn added, "I'll meet you in my room in a little while. I need to tend these two."

Sylvr planted a soft kiss on Meryn's shoulder, running her fingertips up Meryn's arm before she strolled from the room. Meryn looked thunderstruck for several seconds, as though she might race after Sylvr, then shook her head.

"That girl will be the death of me."

"Oh?" Camion asked.

I was surprised to find my own amusement marked on his face, though more subtly. Meryn shot a glance between the two of us, rolling her eyes.

"Do you see her? I couldn't find another girl like her if I searched a thousand lifetimes." Meryn sighed. "All right, Camion, you first."

He winced but removed his shirt. The steady rise and fall of his chest became slow, too slow, too measured. I knew he was waiting for the reaction, for the fallout or surprise.

Whatever Meryn made of what she saw, she didn't comment. Instead she cleaned his wounds as carefully as she had Andimir's, an appraising brow arched at me. "No chance you can use your magic to speed his healing?"

I tugged at my magic. Pulled. But all I found was a dark, bottomless chasm without even a flicker of life inside. "I can't . . . I can't get my magic to respond."

"The venom can do that." Meryn sighed. "I hoped we had caught it fast enough. You'll see your powers again, tomorrow likely, but until then, natural healing will do."

Camion frowned. "And if the venom was left long term?"

"If I had left the venom in you, all three of you would have died within a few hours. The fever hits first. Then the boils. Gasping for air. And death."

I shuddered. "Not exactly a pleasant way to go."

"You're welcome." Meryn smirked.

I considered the vial of antidote and shuddered again. The venom was definitely worse.

When she finished with Camion, she moved to me and started on my arm. I jerked away the second her cloth touched my skin, wincing at the burn that renewed.

"The skin is tender, but that shouldn't last long," Meryn commented. When my face scrunched again, Camion dropped to my side, gripping my free hand, before Meryn added, "Not all of your army is loyal to Drask. Or Devlyn. The information might be useless because I don't know who, or how many. I only know it's the truth."

"Not useless," I hissed, seeing the distraction for what it was as the burn reignited. "Some of my men might fight for us, if they see that I've returned."

"I agree. Unfortunately, that also means putting you on a battlefield, and I'm not sure I'm keen on that idea. Especially without my full powers."

Her grip tightened as I tried to wiggle away. Camion's thumb ran slow, gentle patterns along my hand.

"I don't plan to sit out on the fighting."

"You might not," Meryn replied, "but you know no one will support your decision. Especially since we still haven't found Annalea."

"Audri has heard rumors about her. She's alive. You know I don't care about a palace or titles. If Thrais is completely overtaken, if I don't survive and Annalea—" I cut the words off, swallowing hard. "Help Audri and Phelix protect my people, if it comes to that. Please."

"We won't let it come to that."

I searched Meryn's eyes. Her hands paused on my arm. "Audri and Phelix will help, if we ask. If we get them a message, we might have an army to fight an army."

"If we can get them a message fast enough," Camion murmured doubtfully. "The group they're bringing north now is only a fraction of their forces.

Meryn released my arm, pulling various herbs toward her for a poultice. "I have another alternative, as well."

I shot Camion a quick glance. "We're listening."

"The dryads."

A frown curved my lips. "I didn't get the impression the dryads were interested in fighting."

"They're not. But they will."

"The dryad we met seemed so . . ."

"Frail?" Meryn nodded, packing the poultice around my injury before slowly bandaging the herbs down. "Well thankfully one of them asked a silly little nature witch to carve protection runes into their bark. I'll have to do more, for any who are willing to join and haven't been marked, but the runes will protect the dryads from fire, if nothing else."

"And you really think they'll join our fight?"

"If you think the Titans are going to let the dryads live in peace, you would be wrong. They remember their reign. And they'll understand our need for better fortifications, especially after tonight."

"It's a start," I admitted. A beat of silence passed before I asked, "Why did the soldiers attack? The wolves? And a temple no less . . . I can't fathom it."

Meryn waved her hands, gesturing for me to remove my shirt. I did, leaving my underthings in place as she examined the wounds. Her eyes wandered over me, and I didn't miss her sharp intake of breath. "Oh, Nat . . ."

"The attack. Please."

Her gaze lingered on the new scars, as did Camion's. His jaw clenched, but Meryn murmured, "I haven't had the chance to say this yet, but I'm sorry about Jyn. I wish I had been there."

"We're all playing the blame game with ourselves," I whispered. "But the blame is only on those who killed him."

"I know," she said. I glanced up to see the tears spill onto her cheeks. Meryn. Strong, stoic Meryn. "I'm going to miss him."

"We all are."

I freed my hand from Camion's, leaning to pull Meryn into a hug. She freed herself quickly, dabbing at her eyes with a corner of her skirts.

"I have to bandage you. Don't let me fall into that hole. We have too many things to do and I fear . . . I fear I won't come out."

"Deal," I said. "But only if you'll do the same for me."

Meryn nodded sadly. "That's what friends do."

Chapter 14

"You don't have to come. In fact, I think I might insist you stay behind."

Camion glared at me over his crossed arms. "You can't be serious."

I glanced around the table for support—at first Meryn, then Sylvr, followed by Andimir, and Lucian. The men looked away, fidgeting with the weapons and armor crowding the surface in front of us. Sylvr's eyes lifted to Meryn, and my friend nodded slowly.

"She has a point, Camion," Meryn said finally. "You slept for a full day after the Marawolves attacked."

Camion's gaze dropped to the table. She was right and the guilt was all over Camion's face. Unfairly, I thought, considering we hadn't expected him to be in full fighting form.

"I can't let you go in there while I sit here doing nothing," Camion argued.

I reached across the table, waiting until he relented and

dropped his hand onto my waiting palm. "There are plenty of things for you to do here too. None of the Titans should be in Thrais, not yet. Audri has aid on the move; they'll be here tomorrow, mid-morning at the latest. We can do this without you."

"You shouldn't have to." His fingers tightened around mine. "I should be stronger than this by now."

"The fact that you're alive at all means you're stronger than most of us," Andimir said softly. "But you have to heal. Nat's right. You're no good to any of us dead."

"Don't forget that while Nat healed your physical wounds, she can't heal the effects that starvation, dehydration, and abuse had on your body," Sylvr said. "You're going to need time for those."

"Taking time to heal isn't weakness," I added.

Sylvr shrugged. "Why don't you help me tomorrow? I need to gather supplies for our trip to Starberry."

"And I could use extra eyes on Callithyia," Meryn said. Sylvr nodded. When Meryn met her waiting gaze, a pink flush crept up Sylvr's cheeks, one that made the corner of Meryn's lips quirk up. "Right before we gathered together," Meryn continued. "Devlyn sent a contingent of soldiers to guard the temple, but we can't trust where their loyalties lie."

"Wouldn't he go after Sylvr?" Andimir asked. "She is the guardian of your life essence after all."

Meryn shook her head. "Drask doesn't know that. Nor does he know, as far as I'm aware, that the stone has a guardian. And we better hope it stays that way; if he suspected, he would come for the High Priestess of Nahara's temple first."

"In general, be extra careful of your comings and goings," Sylvr said. "Make sure no one is watching when you go in and out of the secret passage. That'll be our last defense, if they come back."

Lucian leaned forward. "Where did Valdis get those Marawolves? I've never seen them before."

"No idea," Meryn admitted. "I don't know much about them, only the barest information about what they look like and their venom. Which, by the way, holds great value in certain circles."

"And you collected a few vials, didn't you?" The corner of my mouth twitched.

Meryn gave me an innocent shrug. "Never let an opportunity pass you by."

"I should go, then," Camion said. His tone was teasing but sadness lined his eyes. "Can't let the opportunity pass me by."

I touched his arm. "You know that's not what I meant."

"Look, Camion," Lucian started, "I know you don't have a lot of reason to trust me." Camion's eyes grew wary. "But you have to know I'll do everything in my power to keep her safe."

"I appreciate that."

"And"—Lucian reached into his pocket—"I've been meaning to give you this. Never felt like the right time."

He held out his hand. The object on his palm caught the light. I sucked in a sharp breath. A rose gold ring set with a stone of rough pink quartz. Camion's ring, the only thing he had left of his mother beyond fading memories.

Camion's jaw clenched, but not with anger. Whatever thoughts were running through his mind, his eyes welled up with tears. I brushed my thumb over his fingers as he lifted his free hand to take the ring from Lucian.

"Thank you," Camion managed. "I thought this was gone."

"My father has an armory of sorts in the prison. Everything he takes from the prisoners usually goes there. I went back in before I returned to the cave that night. Most everything was buried, but that caught my eye and I remembered seeing it once. I'm sorry I didn't find the chain."

Camion nodded his head as he stared at the ring, a single tear sliding free. "I can replace the chain. This . . . this was my mother's. I can't say how much it means to me. Thank you."

Lucian offered a small smile. "Glad I was able to get her ring back to you, then."

"That's oddly kind of you, Lucian," Meryn said.

"Look . . . I'm still sorting through all the deceptions, but I see now how I've been raised to believe I'm entitled to things I'm not." He glanced my way. "To *people*. That's not an excuse. But I'm trying to do better."

"He's been doing really well," Andimir said, as Camion and I motioned our agreement.

"I won't disappoint you all."

"You better not," Meryn threatened, but her tone was light.

"I'll stay here tomorrow. I'm at your disposal Sylvr." Camion's eyes were still locked onto the ring as he spoke. "Whatever you need."

"Thank you," Sylvr said.

"Start by eating some food." Meryn shoved a basket of biscuits at him. Camion sighed heavily but grabbed one, taking an over-exaggerated bite. She rolled her eyes. "You don't have to be such a grump. You're reminding me of—" Her words fell off abruptly and she froze in place, realizing what she had been about to say. My fingers brushed the daggers sheathed on my hip.

Camion swallowed quickly, eyes locked on my fading smile. "I said I would help. I didn't say I wouldn't complain about staying behind."

I offered him an appreciative smile, but it barely curved my lips.

Spirits.

I missed Jyn so much.

***

My boots crunched through the underbrush, even as I took each step with the utmost caution. I itched to reach out and run my fingers along the stone wall that was only a few paces away. My home. I longed to be on the other side—safe, warm, happy. Training with Camion in the bright sunshine, with Jyn hovering a touch too close, and the scent of Meryn's baked goods in the wind. Or even drinking tea with Annalea in the library . . .

I stumbled. Andimir gripped my arm, brows scrunching as his eyes narrowed on me. I shook my head, waving a dismissive hand. He released me, frowning slightly, but I needed to get my head on straight. Araenna might depend on it.

The dryads were to meet us against the back wall of the palace. Meryn hadn't fully pleaded our case yet; we were running into the forest on the blind hope that they would agree and we could launch an assault before Devlyn had time to prepare. Audri's forces arriving in Thrais in the morning would set off too many warning bells, unless we were already inside the walls.

My fingers tightened around the hilt of one of Jyn's daggers, even as my thoughts dipped to the bow I had lost. A small loss compared to the weighted grief that pressed down on my chest. But I loved the bow Camion had made for me. The stolen bow I had taken from Edra wasn't quite the same—even the weight of it sat differently over my shoulder.

A soft, yellow-green glow emanated from the rear wall. Panic zipped up my spine, clenching my lungs tight, but Meryn was relaxed. Still, the impulse to draw the dagger trembled through the tightened muscles of my arm.

"Tiny one," a familiar voice said. The sound was gentle, floating past as though carried on the winter wind that blew by. I tugged my cloak around my shoulders. Andimir's hand went to the elm-wood pendant at his throat. Meryn had insisted each of the men slip them on before we left the temple, protecting them from the dryad's immobilizing speech. We all remembered what had happened last time we met the dryad's, the way Jyn and Camion had frozen in their tracks.

A figure stepped from the shadows, glowing faintly in the dark of the forest. She was as I remembered her: tall and lithe, clothed only in the branches that slithered and moved over her green skin. Her hair fell around her thighs, fluttering with each step. Andimir stilled beside me, nearly tripping Lucian. He grabbed my arm, his expression wary.

"Her?" he whispered.

"She's the one."

The dryad looked toward our hushed voices, tilting her head slightly. "Oh, young one. You have suffered much. I fear you still have much more to weather before your journey is complete."

"Unfortunately, I assumed as much," I said quietly. Her dark, whiteless eyes studied me for a moment before I added, "Is there a name we might call you? I feel disrespectful not addressing you in proper terms."

"Dryads are not named, as you are. We grow from saplings, often spreading so rapidly there is simply no time for such things." She paused. "You might call me Kalïa, though. In our tongue, this is an equivalent to 'leader.'"

"You don't speak the common tongue natively?" Andimir asked, voice low. Some courage had returned to his expression.

"No. Most of us do not speak common tongue at all. I am the speaker of the dryads. I know many languages."

"Will you help us take the palace?" Meryn interjected, quietly herding us back on track.

"What is your plan?" Kalïa studied the hesitation on her face. "You have no plan, tiny one?"

"We didn't want to plan for your assistance, if you were unable to provide any."

Kalïa nodded slowly, glancing around at our group. "I can understand this. Especially given that you are few in number. We also lack numbers. Do you have no one else? I do not like the odds of success presented here."

"We have a force coming from the south, but they likely won't arrive until mid-morning."

Kalïa dipped her head into a slight bow. "Then we shall do what we can to prepare for their arrival. If we strike, are you ready to fight?" We nodded and a small grin tilted Kalïa's lips. She looked over her shoulder, gesturing toward the trees. "Come, friends. Show yourselves."

For a moment, nothing happened. Then soft creaking filled the forest, and dryads of all shapes, sizes, and color stepped from between the shadows. None before us were so tall as Kalïa, but many had the fierce determination of warriors written across their expressions. After a moment, the group fell as one, bowing their heads before me and Meryn.

"Rise my friends," Kalïa said. "For Queen Natylia and our revered Titaness have invited us here as equals. To assist them, not serve them."

They rose and approval flickered across many of their faces. Under the soft yellow-green glow the dryad's emanated, I could see the hastily scratched runes where Meryn had etched her marks on their bark what now felt like so long ago.

Kalïa's gaze followed mine. "The men in your walls will expect fire to work against us. These runes have had long to sit on our bark, to collect magic. They cannot harm us with their flames. This will give us an advantage."

"Oh good. I was wondering how we were going to combat fire with sticks," Andimir muttered under his breath.

I shot him a warning glance. He winced apologetically.

"He has . . . a valid question," one of the smaller dryads said. She stood around my height, her skin as pale as the white birch trees scattered around us. "We are . . . vulnerable . . . to fire without runes."

Kalïa patted the dryad on the head, earning a shy smile. "Sólaya—second, in our language—has only recently begun to master the common tongue," she explained. "She is training to be my replacement, when the time comes."

"So, what are we going to do?" I asked.

"We are going to retake your palace, Queen." Kalïa peered at the wall beside us. "Until daylight breaks, we will focus on the guards along the outer wall, the rear door, the front gate. When they catch onto us, we will have little time. We will need to move quickly. We are not unaware of what goes on in the world. We cannot let the Titans return."

"We know . . . their rotations," Sólaya said, "we've been watching . . . since Nahara returned . . . to Thrais. Before the day . . . breaks the sky . . . they will change."

"I must warn you, Your Majesty," Kalïa added. "A great deal of darkness resides within your palace walls. You might not find a home inside when we are through."

Shivers ran the length of my spine. "What do you mean?"

"A great many . . . of your men . . ." Sólaya fidgeted, looking up at Kalïa. The elder dryad nodded, willing to supply the word.

"A great number of your guards are Risen."

My stomach churned. "Risen?"

The dryad nodded. "Some went eagerly to their new master. Some . . ." She paused, tilting her head toward the wall. Her body stilled, as did the branches that trailed her figure before she said, "Some would have died for you. Many. They will not be eager to fight you, but they will not have control over this. They will likely reveal themselves as Risen most quickly."

"Valdis was here? Raising my people?"

Kalïa nodded. "Any who didn't come willingly."

"Can you render the men immobile so we can capture them? With your voices?"

"If we could, we would." The dryad leader sighed. "The range at which our voices are effective is limited. But more importantly, they have no effect on the Risen."

My shoulders sagged. "Is there hope that any of my guards

might be saved?"

"There is always hope, young one. When all is too heavy and the world feels dark, the light will shine out. The sun will rise, the night shall fade. And with each new light, there is hope."

Chapter 15

As the night sky turned to grey and the sun slowly started its stretch into the morning sky, we began our assault. Almost a dozen dryads spread out to pick guards off the walls, one by one, so quickly and silently that they had no time to alert the others. Their attempts at crying out were muffled swiftly by long, slender branches that slithered up the stone to wrap around their throats. The silence was deafening against the thuds of motionless bodies. I winced, even despite Kalïa's assurance that only the most loyal had been assigned to the wall.

"Well, at least they're efficient," Andimir whispered.

"That's one way to phrase it."

Meryn smirked. "You doubted them?"

"Maybe," Andimir admitted.

I crept forward, following Kalïa until she reached the small wooden door in the rear palace wall, the one we had crept out of the first time we left. The etching along the surface was engraved on both sides: two intertwined trees with a star in the center. Kalïa's dark eyes turned expectantly in my direction and I sighed, running a sharp blade down the side of my arm—a new scar, to match the old. Smearing the blood over the rough wood struck a familiar chord of memories. My heart clenched at the differences. At Camion being left behind; at Jyn no longer by my side; and at Andimir, who rose to try to fill his place. I glanced at Lucian as the glittering magic scattered across my skin. His yellow eyes were locked onto the door in front of me, lips parted in shock.

"That's how the door opens?" He shook his head. "I would never have imagined—"

"Neither did I, until I had to," I whispered. "How about we keep this between the group?"

His jaw snapped shut. Then he nodded tightly. "Your secrets are safe with me."

Andimir leveled a wary gaze at the prince. I could tell he still warred with trusting Lucian but, after a second, his head bobbed in approval. Even he could see the better side that Lucian was showing. If Jyn were here, he would—

I blew out a slow breath, releasing the clamp that tightened around my chest. Jyn would want me to focus on what we needed to do. Reclaiming my palace would be a major victory for us. I rested my palms against the wooden door then gently pulled.

The silver of Jyn's dagger glinted in the light splintering through the leaves above us. I tucked the blade closer to my side, into shadow, and waited for the creak of aging hinges as the door opened all the way. The sound never came, but underneath the grass rustled softly, a gentle sound that made me hesitate.

As the door opened, metal chinked together from two guards

who spun on us. Before I could lift my dagger in defense, the dryads had them. Branches wrapped the guards securely, then dragged them out the door and pressed them up against the wall.

"These two do not feel as the others," Kalïa whispered. "There is not so much darkness in them. They might yet remain loyal."

"And if they aren't?" Andimir's brow furrowed.

"We deal with them," Meryn answered, stalking closer to the two guards. Their eyes widened, in fear or recognition, I wasn't sure.

I cringed at the thought, then tugged my hood away from my face, letting the lining rest on my hairline. Light caught my face and the guard's expressions relaxed. Kalïa lifted the branch covering the mouth of one.

"Your Majesty?" he asked softly and dipped his head.

"What do you know of what's happening inside my walls?"

He met my gaze with a frown. "Nothing good, Your Highness." When he paused, I waved him on. "I don't know all the details. Devlyn is a traitor. When you and your sister vanished, he claimed the throne as an advocate to the north and brought down a small contingent from Wydus. He equipped them in your colors, tossed them in with our men. Then Drask came and . . ."

"And?" I pressed.

"He demanded loyalty. Said he was calling in the treaty for the protection of Thrais. Anyone who protested was forcibly removed from the palace grounds . . . and, when they returned, they were different."

"Different how?"

The guard looked at the ground. "They didn't protest anymore."

I winced, then glanced between the two of them. "And you two? Where do you stand?"

"I'm loyal to Thrais. I'm not the only one. But I cannot speak for her."

I turned my attention to the guard beside him. Kalïa freed her mouth and, for a moment, the guard simply stared at me, eyes wide.

"You abandoned us. Before I state my loyalties, I at least want to know why."

"There's a lot to tell," I said levelly. "But suffice it to say, Princess Annalea and myself were tricked, then betrayed. We didn't knowingly surrender the palace into enemy hands. I will gladly explain in detail at another time."

The guard studied me for several long heartbeats, then inclined her head. "I am loyal to Thrais, Your Majesty. I'm glad that you haven't forsaken us."

"I would never. Not without dire reasoning."

"Then whatever your plan, you have my sword."

"And mine, Your Highness," said the first guard.

"I am grateful."

Meryn stepped forward. "Do you know where the other guards are stationed?"

The female nodded slowly. "Some are our friends . . . What will you do with them?"

"That depends on what I see in their hearts," Kalïa said. "Hearts are more reliable than words."

"What will you be looking for?"

The dryad was silent for a moment before she said, "Darkness."

"But you said these two had darkness in them?" My question was softer, barely more than a whisper. But the dryad heard.

"Everyone has darkness in them. Darkness, but also light. There is a balance to all things. When there is imbalance, there is turmoil." Kalïa closed her eyes for a moment, sighing deeply before she added, "Many of those I sense in these walls have been flooded with darkness. They will not find their way back."

The first guard shuddered. "There's a person stationed at every door. Every entrance to the palace grounds. And the palace itself has full guard rotations every few hours."

"Thank you. No point delaying farther," I muttered. I tugged my hood low, concealing my face in shadow again.

Kalïa lowered the guards to the ground. Sólaya straightened beside her and said, "You will stay . . . with us . . . or you will stay here. One hint of . . . deception . . . and you will not live to this night."

"Understood." They said in unison.

We crept through the door, slinking along the shadows toward Meryn's home. A guard paced restlessly outside, unaware of the dryad's tangled branches slithering toward him until they were already around him—groping, twisting, pressing him down until he was silent.

"Only one guard on my home?" Meryn scoffed quietly. "I'm insulted."

"I mean, I wasn't scared of you either," Andimir whispered.

"Wasn't?"

"Well after you lit Jyn on fire that changed pretty fast."

Meryn narrowed her eyes on him. "We'll discuss this later."

Morning light crept over the walls now. If we didn't get to

the guard quarters and Devlyn before the sun broke the trees, we would lose the shadows.

The dryads melded seamlessly into those very shadows, pulling guards from their posts like weeds. Some of the guards didn't survive. Others were left to join us or flee . . . but their numbers were miserably few.

We were almost to the guard quarters when the bell clanged. My eyes rose to the flash of silver at the front gate, to the sentry whose attention was fixed on our position. My heart hammered inside my chest, my fingers tightening on Jyn's dagger.

Frazzled guards and soldiers ran from the garrison, the battlements, the palace itself. The lawns and gardens filled with armored men and women who looked disoriented as they tried to place the threat.

"Here!" Devlyn's voice rang out loudly above the sea of clanking metal and hurried conversations.

Groups turned in unison. A chill ran the length of my spine. Their attention was too precise, too meticulous in the chaos.

"Risen," I whispered to the others, moving backward until we were grouped, backs together.

"Not all of them," Meryn gritted out. "How do we tell the difference?"

"If they attack you, assume they're fair game," Andimir muttered.

"Identify yourselves," Devlyn said, swinging a blade in his hand as he strolled closer. His expression was one of smooth arrogance. I frowned.

"I hear you're the acting commander of Thrais," I called out.

He paused. Recognition lit his eyes and he stumbled, recovering quickly. "My queen vanished into the night. I did what was necessary in her stead, especially since she's been presumed dead."

"I didn't realize I was dead."

I pulled my hood away from my face, letting the soft glow of morning sun hit my face. Gasps rippled across the guards. Several dropped to kneeling positions. Not enough. Not even half.

That didn't bode well.

One of the guards still standing eyed me warily. "How do we know you're who you say you are?"

"Because I also believe she's who she says she is," Lucian said from my side, lowering his own hood. "And if the verification of a second royal isn't enough, I'll be happy to call in Queen Audri and King Phelix as further evidence."

At the sight of those yellow eyes, Devlyn paled. More soldiers dropped to their knees, bowing their heads. Closer to half, at least. Better.

Devlyn cleared his throat. "And yet you've led an assault against your own palace?" He gestured at the dryads lingering behind me.

"Because I don't believe you've been completely truthful with my men." I gestured to Kalïa. "And she can tell me which of you are truly loyal."

Guards and soldiers were shooting nervous looks at Devlyn now, confused. All but the Risen, who stood firmly focused on us, weapons ready. They didn't twitch, they didn't move. Not even to blink.

"I'm not sure what you mean, Your Majesty." Devlyn paused to clear his throat, but his knuckles whitened where he gripped his sword. "I'm quite relieved you're safe and well . . . and under the protection of the prince, who must have found you and brought you back to us as his father asked."

"I did nothing of the sort," Lucian said. "I offered my services. Nothing more."

The frown on Devlyn's face deepened. "Well now. This is a surprise, after the number of times the queen publicly embarrassed you."

A rustle of confused agreement shivered through the guards and soldiers. Questioning, believing Devlyn's act, and the restlessness encouraged him. "And where is Jyn, the one who never leaves my queen's side? Or that new beau for whom she's been scorning you? I'm sensing a deception in our midst."

More of the men and women were questioning our presence now. I frowned. "I would not deceive my own people."

"Of course not. If you're *really* our queen."

Devlyn's accusation had the crowd rising to their feet, anger in their voices. I winced. I didn't have Jyn. I knew I looked different, but surely . . .

"None of you recognize me?" I asked. "None of you can see the queen who you've lived with and served for so many years?"

Silence fell then. A few guards exchanged glances, and I caught sight of a guard who had been stationed outside my room after my mother's murder. I met his eyes firmly. "You heard everything I went through after my mother died. Every single tear. You would deny me now?"

He blinked slowly, then dropped to a knee, bowing his head. The guards who had stood in anger shifted uneasily. Meryn and Andimir stepped forward, revealing their own identities, and at the sight of the nature witch, many more knelt before me.

"These are hard times and rumors of Titans abound," Devlyn said. "Until I know you are who you say you are . . ." He glanced around. "Apprehend the prisoners. We will interrogate you until I can determine the truth. If they resist, kill them. They chose their fate."

The kneeling soldiers exchanged uneasy glances, but the Risen didn't hesitate. As one, they rushed forward. The men drew their blades. Meryn pulled fire to her fingertips. I unshouldered my bow.

They attacked.

Our group scattered quickly. Meryn raced to help the dryads, whose limbs creaked and groaned as they moved for the Risen. Lucian vanished from my side, replaced quickly by Andimir.

"Fight with me, Nat. Like we trained."

I nodded, pulling my bow string, loosing an arrow. The point nicked a Risen's throat, his dark blood spilling free. He still moved, too close now. I drew a dagger and slammed the blade into his stomach. My hands shook, but I tried not to think too much about what I had done, about the fact that I had stabbed a person, that my hand was now covered with his blood.

A person.

No, a Risen.

"Take the head."

Andimir's voice broke my thoughts. I glanced up for a split second, but the Risen had recovered, twisting himself free of the dagger impaling him. Andimir swept around me and sliced his sword clean through the Risen's throat. The body slumped to the ground. Andimir grabbed a fistful of hair on the severed head and lifted.

"How do you know to do that?"

"Jyn," he muttered before twisting to take the brunt of another attack. "We'll have to burn them later."

I stepped up beside him, gritting my teeth as my blade sank into the Risen's neck. He gurgled and fell, and Andimir quickly moved to remove the head. We continued like this, a well-tuned machine, struggling our way through Devlyn's men.

The bell sounded again, a series of clangs that didn't mean anything to my people. Andimir covered for my momentary hesitation, knocking a Risen back before he could sink claws into my arm. The main gates opened wide. For a moment, I thought Phelix and the southern army might have arrived.

But the faces that greeted us weren't friendly. Risen raced through the gates, at least two dozen, joining the frenzied fighting. Most were not armed beyond teeth and claws, but that didn't stop them.

Loyal men fell to the onslaught. Meryn was little more than bursts of orange and red in my peripheral. The heat from her flames blasted across the battlefield in waves. Lucian was making his way toward me and Andimir, incapacitating Risen with the precision of one with royal training. Beyond him, the Risen seemed to have recognized the real threat, because each of the dryads contended with a small fray of the darkened humans swarming their branches.

Andimir vanished from my side.

I moved to help him but two Risen sprang up on my exposed side. Jyn's dagger was ripped from my hands. The larger of the two stole my bow and snapped it in one swift motion. Terror built in my chest and I started to scramble for a weapon. They realized my intent, lunging for me again. I pulled for my magic, each tug desperate and furious. But, before I could release even one glittering tendril, I was on my back, pinned beneath the two Risen. I struggled to push them off, every kick and thrash in vain. Their claws dug into my skin where they grappled for my throat and the warmth of hot breath grazed my cheek. I recoiled, my magic alongside. Teeth snapped in my ear. Panic rose higher in my chest.

A blur of gold flicked past my vision.

At first, I thought I had imagined the light, or that my magic had finally responded. Then I was free, breathing, scrambling for Jyn's dagger to slam into one of the Risen. I spared a glance in Andimir's direction. The Risen he was fighting had him pinned against a palace wall, his arms locked at his sides.

I bolted across the gap, slamming my side into the Risen. He growled at me, an inhuman, animalistic sound that shivered up my spine. Then I had my blade lifted, aimed for his throat—

But a silver blade flashed in front of mine before I could finish my stroke, a blade etched with shimmering golden runes that easily swept the Risen's head from its neck. Andimir gaped, wide-eyed and blinking.

"Thank you," I panted, looking over my shoulder as the Risen slumped to the ground.

I froze.

Blinked.

"You— You, you—" I stammered on the word, eyes burning. I stumbled back a step, not trusting my eyes. My mouth continued to move, even when the words fell off.

"I love you too, Princess. Talk later. I promise." He paused long enough to offer me a warm smile, then glanced at the daggers in my hands. "Can I have those back?"

I held them out without thinking and Jyn grinned again, giving me the Elven dagger he wielded. "Be careful, it's sharp."

He was gone before I could process the emotions overwhelming every inch of my body. I stared hard at my friend until I realized what was bothering me most immediately.

Jyn had always been an imposing presence. Well over six feet, with golden-toned skin that only made his dark eyes and black hair appear more striking. But now . . .

Now Jyn was decked in brand new leathers that accented the lean muscle of his frame better than any he had worn before. Sheathes hung across his shoulders and lower back, and daggers peeked from his boots.

But more striking than all the rest was the golden aura that pulsed in the air around him. From his boots to the tips of his pointed ears, a soft warm light danced around his skin.

Jyn had his powers back. After all those years of resisting his Elven rights and lineage, he was fully powered, an immortal Elf once more.

Elven strength suited him.

Jyn moved, cutting through the opposition as though they weren't well trained soldiers. The Risen didn't stand a chance. Between him, the dryads, and Meryn herself, the Risen began to fall rapidly.

Andimir and I together dispatched an advancing Risen. I barely dodged the claws that stretched for my face. Jyn lifted his daggers and sliced through another pair of Risen who had turned their attentions on us. In that same moment, a different Risen moved for my guardian. Jyn killed it with ease.

Then he shouted over the fray, "Oh, and I brought help," and gestured toward the gate.

Another figure stood there, golden aura shimmering around him as he combated anything that came too near with easy precision. Andáerhyn. Commander of the Elven Militia. I glanced up at Jyn, brow furrowing in confusion. I wanted to talk; I had so many things to say, so many questions to ask. Jyn knew. He offered a half smile. "We have a lot to catch up on."

"We do." But, reluctant as I was to admit it, we had a palace to reclaim first.

I glanced around. Most of the Risen were dead, the Elves having thinned their numbers considerably. Andimir and I began to scour the grounds for Devlyn. After the second wave, he had disappeared, and I hadn't seen him since. By the time the morning sun was past the trees, we had still seen no sign of him.

A horn sounded nearby. I turned to see, wary of letting my hopes rise, and froze. A throng of soldiers on horseback poured through the gates.

"Phelix," I whispered. An invisible weight lifted from my shoulders.

Andimir and I exchanged a glance. With the southern army here, the remaining Risen would be decimated quickly. But what of Devlyn? Where had the traitor slithered off to?

I shoved down the emotions threatening to erupt at Jyn's appearance. My eyes skimmed the grounds, searching around the clusters of soldiers, horses, and the few Risen who were cut down as they tried to flee. As quickly as it had begun, the battle was over.

But I knew this was only the beginning.

Still, a relieved sigh slipped free, gratitude that my friends were all alive and relatively unscathed. My gaze landed on Jyn again, and stuck. When he met my eyes, I bit down on my lips, resisting the tears that burned in my eyes.

Then I was swept into an embrace that flooded my senses with coconut and hazelnut. I didn't try to stop the tears then.

"Shh, Princess," Jyn soothed. "I've got you. I'm here."

"I thought—" I clung to him, sobbing on his leather-clad chest, hoping against hope that, if I held on, I could believe he was real.

"I know. I know what you thought. I'm sorry. I'm so sorry." His arms tightened around me. "Andáerhyn wanted to send word the moment I woke, but Izoryian wanted to make sure that my immortality took. That I really healed, and not temporarily. He didn't want to give you hope, if something went wrong."

"And now?"

"And now I'm here. Apparently with perfect timing."

I nodded against his chest. Voices begin to chatter around us, a more official end to the battle. But then a voice cut through close to my ear.

"Jyn?" The word was almost whisper soft.

"I owe you, friend," Jyn said to Andimir in response, a warmth in his tone that he usually reserved for me.

"You're not mad then?" Andimir said.

I felt Jyn shake his head. Mad? I drew back, wiping at my eyes with the bare patches of my sleeves.

"Why would he be mad?" I asked. Andimir gestured the

length of Jyn's body and then I realized. "Oh. Because he has his powers back?"

Andimir nodded, his face pale. "He never wanted this."

"You're right." Jyn's gaze was steady on Andimir's face when he added, "But I wanted this; I wanted my family back."

He tugged both of us into a crushing hug, then added, "If I had to get my powers back to stay with you all a little longer, I can live with them."

"Your powers suit you," I said, stepping back.

Jyn's eyes lingered on my face, then followed the still-thin lines of my hands and face, the scars that I knew peeked around the edges of my shirt and leathers. His smile faded into a frown.

"Well, well, well. I heard a rumor you were dead." Meryn bounced to my side, sweat beaded on her forehead and blood splatters down her front to match the rest of us. Her eyes were locked onto Jyn, though, now glittering bright with tears. When he smiled, she pounced, wrapping her arms around his neck. "I'm glad it wasn't true."

"Technically"—Jyn grinned over her shoulder—"I did die."

Meryn leaned back, gripping his arms. "What do you mean, you died?"

"Izoryian felt my pulse fail, as did Andimir." The Elf slid a brief, apologetic glance in Andimir's direction. The latter waved him off, even as his throat bobbed. "Izoryian believed that if he returned my immortality, I might live, since my life aura was still strong."

I swallowed. "So, your soul was still—"

"You could say that. Seems as though Izoryian was right. Returning my immortality rejected the toxins in my system, restored my strength and well"—he waved a hand at himself, snorting in disgust—"added this nonsense."

"You died, though," I croaked. Saying the words aloud made my chest ache.

"I did, Princess," he said gently. "But as you can see, I'm fine."

"How did you leave Eythera?"

"Now that"—he paused to throw another glance around the grounds, surveying the lingering chaos—"is a story all its own. Izoryian and Andáerhyn spent days convincing Eáryn that I needed to be allowed to leave. And Izoryian wasn't sure that removing my immortality so soon wouldn't have lasting . . . negative side effects." He grimaced.

"She let you leave?"

"Not without a fight." I started at that voice, and at Andáerhyn who crept up behind us. "She doesn't like us being involved in 'your war.'" He grinned broadly, his sword slung loosely over his shoulder. "I haven't had a fight this good in ages. I can't *wait* to see what else you have planned."

"This wasn't planned," I said, but the corner of my lips twitched.

"Regardless. This was fun. What now?"

"Well, I haven't found Devlyn, so maybe start there," Lucian said, coming up beside Andimir. Jyn's eyes narrowed on him. The prince paled. "I thought you—"

"Yeah, you didn't get so lucky." Jyn glared at him, then turned to me. "Why is *he* here?"

"I wouldn't be here, if he wasn't," I murmured.

The annoyance on Jyn's face faded into concern again. "Princess?"

"Later." I looked away, but not quickly enough to miss the look Andimir shot Lucian. The apologetic, reassuring glance.

"Then we need to find Devlyn?" Jyn asked. I nodded. "Is he not safe? Do you think the Risen got him?"

I glanced at Andimir, then back to Jyn. "You . . . don't know?"

"How could I? Natylia, what's going on?"

"Devlyn betrayed us. Proclaimed my throne abandoned. Filled my ranks with Risen. He attacked us when we arrived and tried to convince my men that I'm not actually their queen."

Jyn's concern exploded into rage. "He *what?* He better hope we don't find him, because I'll kill him myself." His eyes darted around the field. Then he froze, looking slowly back to my face. "Princess. Where's Camion?"

"He's fine. Or safe, anyway."

"We find Devlyn, then" Jyn growled.

Lucian glanced toward the army piled at the gate. "Did anyone see him leave?"

"We can check with Phelix," I said. "See if they saw him dip out. Lucian, can you ask the dryads if they saw him leaving through the back? Take Andáerhyn with you."

The prince's head dipped in agreement before he strolled off, the muscular Elf Commander following at his heels.

Meryn gripped my arm gently. "We should check the palace."

My gaze landed on the large front doors, then scaled the stone walls. The last time I had been inside my own palace, I had watched my sister ride away. I had trusted Devlyn.

What had changed within? Did I want to know?

I took a steadying breath. "Let's go." Before I moved, I turned to Andimir. "Go to Phelix. Tell him that I've granted you power to speak on my behalf if needed, but also tell him where I am and who we're looking for. If he needs verification for anything, I'm not far."

Andimir didn't argue, casting another appraising glance at Jyn before he split off to weave his way through the crowd. Jyn and Meryn were at my flanks, his daggers and her magic at the ready, as I strode for the palace. I tried to ignore the thundering rhythm of my heart in my ears as I reached for the handles.

And shoved the doors wide.

Chapter 16

My breath caught as we stepped into the main foyer. A swell of emotions rose in my chest. I hadn't expected to feel so overwhelmed. But the familiar art, the expensive rugs . . .

I had begun to believe I would never see my home again.

Tears pricked at my eyes. I had hoped that, if I were lucky enough to return, Annalea would be with me.

I brushed away the tears that slipped down my cheeks, hyper aware of Jyn's hand on my shoulder. My gaze slid to the dining hall, where the doors sat slightly askew.

"We should search the lower level first. If he's upstairs, we'll find him as we go," Jyn said.

"We *will* find him, Natylia," Meryn added.

Jyn tightened his grip on my shoulder. "We stay together. We fight together."

"Yeah," I murmured, reaching up to squeeze his fingers. "I missed you."

"I came back to you as soon as I could."

"I know you did."

"We should talk—"

"Later." I emphasized the word, striding across the foyer.

Behind me, I heard Meryn whisper, "Good luck getting her to talk."

"Oh, she'll talk." Jyn's response was low, but I could hear the determination.

I set my shoulders. They meant well, and I did want to talk to them. Camion wanted to say the words. I watched him fight to share his trauma almost hourly. But . . . I didn't know how. Neither did he.

How did I explain my hurts compared to everything else going on? How did I share my pain when my friends had given so much for me?

I released a heavy sigh, refocusing myself on our search. The dining hall was empty: no scattering staff, no hints that there had been any kind of fight outside. I tilted my head to listen for footsteps, but none greeted my ears. My brows drew together. Where were my staff? Had they sought safety during the fighting?

Jyn moved for the kitchens, and I followed. His steps were too fast, like he knew what waited. Maybe he did—I wasn't familiar with what his new Elven abilities could do. He pushed open the door. Clouds of smoke poured from the room. I coughed and sputtered, waving my hand to clear the air. A hand gripped my arm, long enough to pull me back, but the smoke followed and bled into the dining hall.

"Nat—"

"I know," I managed between gasping breaths. The kitchens

were well and carefully staffed. Burnt food almost never happened, but to this degree? It was unheard of. Mistakes like these didn't happen.

"I'll go in first," Jyn said. His fingers tightened around the hilts of his daggers.

He stepped around me and Meryn. We followed closely, listening for any sounds of life. Meryn scanned the room behind us as we moved, watchful and wary. A haze hung in the air, an acrid burn that tore at my throat. For a moment, the only thing I noticed to be amiss was the bread left on the baking rack, now crumbled to smoldering ashes above the fading fire.

Then we spotted them.

Shoved hastily into the pantry, the door not even fully closed behind them. Unmoving, piled on top of each other in a way that immediately dropped lead into my stomach. I took a hesitant step, then another. Jyn pulled the door fully open, then crouched to check their pulses.

"It's them," he murmured. "The kitchen staff." He stepped in front of me, blocking my view as he put his hands on my shoulders. I brushed him off and he frowned.

"But I— but they—" My stomach twisted. I was going to be sick. Most of the kitchen staff had been with us since I was a child. They may not be close to the family, but they were certainly friends and they hadn't deserved . . .

Where was Raye?

Meryn's eyes were locked on the bodies. "We'll give them proper rights later. They'll be taken care of, I promise you. But we have to find who did this before they escape. Be that Devlyn or someone else."

I nodded numbly, the lump in my throat too tight to let me speak. I wasn't sure what I would say, if I could.

We searched the remaining nooks of the kitchen, then moved through the dining hall to the next room. They were all clear— not a sign of life anywhere. Not the ballroom, the Council Room, nowhere. No sign of Raye, my own maidservant, the girl who had been trying to earn money to send to her family before I left. Her absence made me uneasy, but maybe when we were farther upstairs . . .

"We have so much staff, I don't understand—"

"We'll find them, Princess. One way or another."

The "another" was what I was afraid of.

"We don't know what happened. They might have hidden," Meryn offered. "We need to keep moving."

Our search of the second floor was almost as fruitless as the first. Almost. The last room we searched was the library. Books were scattered to the wind, tossed across the floor, pages ripped from the volumes. And toward the back, as if they had tried to hide, a group of attendants lay slaughtered in cold blood.

"The blood is dry," Jyn murmured. "They did this recently, but not today. Not like with those in the kitchen."

Meryn leaned in, her nose wrinkling slightly as she examined the bodies and said, "Two days ago, tops. Maybe Devlyn got impatient . . ."

"Maybe that's where the rest of your staff went," Jyn murmured.

"You think they're all—" I choked on the words, swallowing hard against the bile in my throat.

"Not necessarily." Jyn clarified, "I meant, if he got impatient and started murdering people, maybe the rest went into hiding."

His words weren't a comfort. I looked around at the shelves; I couldn't spot a book that hadn't been disturbed.

"What were they looking for?" I asked, mostly to myself.

"We can search for clues later," Jyn said gently. "But think while we move. Is there anything, *anything* your mother had that they might want?"

I shook my head and followed him into the hallway again. My heartbeat thundered to a gallop as we climbed to the top floor. Our rooms were here, our private and family quarters. We crested the third-floor hallway and I fell to my knees.

Guards. All dead on the floor. Half a dozen loyal men and women in Thraisian colors. As I looked from one body to the next, I held in the sob that tore at my throat. The blood was dried, like they had fought to protect my staff, and I realized that they were probably the reason we had found so few bodies. Whoever attacked them, Devlyn or otherwise, these guards had bought them time . . . and paid with their lives.

I should have been here.

Meryn dropped beside me, looping her arms around me. "We'll find out what happened, I promise you."

I clenched my jaw and nodded, staring at the red carpet that was now splotched with brown and crimson. Instead of the hole now threatening to swallow me up, to lure me into a darkness where I could grieve and wallow, I needed to use my grief as motivation.

Jyn gripped my arm and helped me to my feet. I winced as we stepped over the guards, hurrying for the chambers my parents had once occupied.

The room was wrecked.

The mattress had been slit open, all the jewelry boxes, books, and papers were thrown around. Dresses had been torn from the armoire. I checked the safes behind the paintings and, while it was clear attempts had been made to open them, the jewelry inside remained untouched. The safe under the floorboards hadn't been tinkered with at all.

"I can't determine anything from this mess," I admitted with a sigh.

"Onward then," Meryn said. Her tone was reluctant, maybe even defeated.

My steps dragged as we moved for my sister's room, my fingers hesitant on the polished doorknob. I turned, pushing tentatively.

Her room was untouched. A thin coat of dust covered the furniture and floor, not even a speck disturbed beyond our own entrance. I didn't let myself linger, even as my mind raced through possible explanations. But none of the other rooms had been touched either, and that left only my and Jyn's chambers.

If Devlyn thought he could hide in there, he was dead wrong.

I pushed open the door. My room was trashed. More books were strewn across the floor, the mattress askew on my bed. Pillows were ripped open, their feathers spilled onto the floor. I glanced at Jyn, who opened the door to his own room—destroyed.

"What were they looking for?" I asked again.

"I guess that depends what Devlyn knows and what Valdis suspects," Meryn said uneasily. Her gaze was focused on the bed, on the torn and scattered sheets. "They could be looking for my—"

"That's possible," Jyn interrupted as he stepped past me, moving for the bathing chambers in the room beyond. He opened the door and jerked to an abrupt halt. "Don't say important information here, we don't know who's listening. And don't follow me, in case there's a trap."

I eyed his back, and the door as it closed behind him. Meryn caught my eye and we moved.

Jyn looked up when we opened the door, then quickly stepped into my path. "Princess, I think you've seen enough for today. Please. Go back."

Warning bells clattered in my head, but I nudged past Jyn, ignoring the golden aura that thrummed around him. The room seemed empty, my steps hollow in the stone space. A dark, dried red-brown stain ran the length of the floor, a wide streak that ran into the large bath in the center of the room. A strange sense of déjà vu ran through me.

I didn't know what to expect. But my chest clenched when I caught sight of glazed blue eyes staring up at the ceiling.

"No, no, no . . ." I dropped my dagger, then lowered myself into the empty bath. My fingers brushed platinum curls stained with blood as I sought a pulse.

Nothing. Raye was gone.

She had been so young.

I expected my tears to break free, but instead anger trembled through my limbs. I hadn't been here. She had died, others in my palace had died, and I hadn't been here to protect any of them. And, deep in my heart, I knew Devlyn was behind this senseless slaughter.

"Find him," I snarled, at no one in particular. "Find him and I will kill him myself."

"Princess. This isn't a road you want to go down."

I climbed out of the bath, retrieved my blade, and clenched the hilt tightly in my fist. "I'll do what I need to. I have had enough of death and murder and not feeling safe in my own home. And I'll be damned if it's my sister next time."

Jyn clenched his jaw. His gaze dropped to the floor. Meryn shuffled uncomfortably.

"Nat?" Andimir's voice rang out from my room. I looked toward the door as he leaned around it. "Nat, we found him."

"Thank you." I strode across the room, determination fueling my steps. I would make Devlyn talk.

Then I would make him bleed.

***

Devlyn was in the dungeons, cornered against a wall with a sword in each hand. No one had tried to get close to him yet. Their focus was entirely on assessing his weapons: how many and if they were poisoned in any way.

Across from where I stood, Phelix barely managed to restrain Andáerhyn, who was grinning ear to ear. But as I neared, the king inclined his head and said, "Your Majesty."

I glanced at the faces around me, but when I met Jyn's eyes, I knew he would be furious if I entrusted this next job to anyone else.

With a heavy sigh, I said, "Jyn. Restrain him."

His eyes lit up at the command. He unsheathed his daggers

and stepped forward. "My pleasure."

Jyn rolled his shoulders, spinning the blades in his hands. Andáerhyn and Phelix stepped aside, letting him pass.

Devlyn stilled, then scowled, straightening his posture. "Surprised to see you walking, boy. Valeria's poisons aren't easily survived."

"Good thing I'm not easily killed."

Devlyn paled at that, lowering his guard long enough to take in Jyn's new golden aura. His jaw clenched but that earlier moment of swagger was gone. And when Jyn swung for him, Devlyn barely managed to deflect a blow before my friend had him on his knees, unarmed.

"Traitors!" Devlyn snarled. "Filthy, stinking traitors! You stand here with our enemies, you betray the kingdom that *raised* you. Wydus made Thrais as powerful as you are today. You would be nothing without Wydus and the generosity of Drask and Kathryn."

"And you would be nothing without Thrais," Phelix reminded him, his fingers wrapped tightly around the hilt of his blade. "You would do well to remember who has fed, housed, and employed you for the last few decades."

"A façade," Devlyn snapped. "Do you think I didn't have a deal with Wydus then? Do you think I didn't try to send them what they wanted?" His eyes locked onto me. "I should have known you wouldn't listen—both you and your sister. I should have told you to go anywhere *except* Wydus. Drask could already have been done with all of this."

I tried to ignore the fury trembling in my arms. Despite it, I managed through gritted teeth, "Where is my sister?"

"How would I know?"

"If you lie to her, I'll start taking limbs," Jyn threatened. He lifted his blade until the golden runes glittered in the torchlight. Andáerhyn moved to slap cuffs on my former Guard Captain, but Devlyn's eyes never left Jyn's dagger.

"I. Don't. Know," Devlyn spat out. His confidence had dimmed, though, as he added, "I haven't seen her since I sent the two of you away."

"And my palace? My staff?"

"I was looking for an object." Devlyn met my eyes with a sneer. "Anyone in my way was eliminated."

Heat roared to life in my veins while magic gathered across my hands and up my arms. Phelix staggered back a step, his eyes wide. Concern etched lines around Jyn's eyes for the third time. He reached for my arm, but I shook him off, taking a step toward Devlyn instead.

"They were innocent people. And you killed them because they were in your way?" I was shouting. I didn't recognize the wrath in my voice. My hands shook. I balled them into fists. "What were you looking for that they were such an *inconvenience?*"

"You think I'd tell you? You spoiled little—"

My fist, wrapped in sparkling magic, slammed into his jaw before I could think the motion through. The hit was an immediate shower of ice water to my rage. Devlyn's head lolled and Jyn winced.

"I couldn't—" I glanced around at the faces watching me carefully. "I don't know what came over me."

Jyn leaned forward to check his pulse. "He's fine. Useless to us now, but fine."

"He's only useless until he wakes up," Andimir said. I didn't miss the approval in his tone.

I huffed, rubbing my sore knuckles. "Can two of you move him to a holding cell on the other end of the dungeons? As far from the main doors as possible, please. I would like a word with King Phelix and Prince Lucian."

"I'm staying," Jyn said firmly.

"You would be of more help moving him," Meryn countered. "You and Andáerhyn will be faster, too. I can stay with Nat."

Jyn stared at me for a long moment, waiting until I inclined my head slightly before rounding on Devlyn. The former Captain of the Guard was whisked away before anyone could so much as offer to help Jyn.

"Should I—" Andáerhyn gestured to the door.

"Might as well stay." Sighing, I turned to Phelix. "How are your men faring?"

"No losses, minimal wounds. Your dryad allies and the men who remained loyal to you made sure we were only cleaning up scraps." He glanced at Lucian, then asked me, "You trust him?"

"I trust that he won't go reporting back to his father."

"I would never." Lucian raised both palms in a gesture of surrender as the king's eyes studied him. The door banged open. Jyn snapped it shut before the prince spoke again. "I saw what my father did to her, to Camion. I don't need more convincing. If you ever had reason to doubt my loyalty to you, believe that what I've seen has severed any love I had for him."

Jyn's eyes widened. "Drask betrayed us too? Princess—"

"Later," I said evenly.

A guttural growl rumbled from his throat. "No, not later. Now. Tell us what happened to you."

"Jyn maybe you should—" Meryn started.

"No. Enough excuses. Enough hiding behind your fears. Talk to me. I can't help if I don't know what happened."

Phelix shifted in front of me a step, protectively, and Lucian shuffled uneasily. Andimir dropped a hand on Jyn's arm but he brushed him off.

"Natylia, we deserve to know what you saw," Jyn snapped. "What you heard, what plans could be made. You have to talk to us."

I spun on Jyn, my eyes burning with tears and my hands quivering for reasons that had nothing to do with fear. I struggled to find the words, and when I did, my voice quavered with raw emotion.

"Camion and I were tortured to within inches of our lives. By Drask, or Valdis, or whatever name he's going by now. We almost died, because I have so little control over my magic, and we would have died, if Lucian hadn't managed to save us. I want to tell you all the details. I've been trying to tell Meryn for days. But it's not so easy when your dreams are filled with icy stone rooms and moats full of blood."

I shoved past him. Kalïa would likely be wondering where I was, and I didn't have the capacity to go further into detail at the moment. Jyn called my name, a note of apology in his voice. I ignored him.

Everything would be so much simpler if I could simply tell them what went on. Every detail. But the words were hard and burned like acid on my tongue. The betrayal was too consuming.

So much so that, whenever I looked into a mirror, all I saw were the sharpened lines of my face, the new scars next to the old. The sting of whips rose fresh in my mind every time.

I needed to heal. Spirits, Camion needed to heal.

Kalïa stood near the palace's back gate, sorting Risen bodies from human along with her fellow dryads.

"I cannot sense them all," Kalïa said as I approached. "Not the humans, anyway. You may still have traitors amongst your ranks. Be wary who you gift your trust to."

I eyed the human casualties, laid out in neat shoulder-to-shoulder rows. "There weren't many human deaths, then?"

"No. Your Elven allies greatly unbalanced the odds. In our favor."

"And your own losses?"

Kalïa dipped her head. "We lost one, but only one. She will be honored in the forest when the time is appropriate."

"I'm glad to hear that, but I'm sorry you lost anyone. What should we do now?" I gestured at the Risen.

"We burn them. You don't want them to be raised again."

"Can you see it done?"

Kalïa nodded. "Anything, Your Majesty."

Chapter 17

We cleared the palace, checking every corner until we were sure no one else remained inside, dead or alive. It was the work of hours. More of my people were found in the servant quarters, slumped across the floor and over furniture.

Outside, we were slowly gathering my people, those who had remained loyal to me, for the Temple of Nahara. They would later be prepared for burial before they were laid to final rest in a cemetery not far away. As to the Risen, we were putting them into a pile to be burned in a forest clearing. Meryn would oversee the fire once we had some of Phelix's men installed into guard positions, after she returned from retrieving Callithyia.

She and the High Priestess returned in the early afternoon, Sylvr and Camion at their heels. Sweat drenched my brow and my limbs ached from lifting body after body. But when I met those green and blue eyes, something eased in my chest.

He crossed the field to me before I could move, gathering my hands in his as his eyes scanned my face anxiously. "You're not hurt?"

"I'm fine," I assured him, brushing my thumbs over the backs of his hands. "Or mostly. Did Meryn tell you?"

His brows pulled together. "Tell me what?"

"Jyn's alive."

Camion's eyes shot wide. "*Alive?*"

"Alive. With full Elven powers in tow."

"He has his powers?" Camion paused, processing my words. "Shouldn't you be more than fine, then?"

"Yeah. But he pressed too hard and I got angry . . ."

"And there's never a point where the two of you haven't figured an argument out."

I freed a hand, brushing my fingers over his cheek. "You're right." When he stepped back to study me, I added, "I'm fine. I promise. A few scrapes and scratches but no worse for the wear. We're going to interrogate Devlyn again. Or try, if . . . if I can contain myself."

I winced when he frowned in confusion, then awkwardly explained. No judgment filled his eyes, only concern.

"I should have been here."

"You were where I asked you to be," I said softly. "I appreciate how hard that was for you."

"That's not an answer."

"I'm fine. I had a momentary lapse in judgment."

His hand tightened around mine, but he nodded. I turned to study the palace grounds, seeking Jyn but only spotting Andáe-rhyn's golden glow. Lucian was near the gates with Phelix, who was ordering his men around while Meryn helped Sylvr tend the injured.

"We should go to the dungeons," I said quietly. "I don't think Jyn should be left alone with Devlyn any more than me."

Camion's brow furrowed at that, but he followed my lead. The entrance to the dungeons was outside, near the armory. I pried open the heavy door and didn't have to set foot inside to have my concerns validated. A voice growled out a threat—too low to understand but too clear to be mistaken for anything else.

"You should tell me what you know before she returns. She needs the information you have, but her patience is running thin," I heard Jyn say.

I strolled closer, to a cell near the end of the row. Devlyn was chained to the wall, in a fashion similar to how I had been chained up. I stumbled at the sight, backing up a step and swallowing hard. Jyn glanced up at the sound of my boots. Before he could move, Camion's hand was on the small of my back.

"You don't have to do this," Camion whispered.

"I do," I murmured back. "I've had enough betrayal to last a lifetime."

His fingers tightened on my shirt. "I'm here."

"I know. Thank you."

Jyn stepped out of the cell. Camion moved forward to clap him on the shoulder but Jyn pulled him into a hug.

"I'm glad to see you alive, my friend," Camion started.

"Alive and well." Jyn smiled faintly. "I'm glad to see you're all right as well. Thank you, for taking care of her."

Camion's eyes met mine. "Don't be fooled. She took care of me."

"Indeed." Jyn studied my face for a moment before I looked

away.

But all I saw was the cell, the chains. I took a deep breath and calmed myself by homing in on the differences. Devlyn sat on a chair, even though his arms were chained out above him. The shackles on his ankles were over his boots. He had been stripped of weapons, but not of his clothing.

We weren't cruel to our prisoners. Our dungeons were heated with fireplaces, there were windows that could be opened and closed to let in fresh air. Devlyn wouldn't be thrashed and beaten and drained—

I cut the thought off sharply. I didn't need to dissect the details that far. Lingering on the past wouldn't change anything.

"I can handle him," Jyn said softly. "But if I'm entirely honest, I don't think he knows much more than he's already let on. I think he's more of a puppet."

"He fooled us for years. Which is why I *should* interrogate him."

"Princess, earlier . . ."

"I lost my temper. I'll be more careful. I feel bad enough."

Jyn frowned. "I'm not saying you weren't justified. I'm saying I'm worried about you. Both of you."

His eyes were locked onto Camion, whose gaze was pinging around the dungeon. I stilled, noting the straight set of his shoulders, the line of his jaw. "Camion, why don't you see if Meryn could use a hand? She needs to oversee the disposal of the Risen, but she's also needed for healing. Maybe you can do some bandaging for her or help Callithyia with transporting our fallen?"

Camion's focus snapped to me. "I don't want to leave you again."

"I know, my love," I murmured. "But this is too soon for you and we both know it. I'll find you as soon as we're finished."

I saw the indecision—the defeat—flicker across his face before he nodded. I grabbed his hand. "You're not a failure. You need time. We both do. But I'm angry, and that helps. I can do this without you for now."

"I'll take care of her, Camion," Jyn murmured. "You know I will."

"I know." A muscle ticked in Camion's jaw but, with another glance around the dungeon, he nodded once more. He brushed his lips to my forehead before he strode toward the door, casting another hesitant look over his shoulder before he stepped out.

I took a long, slow breath while pulling at my magic. Warmth tingled up my fingertips. Jyn's brow creased but I stepped around him, moving for the man locked in the cell.

Devlyn glared in my direction, a sneer twisting his expression. "I've told you all I'm going to. Why not save us both time and finish me off? I can tell you want to."

"How long?"

"What?"

"How long," I gritted out, "have you been working with Valdis?"

Devlyn faltered then. His angry expression collapsed into confusion, then distrust. "Who?"

"How long have you been working with Drask?" I rephrased.

"Years," he answered, staring at me thoughtfully. "But that's not what you asked. Why do you think I'm working with a Titan?"

"You don't know?" Devlyn blinked up at me, a dismissal and

refusal that made me frown. "Drask *is* Valdis. One and the same."

I saw the backpedaling start in his eyes and then spread to smooth out his expression. I chanced a look at Jyn, who grimaced. When I focused on Devlyn again, he shook his head.

"Natylia, I didn't know. I swear to you, I didn't know. I wouldn't have worked with him, if I had."

"I don't think it matters whether you knew or didn't," I said callously. "If you have no more information, you've worn out your use to me."

Jyn pulled his daggers free, taking a step closer.

Devlyn's expression darkened. "I know nothing else. I took your palace because you were too stubborn to do what needed to be done. Drask was going to combine the kingdoms, but you, and your father before, refused him. I was going to oversee the armies of both kingdoms, with all the glory and luxuries of my position. You ruined everything. Drask only did what was necessary."

"What do you mean he did what was necessary?" I asked. The glittering magic began to climb my arms again. Jyn twisted his daggers in his hands, but his attention was split between my trembling limbs and the man chained before him.

Devlyn's eyes were locked onto the daggers and the Elf wielding them, his mouth opening and closing as he weighed his words. Then he met my narrowed eyes and said, "Your father didn't have heart problems, Natylia, unless you consider marrying a filthy commoner a heart problem. Your father was *poisoned*."

"You're lying," I said. Anger began to thrum in my veins. "Mother would have told me."

"I would be willing to wager there's a great many things your mother didn't tell you."

"Like what?"

"Let's start with the fact that Valeria poisoned your father. And when they suspected your mother might fill you or Annalea in on the secret, Drask had her taken care of too."

"He . . ." Jyn gripped my wrist, squeezing gently. I continued, ignoring him. "He murdered my parents? Because they wouldn't combine our kingdoms?"

"He was searching for something. I don't know what. The Scepters you went chasing, maybe. He thought if the entire northern half of the continent belonged to him, he would be unhindered."

"I thought you didn't know anything else," Jyn snarled.

"It's too late for any of these plans anyway. Drask had alternative methods to get what he wanted." Devlyn took in my thin form, the scars and lines of exhaustion. Some of his confidence returned. "I dare say he already got it too. In one way or another."

I ignored the taunt. "Is that it, then? My parents, murdered at his hands? That's all you know that may be new to me?"

"Isn't that enough?" Devlyn quirked an eyebrow. Jyn took another step forward, the scowl on his face more menacing than usual. Devlyn's throat bobbed. "But you're right, that's not everything. Your sister? There's a kill order on her head. We suspect her guard overheard, but I can't promise you she's still alive. And that boy you're so infatuated with? That dirty commoner? He'll die soon enough. How much do you know about your beau's lineage? Because Drask wants him. I don't know why."

"He already got what he needed," I ground out. "So, you really are useless to me."

"I could still lead your armies. Call it an . . . amnesty agreement."

"Not a chance. I left them to you before. I can't believe you didn't suspect, with Risen among your ranks."

"Oh, I knew about the Risen. Best soldiers I've ever led. They follow without question. I knew Drask had access to necromancy. I didn't know he was *the* Valdis, though."

"And at no point did killing and raising soldiers strike you as immoral?" Jyn snapped.

"You do what's necessary in a time of war."

My eyes narrowed to slits. "This is war, then?"

"At first, I would have said no." Devlyn grinned. "But if you're planning to stand up to the Titans? Yes. This is war. And you're not going to win."

Chapter 18

"**I** can't believe we spent an entire afternoon cleaning your room. How much stuff does one person need?"

Out of the corner of my eye, I saw the small hint of a smile on Camion's lips. But I rolled my eyes and sighed, hitting his chest with one of the extra pillows. He feigned indignation but didn't retaliate, even though a pile of pillows was easily within his reach.

Camion wasn't wrong, though. We had spent half the day between repairing the mattress and cleaning the scattered remains of books. And that was before the dumped-out jewelry boxes, the dresses and clothing that lay everywhere imaginable, and the soot streaks from the fireplace ashes.

We were exhausted, sore, but together in my room. I had thought I would be comforted returning here. But, as my gaze roamed the familiar walls, nothing felt the same.

Warm arms wrapped around my stomach and I smiled faintly.

A sliver of safety warmed my chest and I fell into it, fell into Camion. I rested my head on his chest and listened to the heart-beats that thrummed gently next to my ear.

Deep sleep was a net of comfort that morphed into vibrant dreams. And then nightmares. Memories of Drask flooded my mind—yellow flecked eyes and that sneer of a smile that no longer reminded me of the man I had once called family. His taunting voice echoed through the nightmare. My hands clenched into fists, but I couldn't move them. I felt his breath on my cheek, the whips on my back, the chill on my skin.

I didn't see, only felt. I was trapped in my mind. Chains bit into my skin. My wrists ached. I tried to breathe but the air was fire in my lungs.

No, no, no, no.

I wasn't here. This wasn't happening. *I was free, I was free, I was safe*—I was with Camion. Arms looped around me tightly, soft whispers in my ear. My chest ached as I fought them off, squirming, desperately trying to pull in a breath. The magic in my veins thrummed to life, filling my mind—

"Natylia, *stop.*"

Camion's voice. Filled with concern and . . . fear?

Air whooshed into my lungs, extinguishing the burn. I thrashed against the arms holding me. Then I felt myself falling. My eyes shot open. Those same arms reached out and caught me right before I hit carpet.

Fire was bright in my vision, dancing on the blanket, over the translucent draping above the bed. I pulled my magic back after a second's thought and the flames extinguished. Camion groaned, lowering me the rest of the way to the floor.

"Sorry, I'm still—" he panted, "still trying to get my strength back."

I blinked.

"What did I do?" I whispered. Tears welled up in my eyes. I drew my knees to my chest. We would never be past this. *I* would never be past this. Some days, I felt like I could conquer the world, but others . . .

And I was supposed to rule a kingdom. I was supposed to *lead* a kingdom. To battle. Maybe to war.

To war?

My heart constricted.

"Tyli?" Camion's voice was soft.

I hugged my legs, burying my face in my knees and let the sobs shake through me. Betrayals, torture, deaths, my missing sister, Jyn's return, fighting for my palace, the never ending guilt over Camion that was eating me alive . . . the whisper in my ear that grew louder every day, insistent that we couldn't win, couldn't save my people or the people that I loved.

Camion's warmth pressed into my side. His fingers ran a steady path the length of my spine, up then down. Back and forth, until I could catch my breath again. Then I slid an inch away, hating myself for leaning on him when I knew what he had suffered.

He slid back into my side. "Enough, Natylia."

I balked at the sharp tone in his voice, wiping at my cheeks as I looked up to meet his eyes. "W—What?"

"Enough," he repeated. The word was softer though. He reached out, tilting my chin, pressing a soft kiss to my lips. "Don't try to create a distance between us that doesn't exist. That I might lose you, because you keep pushing me away, hurts more than I can even try to say."

"Camion I . . . I'm sorry."

"You truly have nothing to apologize for."

I shook my head, taking in a long breath. "You've stood by me. From the very beginning. Before I knew I needed you, before I deserved you in any way. I've broken your trust, I've *hurt* you. And knowing that I was even remotely the reason you were . . . you were . . ." Camion started to open his mouth, but I waved him off, swallowing back the burning lump in my throat. "I need to get this out. Because you're right. I need . . . I feel trapped in the past. I can't let go of all the hurts weighing me down and they're hindering me from becoming who I'm supposed to be. And, again, I'm hurting you. And I'm sorry. I am."

"Tyli, you can't expect yourself to be strong all the time. I've been failing at that lately myself and it's hard, impossibly hard. But you know what? We're getting there." He sighed, running his thumb over my cheek. I lifted my own hand, clasping his, leaning into him. The half smile he offered made my heart flutter.

"Let's talk," he added quietly.

"I thought we were." My lips twitched.

"Let's talk about what happened. Now. Let's tear off the bandage and put all the words into the world so we can move on."

"I don't know if I can . . ."

"I'll go first."

I met his eyes. Took a shaky breath. And, after a long moment of consideration, I climbed into his lap and buried my face in the crook of his neck.

And then he started to talk.

His voice was a soft rumble through his chest, gentle and soothing against the words he struggled to speak. But he took his time and told me every detail. Every lashing, every cruel manipulation to cause him pain. Each word that Cybele whispered to him as he stumbled in and out of consciousness. He paused, when he couldn't hold back the tears, and I held him until he took a breath and pressed on.

His courage gave me strength. *He* gave me strength, even when my throat stuck and the words wouldn't come. But once they started, they were a flood. And telling Camion, telling a person I trusted implicitly, was therapeutic.

Camion was right, though. With every word I pried another thorn free, released another hurt. I knew the wounds would need time to heal, but they were laid bare, cleansed of the toxic fear that held them in place. And when we curled up to sleep late in the night, a weight had lifted from both our shoulders.

Weight we should have never carried alone.

***

A floorboard creaked, louder than the uncomfortable groan of trees outside my window. I shot upright, scanning the room for anything that seemed out of place. Camion snored gently beside me, and I knew Jyn would never have made a sound.

A shadow moved. Rage ignited in my veins. Valeria grinned at me, her hood tossed back, her pale skin bright in the moonlight from the window. Dark hair fluttered around her shoulders, but it was her eyes, her bright crimson eyes, that sent a shiver trickling down my spine.

"Well this won't do," she whispered, the sound barely more than a soft caress in the night air. "You should be asleep. I didn't track your Elf this far only to have him warned of my arrival."

She moved for the window. But I was already up, magic springing from my lifted fingertips. I had her pinned in tendrils of glittering magic before she could escape. Camion yelled from behind me, but I didn't hear the words. I was too focused on my power, on letting the threads creep up her chest. Tendrils of my magic twined around her throat and tightened as her eyes grew wider and wider.

"You . . . have . . . magic?" she gasped. Clarity shone in her eyes. "That's why . . . he wanted you."

"And you handed me over," I growled. "You hurt my friends. And then you had the nerve to come back and finish the job?"

My magic continued a slow crawl up her jaw and slipped over her mouth. I could feel the depths of my power draining slowly. On my side, the scar ignited almost as bright as my anger. The tendrils extended, holding her in place even as she struggled.

Valeria's breaths became wheezing pants. Jyn's door banged open. I heard voices but not what they said. My entire focus, all of my being, was trained on ending the Vampyr in front of me. Whether I could or not was inconsequential.

For a moment, I thought I would hesitate. A warm hand gripped my arm—one of the two men, trying to rein me in.

But I didn't want to be stopped.

So, I didn't.

The coils around her throat tightened, sharpened, until they bit into her pale skin. They changed too, from blue and purple sparkles to a deep, velvety black flecked with silver. Valeria clawed at the magic, tearing her fingers, staining her nails with blood.

"Natylia." Jyn's voice was firm in my ear. "Don't do this to yourself. Pull back."

Heated anger rose in response and filled my mind until I saw nothing but red and the dark tendrils.

"Princess, please," Jyn pleaded.

My hands tightened into fists. My magic followed in kind, clamping down on the Vampyr.

"Tyli, stay with me." Camion's voice gave me pause. "Don't become who they want you to be. Don't let your anger control you. We need you." His breath was warm on my ear when he added, "*I* need you."

The hatred flooding my veins stuttered, then loosened. My magic swirled, softened. Sparkling blue and purple filled the space again, then Jyn was across the room and Valeria collapsed into his arms. He whisked her away without a backward glance. I didn't know what he intended to do with her—kill her, interrogate her. She would heal rapidly enough for questioning in a few hours, if he let her live.

I became more aware of the ache up my side. My hand rose to the scar that sat above my ribs. Camion's hand covered mine, his movements slow and deliberate—soothing.

"Are you okay?"

I blinked. For a moment, it had seemed like time had slowed and was only now beginning to catch up. Then I met his eyes, that bright blue and green glittering down at me.

"I almost . . ."

"I know," Camion murmured, opening his arms to pull me in

tight. "I'm proud of you. The Tyli I knew only a year ago wouldn't have held her own against an army of Risen *and* a Vampyr. You're incredible."

"This was different," I said, staring out the opened window. "I've killed before but . . . this was the first time I really truly *wanted* to."

My eyes flitted to my hands. The skin was the same as before: flecked with small scars and calluses, smooth and pale in-between. But that magic . . . I didn't think I had ever seen magic that color before.

As if reading my thoughts, Camion asked, "Did you know you could do that?"

I shook my head. "I didn't even know magic that dark existed."

"Did you notice anything different when you cast it?"

"Only one thing," I murmured. "That magic was completely fueled by hate."

Chapter 19

Phelix met each of our waiting gazes, then his eyes lingered on mine. "Our advance scouts spotted Eurybia moving south. She might need to supplement her powers and, if she does, the only place nearby with enough water is here"—the king pointed to Starberry Lake on the map spread before him—"but if her siblings haven't made a move on the palace yet, they could be grouping. We might want to prepare for an assault."

"I don't have enough men to withstand all five Titans," I said. "We don't know who of my soldiers is truly loyal, let alone willing to risk their lives so haphazardly."

"Kalum will lend you all the strength we have. Audri will bring a larger regime in the days to come. As to the rest . . ." Phelix's eyes lifted to Jyn's. The king had really come out of his shell under pressure, I noticed. Maybe the plate armor weighing down his shoulders gave him more confidence, because he was fearless when he said, "I'm hoping you have better news?"

Jyn sighed, crossing his arms over his chest. Andimir, perched on a desk slightly behind him, shot Jyn a concerned glance.

"Not particularly." Jyn sighed. "Valeria is taking her time healing. I'm not sure if it's residual from the magic used on her or because we haven't given her human blood. We might need a few more days before we can interrogate her."

Camion slid me an uneasy glance, that strange, dark magic still a weight on our shoulders. But before anyone could comment, the door groaned open. A ripple of tension crashed over the room, a wave of tightening shoulders and drawn weapons. Lucian sprang away from the door frame he was leaning against.

I was the first to ease my posture when I recognized Andáerhyn.

"Sorry," the Elven commander said, lifting his hands. "I might be able to help. Not with the Vampyr—I didn't mean to listen in, sorry—but I do have some information."

Jyn waved a hand for him to continue. Andáerhyn wagged his eyebrows at Jyn, a grin on his face. He leaned on the back of the chair Meryn had sprawled over, sparing a quick glance at Sylvr, whose head currently rested on my friend's stomach.

"I can't confirm this," Andáerhyn continued, "but Izoryian was planning to enlist Elves to join your fight. Eáryn wasn't thrilled with the idea . . . but they let me come. They let *us* come. If you're lucky, you might find a force of Elves at your side."

"But is that enough?" Camion asked thoughtfully. "I can work, day and night. Forge as much as I can, as fast as I can. But I know that between Thrais's armories and my own work, we would be stretched thin. Replacement gear would be nonexistent, even if I could outfit the entire force."

"What of the Dwarves?" I asked. "Would they be willing to join us? They could help you. Their craftsmanship is legendary."

Andimir shrugged. "If we could get a ship down the coastline, maybe. If Eurybia did move inland, that would eliminate the largest threat to doing so. But I couldn't counter the others, and Boreas has wings."

"I could send a missive to Audri." Phelix leaned on the broad table between us. "She could send one of our smaller ships south virtually undetected."

"I should go with them," Andimir said. I studied him, confused. "Remember? I've worked with the Dwarves before. Pirate or no, I have an amicable relationship with them. Maybe I can at least barter with them for weapons and arms, if they won't fight."

"You would ride south? Alone?" Jyn's gaze was sharp on Andimir.

"With minimal stops, I could be there in a bit over a fortnight. At most."

"Assuming you weren't attacked by bandits." I frowned. "I'm not sure I love the idea of you traveling so far by yourself. Nor that we would need to wait so long to gather forces."

"You're going to have to wait regardless," Phelix pointed out. "You don't know for sure that the Elves are coming. We need to send out spies. We need to find out exactly where the Titans are, what they're up to. Your men will need interrogated, and those deemed safe will need extra training."

"We need to retrieve your life essence," Sylvr said. Her tone was low, meant for Meryn, but we all heard the words.

Phelix hesitated, scanning the faces around him. "Her what, now?"

"Her life essence," Jyn said. He looked pointedly at Meryn though, waiting. The people in this room were our closest allies. If we were to move forward, they needed to know.

Meryn winced. Every eye in the room was locked onto her. Meryn glanced around, then sighed. "Fine. But this can't leave this room. Not yet."

Jyn locked eyes with the prince. "If it does, I'll find the leak. Mark my words."

"Don't look at me," Lucian said. "I won't utter a word."

Seemingly satisfied, Meryn murmured, "I am . . . Nahara." Her nose scrunched as the words fell off her lips and Sylvr reached up, brushing her fingers over Meryn's wrist.

Phelix straightened, his expression incredulous. "You're who?"

"Nahara."

"As in—"

"As in the Titan, yes. But I don't remember anything about her. Not anything more than I've learned since I've lived in Thrais."

"How do you know for sure, then?" Lucian asked. He looked the least phased of everyone around him. Maybe after his father, nothing surprised him anymore.

"Because her legacy has been passed down through the Priestesses of Nahara for a long time," Sylvr said. "And because I was the one to hide the stone that is her life essence."

"What about your dragon?" I asked without thinking. "The one we found in those Dwarven ruins?"

Eyes widened around us, but Meryn shook her head. "I don't know where he is."

"You have a dragon?" Lucian considered when she nodded, then looked at Sylvr. "And you told her she's this . . . Titan? Deity? And now we have to find her life essence?"

"We told her, actually," Andáerhyn said. "Or Izoryian and Eáryn did. But she returned to Thrais afterward."

"I don't know those names," the prince admitted.

"Izoryian and Eáryn are the Lord and Lady of the Elves, respectively," I said.

"The life essence should be our most immediate task, then," Phelix said, returning his attention to me. "None of us can deny how beneficial it would be to have a Titan on our side, especially one as powerful as . . ." His words trailed off as he glanced at Meryn and assessed her slight frame. A small frown tugged at his lips. After a moment, he shook his head. "While we find her life essence, Andimir can go south and meet with my wife. She can bring the bulk of the army north, and we can send a small contingent south as an escort."

I nodded. "In the meantime, I can send a spy north, to scout the ruins of the Wydus prison. I don't know if Drask—" I glanced apologetically at Lucian. "I don't know for sure if Valdis and Cybele survived the collapse or not."

"We should assume he did," Phelix said, "Especially if the other Titans are still moving. You might have managed to slow him down, though. Still, couldn't hurt to have the area scoped for any other useful information. Cybele was with him?"

"Yes."

"Assuming this, we know that the next thing he needs to do is go south to retrieve his son." The king realized what he said as the words fell free, but Lucian shrugged. Phelix frowned again.

"We might as well consider Lytalian lost."

"I can't accept that," Andimir said, straightening. "I can't let those people die."

"You're going to have to. Those islands are too far to be defensible without preexisting forces. Of which they have essentially none." Phelix rubbed at his temples, pushing curls back from his forehead. I could understand how the king felt. No part of this was easy. "None of us like preparing for the possibility of war. We like war even less. But the worst part by far is that you can't save everyone. You can't. Humanity will see heavy losses before this is over. All we can do is save as many as we can."

"I won't accept that Lytalian is going to be abandoned to their fate."

"They did choose to secede from the mainland rulers," Lucian murmured. "Technically, they chose to separate themselves from our protection."

Phelix nodded in agreement. "We don't have the men to send there, even if they hadn't. We're already going to need to evacuate the southern cities. Once Thanatos hits the mainland, death will roll out at his feet. We have to prepare a unified front, or we won't survive."

"We should fortify Thrais," Camion said. "It's the middle of the kingdoms. We already expended energy and people to reclaim it. Let's use the palace. More people will be able to travel here faster anyway. Our best chance at building an armed force lies in getting them all to one location."

"So, Thrais becomes that one place," I said quietly. There was logic to his words, but a nagging feeling tugged at my gut. "But what if we lose the village? What motivation will people have to fight, if they think we can't protect them?"

"They'll fight for their homes," Phelix said. I frowned, so he added, "If you lose Thrais, I will help you rebuild. Kalum will help you rebuild."

"Help me take my throne from my father and Wydus's resources are yours as well." Lucian's jaw flexed. "I don't know where my mother stands in all this . . . but I won't allow him to continue to rule our people, if he thinks that ruling them means he can turn them into the monstrosities we fought yesterday."

Jyn snorted. "You won't have any people left to worry about, by the time he's through."

Lucian's nostrils flared, but he held his temper. "Isn't that the point of all this? Saving as many people as we can? Or is that exclusive to your kingdoms because my father is the antagonist?" He pushed off the wall, fire in his eyes as he added, "From where I'm standing, you're all too willing to condemn to death anyone who isn't your people. You've been wronged, I don't disagree. But I don't see the world in black and white. Maybe you should consider those of us stuck in the grey."

My gaze was locked onto Lucian. On the flames that turned brilliant, shining deep within his eyes. The inferno dimmed then brightened, into the purest, brightest light I had ever seen.

"Lucian," I murmured, glancing down to his clenched fists. His fingers shimmered with purple and blue magic that ever so slowly faded to a glimmering white that danced across his skin. "Lucian look at your hands."

The prince's brows scrunched together, but he looked. And stilled completely.

In an instant the magic blinked out.

Meryn took a step toward him, her face bright with awe.

"I—" Lucian studied his hands. His jaw clenched, then he managed, "I need to go."

Before any of us could utter a word to make him stop, the door was closing at his heels. A beat of silence passed.

"We should talk to him," Phelix said finally. "He needs guidance and companionship more than ever right now. Don't let him shut us out. The prince could be a good man, yet."

"He already is," I murmured. "I used to miss the boy I was friends with. But he wasn't gone. He was lost. Still is."

"I need to examine that magic," Meryn said. "I've never seen anything like it."

Sylvr stared a moment too long at her wife-to-be. "Your life essence would help with his magic, you know."

"I know."

"He has a point," Andimir muttered. "I'm not happy that you're so willing to sacrifice Lytalian."

"If you can think of a way to save them, we'll try," I said gently.

Andimir's expression softened. "Let me try to evacuate them after visiting the Dwarves. The trip is a straight line. We could get them to Edra or, at the very least, Seryn."

"You would be gone months if you went to Edra." Jyn frowned. "You might miss the fight altogether, which would defeat the purpose of sending you to the Dwarves."

"I'll take them to Seryn then, or Dalbran. An extra fortnight, if seas are clear. I'll push the crew and work the rigging myself. Please. Please give me this chance."

I nodded. "You're right. And Lucian's right. We need to try to help as many people as we can, and Lytalian is in the direct path of the Titans. If you can go to Dalbran, you can spread the word for them to be wary." I paused to consider. "Should we evacuate them?"

"No, don't," Camion said. "Let them try to retain some normalcy while they can. Evacuating the south will cause panic enough."

"He's right." Phelix gestured toward Camion, then added, "I'll get my men settled into full rotations. We can begin interrogations on your people tomorrow, if you like. Then we should make preparations for your trip."

Jyn arched an eyebrow. "That seems . . . directive."

Phelix inclined his head. "Only offering my assistance. Natylia is fully in control of her palace and assets, as well as the assets I've offered to her service. You can ask any of my men who they answer to right now. They will say Natylia, every one of them, until this is over."

"And I thank you for that," I said. I turned narrowed eyes on Jyn. "We would be wise to take advantage of Phelix's knowledge in this situation. Neither of us have much expertise in battle or war."

Andáerhyn grinned. "I do. And I'm willing to offer my expertise."

"For what price?" Jyn scoffed.

"I'm sure we could work out a suitable deal." The Elf shot Jyn another pointed look.

Andimir bristled, clearing his throat.

But Andáerhyn winked at me, fully aware of Andimir's apparent annoyance and the amusement that twitched the corners of Camion's mouth. "I wouldn't ask anything of you, queen," he said with a more sincere smile. "I'll help where I can. Tell me what you need."

"I appreciate that," I said. "That leaves my final concern."

Camion nodded slowly, knowing before I even said the words what I was going to ask.

"My sister. Can you help me find her?"

"We've sent our best spies to look for her," Phelix said. "I'll see if I can send more."

"Send mine. If anything can motivate them to prove their loyalty to Thrais, then safely returning my sister, their princess, would convince me."

Phelix dipped his head. "As you wish. After interrogations I'll send out every available party to search for your sister."

I slowly inhaled, taking a full moment to process all that had been said. I considered all the faces surrounding me. A pang ached in my chest. Lucian wasn't here. Lost. Not gone. But I didn't miss my own reaction to his absence.

"I appreciate you all." I attempted a smile. "I hope you know that."

Chapter 20

I studied myself in the mirror. My corset dug into my ribs painfully. I tugged at the soft bone-lined silk in an attempt to ease my discomfort while waiting for Meryn or Camion to loosen the back. Meryn had laced me into this dress earlier this morning and I was dying to rip the gown off. Jyn thought my formal attire might be best for addressing the soldiers and my people—that I might be taken more seriously. But when I looked at myself, I didn't see the gown and the soft braids in my hair. All I saw were the lines of my face, the scars, the dark circles. I was too thin, too battered, too . . . tired.

I was so tired.

We still had so much to do, though, and I wasn't going to let my people down.

Spirits, I wasn't going to let *my friends* down.

Early in the morning, we had ridden into Thrais to make an official announcement of reclamation to my people. I don't know what I had expected . . . joy, maybe, or relief. But uncertainty shone from their faces as clear as the morning sky was bright. They couldn't deny the disturbing events of late: Thrais being pushed into Wydus's control, the Risen that had ambushed the palace, and the scattered few who had escaped back through town late in the evening. Many of my people seemed to hold me accountable, because I had left in the first place. None seemed to care that I had been acting on the behalf of the kingdom, or that we had dispatched the Risen ourselves upon returning. I wondered how much of their disbelief was honest and how much was simply fear. Because I saw that too.

I sent out spies in the early afternoon, the few we were mostly confident were loyal. Mostly confident was the best we could hope for. Several were sent in each direction to scout out information; not only for my sister, but to find where the Titans were. No news had come from the north in quite a while and I wanted to know Drask's location. His absence since the collapse was disconcerting. Maybe he was waiting on my next move. I needed to know with more certainty.

Lucian asked that I use one of my spies to get a message to his mother. The request was simple enough that I didn't hesitate; I knew he wanted word of her safety as badly as I wanted to find Annalea. Sifting through soldiers and fortifying my palace seemed all that much more tedious while waiting for information. But my palace was still a mess. The murdered staff had been removed to prepare for burial, the deaths scrubbed from the floors by volunteers from Phelix's own men. I was grateful for them. Grateful to the southern kingdom in general, for coming to our aid when no one would blame them for abandoning us.

"Do you need help?" Camion's voice was a welcome distraction. When I nodded, he shut the door behind him. "We have a prisoner to interrogate."

"Which one?" I muttered darkly.

"Devlyn."

"I hate the questioning. He won't answer anyway."

"I know." Camion's fingers moved lithely up the ribbons on the back of my corset, slipping the silken cord free. Slowly, breathing grew easier. I sucked in a breath with relief.

"We should send the dryads a gift for helping as much as they did. Water? More runes? What do you gift a dryad?"

Camion shrugged. "I'm sure you'll think of something."

"Unlikely." I groaned. "I've been considering options all morning."

Camion brushed a strand of hair off my cheek, a small smile on his lips. I gave him one of my own before he said, "I miss that. Your smile. Your happy."

"I could say the same to you."

His smile widened a bit. "We'll get there."

I rose to my toes and pressed my lips to his jaw, his cheek, his lips. My heart skittered with joy when his neck flushed, and that smile finally reached his eyes. Then I turned, sighing heavily as I pulled the corset off. Camion unfastened the hooks up the back of the gown underneath, then pressed a kiss to my cheek.

"I'll tell Jyn you're almost ready."

"Don't bother," Jyn said, the door swinging open. "Change quickly. Valeria's coherent."

***

"You can't sit silent in this cell for the rest of eternity," I snapped. My temper was high, heat red in my cheeks and neck. Valeria had been refusing to speak when I was in the cell, and when I left, she said nothing of merit. Taunts, directed at Jyn, Andáerhyn, Phelix—whoever stepped in.

Even with her slowed healing, she healed too fast to rough her up. We had to continuously sacrifice one of our strongest to guard her cell, because none of us were truly sure what she was capable of, weakened or not. She had spent two days weak and barely able to take sustenance. Now we needed to make a decision about what to do with her and Devlyn, then move on.

Besides, I didn't like the extra close eye Jyn was keeping on me since she had been found in my rooms. Even Camion seemed uncertain what to make of the change in me, the seething anger that bubbled up so quickly. I confessed that my fury hadn't truly left. The rage was always there, stewing right under the surface, and the confession had made both men squirm.

So much so, that we kept the specific details of that encounter between the three of us.

Valeria's ruby eyes were focused on my face, hate etched in each line. She must have sensed that my patience was thin because her mouth opened as I started to turn away.

"I want the Elf."

"Excuse me?" I crossed my arms over my chest. Jyn was in earshot, hidden around a corner. Valeria might be able to smell him. I hoped he stayed put.

"I want the Elf. Then you can do what you want with me."

I frowned. "His life isn't on the table."

"He seemed to think my brother's was," she spat. "I deserve to strike him down before you take my life."

"Is that what this is? A revenge chase?"

"I would kill you all, if I could. But I'll settle for that murdering Sahrian."

"What's stopping you?" I smirked, staring pointedly at the chains and cuffs holding her in place.

Valeria rolled her eyes. "You think these could hold me, if I were at strength? No. Your magic sapped me. Until I feed, I'm stuck here."

"If you're trying to get us to lighten your guard, you're failing miserably."

"No, you foolish girl." She spat the word "girl" as an insult, her accent thick with anger. "I want you to give me what's mine."

I studied her for a moment, then shook my head. "Fine. If you have no information, I'll leave you to rot until we decide what to do with you."

"Even if I did have any information of value to you, what would it serve me to tell you?"

I shrugged. "You choose the method of your punishment. We can draw this out or we can kill you now. But I need information first."

"I don't know anything about your sister. Finding her was Cyrus's job."

"Oh?" But I stilled at the confession. She wouldn't give even that much information so easily, so what was the catch?

Valeria grinned up at me, the dark crimson circles under her eyes prominent in the dim torch light. "Don't worry. He found her before he died. Good thing he was too clever to pass away without sharing the details."

"I won't be bated so easily," I snapped.

"Fine. Don't believe me. Your sister is being guarded. Dwell on that."

"Guarded by Raul?"

Valeria shook her head slowly, savoring the confusion on my face. When she grinned, I turned to leave but the Vampyr spoke again.

"You shouldn't protect the Elf."

"And why is that?"

"He's a dirty Sahrian. Valdis might take pity on some of the humans but not if they cast their lot in with them."

"I think you've made a mistake," I said, my voice lethally calm despite the fury flooding my mind. "You think I want Valdis's *pity* at the end of this? No. I want his head."

I spun away before she could say anything else. By the time I reached the main corridor, where Jyn stood waiting, my fists were trembling. My words were far more courageous than I felt.

"Princess." Jyn caught my eye and held his arms wide. "I'm proud of you."

I sank into the embrace. "I have no idea what I'm doing."

"You're doing the best you can. That's enough."

"We can hope." I pulled away, tugging at the hem of my white shirt. "What do we do now? What if what she said was true? What if Annalea was captured?"

"We wait her out. I'm not about to let her feed." Jyn paused to consider my other questions. "She said Annalea was guarded, not if her guards were friend or foe. For now, let's hope it's the former."

"Jyn—"

"Princess. There's nothing we can do this exact moment. I'm sure your sister is safe. If your spies find anything, I'll alert you immediately, or Phelix will. Trust us."

"I do," I murmured. "To breakfast, then?"

Jyn nodded, falling into step beside me. "Everyone should already be in the dining hall. Phelix checked the rotation personally this morning, but his men seem to be settling in well. Nothing in Devlyn's quarters hinted at why they ransacked your palace and, as of last night, he still wasn't saying."

"What are we going to do with Devlyn and Valeria? In the end?" I paused to shove open the main doors.

"Honestly, the call is yours. We can have them executed, but there's great risk in releasing Valeria long enough for that. Devlyn will be easier in that regard, but I know that's still—"

"Painful," I agreed, wincing.

Jyn grabbed my arm before we stepped into the dining hall, pulling me to a stop. Then he squared up, arms crossed, shoulders rolled back. "Are you okay?"

"What?"

"Honestly, truly, regardless of what you can and can't comfortably talk about. Are you okay? I'm sorry I pushed before . . . but I've wanted to ask since."

I paused and began nodding slowly. "I'm getting there. After we"—I paused, glancing at the guards around us—"After we do what comes next, we'll sit down and have a conversation. I promise you. Camion and I only exchanged our full stories yesterday. We're a bit raw."

Jyn put his hand on my arm and squeezed. "I'm here when you're ready. And I promise you, I'm not leaving you again."

"I know. Thank you."

I shot him a small smile, patting his hand before I turned to the dining hall. The table was already spread with food; I couldn't imagine who had done so, but I was appreciative, nonetheless. Each side was lined with my friends, my family. Warmth rose in my chest at the sight.

Sinking into my seat, I leaned into Camion's arm. His lips curved into a half smile.

"What have you been up to?" I whispered to him, as the rest of the group chatted about breads and fruits and our next moves.

"Phelix and I took stock of your armory. There's less than when we were here last, but still a fair amount." He hesitated. "We don't have enough, though. Not to outfit everyone."

"We'll make do," Phelix interjected.

"Eavesdropping?" I smirked.

The king smiled. "I couldn't help myself. I heard my name."

"We'll leave in the morning," Meryn said. "Spies or no. We can leave Fetian with Phelix."

Andimir frowned. "I'll be leaving in the morning as well."

"Not with us." I said quietly. He nodded. I winced. "I still don't like this."

"You know there's no other way."

"And we have to retrieve Meryn's life essence." I sighed. "With or without you."

Andimir dipped his head apologetically. Jyn studied him for a long moment, words forming that he bit back. I stared down at my plate, shuffling around a starberry that didn't even sound appealing anymore.

"Did you try to retrieve the stone by yourself?" Jyn asked. His eyes were locked onto Sylvr.

"Of course, I did." She leveled a measuring gaze on him. "But when I heard about the patrols, I knew I couldn't take them on alone."

"You know she can't go up there by herself," Meryn said, squirming in her seat. "If anything happened to you—"

"Or your life stone," Sylvr interjected. Her voice wasn't sad or blaming. More like a woman who had accepted that her fate was to be the stone bearer for Nahara. I wondered if she had ever imagined she would fall in love with the Titan and how long she had been carrying this burden. Was she human? How old was she?

"So, are you a Titan?" I asked bluntly.

"You can't ask people if they're Titans," Andimir groaned, pressing his forehead into his palm.

"But I did."

Sylvr glanced between the two of us, a deep scarlet flush coloring her cheeks. "I'm not a Titan, no."

"Then what are you? Because Izoryian and Eáryn hinted that you aren't exactly human."

"I'm a Nereid," Sylvr shrugged.

My mouth fell open.

"You're a what?" Camion asked for the table.

"Twice a year, during the Dýo Meteor Showers, I can choose which form I will take for the next half. Human or Nereid. Usually, especially since Meryn arrived in Thrais, I've been defaulting to the human form. But the winter shower is coming soon and I'll be able to make the choice. I could retrieve the stone easily then. But I would no longer have my legs, and prolonged absence from water would slowly kill me."

"You're a fish," Andimir gaped.

"Not technically. My upper half retains my humanoid form. My lower half becomes that of . . . well for lack of a better phrase, yes, a fish."

"We would need to leave you in the lake?" Meryn murmured. I could tell she was torn about the idea, about leaving her betrothed behind while we fought the battle to come.

"Yes. Unless you could provide a sufficient and constant source of water here."

"The communal baths in the servants' quarters," I offered. "They're fairly large pools. You could live there until the next shower passes?"

Meryn nodded. "And if you wanted to stay in that form occasionally, I'm sure we could have a pond created in the palace walls?" She lifted an eyebrow in my direction.

"Of course," I said. "If we can find a spring, that would be simple enough to set up."

Sylvr's cheeks darkened. "You're kind, but that's a lot of trouble to go through for me. There might be another way."

"Another way to breathe and see underwater? To find a rock in a chest? Call me skeptical," Jyn scoffed.

"There might be a potion, or a spell, or an herb."

My magic sparked at the thought. Shimmers burst to life along my limbs. Camion studied me, concern etched along his brow.

"Why is your magic—" He waved his hand at the sparkling colors.

I shrugged. "My magic hasn't been entirely predictable in a

while."

"Are you angry?"

"No," I said. "Not right now, anyway. Surges of anger come and go, like mood swings but faster, and only ever that wild fury. I need to use my magic, but whenever I do, I'm always exhausted, as though there wasn't enough to start with. Until I'm angry again, and then my powers feel restored. But as soon as I use them, I'm even more tired."

Jyn blinked. "I don't like the sounds of that."

"I feel like I'm trying to burn myself out, but not intentionally," I murmured.

"What if you're tied to the Titans?" Meryn asked quietly. She looked at Sylvr. "Is such a thing even possible?"

"She could be. If her magic is in the Scepters, any time Drask is using them, or more directly the Stave itself, they could trigger a response in Natylia. Or she could be directly tied to Thanatos himself, and his emotions, in passing. Her magic did recharge the life essences that repowered his, which allowed the Scepters to be combined and potentially break him free." Sylvr shrugged. "It's probably harmless," she continued. "Keep an eye on your emotional swings and those of your powers. Make sure you're aware of anything that triggers your abilities."

"Natylia used to be able to track the Scepters using her powers," Jyn observed. "Could she still do the same thing with the Stave?"

"Possibly," Sylvr admitted. "But I'm not sure why you'd want to do such a thing. You'd likely find four extremely angry Titans on the other side."

"And at the moment, we should be more worried about Eurybia," Phelix said.

"We may see her at the lake," Jyn said. "Another possibility to prepare for." He tugged at the point of his ear unconsciously. "If we could take down Eurybia on her own, we would stand a much better chance against the others."

"You're right." Andimir grimaced. "But how do you plan to take down a fully powered Titan on your own?"

"Who says she's fully powered?" Jyn grinned. "Assuming that Drask—Valdis—is using the Scepters to release his captive son, they could all be in the south right now. She might still be at a power disadvantage, with her life essence stuck in the Stave. Andáerhyn and I could handle her, if so."

Andáerhyn smirked. Andimir shifted uncomfortably in his seat. "You two might be strong, but I'm not sure I like the idea of you trying to face off against that Titan so . . . alone. And if I'm going south tomorrow, I won't be able to help."

"I can send some men," Phelix offered. "Tell me how many you need."

"I don't think we should endanger more of your men," Camion said. "They're already offering so much."

The king nodded. "Reasonable. Though, I'm not really sure it's wise to confront her regardless. She's bound to be strong, full powers or no."

"They all are. Isn't our only chance picking them off one at a time?" Andáerhyn argued.

"Possibly," Sylvr admitted. "The only way you're going to manage to kill any of the Titans is if you can get their life essence stone free of their chest—and that's assuming Thanatos is free and they've all had their life essences returned. And if that's the case, we're in trouble anyway."

"How will we know if she has her life essence back?" Jyn steepled his fingers together, waiting intently while Sylvr fumbled to explain.

"Titans at full strength will give off an . . . aura," Andáerhyn said. Sylvr smiled appreciatively. "You'll be able to feel the change, now that you have your powers back."

Jyn frowned. "When Meryn gets her powers back, she'll *feel* different?"

"Yes. There will be almost a warmth emanating off her. I'm always reminded of standing too close to a fireplace."

I raised an eyebrow at Andáerhyn. "You've been around many fully powered Titans recently?"

"Do you think that the five we're facing, and Meryn, are the only Titans to exist? Because that would be a dangerous oversight." He paused. "Besides, I fought with Nahara before, remember? When the Titans were free last time."

"I had forgotten," I admitted. "How many Titans are there?"

"Quite a few. I suggest you try to enlist some of them."

"We don't even know where they are."

"But I do." Andáerhyn grinned. "And at least one of them is in Morland."

I sat up straighter. "Who?"

"Berit."

My brows pulled together.

"She's the Titan of Prophecy," Meryn explained, then to Andáerhyn, she asked, "How long has she been in Morland?"

"Since shortly after Natylia returned," Andáerhyn said. "She probably thinks she can protect Natylia or Nahara. Or that she can help in general. So, she's slowly been migrating south."

"How do you know this?" Camion asked.

"She's been there for a while. I'm more surprised she hasn't made her way to Thrais yet."

Sylvr sighed, a long, exasperated exhale. "Berit is known to you as Helyna, Natylia."

I blinked and looked at Jyn. He looked equally confused. The only Helyna I knew was an older woman with pale blue eyes and silver white hair. For a long time, she had been like a grandmother to me. But I hadn't seen her since . . .

Since my coronation.

I was supposed to believe that slight, soft spoken woman was a Titan?

"You have to be mistaken. Helyna? There's no way."

"Helyna, yes." Sylvr lifted a shoulder. "Her husband Wyatt is a mortal, so she let herself age magically to keep up with him. She'll likely resume her real appearance after he's gone. If we find her, she might be able to lead you to others who are willing to help you. Many of the Titans likely desire to continue the lives they've built for themselves."

"And the others?" Jyn crossed his arms over his chest. "What of the Titans who would stand against us? You think we should risk adding to their ranks?"

"Well, that's the reason I'm suggesting we ask Berit first," Sylvr said. "She should know where the others' sympathies lie. And if she doesn't, we can pass them over. Simple enough."

"Aurial and Marinus would likely join your side," Andáerhyn offered. "Marinus won't love the idea of killing his daughter, but the fact that Valdis corrupted her so easily has never sat well with him."

"How does one corrupt a Titan?" Andimir asked.

"Have a handsome Titan son," Sylvr scoffed, shooting an apologetic glance at Lucian. The prince didn't acknowledge the reference to his half-brother. "Thanatos wasn't always so . . . cloak and dagger. He was attractive, and powerful, and his father's abilities rivaled Nahara's. He held so much potential . . . But with that kind of power comes an ease of corruption. His father wanted more and he dragged Thanatos along with him. Naturally, Thanatos dragged his friends along too. For what is a powerful leader without servants to do your bidding?"

"So, he corrupted her with power?" I asked.

"Exactly." Sylvr nodded. "Thanatos gave her a taste for the finer things, showed her how the world could be if Titans ruled. Though, he didn't have to try very hard. They all hated humanity already. He offered her a poisoned apple and she ate every last bite."

"And what of Aurial?" Camion asked.

"She's Boreas's mother," Andáerhyn answered, his tone lower than usual. He swallowed hard, then explained. "Aurial was a good friend of the Elves for a long age. Her absence has been felt keenly by those of us who fought the Titans in that initial conflict."

"Where did she go?" I pushed. "Why would she help us?"

Andáerhyn lifted a shoulder. "Berit might know where she's hiding. Aurial is a good soul. Her kindness knows no bounds and she would feel personally responsible for Boreas's behavior. Even if she shouldn't."

"We can't guilt her into this," I murmured. "This could be a full-scale war, if we can't stop them fast enough."

"She knows," Andáerhyn added. "As I said, she was there for the initial conflict. She knows the risk that her involvement would be."

"And her powers?" Meryn pried.

"Aurial is a Titan of air," Sylvr said.

I frowned. "So, she could be literally anywhere?"

"No. We can ask Helyna. We're going on chances here. But if you hope to beat those five, you need to find more allies."

I glanced around the table, studying each face in turn. Then I locked eyes with Andimir and the breath left my lungs. "Do you have to leave tomorrow? Are you sure you're ready?"

Andimir smiled faintly. "We're all leaving tomorrow. Seems as good a time as any. I still need to pack, though." He darted a glance at Jyn, then met my eyes again. "I'm working up the courage to say goodbye."

"Don't say goodbye then," I said. "Say you'll see us soon, and then return swiftly."

A small smile curved his lips and he dipped his head into a mock bow. "As you command, Your Highness."

"I suppose that means breakfast is finished?" Meryn asked. There was an oddly definitive tone to her voice, a finality that broke my heart.

Tomorrow morning, Andimir left with the sun. And yet again the wheels began to turn, ready to crank us back into motion and fling us into the jaws of chaos.

Chapter 21

I almost didn't see Andimir off. I almost hid in my rooms, feigned a stomachache, and let him go. The last time I had watched someone leave our gates, they didn't return. No news of my sister had to be good news . . . but Valeria's words haunted me. Guarded? By what or whom?

In fairness, only one spy had returned so far and he had no news at all. Nothing of the Titans, or my sister, or the ruling parties of Wydus. Nothing definitive, anyway. Rumors were swirling that the royals had disappeared. A few voices were heard muttering curses on Thrais or Kalum, saying we had partied up to destroy our northern allies after Lucian persisted with his advances.

The lies were laughable, especially when Lucian himself was staying in the palace with us. The lack of solid information, however, was not. I had hoped that after several days in Thrais, my sister would return home, or reveal herself—but nothing. Our small victory was inconsequential in that regard. Maybe she was safer this way.

Wherever she was, I missed her desperately.

For the moment, I stood in the stables, helping Andimir with one of the finest horses we owned. She was even-tempered, fast as lightning, and clever to match. But as he ran his hand over her mottled black and white neck, the heavy weight of parting settled in my chest.

"I'll come back, Natylia. You don't need to worry so much."

"But I always worry. Why wouldn't I worry?"

Andimir grinned, but the expression held no warmth, only sadness; the kind that dragged at the soul until there was nothing left but emptiness. Another absence. Another separation. My breaths became labored. We couldn't protect him if he wasn't here. If he died—

"Don't give me that look, Nat. I'm not going to die."

"You don't know that," I murmured. I helped tighten the cinch of his saddle. "You don't know that any of us will see you again."

"I'll see you again, Natylia. Have a little faith."

The sound of footsteps over hay broke through our conversation and I turned to see Jyn striding our way.

"She's right, you know," Jyn said. "You don't know that you'll be back. You don't know that we'll be here, if you do."

"You two are absolute rays of sunshine." Andimir dropped the horse's reins though and came over to the other side. Clapping each of us on the shoulder, he said, "I'll be fine."

"I've said that before." I gave him a pointed stare. "Look where that got me."

"You're still alive and kicking, aren't you?"

I grunted at the words but nodded my assent.

Jyn sidled up next to Andimir, their arm's brushing as Jyn double checked the horses gear. I knew he wasn't doubting me. He was Jyn. If he wasn't sure and anything went wrong, he would carry the blame to his grave.

"Get any closer and I'm going to start wondering why I didn't at least buy you a meal first," Andimir muttered as Jyn stepped closer, nearly shoving him out of the way so he could get to the bridle.

"You'd need to buy me more than a meal," Jyn retorted.

Green eyes locked onto Jyn's, steady as he said, "Noted."

When they held each other's gaze for a moment too long, I cleared my throat. "I'm going to step outside. I need to find a better hoof pick to check her shoes."

Andimir's hand fell from Jyn's shoulder. Their eyes dropped to the ground in unison, Andimir's cheeks darkening. I smiled to myself but didn't say a word as I left. I knew no one deserved happiness as much as the two men behind me. And if they found that with each other, who was I to stop them?

"What are you smiling about?" Andáerhyn startled me. I blinked at him.

"Nothing important." But the small smile still lingered on my lips.

The Elf's eyes narrowed. "Why don't I believe you?"

I grinned, glancing around the small tack shed. "Help me find a hoof pick? I want to check Andimir's horse one more time."

"There should be a few of them . . ." His voice trailed off and I looked up, only to see him rifling through one of the drawers.

"You've been down here often?"

Andáerhyn shrugged. "I like animals. They're more consistent than people." He held out a hoof pick. "Yours *and* mine."

I tapped the hoof pick off my palm, nodding my agreement before I gestured for him to follow my intentionally slow pace. By the time we opened the barn door and began striding down the rows of stalls, Jyn and Andimir were standing suspiciously far apart. If Andáerhyn sensed the tension, he didn't comment. I was surprised at his silence, though. Jyn was positively glowing, in a way that had nothing to do with being Elven. A small smile tugged at the corner of my lips.

And then we were moving too fast, gathering at the gate to send Andimir off. I didn't know what to say that I hadn't already. Once I had imagined Andimir as a major part in my life. Now he was, in a different way, and the thought of him being gone again . . . I didn't want to imagine it.

"Safe sailing," Meryn said, looping her arms tightly around Andimir's waist. "Come back as fast as you can."

"I will. I promise."

Sylvr hugged him next, then Andáerhyn, who pulled the pirate into a tight bear hug and lifted him from the ground. "Good luck!"

Andimir shot him a bewildered look when he was solidly back on his feet. "Thanks."

"Stay safe, old friend," Lucian said next, holding out his hand.

"Thank you." Andimir paused. "I'm proud of you. You've always been better than you've been acting."

"I know." Lucian bowed his head as he stepped away, a gesture of respect—not shame, for what might have been the first time since he had found us.

"You're a brave man," Phelix said, shaking Andimir's hand. "I hope you're able to save Lytalian."

"Me too, Your Highness."

Jyn was next but the two didn't exchange words, only handshakes. I imagined they had said what they needed to in the stable. But I didn't miss the look that passed between them, or the way Jyn's grip tightened subtly when Andimir moved to pull away. I reached out to Jyn, resting a hand on his arm. He didn't acknowledge me, but his jaw flexed and his gaze dropped to his boots.

Camion moved forward, pulling Andimir into a hug of his own.

"I'm honored to call you a friend and brother," he said, as Andimir clapped him on the back. "Come back safe."

"And I you, brother." Andimir glanced my direction, then Jyn's and Meryn's. Then his eyes landed back on Camion. "Take care of them?"

"You don't even have to ask."

I was last. For a long moment, I hesitated. He knew my thoughts, my fears, could read them all over my face. Without hesitation he swept me into a hug, filling my nose with the scent of sea and roses and leather.

"I'll come back, Natylia. You can't get rid of me that easily."

"I did once." I laughed but the sound was choked, cut off by the small sob that broke free.

"Nat . . ." Andimir squeezed me tightly. "We'll find your sister. We'll beat these Titans. And I promise you. I'll come home."

My heart warmed. Home? Andimir thought of Thrais as home?

"Be safe, Andimir. I can't imagine a life without you in it."

"Nor I you, Nat. Hey . . . hold onto this while I'm gone?" I looked down at the hand he freed, at the compass with the cracked glass that he carried everywhere.

My brow pulled together. "Are you sure? Won't you get lost?"

"I'll use the stars."

"Are you sure they're reliable?"

"More reliable than the compass, for sure." He stepped back to look around at the small group around him. "Good luck retrieving the stone. I hope you find the box."

"We will." Meryn reached out to squeeze his hand. "I'll take care of them until you're back."

Jyn scoffed. "*We'll* take care of them."

Andimir gave him a smile before he mounted his horse. Then he said, "Take care of each other. I need you alive."

And then he was gone.

I didn't move until he was out of sight. Camion waited with me, his hand gentle on my back. By the time Andimir had vanished, the others had our horses ready and bags packed. Andáerhyn was to stay behind with Phelix. The king could use a second hand should anything happen, and we were more sure of Andáerhyn's loyalty than most anyone we knew. We would need luck and sheer numbers, if we ran into Eurybia . . . that, and Jyn's abilities. If all went well, we would gain a fully powered Titan of our own. Maybe a few.

But that meant we needed to visit Morland first, before heading to Starberry Lake.

The small city was out of the way, but if we let Helyna know that we needed help, she might be able to trigger a chain reaction. None of us were keen on the delay. But the Titan would need time to spread the word, and if we waited, she wouldn't have it.

Fears filled every corner of my mind, dark and coaxing, easy to sink into if I willed it or let down my guard. My heart had been reluctant to say goodbye to Andáerhyn and Phelix. Leaving the palace was harder this time. Hard because I had to leave my people after only days ago having declared my intentions to protect them. Harder still because I had begun to feel at home again.

But hardest of all was trusting my kingdom in the hands of allies once more. I knew how that turned out last time. I was still fighting to reverse the damage.

And there was much to do.

So much to do.

After all, we only had the weight of the world on our shoulders.

***

I dismounted in the central square. Morland had been designed in a circular fashion, with a ring of shop fronts that bled into the homes of its citizens. The city was similar to Thrais, but slightly larger, and unlike Thrais, the buildings were primarily built from wood.

None of this drew my attention though.

My horse nickered uneasily, the reins shaking in my hand. I cast a wary glance around, but no eyes met mine beyond Camion's and Jyn's. No scent of baking food wafted on the wind, no pound of hammer on anvil to speak of their smithy.

Morland was empty.

"Nat, when was the last time you were here?" Meryn asked quietly while dismounting beside me. She stepped up to my side, her arm bumping mine.

"A while. I can't remember when. You?"

"A few moon cycles, tops." Her eyes scanned the buildings. The doors and windows were in various states of open and closed. It was as though a small city's worth of people had simply vanished.

Camion's nostrils flared. "Do you smell that?"

I sniffed gingerly and recoiled. Rot, decay. Mold. "What happened here?"

"I'm not sure," Jyn said. "And I'm thinking we don't want to find out, either."

A door squeaked behind us. I spun, pulling my bow free. Lucian drew a sword as well, Camion sliding off his horse and coming to my other side. His steps still lagged a bit, even after training with Jyn and Andáerhyn for a few days. I knew the feeling. My body still wasn't quite as responsive as I was used to.

My gaze skipped over the buildings around us. Waves crashed against the beach a few dozen yards away, but there was nothing else. No birdsong. No irritating chirp of insects.

I exchanged glances with Camion. The road was barren, not a single sign of Morland's inhabitants.

"Should we move on or search the buildings?" Sylvr asked finally.

"We should move on," I said, keeping my eyes trained on the city. "I have a really bad feeling about this place."

"Should we make for Falmar, then?" Camion glanced around.

"I have a feeling that little of what we find here will be of use to us anyway."

Jyn and Meryn conceded to that. Lucian hesitated, but then nodded. We moved for the horses. The men had sheathed their weapons, my bow now back over my shoulder, when a screech broke the stillness.

I whipped around, sliding my bow free once more and nocked an arrow on reflex. In the center of town stood a figure, humanoid and tilting its head as though pondering us. The person took a step closer and I flinched. No, not a person. *Risen.*

Her skin was mottled purple, the red veins in her eyes thick and bright. Her dress was thin, fluttering cotton—the typical style for the humid heat of Morland—but drenched in dark, blotchy stains.

Blood.

The Risen opened her mouth, releasing another unearthly scream. Goosebumps sprang up on my arms.

Jyn grabbed my shoulder, pulling me backward, away from the Risen now baring her teeth at us. Teeth filled with the dark remnants of a meal I didn't want to know about.

Her lips pressed together, drawn up in an evil smirk. Then other doors began to open. My heartbeat thundered in my ears. Risen. A dozen, maybe two. I lost count as the decaying bodies shoved their way from homes and shops, from attic windows where the bone-shattering fall only slowed them down.

"We should—" The shrieks of our horses cut off Sylvr's words. Camion and Meryn tried to hold tight as the animals tugged and bolted. The leather reins slapped against their mud-splattered arms as each horse slipped from their fingers.

Camion slid a dagger free and side-stepped in front of me. His blade trembled, though. I moved from behind him and rested my hand on his arm. "Together."

He nodded in response, his eyes tracking the Risen now shambling across the stone road. Jyn moved to my other side and nudged Meryn and Sylvr behind him, while urging Lucian to his exposed side. Meryn huffed, then shoved past Jyn's shoulder.

For a heartbeat, the Risen froze and examined their prey.

Then they were on us.

My bow was knocked from my hands. I tried not to think about what I was doing as I wrenched a dagger free and slammed the blade into the stomach of the first body. Near-human eyes stared back at me as the Risen squirmed to be free. I jerked the dagger loose. Dark blood splattered my leathers as I shoved the undead woman away. She staggered, then lunged for me again. I spun away from her attack. She fell on her face against my swift movements and I seized the distraction, rushing to strike before she stood up.

"Their heads," Jyn panted, kicking a decapitated corpse away as he dodged the mangled fingernails of another reanimated corpse. "Don't forget we have to take their heads."

Jyn pulled the Risen I was fighting away from me and ripped her head from her shoulders. I took the pause to glance around at the others. Camion struggled to my right with two Risen who clawed at his face. I twisted, thrusting my blade through the neck of a man who looked far too young to be dead. Warm liquid sprayed my face as he gurgled and spewed the blood dripping from his lips. Then he fell. I didn't have time to pause or swallow back the bile rising in my throat.

They kept coming.

Within minutes, we were completely surrounded. My dagger was pulled from my hand. Claws ripped at my back, my face, my hair. Camion went down. I struggled toward him, screaming at the Risen, frantic when I couldn't seem to reach him. Hands groped for my throat, fingernails raked my skin. I searched for my magic, pulled, but my power wouldn't respond. Pressure grew on my throat. The claws found purchase and blood trickled down my skin.

Sliding my feet up, I bucked my hips and kicked the Risen off me. I scrambled for Camion on hands and knees and then threw my shoulder against the Risen he wrestled with. But the reanimated being didn't budge.

I looked around for help, but I knew none was available. Jyn was fighting a group on his own. Meryn protected Sylvr with blasts of fire. And Lucian was trying to defend them both.

The toe of my boot tapped my dagger hilt and I kicked it up, reaching until my fingers brushed the cool metal. When I had the weapon gripped tightly, I twisted to slam the blade into the Risen's side. He lurched toward me, teeth bared. The slight shift in attention gave Camion enough of an advantage. He flipped himself over the Risen and buried his dagger's blade deep into the man's neck.

Preparing for another attack, I spun looking for my bow. But no attack came. Jyn had become a whirling mass of gold and silver, slamming his dagger into anything that moved for us. Every movement was smooth, calculated, as fluid as running water.

A Risen dove for Sylvr. Meryn moved to shield her, but Jyn was there before she could. The Risen was slain before the corpse could even sink a nail into either Meryn or Sylvr.

I heard a grunt of frustration and turned toward Lucian. Dark, decay-mottled hands—dripping with blood—were wrapped around Lucian's blade as the Risen tried to wrestle his sword from him. She snapped at his face. Jyn flew forward, dispatching the Risen with a look of indifference that had my jaw falling open.

I simply stared, wide-eyed and bewildered.

Jyn had always been powerful, always stronger and faster than the rest of us. But he cut through the Risen as though they were nothing. Mere insects.

For the first time in a long while, a small glimmer of hope rose in my chest. If the Elves would fight for us, even a few, we might actually stand a chance against the Titans.

I clapped the dirt off my hands, pulling myself to my feet. My gaze ran over the city, over the road now soaked in dark blood and the bodies that had fallen in heaps. Helyna was not here. If she had been, she was gone now.

"I can burn the bodies, but we'll need to pile them up," Meryn said. "We don't want Valdis to stitch them back together."

"That's . . . a disturbing image." Lucian winced.

My attention fell to Camion, to the claw marks that sliced up the side of his throat. Out of reflex, I touched my fingers to his neck and closed my eyes. I breathed slowly, pulling my reluctant magic up, trying not to let the frustration over my lack of magical control dominate me. A minute passed before I felt his skin begin to knit together beneath my fingers. I opened my eyes.

"Are you all right?"

His shoulder lifted. "Yeah. Thanks."

I frowned. Inadequacy was written all over his face. Meryn offered me a bandage drenched in water and I put the fabric to his neck, gently cleaning off the blood. Camion winced, and when I was done, I brushed a soft caress over his cheek.

"You're not useless."

"How do you know what I'm thinking?"

"I don't. I know you."

"I'm glad you do." He offered a half smile, but it faded too quickly.

"You have to heal, my love. I'll cover you until you're back to full strength."

"You're not at full strength yourself."

"Then I'll cover you both," Jyn said with a grin. "I dare say I handled this pretty well."

I smirked. "You dispatched a few."

"More than a few."

"A handful."

"Definitely more than a dozen."

I smiled up at him, grateful that a flicker of light had returned to Camion's eyes. Then I looked around, studying each person for wounds. Meryn and Sylvr seemed unharmed. Jyn was fine. He moved away quickly to stack bodies.

Lucian had some minor scratches, small ones that took me all of two minutes to heal. He stared at my fingers afterward, where they still rested on his arm, and said, "Thank you. I still feel like I don't really deserve your help."

"Everyone deserves help. Especially when they're trying to do the right thing."

His eyes filled with tears and his jaw flexed. "Thank you."

"Of course."

"Can you teach me to do this?"

I studied his face for a moment, considering. "I can try. Have you been able to pull up your magic again?"

Lucian shook his head. "Not at all."

"We'll work on it," Meryn said, squeezing his arm gently.

"Most people aren't able to use their magic for years after manifestation." Sylvr looked from Lucian to me. "And when they can, the powers are usually unbalanced, unpredictable. Thus, Natylia's struggles with her connection to the Stave."

"We should move for Falmar," Jyn interrupted, his eyes steady on the pile of burning Risen. "If Helyna is all right, she might have gone there. And if not, we can't delay getting Meryn's life essence too much longer."

Meryn shifted on her feet uneasily, tugging at a strand of copper hair. "We could."

"No," Sylvr said. "They're your memories. Your past. You deserve to know all the things you've been through, all the things we've all been through. But most importantly, you deserve to have your powers back."

"What if . . . what if I can't control them, as you said? What if they're useless to me because I don't know how to use them?"

"You'll know what to do," Sylvr said. "Titan abilities are ingrained from birth. The only reason they seem so unfamiliar to you now is because you don't have them. Powers are only difficult to control when they're brand new."

"And once I have them? Then what? I can destroy the others?"

Sylvr shrugged. "I don't know the full extent of your abilities.

I know you were powerful. I know you could stop Valdis, if you wanted to. As to how easily that might be done . . . I don't know."

"To Falmar, then?" I asked, looking around.

A small chorus of voices rang out, "To Falmar."

Chapter 22

Falmar was a small, private township tucked into the forests north of Starberry Lake. I hadn't been there often, only a few times when I was younger. But the dark, wooded town had a quiet appeal, cradled tightly by the forest it was hidden within. They made use of the lake and river to hold a steady export on building supplies; they chopped the trees, carted the logs downriver, and transported firewood. Falmar was prosperous but small, and my memories were still filled with the heavy scent of cedar that saturated the city.

Wooden homes were built among the trees, some even built directly around them. I had always been curious what those looked like inside, but after seeing Edra, I could imagine the beauty they held. The few shops they had weren't the focal point of the main square; the cobblestone-pathed center of Falmar was split by a massive, ancient tree that canopied the town and blocked most of the sunlight. Nestled into an open corner, a smith was tinkering away in his forge. The aroma of baking treats wafted along the air. My stomach rumbled aggressively.

"We can get food," Jyn offered. His eyes were locked onto the inn. "And if we ask for Berit—I mean, Helyna—we might find her faster than trying to go door-to-door."

I nodded my agreement.

A small yip caught my ear and we spun in unison, Jyn's hand falling to his blade hilt. Camion stared down at his feet, as though his boots had made the sound. Then he looked up.

"I feel—"

He didn't have to finish. We all saw the slight shuffle of his pant leg, the pressure mark as though something leaned into him. Jyn tilted his head in confusion, but Meryn reached into one of her pockets and pulled out a vial, blowing a soft puff of glittering magic toward Camion. Each spec glowed softly as it fell, and where they landed the soft shape of the Zylarra took form.

"Bioluminescent mushroom powder," Meryn explained. "I had a feeling we might keep coming across this one."

"Neat trick," Lucian said, his eyes wide on the little fox-like creature.

With Meryn's powder on the Zylarra's back, her soft silver fur caught the light. Camion knelt slowly, very slowly, careful not to scare the tiny animal away.

"Still following us?" he asked. "I feel like you need a name, if you're going to keep following us. What about . . . Lethe?"

She yipped at him happily, then bolted into the brush, returning before Camion could even straighten. He lowered his hand to pet her again and she snuffled her nose into his palm. Camion's brow scrunched together.

"Cam?" I asked warily.

He held out his hand. A small ring, inlaid with amethyst, sat between his fingers. I took a step closer, tilting my head slightly when I recognized the engravings on the sides.

"My . . . my mother's ring?" I plucked the ring from Camion, letting the silver catch sunlight. There was no mistaking this ring. Those engravings were gryphons, the symbol of Thrais, with stars on their chests. This was a gift to my Mother, from my Father. The amethyst used was half of a larger piece; the other was in a helm that my Father hadn't donned for a long age before his passing.

Jyn's eyebrows shot up. "Your mother's?"

"How did you get this?" I asked Lethe.

In response, she scampered behind Camion's ankles, as if he could protect her from interrogation.

But it was Lucian who said, "Is that what she stole from Eurybia?"

My jaw slipped open. I looked at the little Zylarra, who yipped as if in confirmation.

"I guess that answers that," Meryn murmured.

I studied the ring. I wasn't sure what to make of its sudden appearance. The gryphons reminded me of home, and my sister, and made my stomach twist and ache. But more, I couldn't understand what the Titans would want with a simple ring.

"We should get inside. We're drawing attention," Jyn muttered.

"What about—" I gestured to Lethe, who was basking in Camion's affection.

"Do you want to come inside with us?" Camion cooed at her.

I shot him an amused smirk but the Zylarra paused, glancing the direction he pointed. Then she licked his hand and bolted into the underbrush.

We waited a few minutes to see if Lethe would return. When she didn't, we climbed the small pile of stone steps up to the inn, gripping a twisted railing before we pushed open the gnarled wooden door.

Inside, the inn was much the same: rough chunks of wood had been cut into jagged shapes and fitted together to make not only the structure but the furniture. I perched on the edge of an uneven seat, hood pulled up over my face, Camion's hand a warm, reassuring weight on my knee. Meryn approached the innkeeper, a bright smile on her face.

"Need some food, lass?" the innkeeper asked roughly.

Meryn nodded up at him, leaning on the bar. "My friends and I are famished. We have plenty of coin . . . but I have a question for you as well."

The innkeeper's bright silver eyes skirted over our hooded features, scanning the swords on Jyn's back with curiosity. "What kind of question?"

"We're looking for a friend of ours. Last we knew she was in Morland, but the city was deserted. We have concerns that she was taken, maybe by King Drask."

"Morland is deserted?" The man's eyes snapped fully to Meryn's face. "What do you mean Morland is deserted?"

"The few people we saw weren't people," Meryn answered cautiously. "We saw no one else."

"That's . . . that's unfortunate," the innkeeper said, and sadness flickered in his eyes. "I had a cousin in Morland. We had heard rumors the Titans were roaming. I assume that means the Risen have returned as well?"

"I'm so sorry for your loss," Meryn offered. She extended a hand, resting it on the man's arm. "But yes. The Risen are returning. You've been involved with them before?"

"I . . . I enjoy history."

"You've seen no one from Morland come through?"

"No." He shook his head. "Not in a long while, though I suppose that makes more sense now. Has the king been made aware of his territory loss?"

"As far as I know," Meryn said.

"And Thrais?"

"They're doing what they can to prepare."

"Is Devlyn still in charge?"

"No," Meryn said, in a tone that said she didn't want to answer any more questions. She retracted her hand and the innkeeper reached behind him, pulling mugs off the wall even as he studied Meryn's face. "How long since you've seen anyone from Morland?"

"It's probably been a moon cycle." He considered as he filled each mug with tea, pushing one toward Meryn and stacking the others on a tray. "Maybe longer. We don't get many outsiders in general, so they tend to stand out."

"And you've not seen anyone who went by the name Helyna?"

The innkeeper carried the tray to the table, distributing a mug to each of us before making another loop to bring a pitcher of milk and a bowl of sugar cubes. Then he shook his head. "I've seen no one by that name. As I said, we haven't seen any visitors in a while. The most recent has been staying here. Petite lass. White blonde hair. Insists on carrying her damned owl everywhere."

He didn't sound annoyed, more amused. I looked toward Jyn, who shook his head slightly. Meryn looked confused, and I wondered what about the woman's description had struck a memory.

"Did she give a name?"

The innkeeper shook his head. "Afraid not."

"Well, thank you for your help," Meryn said. "And we'll take whatever you're serving, whatever your cook is making smells amazing."

A dark flush spread up the man's cheeks, above his dark beard. "Thank you."

He vanished into the kitchen, returning to serve up steaming piles of eggs, spiced sausages, bowls of fruit, and soft, warm bread. Once we had loaded our plates, we began to talk in low voices. When the innkeeper lost interest in our conversations, Meryn mentioned the blonde-haired patron.

"Helyna could have swapped disguises," Meryn whispered. "But I think that's unlikely. Especially with the owl."

Lucian tapped the edge of his plate with his fork, voice low when he said, "What's with the owl?"

"The owl is a trademark of another Titan," Meryn murmured. "One I didn't think we would find so easily."

The innkeeper returned to refill our tea, offering Meryn a shy smile when she complimented the cooking again. Sylvr scooched a touch closer and a grin broke on Meryn's face.

"Worried?" Sylvr shook her head but Meryn reached beneath Sylvr's hood to tap her nose. "Don't be."

"So, what should we do?" I absently pulled Andimir's compass from my pocket, running my thumbs along the uneven sides, and sighed heavily. "Should we go for the stone, or stay and hope that this . . . person? Recognizes you?"

Meryn frowned. "This person, as you called her is, if I'm guessing correctly, Aurial. Which would save us a step. But she might not believe us without Helyna. Or more specifically her powers—Berit's powers."

"Then we should go for the stone."

"Yes. Probably."

"We're not close enough to the meteor shower, though," Sylvr said quietly. "I won't be able to help. Not with my Nereid form, anyway."

"You mentioned there might be another way," I said quietly. "A potion or a spell?"

"We might be able to find one . . . I do know of a lavender-colored potion that will let us breathe underwater," Meryn offered. She looked up when the innkeeper passed by again and raised her voice. "Sir, can you tell us, does Falmar have an apothecary nearby?"

"A small one, yes. Zemira makes potions, medicines, herb bundles . . . Two shops down on the left, slightly more tucked into the trees."

"Thank you." Meryn smiled. The man nodded shortly as he pulled out a cloth to rub down the bar, but several more seconds passed before he stopped listening.

"Even if we find these potions, how are we supposed to see under the lake water?" Lucian whispered skeptically. "And we don't know what lives there."

"No, we don't," I said. "But we need that stone, regardless. And unless we plan to wait until the meteor shower for Sylvr, we need to take this chance."

"I might be able to cast some light underwater," Meryn said.

"And if you can't?"

"It's a risk. We could always try to find some bioluminescent plants and shove them into a bottle. Create our own lights. But I'm not sure where they grow this far north. Or if they'll cast enough light underwater."

I rolled the compass along the table under my finger. The metal made a small popping sound. My hand stilled. Then a soft swear slipped from my lips.

"Did you break Andimir's compass?" Camion asked.

"Break it more, you mean." Jyn laughed, but I rolled my eyes.

"I don't think so?" I picked the compass up, examining the thick line that had appeared down the center. "Maybe I did."

Meryn held out her hand expectantly and I handed it over. She slipped her thumb nail into the crack, prying gently. I winced when she applied pressure, when the metal fought against her, but then the seam popped open and confusion replaced the slight guilt I had been feeling about further breaking Andimir's compass. Meryn held it out so we could all see the groove in the center, as well as the engraving across the smooth, opposite side—two bare trees, twisted around a star. The royal symbol of Eythera, of the Elves.

"So, the break was intentional." I frowned. "But why the symbol?"

"I don't know." Meryn's brow scrunched even more as she watched Sylvr, who was fidgeting with a chain around her neck.

After a moment, she pulled the necklace from under her shirt. The pendant was familiar—the one we had found in the Dwarven ruins, in Thastrag, while hunting down the Tellus Scepter. A tiny golden pendant etched with two dragons, wrapped tail to nose around a single star.

"Natylia, that ring . . . the one the Zylarra brought . . . I have a hunch. May I try putting them together?"

I didn't hesitate to pass Sylvr the ring, though confusion and curiosity were thick in my mind. She examined all three items, then slipped the ring into the grooved slot.

"The one thing we've been missing for this trip is the key." Sylvr spoke as she worked at fitting the pendant over the ring. She shot a nervous glance at the innkeeper. "Meryn's . . . *gem* is in a box. And for that, we need a key."

Meryn turned a skeptical eye on her. "You didn't think to mention this before?"

"To be completely honest, the lock on the box is made from mithril. Hard to break, but not impossible. That, coupled with the need for your magic, will keep the box holding your life essence effectively sealed—but not so much against you. Having the key will save us some time."

"And you think it's—"

"In here, yes." Sylvr gave the pendant a firm twist and another layer of the compass bottom fell away. A tiny golden key fell into her palm, which she held out to Meryn. "I believe this belongs to you."

"Did Marinus know?" I whispered. "Is that why he made sure Andimir had his compass after Eurybia attacked us on the ocean?"

"I wouldn't be surprised," Sylvr said. "Marinus was never a fan of wiping out the other races."

Meryn leaned in, brushing a soft kiss against Sylvr's cheek. "Thank you."

Sylvr winked. "This *is* kind of my job."

"And you're so very good at it."

Chapter 23

The apothecary was less of a shop than a brew station. A tall woman swirled around the room, dropping ingredients into the half-dozen kettles and cauldrons that spanned the wide space. Her dark skin was spread with tattoos of silvery vines, and each time she paused to check a brew, they were spotted with purple flowers that opened and danced with her magic. Every surface was spread with dried herbs, empty bottles, half-filled bottles, and random bits of exotic creatures I didn't care to identify.

Meryn's eyes lit up as she scanned the room. The apothecary witch paused her dancing long enough to appraise my red-haired friend, then her stormy grey eyes skirted over the hoods that concealed the rest of us. Silver jewelry glinted from her face: piercings in her eyebrows, lip, and nose. Her clothing was made from a patchwork of leathers and fabric she seemed to have sewn together herself, but they still exposed a fair bit of tattooed skin, even behind the apron tied at her waist. I had never seen a woman so wildly well put together.

"I don't abide hoods in my store. Remove them or out with ye." Her voice was heavy with an accent I didn't recognize. I turned my eyes to Meryn.

"My friends need to retain as much secrecy as they can. Are you willing to make an exception?"

"And ye' are?" White locs spilled over her shoulders, a bright rainbow of beads and threads woven in. The woman leaned against a table, crossing her arms.

"My name is Meryn. I run the apothecary in Thrais."

"Oh?" After a moment's pause the witch straightened. "I am called Zemira. I recognize the name, and it's a reputable one, so I'll allow yer friends to keep their secrets. But I can revoke that in a second."

Meryn nodded. "That's more than reasonable."

Zemira eyed the blades on Jyn's back. "Those stay in their sheaths."

"Don't give me a reason to pull them out," Jyn muttered under his breath.

Meryn scowled at him. "My friends will behave themselves. We're actually looking for two rather specific things."

Zemira's eyebrow lifted. "I might have 'em."

"We're looking for water breathing potions. Six of them. And potentially a water-resistant light source."

"Going for a dive in the lake?" Zemira cackled at her own joke, turning to a closed door tucked against the back wall. "Let me see what I have."

Meryn glanced at us, her eyes wide with amusement. A dive in the lake might seem crazy to the shopkeeper, but the witch was spot on. Maybe she assumed, correctly, because Starberry Lake was so close.

Or maybe, the fear I was trying to suppress was true. Maybe we weren't the first to go diving in the lake recently.

"I have these," Zemira said, stepping out again. A dozen crystal bottles were perched in her arms, the liquid within a lavender color with specks of silver that glittered in the light. She dumped them onto a table, on top of a stack of parchment with hasty, scratched lettering scrawled over the front.

"They're a gold each. They'll last ye' a full day. Ye'll see no effect outside of water, only in. Ye'll know they've faded when . . . well, when ye' drown."

"Ominous," Jyn muttered.

"These are perfect, thank you," Meryn said, loudly enough to mask Jyn's comment. "Any suggestions for the light?"

"Plants in a bottle?" Zemira shrugged. The beaded silver and crystal headpiece on her brow shifted in the light. "I may have another option." She scanned our group. "I'm not sure ye' can afford it, though."

Lucian scoffed. "And what gives you—"

"Money isn't an issue." I cut the prince off with a pointed glare in his direction. He didn't need to see my face to understand. "What do you have?"

Zemira reached into a hidden pocket, drawing out four long, teardrop shaped bottles. Flecks of a silvery-colored substance shimmered inside. She shook one, as though we should understand what we were seeing. Sylvr looked bewildered and even Meryn's brow drew in confusion as the particles caught the light, reflecting rainbows. With a long sigh, Zemira closed her eyes and gripped a vial more tightly. Without warning the room filled with bright, blinding white light.

I scrambled to cover my eyes. The light began to fade a moment later, and Zemira cackled softly as she dropped the vial onto one of the tables. Meryn stared at them with understanding in her eyes.

"Star powder," she murmured. Sylvr nodded her own confirmation. "One of the most rare materials in the world, nearly impossible for the average apothecary to afford." Meryn's eyes narrowed on the witch. "How do you have four vials?"

"Not asking questions is part of the price."

Meryn sighed. "Fine." When she realized the rest of us hadn't reacted to the revelation, she added, "Each of those vials contains a crushed star."

"From the sky?" Lucian sounded bewildered.

"Have you seen stars anywhere else?" Jyn scoffed. I swatted his arm and he added, "He set me up."

"From the sky," Zemira interjected. "When a star falls, if ye're lucky, ye' might gather it."

"And crush them into powder?" Camion sounded sad at the thought.

"Yes," Meryn admitted. "But once stars fall from the sky, they don't glow as they do in the heavens."

"Until ye' crush them," Zemira said gently. "In the darkness, any of those will glow as brightly as though they were still in the sky. Under the sun, ye'll see not a hint of that light . . . unless ye' power them like I did. The potion they're suspended in is magically charged."

Camion's grip tightened slightly on my hand, but he said

nothing more. Instead, Meryn asked, "And what will these cost us?"

"Ye' know their rarity. What do ye' think they're worth?"

"Honestly?" Meryn stared at the little vials for a long moment. "At least a hundred gold each."

I winced at the number.

Zemira nodded. "A bit under value, but I'll give them to ye for that."

Between the six of us, we had the gold. But four hundred gold pieces would completely drain our purses. Meryn looked at me expectantly and I considered.

"We'll take three of them," I said after a moment. A bit under a hundred gold would still give us some wiggle room if anything happened in the lake. We didn't want to empty our gold supply, and we could swim in pairs—a star to two people.

Jyn took a step closer, bending to look at the vials more closely. "Do the stars ever fade?"

"No." Zemira studied him. "But dark places usually lack light for a reason. If ye' use them, be aware of the things ye' might attract. Some might not care that ye're in their home . . . and some may be provoked with starlight in their presence. Be wary."

"We will," I murmured.

Each of us pulled some gold free, piling the coin on the table. She pushed the star vials toward us, along with the water-breathing potions, and I passed them out to my companions.

"Thank you," I threw over my shoulder as we turned to leave.

"Ye' might not thank me when ye're done."

∗∗∗

Dark water lapped at the shore, slipping dangerously close to my toes. My cloak was wrapped around my weapons, hidden securely in the brush nearby. We had stripped down, wearing little more than our underthings and carrying nothing more than the lightest or smallest weapons we could tuck into our waistlines.

Camion held our star, staring at the glittering vial with an expression I couldn't quite read. While we waited for the others to hide their things, I moved closer, wrapping my hands around his.

"What are you thinking?"

He spun the vial, watching how the rainbows caught the sunlight.

"It's a bit sad," he said, lifting his eyes to mine. "Something that was once so beautiful has been crushed and shoved into a jar. To be looked at, and used, but never really appreciated."

"True . . . but when they glow again, they'll shine so much brighter than anything we've ever seen. We can appreciate them."

The corner of his lips tilted up and he leaned forward, brushing a kiss to my forehead. "I like that." He paused, searching my eyes. "And we should appreciate them. Maybe they can light our wedding."

I stilled, my fingers unconsciously tightening where they lingered around his hands. "Our wedding?"

"Yeah . . . that's been on my mind a lot lately." Pink spread up his cheeks. "Someday maybe I'll work up the courage to ask you."

My heart fluttered at the admission. At the fear that flitted across his eyes.

"What makes you so nervous?" I reached out to brush my fingertips over his cheek.

He leaned into the touch, then said, "I'm not sure I'll ever be worthy to ask you for everything marrying you will entail. It's not so simple as asking you to be with me forever."

"You're thinking of the crown?"

His jaw clenched, his gaze dropping from mine as he nodded. "Yes. I don't feel right asking you to take me as your . . . your king. I feel strange even admitting that."

"You know that's not what you're asking for, right?" Camion shifted uncomfortably and I added, "I understand what you're saying." I glanced around at the group, at Jyn and Lucian who were trying to decide on weapons, and Meryn and Sylvr, who were speaking in the same hushed whispers that Camion and I were. "Who knows, soon I might not even have a throne for that to be of consequence."

"Don't say that. We're going to win this." He tilted my chin up, pressing his warm lips to mine. "Don't get discouraged."

"The odds aren't in our favor," I countered. "I'm being realistic."

"I think you mean 'pessimistic.'"

I inclined my head in agreement. "Regardless. I love you. I want to be with you. We can figure out the rest later."

"Agreed." He smiled softly. "And when we do get married, we're going to light the ceremony with stars."

"Are you two finished yet?" Jyn asked loudly, and I jumped. He snorted, then said, "We should hurry. We need to get Meryn back to that inn before Aurial decides she's overstayed her welcome and leaves."

"How will we find this . . . stone?" Lucian asked. He eyed the water skeptically. "We could be searching for hours."

"Meryn will feel the stone calling to her, if she doesn't already," Sylvr said. "As long as you're within visual range of her, you should find her life essence much faster. All of you searching an area will be easier than Meryn searching by herself too. And . . ." Sylvr drew in a long breath. "And I don't think I can go with you."

Meryn spun on her. "What do you mean?"

"I don't . . . I don't know how to swim with these," Sylvr admitted, gesturing at her legs.

"Why didn't you tell me before now?"

"I'm sorry." Sylvr buried her face in her hands. "I didn't know how to tell you. I'm useless to you until the meteor showers come."

"It's fine," Jyn said. "You can hide nearby and watch the gear."

Meryn focused on the lake, her expression a war between frustration and sympathy. "You should have told me."

"I didn't know how," Sylvr pleaded.

"Don't worry about it." Meryn slowly met Sylvr's waiting gaze. "Like Jyn said, you can hide nearby. Stick to the shadows, all right? Stay safe?" Meryn glanced at the lake once more, sighing heavily. "We should go."

Sylvr bolted forward as Meryn moved, grabbing her arm and spinning her around. Before Meryn could react, Sylvr's hands cupped her cheeks, pulling her into a kiss so deep that even I began to flush. She whispered into Meryn's ear before she released her again, clearing her throat as she added more loudly, "I'll hide. But I have no way to warn you if anyone comes. Be careful."

Meryn stared long and hard after Sylvr as she scrambled away toward the tree line. She kept watch until Sylvr had ducked between trees and climbed over a massive rock, seeking a suitable hiding place. My friend turned to me with a slow blink. "That was . . . that was some kiss. I'm not entirely sure how I'm supposed to recover from that."

"Cold water should help," Jyn said, toeing the lake with a grimace. "Let's get this over with."

We lifted our vials in a mock-toast, tossing back the lavender liquid. I coughed at the burning that filled my lungs, gasping for air as the enchantment settled. My own magic responded angrily, covering my body in blue and purple sparkles that sent searing pain up the scar on my left side. After a moment, I sucked in a breath of cool air. The potion's magic began to calm. I heard the gasping breaths of my companions around me and waited until everyone was breathing evenly to step toward the water.

I offered my hand to Camion, squeezing tightly as I inhaled once more. "Ready?"

He nodded.

"Are you going to hold my hand?" Lucian asked Jyn with a smirk.

Jyn glared at him. "Not a chance."

"You're right I'm not . . . *piratey* enough." The prince's smirk grew when Jyn's expression fell flat. They were interrupted by a loud splash, the sound of Meryn diving headfirst into the lake. I glanced at Camion, nerves rising in my chest.

"Well," I sighed. "Now or never."

We jumped.

Chapter 24

I ce shot across my skin. The water was chilled as though the lake was fed directly from the snow-capped mountain peaks. I recoiled, nearly gasping in a mouthful of water—then realized I couldn't. Bubbles of air had formed in my mouth and over my nostrils. Breathing was as easy as it had been on land.

I tried to look at Camion, but the darkness flooded with brilliant, glowing white light. My hands lifted on instinct but even my fingers failed to dim the brightness. Several minutes passed before my eyes began to adjust. I blinked, clearing the last of the spots away. Camion was beside me, the radiant starlight in his hand illuminating the lake around us almost as brightly as the sun we had left above water. Fish that had scattered when the glow began were now circling back, warily swimming toward us, as cautious to keep their distance as they were curious.

Lucian, Meryn, and Jyn swam over, the latter two clutching their own stars with wide eyes.

"Overkill," Jyn mouthed, shaking the vial.

Meryn nodded, lifting a shoulder and gesturing us onward. She tucked her star into her breast band, dulling the glow to that of an overly bright lamp. Camion and I flanked her left, Lucian and Jyn to her right, each of us spread out effectively enough to light several dozen feet of lake water.

Plants swayed in the gentle undercurrent. The fish grew braver, swimming close as we searched under rocks and between thick clumps of the underwater forestry. Meryn kept our search steady, her path consistently forward. She paused once, glancing around, the bright lights making her hair glow under the dark lake water.

For a moment I could picture her, the Titan within, even without her powers restored.

Then she plunged ahead and I was left wondering how restoring her life essence would change my friend. Maybe she would be exactly as I had always known her. Maybe the burden of the memories she had forgotten would be too heavy. I wouldn't know, couldn't know, until she did. But, with every second that passed, anticipation weighed on my chest.

I knew I shouldn't think that way but . . . I could lose my best friend.

The realization was a tight knot between my shoulders.

Minutes turned into an hour. Then two. My weakened muscles ached with fatigue, but spurts of healing magic helped push me onward. Every few minutes I would reach over, offering the same to Camion, who repaid me with faint smiles each time.

We followed Meryn, searching with our eyes when she pressed quickly forward, digging into the soft lake bottom when she paused. I couldn't make out the surface of the lake any longer; we were so far down, all I saw was darkness pressing down from above. The sight sent a shudder the length of my spine.

When we were near what I guessed to be the center of the lake, Meryn stopped. She glanced over her shoulder toward us and there was a frenzy in her eyes that hadn't been there before. Without warning Meryn dove straight down, clawing furiously at the sediment on the bottom. Was this what all Titans were like when their life essence was near?

I glanced at Camion. He shrugged, his expression as bewildered as my own.

A dark shadow moved across my vision. I reached out, yanking Camion against me and away from the shape that slowly circled around us. Lucian dove to help Meryn search as Jyn, Camion, and I pressed our backs together. Whatever this creature was, we needed to buy our friends time.

The shape neared, large green eyes glinting in the starlight. Its mouth opened, a slender pink tongue slipping from between rows of sharp, pointed teeth. I restrained the chill that started at the base of my spine, steeling myself for a fight. The creature looped around us, its glare menacing. A pointed snout caught the starlight and wiggled as though it was sniffing.

Then the creature's attention shifted abruptly. Fixated on Meryn.

It lunged.

Jyn dove, a blur of dim golden light as he slammed the blade of his dagger into the creature's neck. Its long dark body twisted, bubbles spewing from between those sharp teeth. The creature snapped for Jyn. Smooth, slippery skin brushed my arm. I recoiled with a hiss, glancing down at the bubbled skin that glistened in the starlight.

"Acid," I mouthed to Camion, showing him my arm.

He winced and nodded, then motioned as the creature's tail snaked back toward us. We moved. Both of our daggers sank to the hilt before we dragged the blades down the slithering mass, careful to avoid the dangerous skin. Dark blood seeped into the water and cast foggy shadows in the starlight. The creature thrashed away again, almost taking our daggers with it.

We regretted our attack instantly. Creatures we hadn't seen, small spiny things with claws and spikes, sprang toward the blood—drawn to a potential meal. They mostly ignored us, focused on the wounded creature. Several paused near my arm. I glanced down. The skin was raw, bleeding into the water. I hadn't felt it. I spared half a second to heal my skin, ignoring the familiar tug at my side.

Meryn and Lucian were swarmed by the sharp-clawed scavengers that, hoping for an easy feast, attacked anything in range. Camion and I dove for them, brushing off the tiny critters as they tried to latch onto our clothing and hook into our skin. A glint of light snagged my attention; Jyn's first dagger was still buried deep into the creature's eye. Then his spare knife flashed, moving up the monster's side in quick, uneven swipes.

I lost sight of Meryn and Lucian. My heart pounded against my ribs, panic rising in my chest to meet it. I reached for Camion's hand, to find only open water. A knot climbed my throat.

Another dark shape appeared and I spun, spluttering on air. Slinking from the depths was a twisted half-humanoid form with horns that rose above her head and fell across her slender back, twining together at their points. Crimson eyes shifted my direction as the new creature's tail slid into view. Everything else we had been fighting scattered, leaving the water dark and empty but for us and her. She reminded me of the way Sylvr had described her own water form—but darker. More wicked and ill intentioned.

Those crimson eyes turned toward Jyn. She dove for him. Bubbles filled the space between them as he brandished his blade, aiming for her slender stomach. The tip scraped across her flesh, a puff of blood added to the churning pool around us. A few of the tiny clawed creatures crept back out of hiding, desperate, but the horned creature clenched her fist and they grabbed at their throats, tearing frantically until they stilled completely and fell away into the water.

My stomach lurched, but a warm glow from the bottom of the lake distracted me. Lucian swam up from our left, his eyes wide, gesturing at us to swim. We moved. Jyn spun around, cutting through the water, but the demon-looking Nereid still followed him. Each stroke of her powerful tail pushed her closer; she was faster in the water, so much faster. I started to go back for Jyn, to help him, but Camion grabbed my arm. Gestured down.

That orange light had grown. Heat spread to my toes, upward, climbing my skin with the glowing light.

The lake exploded.

A blast of pulsing red and gold light burst into our vision. The creature fled, racing away from the warmth that flooded the lake's waters. Our stars were drowned against the brightness. I shielded my eyes for only a moment before I moved my hands away and spun around.

My jaw fell open.

Meryn floated in the water before us, her expression nervous. Power poured off her. The magic thrummed and pulsed around us in every inch of water that her light touched. She blinked, then spun slowly, as though showing off a new dress. I snapped my jaw shut, then dove forward to hug her. She wrapped her arms around me, squeezing tightly.

Nahara or no, she was still my best friend.

Nahara or no, I wasn't afraid of her power.

***

As soon as my head broke water, I could sense the full difference in Meryn. She carried herself differently. Her posture was straighter, her face lined with purpose. But there was a weariness to her too, and I wondered if the weight of her memories was heavier than I had even imagined. Much like the Elves, she now had a soft aura around her. Instead of gold, though, hers shifted between warm hues of orange and yellow that glimmered over her skin and sparkled through her hair.

"This should fade," she said, noticing my awe-struck stare. My cheeks heated and she laughed. "Do I look so different?"

"Not too much—" I started to say, but I was cut off by a chorus of "yes" from behind me.

"Your aura, for one," Jyn explained. "But I understand what Andáerhyn was saying now. You *feel* different. Warmer but also . . . powerful. Wiser."

"Are you saying I look old?"

Jyn smirked. "I'm saying you look like the several-hundred-year-old Titan that you are."

"I'm not old," Meryn scoffed. Her smile faltered as she scanned the beach. Then she jolted into a run, dashing into the tree line to where we hid our gear.

"I wondered when you would return," a female voice said. One that was cold, icy.

Familiar.

Camion recoiled beside me, taking a step back. Jyn shot him a concerned glance. Anger burned in my chest. I clenched my jaw, my nostrils flaring as I jogged to catch up to Meryn, pausing only to grab my sword.

"You're alive?" the voice growled. At that, Camion was in front of me, Jyn at his side.

"Cybele," I snarled, shoving them both out of the way. "I could say the same to you. You'd look better with a pile of rubble on your head."

The olive-skinned Titan dismissed me with a glance, her dark eyes landing on Camion's face. "You're recovering too? I didn't do my job well enough."

His arm shook where it pressed against mine, but I would not let him be hurt. Not again. I took another step forward, drawing her eyes. A lock of her dark brown hair was twisted around a finger, the flowers and berries woven through shifting with the motion.

"Where is she?" I growled.

Cybele's grin spread wide. "Where is who?"

"You know." There was an edge to Meryn's voice that reminded me of my own. Sympathy rose in my chest. The anger rising inside me wouldn't let the emotion live, dampening my compassion immediately.

"Oh, her?" Cybele taunted, gesturing to the brush beside her where Sylvr had been hiding. "I didn't need her."

Thoughts shut off, then flipped on. Camion tortured, broken, and bleeding flashed into my mind. Unconsciously, I took a step to the side, shielding him. Heat rose in my cheeks and neck. Sweat beaded on my forehead. The rage was consuming me. That Sylvr too might have suffered at this Titan's hands ignited the burning fury that seemed to always simmer beneath the surface these days.

"Nat," Jyn said in warning.

Sparkling magic twisted and spiraled up my arms.

Cybele stared for a moment, her expression falling blank except for the eyebrow she lifted slowly. "Much easier to use your powers now, I see? Must be that you're feeling confident." She took a step forward, cupping her mouth to add in a loud whisper, "You shouldn't be."

The magic on my arms began to turn that black, star-flecked color from before when Valeria attacked. Cybele paused then, visibly confused.

"Tyli." Camion's hand was warm on my arm. Pain seared up my left side as my powers pulled deeper, quickly draining stores that were already low after helping Camion and I swim.

"You shouldn't have that power," Cybele said. She glanced around the group, pausing to really stare at Meryn. A slur of colorful swears fell from her lips. "You're back?"

"Yes, sister. Nahara has returned. Finally. Valdis will be most pleased."

The voice came from behind us. I spun on my heel. Eurybia

stood near the lake edge, her ebony skin glittering with water. She stretched slowly, letting her dark locs fall around her shoulders. Her icy blue eyes sparkled with amusement.

"I don't think they liked my underwater form," Eurybia mock-pouted.

"Which one?" Cybele smirked. "I mean, even I've never been very fond of that gaudy fish you do."

"No, the Nereid."

"Ah well"—Cybele's gaze flicked to mine, then her eyes ran the length of my body—"I wouldn't expect them to have good taste."

Both Titan's shoulders shook with laughter. I looked between them, wary, my knuckles white where I gripped the hilt of my dagger. We had anticipated one Titan, not two, and the odds had been slim then. I dared a glance at Meryn, who inclined her head to confirm that Sylvr had a pulse.

Eurybia caught the gesture and frowned. "Cybele. You should report our findings to Valdis. He would be very interested in certain . . . developments."

"You're not going anywhere," Jyn snarled.

"And who's going to stop me?" Cybele drawled.

Eurybia clucked her tongue. "Go, sister. Tell him."

Cybele looked at the faces around her, at Meryn who stood and crossed her arms over her chest. Her eyebrows pulled together, her eyes narrowing.

"Are you sure you can handle . . ." she gestured around at us.

Jyn's grip tightened on his dagger. Small purple and blue sparkles jumped to life on my hands. Camion shifted himself forward, angling his body as a shield between me and Cybele.

"I'll keep them here." Eurybia smiled. "I can handle them."

Cybele hesitated. "Without your—"

"*Go.*"

Jyn and I both straightened. Cybele jerked her head in understanding, then dashed into the trees. Jyn's head twisted in her direction, clearly torn between staying and following her. Jaw clenched, he met my eyes. Loyalty held him in place and, glancing at Eurybia, I was grateful for it. We couldn't take on the Titan without him. Without any of us.

Eurybia had stepped back into the water. Her form grew as large horns sprouted from her head. I winced. She was even more intimidating above water, those crimson eyes glowing as brightly as they had in the starlight. Running wasn't an option— we couldn't leave Sylvr behind. And worse, we wore no leathers, no gear to speak of other than the daggers in our hands.

I shoved the hilt of my dagger into Camion's hand. When his brow scrunched together, I shook my head, taking in a deep, focusing breath before I turned inward to my powers and began to pull.

And pull.

My magic wove up from the depths. The scar on my side burned in protest.

Eurybia cackled before she spoke, her voice was deep, rich, much different from her human form. "You think your magic will have an effect on me?"

She laughed again, but her expression flattened as she raised a hand. Water burst from the lake and slammed into my chest. I flew backward and barely missed hurtling into the rough bark of a tree before I rolled into the underbrush. My magic promptly dissolved from my fingertips. I skidded to a rough stop, then crawled forward, ignoring the stinging pain where my skin had torn against branches and rocks. I pawed through the heaps of our stuff and kept digging until I found Jyn's swords and jerked them out of their sheaths.

The others were still contending with Eurybia. Camion caught my eye, glancing over his shoulder to make sure I was all right. I nodded my head then strode forward. Blood trickled down my arm; I didn't bother to look. Jyn needed better weapons, if we stood any chance.

But he was distracted, jabbing at Eurybia so quickly he was little more than a golden blur. Like a gnat, surveying for the best piece of fruit. Eurybia wasn't amused.

"Jyn!" I called out.

He zipped to my side in a few heartbeats. "Are you all right?"

"Fine," I said, shoving his swords into his hands. "Thought you could use these."

He inclined his head, then he was gone, just as quickly as he had come. But Eurybia's eyes were locked onto Meryn now.

Then I noticed why.

Meryn had become an inferno of living flame. She had done so before, in Thastrag, but this time the heat blazing from her was searing. The rest of us turned and ran for the trees. Camion and I ducked behind a boulder, peering around it.

Eurybia was dragging water from the lake to build a shield, but the heat from Meryn's flames turned the liquid to steam as fast as the crimson-eyed Titan could summon it.

"Give up!" Eurybia screeched. "You can't win this. I'll douse you myself."

"Clever," Meryn said in a voice not quite her own. "It won't save you."

Meryn grew then, larger and larger until she was on Eurybia's eye level. Inside the swirling flames she was a dark shadow, her hands lifted in front of her as though she were trying to control herself. A loud crack split through Eurybia's yelling, like wood that snapped in a fire. Flaming wings burst from Meryn's back, spreading wide until the tips brushed along the trees.

I ducked behind the rock I was pressed against. A spray of hot water rained over our heads.

"You're not going to destroy our world," Eurybia snarled.

"No. Only you." Meryn's ethereal voice sent goosebumps across my skin.

Those large, flaming wings enveloped the other Titan. Thick, hissing steam filled the air, nearly as dense as rolling fog. Eurybia shrieked in pain, but all we could see was a shadow writhing in the fire. Another burst of heat and steam slammed into us. We crouched behind cover and I grabbed Camion's hand, healing the tiny burns that peppered his face and arms. I pressed my free hand to my ear, trying to mute the deafening sound. The air was alive with crackles and hissing and screams. A new wave of heat rolled from the fighting and Camion curled himself around me, creating a barrier between myself and the searing elements. I didn't have time to think or act. To help Meryn.

And then—

Silence.

Chapter 25

I glanced around, to Jyn and Lucian hidden behind trees, to Camion at my side. To Sylvr, whose chest rose and fell in slow, even rhythms. A minute passed. Two. Jyn caught my eye. Nodded.

In unison we jumped up and bolted toward the beach. The two Titans lay collapsed on the ground a dozen feet apart. Eurybia had shrunk back down to her human size. Her skin was covered in burn wounds, her eyes closed and locs splayed over the sand.

I raced for Meryn, in her human form once more. Her pulse was strong under my hand, her skin unmarred. Dark circles lined her eyes, but she seemed all right otherwise.

Jyn grunted loudly and I looked up in time to see him sever Eurybia's head from her body. Lucian, Camion, and I winced in unison as blood sprayed across Jyn's torso.

"Had to be done," he grumbled. "We couldn't risk her being brought back. We're lucky Valdis hasn't returned her life essence.

She wouldn't stay dead as long as it was in her chest."

"Marinus won't love this," I said quietly.

"Doesn't matter. Can you burn the body?"

I cringed at Jyn's request but nodded anyway. "Cam can you sit with Meryn?"

"How can I help?" Lucian looked between us uneasily.

"Check Sylvr," I said, before Jyn could say something snarkier. "Make sure she's okay."

He nodded. Camion passed me, brushing his fingertips against mine as he went. I started pulling up magic, frustrated when it didn't immediately respond. After a moment, I managed to summon enough power to set Eurybia's clothing ablaze.

"Couldn't you have done that?" Camion was eyeing Jyn.

"I . . . I forget that I have magic sometimes."

"Oh," Camion said. "I only ask because Tyli looks—"

"Drained," Jyn finished. His eyes danced over the burn marks peppering my skin, taking in all the new scars I had gained since the last time he had been with us. "Nat—"

"We can talk later." He frowned. I glanced over my shoulder at Camion, who nodded shortly before I added, "Back at the inn. Not here."

He seemed sated with that.

I left long enough to throw on my clothing and leathers, gathering Jyn's in my arms before I returned and handed them off. We stood watch until Eurybia was consumed in fire. Then Jyn stepped into the lake, washing the blood from his skin and underclothing.

"We need to get back to the inn," he said after a moment. "I don't trust that Cybele won't be back."

I studied him for a moment, watching as tiny burn marks and cuts healed themselves. "That's incredible."

He frowned. "It's Elven magic. I shouldn't be able to heal like this. It's not natural."

"For you, for the Elves, it's the most normal thing in the world."

"It's not though," Jyn scoffed, then sighed. "I guess I went too many years without magic to think this is normal."

"But you've always been fine with me healing you?"

Jyn shook his head. "It's not the same."

"I didn't have magic until almost a year ago. How is that not the same?"

"I don't know."

"Jyn." He met my eyes and I offered him a small smile. "I've never seen you look more comfortable in your own skin. Magic or no."

"I'm not keeping my powers. As soon as I can shed them safely, or those Titans are gone, so is my magic. My immortality. I don't want them."

I shrugged, my argument cut off by a soft groan from nearby. Camion helped Meryn into a sitting position. She rubbed at her head.

"I feel like I haven't slept in a moon cycle," she moaned.

"We need to get back to the inn," Jyn reiterated. "We can rest there."

She nodded her agreement slowly. Then clambered to her feet, stumbling over the sand as she hurried to where Lucian sat by Sylvr. When she got to her, she prodded at her, fingertips gently checking Sylvr over.

"There's a nasty welt on her head. Swollen, split open. But that's the worst, I think . . . Cybele must have wanted to question her for some reason. Maybe she thought she knew something."

"Cybele clearly knew nothing about you," I said.

Meryn frowned. "No. And I wasn't aware your magic was changing regularly."

"Only when I feel threatened or someone I love is threatened. Or when I'm angry." I grimaced. "I've been angry a lot lately . . ."

"That's . . . odd," she admitted with a sigh. She paused to close her eyes, rubbing at her temples. "I don't know if you're connected to Valdis or Thanatos, though. My memories have returned but wading through them will take time. I'm inclined to believe you're connected to Thanatos, because Cybele and Eurybia didn't have their life essences." Her eyes opened. "Do you mind healing her? I need to rest before I can test my powers further."

I nodded, kneeling beside the pair to touch Sylvr's arm. After a moment, the blue and purple sparkles poured out and danced across Sylvr's dark skin. The wounds slowly knitted themselves together. My magic was faint though, barely visible in the bright sun. I winced, closing my eyes when my side ached again.

"Do they need magic to unforge the Stave again?" Camion asked softly.

I knew what he was asking: were we still targets? Would they try to take him, me, or both of us for our blood and powers again?

Meryn considered, her spine straightening and her head tilting slightly—the Nahara in her shining through. "That's unlikely. If they were clever, they would have stored an excess of your blood, so you wouldn't be necessary. Especially if they assumed you were dead when they saw you last. But . . . arcana would be necessary."

"Why his blood?" Lucian asked. "He's not royalty, or Elven, or anything."

Camion frowned, but Meryn turned slowly, her movement meticulous and measured. She inhaled slowly, then touched Camion's arm. "I'm remembering . . . I'm remembering that your mother was a smith of great renown. Many of your ancestors were, as well. Their bloodline—your bloodline—contains that of the one who forged the Scepters initially, and the Stave. But a binding agent is needed in a spell with components as volatile as life essences, especially when there are three. I would even dare say a sacrifice was made."

"How do you know this?" Lucian asked.

"I didn't," Meryn said slowly. She tapped the side of her head. "But now I do."

"You think one of my ancestors sacrificed themselves to make these cursed Scepters?" Camion asked.

"I do. Or one of their children, or another relative. Regardless, it's your blood that fused them and your blood that will break them. But we still have to get the Stave from Valdis, and that might be a harder task than you understand."

"Can it be done?" I asked. I wasn't so arrogant as to assume our weak victory against Eurybia was an indication of how every fight would go from here onward.

Meryn watched the last of Sylvr's wounds pull together. Then she leveled her eyes on me. "Honestly? I'm not sure. I wasn't sure then, and I can't pretend that I am now. I don't think it's impossible, even though I know that's not what you want to hear."

Sylvr groaned then, putting a hand to the bandage on her

head. Her dark eyes fluttered open and she jolted upright. "You're—you're okay?"

"I'm fine," Meryn said, her posture slouching a bit. "Did Cybele say what she wanted?"

"I—" Sylvr stared at Meryn for a long minute, blinking several times. "This is an adjustment, I'm sorry." Meryn's brow drew together in confusion. Sylvr waved a hand. "Your aura is blinding. You found the stone?"

"Yes." Meryn reached into a pocket. The stone glowed at her touch, a muted yellow light. When Sylvr took the essence, the stone dimmed, leaving a dragon opal that glimmered bright like flame, mottled with purples and blues.

I looked between them. "What are you going to do with it?"

"My job," Sylvr said. She sang softly over the stone. Her voice was pure and clear, gentle and demanding. For a moment, nothing happened, then the stone began to shimmer and glow bright white. When Sylvr was done, the small dragon opal was half the size it had been. She pressed her hand to Meryn's chest, where a glow blazed through Meryn as though she was lit from within. When Sylvr looked up again, I knew all our faces wore matching masks of curiosity.

"Oh. Sorry. I finalized the return of her life essence. Meryn can use her powers without limit if the stone is on her, but the life essences never recharge properly if they're not returned *to* their Titans. She could return it herself but . . ." Sylvr blushed, shooting Meryn a look that had the Titan lifting a brow in amusement.

"What did Cybele want from you?" Meryn pressed again.

Sylvr's gaze dropped to the grass. "I'm not entirely sure. I think she dismissed me as unimportant, but I'm sure she knows

I'm your sentinel, now that she's seen you. She might come back for me."

"How did she know we were here?" Jyn scanned the trees. "I can't sense her in the area. I felt her leave. She can't have been following us, I would have known."

Meryn frowned. "Who knew we had to come to the lake?"

"Not many. We kept that information between us."

"Who?"

"Andimir, Phelix, Andáerhyn," I rattled them off using my fingers. "Us, Callithya."

"None of them would betray that information unless they had no other choice," Sylvr said quietly.

"You don't know that." Even I heard the bitter tone in my voice. "You never know what someone will sell you out for."

"Andimir would die before he would sell us out. So would Andáerhyn," Jyn said. "I daresay Phelix feels the same."

Lucian rolled his eyes, but I nodded slowly. "Jyn is right. Andimir has more than proven himself. And Jyn has known Andáeryhn for a lifetime. If he trusts them, then so do I."

"Thank you, Princess."

"That leaves Callithyia and Phelix," Camion said.

"Callithyia would never," Sylvr insisted. "Her family have been loyal servants of Nahara for as long as anyone can remember. She wouldn't betray the only life she's known."

Camion shrugged. "Maybe it wasn't entirely her choice."

"We don't know Phelix that well," Lucian offered.

"No," I said firmly. "Suspecting that Kalum was our enemy only served to distance us from any ally that could help with our true enemy. I don't suspect them."

"Who, then?" Jyn asked. "Because someone knew we had to come here." He glanced around. "Speaking of . . . we *really* should go. We're pressing fate staying here this long."

I nodded my head in agreement, climbing to my feet. "As much as I don't want to, I have to admit . . . I suspect the worst. The only person I can possibly think of who would willingly betray us—"

"That shopkeeper," Camion said suddenly. "That witch. Zemira. She knew."

We exchanged dark glances. She owed us no loyalty, that was certain. "Fine, then we should get back to the inn and prepare to leave soon. Even if no one betrayed us, our friends may be in trouble."

Chapter 26

We sat around the inn much of the evening—resting, eating, and drinking our fill. Or pretending to, as we kept watch for Aurial. The innkeeper didn't seem to suspect anything, so taken with Meryn's displays of charm. Sylvr always lingered close at her side, but he wasn't phased. Her flirtations were received and returned, and in exchange he tolerated the hooded friends she had with her. As an extra bonus, he stopped charging us for the food and beverages, even if we continued to tip generously. His eyes lingered on Meryn though, even when he returned to the bar. Her posture was straighter, her eyes dull with the years of knowledge that weighed on her shoulders. I wondered what he saw.

Because her new aura had faded, though still visible in soft, shimmering waves, like the heat above flames. The power had dimmed, but I had to imagine if I could see it, so could the innkeeper. If he did see, he didn't say anything.

As I was ready to give up and turn in for the night, Aurial strode into the inn. I knew her instantly. Her presence emanated the same kind of thrumming power that Meryn's did, though Meryn's aura didn't share the intensity of this Titan. Aurial had a fully powered life essence and the difference was palpable.

An owl perched on her shoulder, a beautiful black and white bird that locked eyes with me almost immediately. He didn't flinch as I held his wide-eyed stare. Then his head bobbed, his beak clicking.

Aurial turned at the sound. Her armor was silvery, scaled, and flowed like water with each of her movements. Two thin braids ran up the side of her head, disappearing into the pile of soft curls tied back from her face.

Meryn turned on her chair, the laugh in her throat cut off abruptly as she met Aurial's eyes. Aurial stumbled. The owl hooted softly, tilting its head to the side.

"I thought you were . . . lost. Dead. Why are you here?" Aurial asked softly.

The innkeeper paused, looking between the women. When none of us moved to lower our hoods, he cleared his throat. "Beer, Aurial?"

"Stronger," she replied, slumping onto one of the bar stools. The owl hooted again at being jostled. A little glass slid down the bar. Aurial caught it without hesitation, the ease of her reflexes on point with Jyn's. She tossed the amber liquid into her mouth, clearing her throat after she swallowed. Her eyes stayed focused on Meryn. "Explain."

My friend licked her lips, like she couldn't decide what to say. We hadn't expected Aurial to immediately recognize Meryn. Maybe we should have.

Aurial glanced around. The room was empty, except for us

and the innkeeper. "None of these are unfriendly faces. Not to you, anyway."

Meryn crossed her arms over her chest. "I trust no one but the people you're currently assessing."

"And I trust no one but him," Aurial countered, jerking her head at the innkeeper. "We're even."

I lifted an eyebrow, thoroughly confused, when Meryn turned a wary eye on the innkeeper. She studied him for a long moment, stepping up to the bar to really access him. Then she held out a hand. Sylvr stiffened, but the man smiled knowingly and shook Meryn's hand.

Meryn jerked away almost immediately, whispering, "I didn't recognize you. And you never said a word. Did you dampen your aura?"

He nodded. "I wasn't entirely sure you were who I thought you were."

"Fine," Meryn said. "Lock the doors. We can talk."

Aurial smirked, striding across the room to lock the door and shutter the windows. When she returned to her seat, Meryn gestured for the rest of us to remove our hoods. We did, but the tension around each of us was palpable.

Meryn met my eyes. "You know of Aurial already. What I should have realized is that our companionable innkeeper here is Caru, known to you as the Ancient of Love." She looked to the two Titans. "Aurial, Caru, I would like to introduce you to Natylia, Queen of Thrais. Lucian, Prince of Wydus. And our companions Jyn, Camion, and Sylvr."

"An Elf?" Caru's eyes landed on Jyn. "I haven't seen one of your kind in a long while."

"Most don't leave Eythera," Jyn said stiffly.

"And yet you were allowed."

"Extenuating circumstances."

"Indeed," Caru said with a smile. I watched him, still unsure that I believed he was a Titan. He seemed so . . . at ease. Even Meryn, who had spent years as a human, was tense where she stood.

"So, is all of Falmar inhabited with hidden Titans?" I asked warily.

Aurial laughed, the sound loud and unbound. "No. Caru and I are the only two in this village. There are others, across the world. But most of them aren't as fond of humans. Or they're hiding, lying in wait for Valdis to return to let them wreak havoc on the humans."

"Well the humans don't want to wait for that to happen," I said. "So how do we stop him?"

"Him? Valdis? I'm not sure there's much stopping him."

"Wait, you said you had a cousin who lived in Morland." Lucian leveled his gaze on Caru. "Who?"

"Berit," he answered hesitantly.

"Berit is dead?" Meryn whispered.

"I'm not sure. You didn't see her. What do you think her odds were?"

"Against the Risen, good. Unless they were still sane enough to take her to Valdis. Then . . ." Meryn winced. "Not good."

"Not good for any of us." Aurial sighed. "Is this why you're here? To find Titans who might help you fight Valdis?"

"Not just him," I admitted. "Boreas, Cybele, and Thanatos too."

"Thanatos is free?"

I scrunched my face. "Potentially."

"Oh." Aurial released a string of swears. "That changes things."

"That's reassuring," Jyn muttered.

"He could wipe out every human in the mainland in a few hours. Easily." Caru hesitated. "Unless we move fast. If we pin him down before he gets too far inland, before he's fully regained his energy . . . well, we might stand a chance at least."

"Kalum is evacuating, as is Seryn," I said. "We're building a force. We're hoping to head them off outside Thrais."

Aurial studied me. "You're willing to sacrifice your kingdom? For this?"

"Not much of a kingdom anyway, if everyone's dead."

"Morland is already lost, as Caru no doubt told you," Meryn said. "The only town we've heard nothing about is Vitic. We don't know if they're safe or not."

Aurial twisted a lock of hair around her finger. "How many Risen have made appearances?"

"Enough to take out the entirety of Morland," Jyn said. "And a few moon cycles ago a man who was supposed to be executed for the attempted murder of my queen was turned as well."

"If Thanatos is released, his father will raise anyone he kills." Aurial paused to consider. "This fight could get ugly. Why not flee? Go through Silverglass and escape north?"

"I have a responsibility to my people," I said quietly. "I can't abandon them, not knowing what awaits if I do."

Aurial studied me once more, then nodded. "I can respect that. I hope you know what you're asking. Not only of your friends, but of yourself."

"I do," I said, glancing around at the faces surrounding me. "I wouldn't ask them, if I knew there was another choice. But they all know I would never hold it against them if they fled into the trees and disappeared, either."

"You carry the weight of the world. And on the shoulders of one so young, even for a human." Caru frowned. "Your burden should not be borne alone."

"What are you suggesting?" Aurial asked.

"I'm suggesting we send that bird of yours to contact some of our old friends. I'm saying we go back to Thrais and fight with our new friends."

"You're too soft."

"I'm a lover, what can I say?" Caru winked. "But I wouldn't feel right if we sat out on this one. This fight is as much ours as theirs."

"You're right."

A door creaked from upstairs and Jyn jumped to his feet, blades in hand. "What was that?"

Aurial and Caru exchanged a glance. "I suppose we should let you in on our little secret, if we're to be allies."

"Secret?" I asked warily.

Caru grinned. "I think you'll rather like this one, lass. It's not often that two Titans serve protection detail for a couple humans."

My brow rose as Aurial disappeared upstairs, my heartbeat jumping to match. Soft voices carried over the landing, then a set of footsteps crossed the room above my head. More talking, then Aurial bounced lithely down the stairs.

"Might I introduce our own little secret," she smirked.

"Though I dare say you already know them."

She lifted her hand, gesturing toward the stairs.

I leapt to my feet as the figures hit the top step.

"Annalea?"

Chapter 27

"Natylia?" Her voice was warm, rich, familiar. I almost fell into a sobbing mess on the floor. I managed to hold my composure, though, at least waiting until she carefully made her way to the bottom of the stairs. Then I fell on her, squeezing her tightly and holding on as though she would float away again.

"Natylia, I'm fine."

"Have you been here the whole time?" I sobbed, pulling back to wipe at my cheeks.

She nodded sheepishly. "I would have sent word but"—she gestured to her guard, standing loyally behind her with a small smile on his face—"Raul said we should wait for you in Falmar. He said he didn't understand strategically why Devlyn wanted us both to go north. I'm so sorry! We didn't know what was safe and, after we heard the palace was taken . . ."

"We've been here for a couple days," I said, rounding on Caru and Aurial. "How did I miss them?"

"We didn't let them in the bar, if there were any guests present. And you were hooded, we had no idea who you were."

I exhaled slowly, letting my quavering breaths steady as I nodded. "True. Okay. How did you end up playing guard to them?"

Caru smirked at my sister, who flushed. "These two aren't very good at subtlety. They tried to hide their identities, but Aurial and I had Annalea's name by the end of the night."

"We didn't even have to work for it," Aurial laughed. My sister flushed darker, but the Titan's expression smoothed out. "Once we guessed who they were, we knew there had to be a problem in Thrais . . . so we offered them shelter and protection. That's all we could offer, but we hoped it would be enough."

"One of the advantages of my abilities is sensing emotions and holding sway over them," Caru said. "When I felt the turmoil in your sister's mind, I made the inn as peaceful as I could so they could relax. Add in that with my powers in place I can make myself undetectable, even if another Titan was looking me in the face"—he paused to wink at Meryn—"and they wouldn't have been safer anywhere else."

"Thank you," I said. "I'm eternally grateful." I really was appreciative that my sister had stumbled into the Titan of Love. He and Aurial had kept her safe. I owed them for that. "And I definitely don't want to think about what would have happened to you," I said to my sister, "if you had gone to Wydus. Or back to Thrais. I'm glad you're here."

"Devlyn betrayed us, then? The rumors are true?"

I nodded, waving to two of the bar seats. Caru saw the gesture and pulled a stack of small glasses free and began to pour amber liquid. I returned to my chair next to Camion, his hand a steady weight on my back as I dumped the drink down my throat.

"I owe you all a story," I said slowly. "I'm only sorry Andimir isn't here to hear it as well."

Jyn stiffened in his seat. "Are you sure?"

I looked at Camion, who inclined his head. I was ready. We were ready. To release the words into the air one more time, to lift more of that burden from our shoulders.

So, I began to talk.

I started from the beginning, my friends filling in the story where they could. Lucian's jaw grew more slack with each word, with every piece of the adventure we had been on after he found us in the forest and after we retrieved the Tellus Scepter. Aurial and Caru listened in silence. When I finished the story of Silverglass Forest, however, I paused to down another shot of the amber liquid Caru slid my way.

Then I leaned into Camion's side, curling into the warmth of the arm he draped around my shoulders, and continued on. The words were harder. I took longer to form each one, the pain of reliving the memories stronger than I had anticipated. Tears gathered in my eyes, but I brushed them away and looped my fingers through Camion's. I was grateful he was beside me for this. I was grateful he was beside me at all, after what we had endured.

Lucian paled when Camion began to talk. Camion stumbled over the words, his jaw clenching in frustration when his voice grew too thick with emotion and he couldn't speak. I leaned over, pressed a kiss to his cheek, ran my thumb across his hand, and offered him the small reassurances I could. Valdis had made him feel powerless, and I knew he still struggled with that. But watching him try to tell a room full of people was far worse than our private conversation. When he still saw them as failings on his part, confessing them was harder. And I didn't know how to help, other than to keep promising him he was more than the nightmares.

When he finished, Jyn rose to his feet and extended his hand in Camion's direction. The latter stared up at him with a lifted brow.

"Not many of us could have kept it together after . . . that," Jyn said gently. "And you're *still* going."

Camion nodded slowly, accepting Jyn's handshake. When Jyn stepped back, I slipped my arms around Camion's waist and hugged him.

"I'm proud of you," I whispered in his ear. "In so many ways."

"And I of you," he murmured, pressing a kiss to my brow.

Lucian leaned forward in his seat, then sat back. Once. Twice. On the third time, he opened his mouth.

"I saw . . . and still some part of me didn't want to believe what had happened. To hear your story from your own lips . . ." His throat bobbed. "My father has to be stopped. And, if we can, I want to save my mother. As long as she isn't in league with him. What he did was . . . I don't even know how to express my disgust. I don't care what has happened between us in the past. If you're willing to accept me, to help me take down my father, I am your brother in arms. From here onward." He looked to Jyn. "And even if you hate me, I'm including you too."

"You don't need *my* forgiveness," Jyn said, his stare cold.

Lucian nodded. "I know." He met my eyes. "I've apologized to you a dozen times. But I don't mind saying the words over and over. I am sorry. For everything I've done to you. For everything my family has done to you. Never again. You will never have cause to question my loyalty again."

"I know," I said quietly. Uncertainty flickered in his eyes, so I added, "Thank you. For everything you've done so far."

"Natylia, I . . ." Annalea's voice was so soft I barely heard her. "You've been through so much since I saw you last. I feel guilty that we've been sitting here, doing nothing."

"I'm glad you were sitting here. One royal must be safe at all times, and I clearly wasn't."

"Two royals," Raul added. I looked at him, confused.

Annalea's cheeks turned a bright crimson color. She buried her face in her hands.

"Annalea?" I asked, sitting up straighter. "What aren't you telling me?"

"I may be . . . we're . . . I'm . . ."

"She's pregnant," Raul said cheerfully.

My mouth fell open. "What? You didn't lead with that?"

"I'm not very far along," she said shyly.

"And I'm going to guess from the expression on his face, Raul is the father?" Raul beamed at me by way of response.

"No, not busy at all." Jyn chuckled, watching Annalea's flush deepen.

I stood, scooping Annalea and Raul into a hug. "Congratulations to you both. We need some light in all this dark heaviness."

"That's why telling you now was such a good idea." Raul grinned.

"Oh, don't act like we planned this," Annalea said.

I smiled at the two of them, leaning appreciatively into Camion when he pulled me into his arms again.

He offered me a sweet smile. "Happy looks good on you, my love."

***

Wind ruffled the down-filled blanket, waking me from my sleep, the scent of pine filling the small room. I pulled the warm blankets back over my shoulders, grumbling under my breath. Camion slipped his arm around my waist, tucking me against him. He nuzzled into my hair, gently kissing the spot behind my ear. "Sleep, Tyli. I'll wake you before dawn."

I rolled to my back. Light hadn't even touched the windows yet. The forest loomed ominously outside. "Have you slept?"

"Some."

His arms tightened around me when I moved closer, curling into his chest. I fell into the soft, steady rhythm of his breathing, almost dipping back into sleep. Camion wasn't going back to sleep, though, his fingers combing gentle trails through my hair. I leaned away, scanning his face, and lifted my hand to brush a thumb across the stubble of hair on his chin.

"Let's get breakfast."

"You don't want to rest more? We have a long trip ahead."

"Not if you can't sleep."

"I can think of ways to amuse ourselves that don't involve sleep," he teased. His eyes were soft and happy, in a way they hadn't been in so long. He was unguarded. For me.

I guided his face down, kissing him deeply and savoring the heat from his hands as they roamed across my skin. When he pulled back, a sweet smile on his lips, a warmth spread in my chest. Without thought, I blurted, "Marry me."

"What?"

"Marry me . . . please?"

"Tyli." Camion traced a finger down my cheek. "I should be asking you."

"Why?" I turned my head to the side, catching his hand and kissing his fingers. "I love you. And the idea of asking makes you uneasy, because of all that it entails." I met his eyes. "But I know what I want. I know *who* I want."

"But . . ." He faltered and I lifted my head, brushing my lips gently over his.

"Marry me, Camion. If I've learned anything these past weeks, it's that our time isn't guaranteed. So, for one moment forget what tradition dictates. Forget everything but you and me and this life we want together. Do you want to marry me?"

"Yes," he said quietly, his eyes scanning my face. "More than anything."

"Then marry me."

"I had it all planned out you know," he said, lips quirking when I glared at his dodge. "You're kind of stealing my moment."

I scoffed. "When were you going to ask?"

"I don't know," he admitted, mischief bright on his face. "But . . . I was going to take you to the pond. In the forest, behind your palace."

"Where we kissed for the first time?"

"Mmhmm. And I was going to pull you into the lake, and when we surfaced, I was going to ask . . ."

"That sounds beautiful," I admitted.

"But you're right. As much as I wanted to ask . . . I'm not sure when I would have done so."

"So, let me ease that weight. Marry me, Camion."

He studied my face for a long minute. So long, I thought he might actually say no.

"You're right, and I love you. Of course, I'll marry you." His fingers slid into my hair, lifting my head as he leaned in, pulling me into another kiss. I trapped his lip between my teeth, biting gently, and grinned against his mouth at his soft intake of air.

Then he pulled away, abruptly, and I tilted my head in concern.

"One condition," he said breathily.

"Anything."

"Wear this?" He freed one of his hands to lean heavily on his other elbow as he reached beneath his shirt. His mother's ring dangled on his fingertips. "I can get you a more elaborate ring later but—"

"This is perfect," I interrupted, tears burning heavy in my eyes. "I don't even have to consider, I agree to your condition. And that you would even offer me this ring means more to me than any other ring ever could. I'll wear this one with pride."

His own eyes welled up and his smile grew while he slipped the ring off its chain and onto my finger. I drank in the sight, tracing my thumb over his lips. He was beautiful, and he was mine. All mine.

Our lives might not seem so lucky but this, us, a love I never thought I would deserve—there was luck in that. I pulled him down again.

"I love you," he murmured on my lips.

"I love you too," I said, lacing my fingers into his hair. "Now, where were we?"

Chapter 28

I picked at the breakfast Caru had laid before me, shoving the soft eggs into a pile with my fork. Each day that crept past felt like another tick closer to our looming executions, overshadowing even the small joys we found. I sighed, dropping the fork.

"We need to get a message to Edra. To Wulfric," Lucian said.

Jyn's eyes narrowed. "Why?"

"Unless he rescinds the orders officially, Natylia's army is technically still under my father's control. At this point, it might be more formality than anything . . . but we can't risk the confusion, if this comes to a battle."

"Lucian's right," Camion said quietly. "Most of Tyli's men don't know war. We don't need them asking questions in the line."

Aurial ran her fingers over her owl's soft white feathers. "I'll send Kotori to Edra first. He'll be the safest bet, no one will catch him. If Wulfric is there, Kotori can bring us his response. If he's gone—"

"We may need to plan for the worst," Meryn finished for her.

A metallic glint caught my eye and I looked down at the ring on my finger. We hadn't announced our engagement to the others yet. Jyn had swept down the hall like a storm as soon as sunlight broke the skyline, pounding on our doors and waking us all up. He wanted to be on the road to Thrais before early afternoon, so here we sat, rushing through a meal before we needed to finish packing.

"When were you going to tell us?" Jyn asked from my left.

I jerked my head up and caught his warm smile before it melted into a smirk.

"Tell you what?" I pushed my hands between my knees.

"Natylia?" Annalea's head tilted to the side, one eyebrow lifted.

I sighed, shooting a glance at Camion. His eyes were fixed to his plate, and he was taking an extreme amount of care spreading honey over a slice of warm bread. I knew he had heard though; his lips twitched with amusement.

"Well, since I'm outnumbered," I mumbled teasingly. Annalea stared pointedly until I lifted my hand, showing her the ring. Her squeal made my ears ring.

When she calmed down, she clapped her hands together. "Oh Nat! I'm so happy for you. For both of you."

"Thank you." I leaned into the arm Camion looped around me. He pressed a kiss into my hair. A round of congratulations filled the room. Meryn reached across the table to squeeze my hand.

"If you hadn't come banging on our door this morning you probably would have already known," Camion teased Jyn.

"Look how long it takes you all to eat breakfast." Jyn rolled his eyes.

"Don't worry, Jyn," Meryn teased. "I'll remember that you eat too fast now to enjoy my blueberry muffins."

Jyn's eyes widened, the shock on his face exaggerated. "You take that back."

Her eyebrow lifted and she grinned. "Sorry, I need to go pack my things."

He narrowed a glare on her retreating back.

***

We were gone before the sun broke the trees.

Our group was too large to be inconspicuous, even with the hoods and cloaks shielding our identities. Jyn walked restlessly to my left, frustrated that having three Titans around was completely blocking him from sensing other threats. Aurial and Caru offered to block their auras a bit, but he turned them down. Meryn's life essence was still acclimating to her body; she wouldn't be able to mask her aura until her powers had settled back into place. Lethe, the Zylarra, trailed happily behind us. Caru could feel her emotions alongside ours, even if we couldn't see her.

We didn't stop until we reached Thrais, and the sight of my home still standing made my heart swell. Aside from Andimir, we were all finally home.

Home.

Even though my palace still crested the tops of the trees, my joy clipped off when we entered the small city. The streets were filled with guards and soldiers from Wydus, Marawolves patrolling in-between. There wasn't a sign of my people. Not a single one.

Jyn loosed a soft string of swears, throwing out his arm to stop us. Caru rolled his neck and shoulders, cracking them as Aurial drew a blade.

At the sounds, half a dozen faces turned in our direction. I dropped my bow into my hand, Camion and Lucian drawing blades of their own. Raul stepped in front of Annalea, but I put them both behind me.

The earth shuddered. A loud crack rent through the air, a flash of lightning brightening the sky.

Smoke poured from the direction of the Temple of Nahara.

Screams filled the air.

My gaze flitted between the eyes locked onto us and the path toward the temple, when hoofbeats reached my ears.

Andáerhyn. Leading a charge of men into Thrais, his golden aura distinct in the fading daylight. He lifted his sword arm in salute as well as in threat, and a wicked grin spread across his face as he barreled into the enemy force.

With him distracting the soldiers and Marawolves, I raced for the temple path. Footfalls followed, but I didn't bother checking to see who trailed me and who stayed in the city. All I could think of was Callithyia and the priestesses, and I didn't want to imagine what might have happened to cause that much smoke.

"It has to be Draven," Aurial said, suddenly beside me. "She can harness the power of lightning and curb it to her will."

"What I'm hearing is I've got a Titan to kill." I didn't appreciate the excitement in Jyn's voice but, as we stepped from the end of the path, my protests lodged in my throat.

A woman with wild, shoulder-length white hair stood in front of the temple, her arms raised high. Another crack of lightning ripped through the sky and blasted into the marble structure. Goosebumps erupted across my arms right before the temple shook and collapsed in on itself.

"Callithyia," Sylvr said from behind, bolting past me, Meryn on her tail.

I exchanged glances with the men and then raced after the women, hoping against all hope that Meryn would stop her before she reached—

The white-haired Titan spun elegantly, as though she was the star of an elaborate play. A wicked grin split her face, her eyes slightly wide and crazed. Her head tilted at the sight of Sylvr, of Meryn, and then she cackled wildly, leering at Meryn.

"Look what's come out to *play*," she crooned. "Too bad I don't have time for games."

Draven threw out her lower lip, an expression that pulled at the dark scar that ran from her forehead through her cheek. Abruptly she changed her tune again, humming and smiling while she danced in front of the temple.

Aurial charged forward, her patience run out. I started to follow. But before I could get far, she shouted over her shoulder, "She's mine."

Her sword lifted and was met by steel. Draven had twisted and thrust daggers up to block.

"Nahara, you brought me *friends?*" Draven squealed in delight. "You really shouldn't have. You know I don't play well with others."

Lightning crackled at her fingertips, then lashed out. Aurial's back arched as the power surged through her, then she collapsed to the ground. Caru moved forward as swiftly as I nocked an arrow. Draven batted both attacks away, unconcerned, before she fled into the trees in another fit of insane laughter.

Caru bolted after her until Meryn yelled for him to wait. I moved to check Aurial's pulse and breathed out in relief. The Titan sat up with a groan.

"It's not so easy to kill a Titan, remember?" she said, spotting the concern on my face. "She didn't even try to take my essence."

I didn't ponder the thought. Instead, I darted after Meryn who had run for the burning temple.

"You can't go in there," I called after her. "You'll die!"

"I won't," Meryn said. Her voice was laced with fierce confidence and I turned a pleading eye on Sylvr. She seemed unconcerned. My gaze flitted back to Meryn.

"Please. Don't."

Meryn shot me an apologetic half smile. A hand weighed on my shoulder and I flinched. Jyn's face held the same worry as my own, but his grip tightened, as though I might run after her as she stepped into the flames.

I thought about it. I was a step away when Camion pressed into my side, Lucian on his heel.

"Don't follow her," Camion murmured. "All you can do is wait."

"I can put the fires out," I argued. "I know I can."

Aurial stood with Sylvr, who was examining the dark lightning marks across the Titan's stomach. "Let her go. She'll be faster if anyone is still alive, and then you can put the fires out. Trust me. She'll be fine."

"But—"

Sylvr glanced up, met my gaze. "Nah—Meryn—has abilities in the flames that most wouldn't. They increase her awareness. She can spread a controlled blaze for miles, specifically picking targets to burn if she wanted, solely tracing their energy with the flames. If you dim the fire now, she won't be able to use those skills to find any potential survivors."

My jaw snapped shut. I didn't know what to say; I didn't know much about Meryn's abilities, and I knew she was still learning herself. But some part of me was still squirming at the thought of my best friend trapped within the inferno before me.

"I don't understand," Annalea said. I turned, having almost forgotten she was with us. When my brow lifted, she added, "Why wouldn't that Titan attack the palace? Why the temple?"

Caru frowned. "Draven was here to bait you. And send a message. If she wanted to put up a fight, she would have. Trust me."

"But how do you know?" My eyes didn't leave the burning building in front of me, even as people ran past with buckets of water, even as my own magic rose to help without summoning.

"Because she didn't use her Titan form, only her human one," Aurial muttered. "Swapping forms, swapping sizes, it's draining for Titans. She would only do so if she intended to fight. She was here to weaken your resolve. Don't let her."

I frowned. "What about Meryn?"

"She'll be fine," Aurial insisted again.

But I couldn't take my eyes off the building. Too many minutes had ticked by, too long with no sign of Meryn between the flames and shattered marble. Every moment the itch to follow after twitched through me and continued until Meryn strolled out, a pillar of living flame.

There was nothing but pure, unending rage on her face.

This wasn't Meryn. This was Nahara. This was the Titan of legends, the one who cleansed the souls before they could pass into reincarnation.

And the fury in her posture was searing.

"They're dead," she growled loudly. The flames on her skin and clothing dimmed with each step she climbed down. "Anyone that was in that temple is dead. All the exits were blocked. Every single one."

"Meaning Callithyia . . ." Sylvr sounded small.

Meryn's expression softened at Sylvr's voice. "Meaning that unless Callithyia was somehow not in the temple tonight, she's gone too."

I was surprised when it wasn't rage that rose in my chest, but sorrow. My fingers latched onto Jyn's and I pulled his hand off my shoulder before gripping it tightly in my own.

"Help me?" I asked him. "It's the least we can do."

He glanced warily at me, then the temple. Then nodded, slowly.

"What are you going to do?" Lucian asked.

"Watch."

I closed my eyes and pulled up my magic. Jyn's answered, but unlike when I had used his blood to heal, I couldn't access it; skin to skin, our magics were completely separate. After another moment, I pulled up enough magic that glittering power covered my hands and arms. Jyn glowed so brightly that the people running past with water paused completely just to stare.

We waved our free hands and the fires extinguished.

Lucian's eyes grew wide. "How—"

"You have to train yourself," Meryn said. "Once you're better at accessing your power, you'll be able to learn to control it. And then, just about anything is possible as long as you have the resources."

Andáerhyn stalked over and slid his arm around the prince's shoulders. "And don't worry. You'll have the resources. I might not use natural magic, but—" Andáerhyn's words fell off and he gestured to the world around him. "I'd say you'll have what you need."

"Who are you?" My sister's eyes were locked onto Andáerhyn, her expression bewildered. Raul was tense beside her.

"Andáerhyn, my lady," the Elf said, dipping into what I would have guessed to be a mock bow but for the lack of humor on his face. "I am a friend of the Queen of Thrais."

"My sister?"

Andáerhyn's smirk returned. "Yes, Your Highness. I'm glad to see she found you again."

Annalea flushed at that, and Raul's hand clenched around the hilt of his sword. "And I, as well."

I stared at the ruined temple, at the loss of life. A dull ache started in my chest and I glanced at the others. "I hate this as much as the rest of you, but cleaning and restoring the temple will take weeks. We don't have the resources to spare."

"You're going to have to leave them . . ." Sylvr murmured.

"I don't want to. We might be able to send some of the men from the village in, see if they can recover anyone. But without the temple, the priestesses, we don't even have the means to bury them properly." I looked up at the broken building, still pouring smoke into the night sky. "We'll have to take care of this after we finish the Titans."

"It's the right choice," Jyn offered.

Camion reached out to push a lock of hair from my face, nodding his own agreement. I stepped away from my friends to grab as many of the passing people as I could. They nodded at my ideas, albeit reluctantly, but agreed to send men in tomorrow to search. I didn't have much hope.

When that was secured, I spun on Andáerhyn. "The town?"

"Safe as it can be. We cleared the Risen and Marawolves that were there, but I can't guarantee there won't be more. We might want to think about setting up camps for the incoming soldiers anyway. Why not intersperse your people between the soldiers for their own safety?"

"That's an idea," Meryn said. "How about we discuss it *inside* the palace though?"

I reached out to grab Annalea's hand, giving it a soft squeeze. "Are you ready to go home?"

"Lead the way, sis."

**

The gates opened when we neared. Phelix waited, sword in hand, his expression wary.

"I'm glad you're so prepared," I said with a laugh as I lowered my hood.

The king visibly relaxed, tucking his sword away.

"I couldn't imagine you would be Titans. I assumed they would walk through the walls. But you can never be too cautious, especially when I sent a group of my men out only to have *that* *one* not return." Phelix grinned, jerking his chin at Andáerhyn. "I'm glad to see you back safe. And the rest of you as well."

"A few of us *are* Titans," Aurial said, stepping forward. Her white hair tumbled free around her shoulders and she winked a blue eye at Andáerhyn. The Elf stood a little straighter at the Titan's attention, and I couldn't help the giggle that slipped free at the sight.

Phelix on the other hand appeared perplexed, his confusion growing when Caru stepped forward and dipped into a short bow. When Meryn released the clasp of her cloak, slinging it over her arm, Phelix lowered his head.

"It is truly an honor."

Meryn huffed. "Don't start that, now. You'll make me feel older than I already do."

Phelix offered a smile, then took his time greeting Lucian, Camion, and Sylvr. Two hooded figures remained, and Phelix cocked his head curiously.

"King Phelix I'm sure you remember my sister—Princess Annalea of Thrais."

"You found her?"

That was pure joy in his voice and it made my heart soar.

Annalea lowered her hood. "She found me. I'm glad to see you again, Your Highness."

"Phelix will do fine," he corrected gently. "And you are?"

"Raul, sir." He dipped into an elaborate bow. "It's an honor."

Phelix waved a hand, waiting till Raul straightened to ask,

"And what of the town? What happened?"

"They were overrun by Risen and Marawolves," Andáerhyn offered.

I frowned. "And the temple of Nahara was completely destroyed."

"Destroyed?" Phelix asked. "By whom? Risen?"

"No. Draven decided to make an appearance." The tone in Aurial's voice said she was still itching to jump ship and chase that Titan down.

"The Ancient of Chaos?" Phelix's eyes were wide.

"The Titan of Chaos and her damned lightning powers," Andáerhyn corrected. "And if it interests you, Thanatos's mother."

I shivered at the thought, at the madness that had glittered in Draven's eyes.

Phelix gestured toward the Palace. "If there's nothing more to do for the town tonight, we should go inside. I have some news for you."

My heart leapt. "Andimir?"

"Sorry, no." He motioned to the palace again. "We should discuss this inside." We followed, loosening our cloaks and leaving our bags in the foyer. He led us into the Council Room, waiting as we squeezed in around the war table, then closed the door. Phelix shuffled a few of the figures around the map on the table, then he looked at each of us, releasing a heavy sigh.

"One of your spies found Audri. She was delayed in the bandit forests, and while I suspect we know where the bandits have gone—"

"Where?" Aurial interrupted.

"Valdis's army of Risen."

The Titan's mouth formed an "o" before she mouthed an apology and gestured for Phelix to continue.

"Audri isn't in immediate danger from bandits, but Boreas has been patrolling the territory. He might be gathering information for Valdis, or watching our armies, I can't say. Audri hides her men in the trees during the day, and they move at night . . . but I'm nervous Boreas will catch on to their movement."

"We can't spare men to help her," Camion said apologetically.

"No, I know. Call it an old married man's concern." Phelix smirked, casting a glance at the ring on my finger, but he continued. "Andimir definitely met with her though, and he was fine when he left. She said he seemed tired, but not discouraged, and he hadn't lingered after she provided her assistance. He raced off with the men and there's been no word since. Not even from Fetian."

I tried to push down the worry that rose in my chest. I tried not to think about what he might be doing, or how much he might be delayed by his detour to Lytalian. Jyn nudged my arm with his elbow, eyes narrowed but I shook my head.

"Anything else?"

Phelix nodded at me. "We've started offering shelter for refugees from the south. None have yet arrived, but the word has been spread. I imagine it won't be long, and then they'll start to fill the streets of Thrais. If you're willing, we can reduce the number in the city by offering some shelter in the palace courtyard, where they can be monitored by guards more easily since it's walled in. We can tell all refugees they can leave with a guard escort or not at all."

"That sounds reasonable. Though Andáerhyn suggested we start preparing shelter for the incoming army as well, and put the Thraisian people in their midst. Because the town is clearly not a safe place for them."

"That's doable," Phelix agreed. "But we would need to over-take the forest land. Is that a concern?"

I shook my head. "No. Use all the land you need."

"What about shelter?" Camion crossed his arms over his chest. "Setting camps outside seems . . ."

"Primitive," Phelix agreed. "We'll distribute as many tents and shelters as we can, but the numbers won't line up. If Au-dri's men gave up their own shelters, when they arrive, there still wouldn't be enough for half the refugees we might expect, plus your own people."

"I have an idea," Camion said, glancing around the room. "Get every available seamstress in town. Refugees, tailors, wives. Anyone who can sew. Have them teach each other how to make rudimentary tents. They won't be perfect, but they'll shelter more people." He turned to Meryn. "Do you think the dryads might help protect them?"

Meryn lifted a shoulder. "I'll pay them a visit tonight. I can't imagine they'll say no."

Phelix's eyes were scanning the map in front of him. But he spared a half-glance for Camion. "I like the idea but where would we find all the fabric for that?"

"Between my mother, my sister, and I, we have hundreds of dresses," I offered slowly. "They might be a bit patchwork, but they'd provide more shelter from the elements than open air."

"Let's do that, then," Phelix said.

I nodded. "I'll send word to the town as soon as we're done here."

"In regards to the temple . . . what of Callithyia?" Meryn asked. "Have you seen her? Is there any chance she survived the collapse?"

Phelix frowned. "The priestesses have all but retreated into the temple while you were away. They allowed a handful of people in every morning for worship, but that's all. I haven't seen any sign of Callithyia since before you left."

"Do you think she betrayed us, too?" I asked Meryn.

She shook her head. "No, but I had to ask in case there was a chance she might have survived."

"So, you think—"

"I think we should have left more guards at the temple and in the city."

***

"Faster."

"Jyn—"

"I don't want to hear excuses, I want to hear your blade blocking mine." He shifted his stance, beckoning me forward. "You've seen too much combat already to be this untrained. I'm not losing you or anyone else again, if I can avoid it."

I slammed my practice blade toward his chest, but Jyn stopped the attack without much effort. "Faster, Natylia."

"Not all of us have your Elven speed," I panted, swinging for him again. "Or your Elven strength."

"You couldn't keep up with me before," he smirked.

"I almost could."

Jyn laughed and I realized how foreign the sound had become, so absent without him around. I paused to listen, only to take a blow to the hip that would almost certainly bruise.

"Princess?" His smile faded but I shook my head.

"I missed you."

"Clearly. I don't think you've hit me once." I sighed, rolling my eyes, but he stepped forward and scooped me into a hug. "I missed you too, Princess. But we have training to do."

He released me and I glanced toward Camion and Andáerhyn, who practiced nearby. Camion held his own well enough when it came to attacks, but his strength still wasn't entirely there. Against the Elf, he struggled, and I could see the discouragement written all over his face. He was getting stronger, even if he didn't see it, but my own fears for him grew every time we trained; I didn't know if he would truly be ready by the time we needed to fight. Hell, I didn't know if *I* would be ready. But at least I had my magic to fall back on when my strength failed.

Almost a full moon cycle had passed since we returned to the palace, a stretch of time that felt longer when most of my thoughts were plagued with worry for Andimir. We still had no word from him. Fetian hadn't appeared, nor the sailors, nor the Titans. Each day that passed only served to set my nerves further on edge, to tighten the muscles that already ached from fear at all the smallest disruptions.

Swordplay helped; I could feel my body growing stronger. I had regained weight and muscle. Camion had too, even if I knew he still only saw what he had lost. But he spent his spare time in the smithy, helping make weapons and armor for the armies, and that helped.

Jyn trained with us both when Andáerhyn was running a guard shift. He and Phelix had personally taken up watch spots over the gate every day, and the Elf never let Phelix stay up there very long. Andáerhyn claimed his endurance was better, so it was his responsibility. I wasn't sure I would ever be able to repay him for his help.

I knew Phelix's motivation to keep watch was a bit different. He was restless. One wrong rumor would send him flying into a saddle to find Audri himself. Even helping find places for all the new people barely kept him occupied.

Caru and Aurial spent their days dealing with messages brought to them by her owl, Kotori. They said there wasn't much news, but after a few days, Celestyna—the Titan of Sun, Moon, and Seasons—arrived. She refused to fight unless she had to; she was still deep in grief over the death of her daughter. Eurybia may have deserved her death, and Celestyna openly admitted that, but it was no less painful to her. Instead, she offered to guard my sister. I welcomed the aid, no matter what form it came in.

Annalea kept to the palace and grounds, endlessly trailed by Raul, endlessly searching for ways to help when I insisted she relax. I didn't know much about having a child, but I imagined it wasn't easy. Mother had always complained of her swollen feet. Our father had tended to her every need without flinching.

I glanced at Camion, vaguely wondering what kind of father he might be. Or if he even wanted children. Absently, I spun the ring on my finger. With the amount of care he had always treated me with, I could see him being amazing with children. Did I want children?

This man made me want things I had always rejected.

Spirits, I wanted *marriage*. Wanted it badly enough that I had slipped into daydreams about my dress more than once. I had even asked Meryn to stand with me already—she had accepted and then cried until the front of her dress was damp.

"Whatever you're smiling about better involve ways to actually keep up with me," Jyn said, poking me with his wooden blade.

"Yeah, yeah . . ." I grumbled and lifted my practice sword.

But we didn't get the chance to continue. As I swung for his chest, a horn sounded outside the main gates. The four of us dropped our practice weapons and moved for the real blades we kept nearby. Lucian and Phelix hurried out of the palace, falling into step beside me. Meryn appeared in front of us, arriving in a pillar of flame that followed her as she spun to wait for us.

"I take it back," Jyn muttered with a laugh, "she's the dramatic one."

I nodded my agreement.

The main gates opened slowly. I bounced on the balls of my feet, my hand tight around my sword's hilt. A fully decked army spilled inside the gates, waving the banner of the Palace of Kalum. Hundreds of soldiers and guards poured into the palace grounds.

Phelix glanced at me. "Are the places for all of the men ready?"

I shook my head. "No, but many of them are. Enough that between the existing tents and my palace we can shelter them for the night until the rest of the tents are finished."

"We need some of your most capable fighters at the front," Lucian said. "Camps can be made all along the southeast side of

Starberry Lake, too. Not only will that give us more space, you'll be able to meet an invading force faster if you have men ready and at the front line."

"Smart man." Phelix nodded his approval. "I agree."

"Darling." The king turned at Audri's voice. "I've missed you."

"And I you, My Queen," he said gently, lifting her hand to his lips.

She pulled him closer, gripping his chin to press a kiss to his lips. When she pulled away, he smiled up at her and the warmth in his expression was enough to make my heart flutter. I toyed with the ring on my finger, spinning the band with what I was sure was a goofy smile tilting my lips. Camion reached over and gently stilled my hands.

"I love you," he mouthed. I squeezed his fingers.

Audri's hair was shorter than it had been before—small curls piled on top, both sides shaved nearly bare. Her amber eyes studied Lucian, but she didn't comment, instead turning to me. "Your Majesty. I'm glad to see you again."

"And I you," I said, dropping into a matching curtsy.

"Meryn, Jyn, Camion," she said by way of greeting to my friends. Her gaze paused on Andáerhyn, her head tilting to the side, an eyebrow raised.

I grabbed his arm, pulling him forward. "Queen Audri, I would like to introduce you to Andáerhyn. He is one of our Elven allies and has been critical in helping with situating and protecting your citizens as they arrived."

"Then I owe you a great deal of thanks," Audri said.

"Glad to help."

Phelix clapped his hands together. "All right then. Let's get to work."

"Actually, I think you have one more reunion first," said a voice. A familiar voice.

I turned, looking into the thinning crowd. My jaw dropped and Kalum's army split, revealing a sea of glittering gold and silver. Izoryian, the Lord of the Elves, stepped forward, dipping into a low bow, a wide smile on his face. "Your Highness. I'm overjoyed to see you."

"The sentiments are shared, my friend," I said, returning the gesture. I scanned the forces behind him. "No Eáryn?"

"No." He sighed. "She doesn't want to partake, even though she gave her blessing to our forces. It's better this way. Eythera needs a ruling figure, regardless of what happens here."

"Well, I can't thank you enough."

"I'm grateful that you didn't give up when you had the chance to do so. You've built up a force, Your Highness. Now let's hope it's enough." I nodded my agreement and he added, "Where would you like my men?"

"We have front line camps. Would they be comfortable setting up there?"

"As you wish," Izoryian said, dipping his head. With a blow of his horn the army turned, a well-polished, solid unit, and marched toward Thrais.

"I can't believe you got the Elves," Lucian said, his voice filled with awe. "You really are incredible."

Chapter 29

A horn sounded. The noise was so jarring and unexpected, I nearly dropped the book I held. Camion adjusted his position, helping me off his lap before climbing to his own feet.

"What's going on?"

"I don't know," I admitted. "We weren't expecting anyone today."

The door to Jyn's room opened and he stepped inside my chamber, daggers in hands. "You all right?"

"Fine, let's go see what the fuss is about."

I strode from my room, aiming for the stairs before Jyn had a chance to respond. My bare feet barely brushed over the red carpet, my fingers wrapped around the hilt of a blade I pulled free from my waist.

Phelix and several guards were crouched around a figure on the floor who leaned back against the wall. As we approached, the king looked up to catch my eye. I moved a bit faster when he said, "You'll want to see this."

"Andimir?" I gasped. I dropped to my knees beside him, dropping my dagger to the ground. Camion fell into place beside me. "What happened?"

"We barely got out . . . with our lives," he stammered. Green eyes met mine, his face catching the light. Cuts ran across his skin and blood dribbled from a wound between his locs that I couldn't quite see. "And Wulfric . . . I found Wulfric."

I held my palm over his cheek and pulled up my magic. "What happened, Andimir?"

"I found Wulfric on my way in."

"I took care of him already. He's settled in a room," Andáer-hyn said. "What else happened?"

"We went for Lytalian. It's gone. We were too late." Tears brimmed in his eyes and I reached for his hand, squeezing his fingers gently. "They're all Risen. The entire island, everyone I had known. If there are any survivors, I didn't see them. And your Titans? They're there. Cybele, Boreas, Valdis, Thanatos . . . all except Eurybia."

"You saw them?" The breath stuck in my lungs. He nodded and I managed to say, "We took care of Eurybia. She's gone."

"It's not enough." His fear was palpable.

Jyn knelt to his other side and squeezed his shoulder. "We'll make it enough. We're family. We fight for our family. Whatever it takes."

The commotion in the foyer had woken more people. Izory-ian now stood behind me, a frown on his face. "Why are they all in the southern islands? What are they trying to do?"

Sadness weighed on my shoulders. "We knew it was a possibility, remember? We thought Valdis might be harvesting souls to raise his own powers. I guess he built a bigger army along the way."

"But why would he gather in Lytalian? Wouldn't he want the other three Titans harassing us on the mainland?"

"They're trying to break the Stave," Meryn said as she strode through the front doors. "At least that's my guess. None of the children are at full strength without their life essences, and they can't get those back until they break the Stave. It served its purpose if Thanatos is free. Maybe they only need something to separate them. More magic?"

Camion winced. "More blood?"

Andimir shook his head rapidly. "No, no. They have magic. They have blood. They're trying to amplify Thanatos's power before moving to the mainland. Using the Stave."

"I saw them trying," Andimir continued. "We didn't run straight into Lytalian. We knew they could be there." He paused, touching the spots on his cheek that I had already healed. "When they saw us, they attacked. Immediately. I'm not entirely sure how I escaped."

"Has anyone seen Marinus?" Aurial asked. Kotori hooted softly from her shoulder. "I wouldn't put it past him to save you."

"It wouldn't be the first time," Jyn said softly.

"They could be here in a few days, if they catch a good wind." Celestyna's quiet voice was almost drowned by all the chatter. "A few ships? Marinus could try to stop them but, if he's wise, he'll wait until he has help. Which means they won't be hindered."

Phelix tapped the toe of his boot. "Andimir, do you know how many days have passed since you saw them?"

He shook his head, sadly. "I can't be sure."

"All right then, we need to prepare for the worst," I said. I looked to Izoryian. "Can you send a few advance scouts to scour the shoreline? See if we can get an updated position? They're not to engage, only observe and return."

Izoryian nodded. "I'll send out the fastest scouts I can. Immediately."

"Thank you." My attention switched back to Andimir. "Did anyone survive?"

"The Dwarves. Garrod, a handful of his men. They survived. They brought weapons, armor. Not as much as they had originally, some of it was lost . . . I rode ahead, but they shouldn't be far behind."

"Anyone else?"

Andimir's tears spilled over before his gaze dipped to the floor. "I truly don't know."

I leaned forward, pulling Andimir into a tight hug. Jyn's jaw clenched before his hand slid down to grip Andimir's.

Camion turned to Audri. "How many men did you send with him?"

"Not many. Less than a half dozen."

"They were good men, though," Andimir said bitterly.

"They were," Phelix agreed. "And they knew the risks when they agreed to accompany you."

"I'm no less sorry for their losses," I said.

Audri inclined her head. "We will honor them properly when there is time. What do you require of us now?"

"We need to move more of the camps forward," Camion said. "Create a solid line, ready to spring to defense. And we need archers at the ready."

Andáerhyn stepped forward then, bowing hastily. "I can send Elves into watch rotations in the trees. The higher vantage point will give us greater warning as well. But they may be at a disadvantage against Boreas."

"We will try to protect your men," I said softly. "Order them to take to the ground, if the trees become unsafe."

"The dryads can help them as well," Meryn added. "They've agreed to help protect the camps, but they don't wish to engage further. They can blend with the trees to keep watch."

"What else do we need to do?" Jyn asked, his eyes on Andímir's tear-streaked face.

"I'm not sure," I admitted. "I hadn't thought this far. I'm kind of winging it."

"I've offered what I can." Camion frowned. "I wish I was more help."

Phelix offered him a warm smile. "You've done well this far, my boy. Have confidence."

"So, what's our plan? Sit here until they arrive?" I sounded as uncertain as I felt.

"No," Andáerhyn said. "You do the opposite. You prepare your armies. You form ranks, assign leaders. Get your people organized. Distribute weapons and armor, as much as you can. Get ready. And when they come for you, you take the fight to them. They're underestimating you. *Use it.*"

I nodded slowly. "You're right. And I can have Wulfric sign a statement tomorrow stating that I've regained control of my military. But we have a lot to do, and fast."

"And you'll do everything you can," Audri said. "But don't

forget you're not alone. We're all in this. And we'll all stand against Thanatos when he arrives."

"What exactly does Thanatos's power entail?" The voice was soft, a bit behind the others, but the familiarity caught my ear. Annalea. I glanced up. She and Raul stood with Lucian.

"Thanatos can spread death. Usually in the form of disease, but also through touch." Meryn frowned, scrunching her face like she did when she sought important information. The only difference was, this time, the information was in her mind instead of the pages of a book. "He used to always wear a pair of dark leather gloves. He only took them off when he felt like he was at a disadvantage, or if he needed to work faster. And those he touched fell instantly. No hesitation. No final words. The chords of their life were rent in half, as though they were little more than yarn."

"And the Elves?" I whispered.

She shook her head. "Not immune. Not entirely. He can siphon their immortality. His follow up blows were always so swift, they didn't have time to react."

"How do we fight back against *that?*" Annalea whimpered.

I moved to where she stood and offered her my hand. Her fingers were cold, but I squeezed them between my own and said, "We will fight them and we will win. Because we have something he doesn't."

"What's that?"

"We have a reason to fight. We have each other."

***

The dining hall was a chaotic blend of sound and scents. I

had insisted on raiding the wine cellar, cautioning everyone to mind their limits, but between those of us inside and the amount we distributed to our waiting armies, we drained the stores in a couple hours. Andáerhyn had coerced me into hiring the musicians who usually played at the inn in town, and play they did, surrounded by the leaders of all the allied factions.

Izoryian stood with Andáerhyn and two other Elves I didn't recognize, but who were almost equal with the Elven commander in size. Next to the three of them, Izoryian looked small. The two I didn't recognize looked wary of the humans around them, as if unsure what to make of this gathering. Fairly, several of the humans were stumbling around as though they had been drinking for days instead of a small fraction of the evening—Phelix included.

At a table tucked far into a corner of the dining hall, Wulfric sat alone, eyes wide and hands twitchy. He didn't really want to talk to anyone and hadn't for the past two days while we scrambled around the palace preparing our defenses, not even more than a few words when he rescinded Wydus's claim over my armies. The man was haunted, but I knew as his gaze spanned the room again and again, that he was grateful for the protection we offered. I only hoped that, once all was said and done, he could return to some form of peace.

"If you don't finish that mug, I'm going to hunt down a barrel," a gruff voice said near my ear. I turned in my seat to find the eyes of Garrod, the Dwarven leader, resting on me. "You need to loosen them shoulders and a good dose of alcohol would be the perfect cure."

I laughed softly, tipping my drink to my lips. He wasn't entirely wrong; the more mead I drank, the more the warm buzz settled in my limbs, making me sleepy. But I needed to keep my wits about me, and I couldn't drink so much that I wasn't functional in the morning. I had to be focused.

Garrod dropped into the seat beside me, his large frame filling the space. He scratched at the ebony beard that curved his jawline and matched the shoulder length hair on his head. He took a long swig from his own drink. "That's better. Now tell me, what's on your mind?"

"Nothing too major. Only the end of the world."

"You know this isn't the end of Araenna right? Win or lose?"

I sighed. "It certainly doesn't feel that way."

Garrod lifted a shoulder, eyeing the small party of Dwarves he had brought with him. "Still, it's true. If the Titans take over, even if they wipe out every race that walks, they'll still exist. The world will go on. And someday, new races will populate it."

"Only to be wiped out by the Titans."

"You're in a cheerful mood," Jyn said, taking the seat to my other side. "Is this the pep talk you plan to use before we run into battle? 'And try not to get yourselves killed before we inevitably die anyway.' Inspiring."

I shrugged. "Do you want me to *lie* about our odds?"

"No," Jyn admitted. "But a little hope can go a long way, Princess."

Garrod nodded his agreement, standing to snatch another drink from one of his own men. "Don't give up before the fighting begins, Your Highness. That's no way to win."

"Or walk out alive," Andáerhyn interjected as he stepped up beside Garrod.

Side by side, the two men were even more intimidating some-how, a tall mass of muscle. The sight gave me a small bit of confidence. They were on our side, and there were more like them. More Elves, more Dwarves. More Titans. There was still hope.

I took another sip from my drink, nodding slowly. "All right. You win this round."

"Besides"—Jyn smirked—"One of us is going to have to fix *that*."

He gestured toward Camion and Lucian, who watched Andimir as he tried to teach them to dance. It wasn't until Camion and Lucian actually started attempting the jerky, messy moves in a way that suggested they had all imbibed too much that I snorted, shoving my face into the palm of my hand.

"I think I should leave you to fix this," I said to Jyn. "It's as much your problem as mine."

"What's that supposed to mean?"

"If you stare at Andimir any harder, he might actually catch fire." I wagged my eyebrows at him.

Jyn's jaw clenched and unclenched. "I don't know what you're talking about."

Even Andáerhyn laughed at that. Jyn's gaze dropped to the ground.

I gripped his forearm, sighing heavily. "Do you want to talk about it?"

"Talk about what?"

"When this"—I gestured between him and Andimir—"became . . . whatever it is."

Jyn sighed heavily. "I don't know. We spent a lot of time together after Silverglass. He saved my life. I haven't been so vulnerable around anyone but you in years."

"And Andimir was his compassionate wonderful self?"

He nodded. "Yeah. He never made me feel weaker than I was. He challenged me, and he never gave up on me. And I started to understand what you might have seen in him. What you saw in him that I couldn't, even when he came back."

"Andimir is a good man, Jyn. If you feel something . . ."

His guard snapped back into place, his expression flattening. "I don't feel anything for Andimir. He's a friend. A good friend, maybe."

"Well it's your decision, but you can deny how you feel, or you can acknowledge that you like him and enjoy your evening." I slid my mug onto the table behind me, only to have Garrod snatch it up with a grin. I waved him on, adding, "I myself . . . I'm going to go join the fools."

But as I strode across the floor, waving at Annalea and Raul where they danced with Caru and Aurial, Izoryian intercepted my path, gripping my hand and sweeping me against his chest. I froze, startled by the sudden closeness, until he put his free hand to my waist and looped us into rhythm with the music.

"You looked like you needed to dance," Izoryian said with a smirk.

"That bad?"

"I'm pretty sure your neck has melted into your shoulders."

I rolled my shoulders back, correcting my posture. "Fair."

"Much better. How are you holding up?"

"Nervously. You?"

Izoryian shrugged. "If anyone stood a chance against the Titans before, it was us. The Elves have always been more resilient, and we scared the Titans. That was enough for a while, I think. Or maybe Valdis was truly so bad at finding the Scepters that he never had a clue where they hid. Regardless. You have a little of all the races, except maybe the Numyra. You have tents filling almost every free space of forest in front of your palace, and I haven't heard a human slur 'Sahrian' at any of my people yet. Those are all incredible accomplishments. If you can't pull this off, maybe it's not our fate to survive."

"You're awfully calm about that."

"I've been alive a few hundred years," Izoryian said gently. "I've seen and done everything I *needed* to do. Sure, there's more I'd like to do. But in every religion, there are better things waiting for us. I wouldn't mind finding out what."

I winced at the thought. "Forgive me if I don't care for you to find out."

"I've had a dozen of your lifetimes and we should have properly taken care of the Titans the first time." He smiled. "I'm ready for the fight tomorrow, whatever direction it takes. Have faith that I will give everything, without hesitation, for your chance at victory."

"Izoryian—" Tears stung my eyes. I freed my hand to wipe them away, and our steps faltered. "I'm so grateful you came. That you pleaded our case. Thank you."

"Of course, Your Majesty," he said with a smile, dipping into a bow. "And thank you for the dance."

He was gone before I could say more, too lithe on those Elven feet. I glanced toward Jyn, who was still distracted by Andimir—I had never seen him so absent in all the years I had known him. I was a second from telling him to go tell Andimir how he felt, when he jumped to his feet, eyes wide. Then I looked toward Lucian, Camion, and Andimir and realized why.

Lucian was covered in that bright, white magic again. He was dancing, completely unaware that his partners had stopped to stare slack jawed. I reached them just as the prince stilled. His magic vanished completely as he took in the eyes locked onto him.

"What?"

"Your magic was showing," I said, still unable to believe he had summoned it again. "Can you pull anything up?"

Lucian concentrated for a moment, then shook his head. "No, nothing."

"He's like you, I think." Meryn sauntered over, dragging poor Sylvr along with an arm draped around her shoulders. "His emotions are getting in the way."

"I can't summon my magic . . . because I think too much?"

Meryn shrugged, slurring slightly as she said, "More or less. Free the feelings, free the magic. Which is why your drinking and loosened inhibitions allowed them to come out. We should get you drunk more often, Princey-poo."

"How much has she had?" I asked Sylvr.

"You don't want to know."

"Great."

"At least witches don't get hangovers?" Sylvr smiled and smoothed a curl from Meryn's brow. She moved Meryn toward a chair, adding over her shoulder, "I'll take care of her."

"Thank you." I studied Lucian again, sighing. "Your abilities might be useful tomorrow, but I don't know how to access them. I can't very well have you drunk on the field. So. Be careful."

Lucian raised the mug in his hands with a smile, then drained the contents in one smooth gesture. "Goodbye emotional restraint."

He started to dance again and I shook my head.

Camion grabbed my hand, pressing his lips to each finger before he said, "You're beautiful."

"And you've been drinking."

"Nope. I never have alcohol. You know that."

I considered his words, and realized I couldn't recall a time I had seen him drinking anything other than water. Not even once. I met his eyes and realized why in a single glance. His father. I should have remembered. My gaze trailed away, guilt gnawing at my stomach until I caught sight of Lucian again.

Then I laughed, and Camion tilted his head.

"You're telling me that was your *sober* dancing?"

His lips curved into a half smile. "Now I can't share all my secrets. You've seen me dance. What do you think?"

"I think you're only good when I'm your partner."

His hand was warm on my waist, pulling me to him. "Good thing I've decided to not take that as an insult."

"Oh yeah?" I raised to my toes to kiss him.

The doors to the dining hall slammed open. I jerked back and instinctively reached for the dagger tucked into my boot. Then paused.

Three forms stood centered in the doorway. A woman with deeply tanned skin stepped forward first, her arms covered in dark tattoos and heavy gold and bone jewelry. Her dark brown hair fell loose under the horned skull mask she wore, half the front missing to reveal the piercings and paint that covered her face.

"Where is the queen?" she barked, in a commanding tone I hadn't heard since Valdis.

But I stepped forward and lifted my chin, Camion and Jyn flanking my sides. "Who's asking?"

The woman smirked. "If you want my aid, you'll learn some manners."

"I am Natylia," I said begrudgingly. "This is Jyn and Camion." I gestured to either of my sides, then crossed my arms over my chest. "How can I help you?"

"You can't. But I can help you." Her smile turned warmer. "I am Ushriya. And if you're going to be fighting Thanatos, I am offering my magic."

Ushriya. The Ancient of Luck.

"And I mine," said one of the men behind her. He was tall and well-muscled, much like Garrod and Andáerhyn, but his skin was a deep golden tone, his straight black hair flowing down to his waist. "I am Juris."

The Ancient of Earth. How were we so lucky? How had they known? Had our message reached Berit, or simply gone on to them?

"If Juris is honest, his real quarrel is with Draven. And since she's sure to be with her son, Thanatos, he's willing to take his chances," the third man said.

This man made Andáerhyn look small. His skin was as dark as midnight and half of his black locs were corded into thick braids. When he stepped forward, Andimir stumbled back a step and I slid him a concerned glance. Then the man spoke again.

"I am Marinus. And I'm here to assist as well."

My heart stuttered. "I'm so sorry about your daughter," I blurted.

Marinus dipped his head in acknowledgment. "I appreciate the sentiment. But Eurybia followed her own path. It's unfortunate it went so opposite of her mother's and my own."

He nodded his head toward Celestyna, who smiled warmly, before Ushriya spoke again. "We've been traveling for days. What can you offer us?"

"You can join our festivities, feast and drink," I offered, "or I can have you led to rooms. Whichever you prefer."

The Titan eyed me, an approving grin settling on her face. "Festivities it is."

"Keep an eye on that one," Caru said, too near my ear. I spun around only for him to chuckle and add, "She'll drain every glass in sight, if you let her."

"Is that all?"

Caru shrugged. "They're good Titans. We're all the safer for their joining."

"I'm glad they're here." I studied the three, watching as Juris greeted Aurial. Marinus stalked toward Andimir with a soft smile on his lips. "I think hope is shining a little brighter tonight."

Chapter 30

Camion thought he was quiet while he dressed and slid on his gear: strapping his sheaths on, checking that they were secure. He examined the edges of his blades more times than I could count, casting wary looks in my direction every so often.

I watched him though and, after a few minutes, he caught me. One glance at the sad, apologetic expression on his face and I knew I wasn't concealing the fear that thrummed through my veins. My arms trembled with it.

He wouldn't tell me how bad things were for him, especially on the cusp of battle. But for days he had sunken into himself, and I knew that a piece of him was forever broken. He wasn't alone. All of our friends were showing the strain.

Meryn had regained her identity as Nahara, most powerful and also possibly most beloved of her kind. But when her memories returned, so did a burden of unfathomable weight. I often wondered if she sensed all the souls in the world, the ones who hadn't been released . . . and the ones lost to fuel Valdis's lust for power.

I didn't know, wasn't sure I dared ask.

But I saw the exhaustion in her eyes, and in Sylvr's as she tried to care for her.

Jyn was steadfast in his unwavering support, but I saw how thin he stretched himself to do so—sitting up late into the night with Camion when I was too tired to function, but Camion couldn't sleep. Frequenting the tavern with Andimir, because knowing where the Titans were and that I was surrounded by an army eased much of the burden he took on as my guard. He stood with Meryn as she babbled loud, stream of consciousness thoughts that made little sense. As though she were verbally un-raveling the burden on her mind. Jyn's eyes always lit with joy, though, when she paused to look at him and thank him for lis-tening.

I knew that Jyn was trying, in his own way, to offer comfort and support to each of us. But his eyes were dull, as though he had been counting the days and ran up short. As though he won-dered how many we truly had left, and was now determined to make extra memories with each of us, just in case.

Our armies were readying outside the tent, much the same as Camion was. I could hear the shuffle of bodies, the deep voic-es thick with sleep, the clatter of weapons being retrieved. We weren't a large force. A few thousand humans at most, plus Elves and Dwarves, all scattered in tents and makeshift shelters along the lake and between the trees, side-by-side with a small contin-gent of Titans. Our enemies had four Titans of their own, who were possibly fully powered with their essences returned, ready to go on a murderous rampage across our world.

The Titans would be indiscriminate when it came to the humans. We looked the same to them. If they did, for some reason, pause to give us a second glance, the favor would not be ours. My friends, my family . . . even I was in great danger of being recognized and pulled from the crowd, only to become an example for the rest of our armies.

We were little more than ants, going to war with buzzards.

And the Risen—we didn't know how many Risen had now come to join their ranks. I didn't envy Andimir, having to cut down those he had once aided with frequency. I knew the fight was more personal for him. For Camion, who had suffered at their hands, for Phelix and Audri who had been pushed down by a tyrannical Titan-in-disguise for far too long.

I also knew that personal fuel fed their fires. And those fires would burn. The rage could fuel them onward or it could overcome them, becoming a lashing, destroying fury that didn't care for the bodies it inhabited.

So, I worried, and I tried not to let the others see how much so. I worried that the small ranks of men would falter. I hoped the Elves would lend them courage and the Dwarves would lend them heart.

But inside myself, I couldn't find the glimmer of hope I needed most.

Once, deep in my chest, I had believed we could win this. That we could fight the Titans and save our lands.

Once, I had believed that if I had one single Scepter—only one—that would be enough.

Instead, we found one Scepter. And we lost it.

A loud voice echoed through the quiet forest morning. If I had to guess, it was Garrod, working off some of his drink. He had gone long into the morning before falling asleep half sprawled across the table. The image almost made me laugh.

Then my eyes snagged on Camion and my fingers slipped into my hair, my gaze falling to the blankets around me. I wasn't sure what words to use. How to say goodbye without removing hope. Without making him think that I didn't truly believe he would return. I wanted him to, desperately.

Maybe I was the one who wouldn't return. Maybe none of us would.

But I couldn't see this battle ending without casualties. I couldn't imagine the who, or the when. Or the how.

"I suppose I would be wasting my breath, if I asked you to stay back," Camion said at last.

"You would be."

"Will you stay to the back lines, at least?"

I sat up. The concern in those blue and green eyes was a match for my own. His raw emotions were almost enough to deter me from arguing. Almost.

"I'm supposed to."

"That's not an answer." He sighed.

"And I don't know how I'm supposed to let you fight without me. To wait."

"You never were good at waiting, Spitfire . . ." Camion murmured. He knelt down, brushing a lock of hair from my cheek. "But your people need you."

"My people have Annalea. They need me to fight for them, so they have a future to begin with."

Camion's gaze fell with his hand. "Annalea might be a fit ruler on paper . . . but you have given so much to do what you know in your heart to be right." He sighed again. "There are rulers, Natylia, and there are truly *great* rulers. You have to survive because you're the latter. Your people need honest, compassionate, loyal leadership after this fight. They need you."

"So not because you love me, then?" I teased gently.

The corner of his mouth twitched. "That helps. Call it motivation."

His fingers stretched for mine, warm where they brushed against my skin. I watched him for a moment, and ignored the clattering footsteps around us, the increased volume of nervous men vocalizing their concerns. After a minute, Camion tilted my chin up and held my uneasy stare.

"What are you thinking?"

"I don't want to do this without you," I admitted in a hushed whisper. "I know I *can*. But I don't want to. I—"

Before I could say the words forming on my lips, our tent shook.

"All right you two, come on." Jyn sounded remorseful as he added, "It's almost time."

Camion exhaled as Jyn stomped away. The words dissolved on my tongue. My heart ached.

"Be careful, Tyli. Don't do anything reckless."

"I can't promise you that," I answered quietly.

"Tyli, please."

I saw the panic in his eyes: in the tight set of his jaw, in the pull of his brow. My heart broke at the concern, the bald fear, but I said, "I can't promise I'll let you die, if I can intervene. Or Jyn, or

Meryn. Andimir, Sylvr. I love you all. I'm not going to watch you die. I couldn't live with myself if I did. Could you?"

His jaw clenched and his eyes squeezed shut. "No," he admitted finally. "No, I couldn't live with myself. Just be careful?"

"That I can promise."

"Come on," Jyn said from outside. "Everyone else is waiting in Izoryian's tent."

Camion reached for my hand and pulled me to my feet. He helped me with my leathers, his fingers warm and gentle where they brushed my skin. He tightened my sword's sheath while I checked that my new bow was strung properly—a gift from Camion, a surprise before we had moved to the camps with the armies. I laced my boots, making sure they were snug over my leathers. I started to check my arrows, but Camion reached for my hand, stilling their movements.

"We can't stall any longer."

I clenched my jaw, but he was right. My arrows were handpicked by him. Checked and double checked, I was sure; he was nothing if not meticulous. But I knew what waited this day, and I wasn't sure I was ready to face it.

"Together," Camion whispered, lacing his fingers through mine.

Jyn waited outside, Lethe at his ankles, eagerly waiting for Camion. Jyn paid the Zylaraa little mind. He was more solemn than I had ever seen him, and the sight made my heart ache anew. This was to be a grim day. The knot in my throat refused to loosen.

Izoryian's tent—the largest of them all—was tucked in the midst of the trees and guarded by a pair of dryads who bowed respectfully as we neared. We didn't plan to involve them in the combat. Helping regain my palace, protect our people . . . they had done enough, and if they needed to flee to survive, I would think none the less of them.

Most of the other leaders were already inside Izoryian's tent, as well as our Titan allies. Phelix and Audri slipped in right behind us, closing the flap. The people around me buzzed with nerves. Tension.

But none of them looked as afraid as I felt. Izoryian's hands were clasped in front of him, Andáerhyn positioned at his side. Garrod was oddly silent, but even he shuffled his feet now and again. Andimir and Lucian stood beside Garrod, arms crossed over their chests, eyes on the cluster of Titans. Only Meryn drew my eye, her expression firm, her attention focused back onto me.

"They'll be on us within the hour," Izoryian said quietly, breaking my thoughts. "We need to mobilize our people and make sure everyone is prepared to meet them face on. They will not stop. The Risen have endless endurance, and some of them will retain slivers of humanity. There may be familiar faces among the crowds, if Morland was taken. Lytalian too. Do not stop. Those faces are merely that—they will no longer remember you. That lingering humanity means nothing to them. Do not let your people falter. If they do, we will fail."

"We can take care of the Risen," Andáerhyn said with a smirk. "They don't stand a chance against my blade."

"Yes, but we are immortal, not tireless. They will keep coming, even when we need to rest. We don't know how many Risen Valdis has been hiding all this time."

"You'll want to split your ranks," Caru said. "You'll want to be able to sleep, if this battle doesn't end in a single day."

"Absolutely," Izoryian agreed. "Which is why every army was split into two. The back ranks will take over for the front, where combat allows."

"And the front line? Those leading the armies?" Marinus asked.

"Andáerhyn and I will lead the Elves," Izoryian replied. "Garrod has asked Andimir to lead the Dwarves with him." My heart stopped, then burst back to life, but Izoryian continued. "Phelix will be leading his own armies, and Meryn will ride out with them all. That leaves the Thraisian forces unattended. Natylia?"

I met Izoryian's eyes. He offered an encouraging smile, but I faltered, too nervous and unsure of what to say. Jyn watched me carefully and shook his head defiantly. I should have known he would never leave my side on a field of battle. But then I knew what I had to do, and I hated it. I hated that the option even existed.

"Camion, are you up to the challenge?"

He tensed beside me, fingers tightening around my hand. "You would trust me with this?"

"With my life and all of my kingdom. You would have permission to speak on my behalf, if needed. I would give you full authority to act with the powers that would be bestowed on you, if you were king, here, in front of the leading parties of every race and kingdom." I took in the small nods of understanding around the room, before I said, "And yes, I mean king. Not consort."

Camion leveled a heavy gaze on me, scanning my face before he swallowed the emotions I saw building in his eyes. Then he bowed his head. "Anything you ask, My Queen."

"I won't make you do this alone, though." Camion tilted his head, his brows drawn together. And so I added, glancing away, "Lucian. Help him. You've been trained to run a kingdom and he's been trained to wield a sword. The two of you will make fine leaders someday. So, work together. Lead my armies. Save our kingdoms."

Lucian dipped into a low bow. "It would be my absolute honor."

"Well, with that settled," Meryn said. I jerked at the abrupt tone of her voice. "Natylia, I know you want to fight. But you're a strong healer. We don't have many, especially with Sylvr doing shifts among the wounded inside the palace. What if you saved your energy for that instead?"

"Like a field healer?" Camion asked warily.

Meryn nodded, eyes still on me. "You could stay to the back line, but I have a feeling you've already been plotting ways around that. If you're a field healer, Jyn can defend you while you do what you can for those fighting. I know you want a purpose, and this might be the best way for you to have that. Would that be agreeable to you?"

"That would be a much better use of my energy," I said, with a glance at Camion. "I wouldn't be in one place for long, either. I'd be a much more difficult target to lock down."

He nodded slowly. "If that's what you want to do, I support you."

I squeezed his hand, a jolt of excitement running through me. I wouldn't be stuck in the back lines. Field healing would keep me in motion, keep my hands and mind busy. Nor would I be as inclined to worry—hopefully.

"Anything else we should know?" I asked, looking now to the Titans.

"These Titans will show you no mercy," Ushriya said. "But they have their weaknesses as well. Damage Boreas's wings. Take Cybele's weapons."

"Leave Valdis and Thanatos to us," Marinus said. "As much as you can."

I nodded. "And Draven?"

"If she shows, which I assume she will . . ." Juris grinned. "She's mine."

"And if they engage with us?" Lucian asked.

Izoryian sighed. "Hope you can occupy them long enough for help to arrive?"

"Try to get their life essences. A Titan can be reborn a million times over with their life essence." Meryn paused, scanning the room. "The life essence of every Titan is in their chest."

"Take them down and carve it out," Garrod said, wincing. "Got it."

"That's . . . a morbid way to put it," Jyn murmured.

Ushriya shrugged. "But true."

I swallowed. "Anything else? This hasn't been reassuring."

"No, but these might be." Ushriya passed each of us a necklace. Dangling from the silver chain was a pendant, a tiny gryphon that flashed blue whenever it caught the light.

"Labradorite," she explained. I glanced at the other's pendants—slightly different, but all gryphons, all small. "They should protect you, a little. I didn't have time to make more. They're not extremely potent, but they'll ward off some magic. Some diseases. It's the best I could manage quickly."

"Thank you," Izoryian murmured. In a louder voice he added, "Say your goodbyes, check your gear, and get mounted up. You have minutes and then—"

Andáerhyn cut him off, excitement in his eyes. "We ride."

***

I was frozen in place. Around me, the people I loved moved for their horses. I didn't know who to say goodbye to first. But when Camion waved me on, I knew he would wait as long as he was able.

"You all right, Princess?"

I startled at Jyn's voice. I hadn't heard him over the soft sounds of shuffling horse armor and the soldiers who filled the stables around us. He watched me for a long moment before I managed, "Not particularly."

"You shouldn't say goodbye." I opened my mouth to argue, but he shook his head. "I know you were planning out your words."

"What if I can't say them later? I don't know if I can live with the regret."

"Maybe." Jyn studied Camion and Izoryian, a short distance away. "But goodbye seems so final . . . so permanent. You know how hard he's been training. He'll fight with everything he has."

"I know." A lump rose in my throat at the thought. Images poured through my mind of the battle to come. I didn't like any of them. "But I sent him out there. On the front line. I don't know what I was thinking."

"You were thinking like a queen instead of a woman in love,"

Jyn answered softly. "Tell him you'll see him later. Because I need to believe that the way you two have changed each other, for the better, means that you're meant to be together. If not in this life, then the next."

A rare spread of raw emotion was laid across Jyn's face, but he wasn't looking at Camion anymore.

"I approve," I said, but my voice was small. Jyn's eyes snapped to mine. "I mean it. But if you think for one minute that I'm going to let you pursue Andimir without a *single* teasing word, you've got another thing coming."

Jyn snorted. "That would be ridiculous. I've told you—"

"You might have one day left. I might have one day left. He might have one day left." Jyn shifted uncomfortably, but I added, "Is today the day to lie about your feelings?"

"My feelings are irrelevant."

"You know that's not true. Do you honestly think once all this is over, if we survive, that I'm going to let you tail me for the rest of your life? Never let you live?"

"I have a job, one that I take seriously."

"And I've never expected anything else from you, my friend." I stepped closer, laying a hand on his arm. "But you're more worthy, more *deserving* of love than anyone else I know. I refuse to let you throw it to the wayside for your twisted sense of honor."

"I owe—"

"You owe me nothing." My fingers tightened, creasing his leathers. "You've done everything my father ever could have hoped you would, and more. You've given me *everything*. If we get through this, I'm going to insist you make some kind of life for yourself."

"You don't feel weird about . . ." he gestured to Andimir, then to me.

"No. I love each of you. You're both good men with big, loyal hearts. I couldn't ask more for either of you."

"Thanks, Princess," Jyn said quietly. His eyes lifted to Andimir a moment later and he sighed. "I think I'll take your advice."

"Hey, when you're done, can you . . ." I stretched to my toes, whispering into his ear.

"Anything."

Jyn moved swiftly. He pulled Andimir into the stables and I tried not to linger on how long they were gone. How long I watched as people scrambled around, readying, while I felt for my magic and hoped my life force was strong enough for what was to come. I sought Meryn, and anyone else I knew I needed to say final words to.

But Andimir left the stables alone minutes later, walking toward his horse, a small smile on his lips. I hesitated only a moment before I ran forward and threw my arms around his middle.

"Be safe. Stay alive." The words fell from my lips in a tangled rush before I could stop them. "Don't stop fighting. Get to me if you need help."

"Nat," he said gently, squeezing me into a tight hug. "I'll be fine. We'll get through this."

I let the words fall on my shoulders. I didn't believe them. But I didn't want to spread the negativity, to voice my doubts. They knew. So instead, I said, "We better. Our story has a happy ending. I refuse to believe otherwise."

"Ours would be a terrible story if it didn't," he smirked.

I pulled away, scanning his face. Memorizing it. "After all

this, I'm hosting a masquerade to celebrate. And we'll eat and drink until we don't fit into our leathers."

"I fully support this idea," Meryn said from behind me. I turned, to be swallowed into a hug that flooded my nose with the familiar scents of herbs and vanilla. "We're going to have to fight for it, is all."

"And we will," Jyn said. I stepped away from Meryn, only for Jyn to yank me against his chest. "We have this, Princess. We've united the Elves, Dwarves, and humans, even though no one seemed to think that was possible. You even managed to find more Titans who are willing to fight *for* us. We can do this."

"Easy," I said, around the lump in my throat.

Jyn's grip tightened. "Easy."

Drumbeats thumped to life in the distance. They were close. So close. I hugged Jyn, ignoring the painful ache of my clenched jaw. I closed my eyes for a moment, listened to the soft chatter of Meryn and Andimir behind me, soaked in the comforting coconut and hazelnut then, with a soft exhale, I released my hold. I had one more goodbye to make.

"Did you get it?" I asked.

Jyn nodded, holding a satchel out. The rough burlap scratched at my palm, the breath I inhaled slow and trembling. None of these partings were easy, but this last one made my heart ache in a different way.

"You're not saying goodbye, stop that," Jyn said quietly. His gaze was steady on my face. I dropped my eyes to stare at the ground.

"Regardless," I murmured.

My steps were heavy with the weight of what needed to be

said. Camion was standing beside his horse. Others were mounting up, riding out. He would be needed for the first group, but I needed five minutes. Only five.

I grabbed his hand and pulled him after me and, without explanation, led him away from everyone else.

Five minutes.

When I stopped, concealed in a nook of trees, I shoved the satchel into his arms. Nervous tremors shook my hands. His brow drew together and I said, "We have to hurry."

He nodded, throat bobbing as he pulled the bag open. His mouth fell open. "Tyli—"

"Wear it?" I blurted, before he could argue. "Please?"

The satchel fell to Camion's feet, a silver helm clutched in his hands. Its design was simple and almost indistinguishable from the plain steel the men used, but with three small differences. First, this helm was made from mithril—rare, precious, and worked on by only the most skilled of smiths. Second, on the back, a tiny amethyst heart was inlaid, barely noticeable unless you were close. And last, a Gryphon was etched up the left side. The symbol of Thrais.

"Tyli this is beautiful. I don't know if I've ever held a piece crafted so well."

"Will you wear it?"

He paused his study of the helm to scan my face, his eyes narrowed. "Only if you tell me why it's so important to you."

Emotion rose in the back of my throat, warmth building in my eyes as tears pooled. When I blinked, they skittered down my cheeks, and then fell to the dirt below. Camion cleared the space between us, tucking the helm under his arm and cradling my face between his hands.

"Tyli?" he asked softly, wiping the streaks from my cheeks with his thumbs.

I took a long, quavering breath, then said, "It was my father's."

"Oh." Camion's voice was gentle. He held my gaze for a long moment, then said, "I'll wear this with pride."

I slid free of his hands and threw my arms around his neck, nearly shaking the helm from its precarious perch under his elbow. Camion chuckled softly as he pulled me with him to rest the helm on the satchel. Then he looped his arms around me and tugged me into his chest, resting his cheek on my hair.

I curled into him, pulled him as close to me as I could. He still didn't seem close enough. I couldn't hug him tightly enough; I couldn't hold onto the warmth I knew was going to be leaving me for battle in minutes time.

So, I breathed in the scent of him. I soaked as much of him as I could into my memories: the soft lines of scars that traced his skin, the tiny hints of stubble along his jaw, the intense way he met my eyes as though he too was memorizing every detail.

"Stay with me," I whispered. My voice was hoarse, the sound barely audible over the pounding drum beats. They were closer now.

"You know I wish I could. But you need me out there, leading your armies . . . and I'm not going to let you down." He paused for a moment. "If the worst happens, know that I love you. And if my death keeps you alive, then it was worth it. It was all worth it." I opened my mouth to protest, but he shook his head. "You can't doubt that, Tyli. Not one minute of one day, not now, not ever. I need you to know I'm doing this because I want to. I *want* to keep you safe."

"I don't want you to die," I choked out. Tears spilled onto my cheeks. A frown curved Camion's lips as he wiped them away.

"Tyli, I will fight for you. But I'll also fight to stay *alive* for you. I promise."

"I'm . . . I'm scared," I admitted, so low I thought he couldn't hear the words.

"Can I tell you a secret?" His throat bobbed. "I am too."

His words rumbled through his body and I leaned into him, savoring the feel of every gentle rise of his chest, the steady rhythm of his heartbeat against my ear. He was woodsmoke and lavender, calm and safety, warmth and home.

Camion was *home.*

"I love you."

"I won't die, Tyli. Don't you dare say goodbye to me."

I heard the crack in his throat, felt his grip tighten.

"I'm not," I said. I felt the soft huff of air that meant he didn't believe me. "I need my king."

He stilled at that. I leaned back enough to meet his eyes, and the corner of his lips lifted, a nervous smile. "That will take some getting used to," he said, clearing his throat.

"Then I'll keep calling you 'my king' until you adjust," I teased, but my smile was half-hearted.

"I won't fail you."

I knew he wouldn't, even as his throat bobbed again. I studied his face slowly. One last look in case . . .

"Don't look at me like that," he whispered, blinking away the tears now filling his own eyes.

"Like what?"

"Like I'm never coming back."

"You're coming back," I said. "I won't accept anything else."

"I love you, Tyli." He leaned forward and caught my lips in a kiss so heart-achingly sweet, I almost didn't let him go.

When he stepped away, my fingers lifted to my lips, to the lingering sensation of his lips on mine. Then the helm was in his hands and he was leaving.

Before he got too far, I called after him, "I love you, My King."

The smile he shot me nearly made me forget how horrible today was destined to be.

Chapter 31

Only the river separated our armies.

I convinced Jyn to stand behind the front line. We could pull back once the fighting started, but I needed to see what to expect with my own eyes first.

Audri stood to my left, Jyn to my right, and we waited, watching the massive cloud of darkness rush toward us—the Risen. The reanimated paused at the water, but not for long, barely phased by the rushing river before they plunged in. A few were dragged beneath the current while others struggled across. They were truly mindless when their masters wanted them to be.

The Risen moved fast. Unnaturally fast. When they broke the shoreline, they would be on us in a minute, two at most. Jyn shuffled anxiously beside me, not happy that we were this close, that he knew he couldn't convince me to move back until the fighting started. My attention flicked to the front, to the solid line of leaders atop their horses. Garrod, Izoryian, Andáerhyn, Andimir, Meryn, Camion, Lucian, Phelix. A stern, straight line.

But when the Titans crossed over, at their humanoid size, the Risen parted to let them through. Their entire front line stopped a few dozen feet from ours, only the water and a small tract of land between us. Our line stiffened. Izoryian's horse shuffled nervously.

The four Titans scanned our gathered armies, then Valdis took a step forward. "Where is the little queen?"

Jyn grabbed my arm reflexively. I froze. Without thinking, I had lifted my foot to step forward. But Jyn had been right to stop me; I couldn't risk devaluing the members we had chosen to represent us.

Meryn slid from her horse, pulling her hood off her face and strolling forward. My heart thundered in my ears. I felt the cold hilt of my sword under my fingers before I realized I had reached for it. The bow slung over my shoulder felt heavy.

Valdis's expression morphed from curiosity to that of a predator who had finally managed to find the meal he was going to devour. My hands shook. I shot a glance at Jyn. Even he had paled as we watched tiny, unassuming Meryn step toward the Titan who seemed to grow a few feet before he even reached my friend.

No. She might look like Meryn, but the woman in front of me could handle herself.

That was Nahara.

And I had never been so proud as I was now, watching her face down an army unflinching.

"Valdis," Meryn shouted for all to hear. "You want me, here I am. Face me and be done with this. Banish your lackeys and leave the others be."

"Nahara," he purred. The sound sent shivers of fear down

my spine. "I knew you'd come out of hiding eventually. I knew I would find you."

"Not exactly hard when I reveal myself."

A smirk spread over Valdis's face, then he waved a hand. Cybele stepped forward, pulling up glittering magic. A snap of her fingers and two miles of river turned into solid ground. Solid, passable ground that spanned the line of our armies. The Risen shuffled, gnashing their teeth, ready to move. Valdis gestured again and Cybele dismissed her powers. A grin darkened her expression, her eyes bright with malice as Valdis crossed the remaining space and closed in on my friend.

He leaned toward Meryn, inches from her face. Too close. Goosebumps raced across my skin. Within me, fear and disgust warred against the need to protect her.

"Unfortunately for you I have another mission this day," Valdis said. "As for the others . . . they found out what you did to Eurybia. If you thought they hated humans before, well . . ."

He lifted his head dismissively and eyed the line of leaders behind Meryn. His head tilted; a flicker of surprise and then disgust skipped across his expression.

"Lucian. My worthless son." Valdis stepped forward again, eyeing the prince. "I wondered where you had gotten off to."

"Where is my mother?" The Prince called out.

The smile Valdis offered him was wicked, maniacal. "Your mother? Oh, my boy. Your human waste of a mother is long dead."

Tremors shook Lucian's shoulders, visible even from where I stood. Phelix reached out a hand, gripped his shoulder. Valdis glanced between them, then focused back on his son.

"I always knew you'd be a disappointment. I wasn't sure how much so, but I never imagined you would find the backbone to stand up to me, let alone to ally yourself with traitors and Sahrian filth."

"One drop of Elven blood is worth more than any breath you've ever taken," Lucian growled.

Valdis laughed. "One drop? Yes, tell me more. Your powers never so much as manifested. You know nothing of blood and its value, my *son*." He spat the last word as though it were poison, then waved a hand once more. One of the Titans moved forward. Without seeing his face, I knew.

This was Thanatos.

His cloak rippled around him unnaturally, as though curled by the dark smoke that rose from him like frosted breath. White hair spilled from under his hood, but none of this identified him to me.

No, I knew him by the way the Risen fell away from him. He was utterly, dreadfully silent, not even a footfall breaking the dirt. But his aura felt like death—like sadness and loneliness. Even from this distance, he felt like the end of all things.

Thanatos stopped beside his father. Valdis gestured, and his Titan son removed his hood. He was handsome, as was his father and Lucian. He shared their sharp jawline and Lucian's bright yellow eyes stared back at us. Dark horns twisted from his head, breaking strikingly from his white hair. But his skin was pale, ghostly, as though he hadn't stood under the sun in all his years of life.

"You thought you could seal him away," Valdis said, his gaze traveling back to Meryn, then sliding smoothly to Andáerhyn and Izoryian. "You thought you could take his life, leave him to suffer." The Titan began to pace in front of Meryn, eyeing her closely. "How does it feel to be wrong?"

My pulse raced. Valdis was cocky, smug, secure in his victory. I watched our front line, watched the leaders exchange glances like they saw the hole in his defenses too—and the casual, over-confident set of his shoulders. If we attacked now, our enemies wouldn't expect it. We might be able to get an upper hand. Something like hope flickered in my chest.

A ripple of indecision traveled through our front line, but then their swords were high and I heard the unified command.

"Now!"

The field exploded into a frenzy. I drew my sword, Audri doing the same. Jyn had his daggers in hand before I could blink, but he jerked me backward and away from the fighting. I tried to resist, but the first Elven rank flowed around us; I stilled, waiting until the Elves were in the fray to fully survey the scene.

Elves raced through the ranks of Risen, slicing through them with minimal effort. I spotted Andimir first, saw the wary hesitation on his face as he recognized the face of a Risen who charged his way. Still, his blade did not falter.

Our people began to fall to the screeching, scrambling Risen. I ducked between combatants, trusting Jyn to keep them off me while I tried to heal anyone with non-fatal wounds. The looks of astonishment on their faces almost made me laugh, but I kept moving. Blood splattered my breeches, as well as mud, and other bodily fluids I didn't care to think about. I kept moving.

I caught sight of Andáerhyn next. Izoryian and Phelix fought at his side, the three of them desperately trying to sneak blows in on Boreas. The Titan was too fast, and what he lacked in speed he made up with skill—and those wings that he threw around like shields.

Phelix took a hit and tumbled to the ground. I scrambled around the combatants, slipping on the damp ground, my eyes locked onto the blood that spilled from his forehead. I pressed a hand to his cheek, pouring a small vein of magic into him while ignoring the sharp stab at my side.

"Thank you," he offered before climbing back to his feet and rejoining the battle.

I caught Jyn's eye, tempted to join the fight myself, but he motioned to Ushriya, who had drawn Boreas's attention away from Andáerhyn and Izoryian. I inhaled sharply, relieving the ache that began in my lungs, and cast another look around for more wounded.

The closer we grew to the front line, the more I was needed. I could feel the draw on my magic—though, not a significant amount yet. Even as I knelt before wounded soldiers, I searched the field. Jyn knew I wouldn't be satisfied enough to pull back until I found who I was looking for.

Camion.

Valdis knew what he meant to me, and if the Titan had been looking for me, if he had taken my absence personally, Camion was in trouble. I couldn't find him, though, nor Lucian or Meryn. My heart thundered against my ribs. I dipped to heal one of the Dwarven commanders and smiled weakly at his thanks. Garrod stepped in, defending him until he found his feet.

My eyes scanned the field once more. If Camion was dead, I would know. I had to.

But my mind wouldn't be so easily sated. The fear pounded through my head as my blade sank into the stomach of a Risen who dove at me. Jyn's eyes widened at my lack of hesitation, at the cold way I shoved the body to the ground.

"We have to hurry," I yelled. "If we can't find him, or Meryn, or Valdis . . . If he kills Meryn—"

"I'll rob you of your sliver of a chance at victory," a voice laughed. "Oh trust me, I know."

I spun. Valdis stood over us and grinned. Jyn flipped his daggers in his hands, warming up his wrists, moving to step between us.

"Don't worry little queen. I've tasted your soul. I can borrow what I need."

Pain shot through my side. I gasped, then stumbled. My knees collided with hard ground. Blue and purple magic poured off my skin, flowing in dancing, sparkling light toward Valdis. He lifted his hand into the magic, spinning it, examining each tendril. I swayed and Valdis released his hold on my magic. Jyn caught my arm.

"How?" I snarled at Valdis. "How can you do that?"

"You think I wasted all the power you left in my prison?" He chuckled softly. "No. Boreas has certain powers with various forms of light, and your magic? It's filled with good, pure power. Thankfully, Boreas made it behave. Unfortunately, I can't take every bit . . . but I can certainly keep you on a leash."

He tightened his fist and my scar burned in agony as my powers swirled forth again. Jyn released my arm, and before I could blink, his blades were pressed against Valdis's throat.

"Release her." His voice was cold, uncompromising. The grip

on my magic tightened, enough that I choked.

"I think not," a familiar voice replied.

Boreas.

The winged-Titan slammed into Jyn's side. One of Jyn's daggers nicked Valdis's throat as he fell away. But Valdis simply wiped the blood off with bland disinterest.

"That's one problem taken care of," Valdis said.

"I wouldn't be so sure of that," I gritted out.

His head whipped to the side, focus broken. My magic was released.

Boreas yelped in pain. Jyn straddled his waist while Marinus and Izoryian pinned his arms to the ground, as well as those white and gold wings. Valdis growled the moment Jyn's dagger sank into Boreas's chest. Ushriya raced over to help and reached into the downed Titan's chest to rip free the bright white moonstone that was his life essence.

Valdis roared, his fury loud in my ears. He moved for Ushriya, but she threw the life essence to Aurial who lithely vanished into the fighting.

"Can you stand?" Jyn gripped my arm again and tugged.

I nodded. My eyes were locked on the Titans, though. If Valdis secured that life essence, he could bring Boreas back to life. It had to be destroyed, or taken far from here. It—

"Princess, we have to *move.*"

Kotori flew over our heads then, the moonstone gripped in her talons. Magic burst around her, but she dodged every blast, in a way no normal owl should have.

But the stone was safe.

And I needed to find Camion.

Soldiers blocked my path, deep in combat with the Risen. I pushed through, offering what magic I could as I went, healing the wounds that wouldn't take me hours or days. The losses were already so high. Too high.

I prayed the outcome was worth the cost.

Cackled laughter and screeches of fury caught my ear. I spun, my eyes darting around the fray. And then I found him, locked blade to blade with Cybele.

Completely alone.

One glance at Jyn and he moved to help Camion. But Valdis was back before I could even take a step, his fingers wrapped around my throat. Jyn was on him and then gone, pulled back by a crowd of Risen. He sliced through them desperately, but more piled on. I struggled for my blade, kicking and clawing against the Titan's grasp.

"Oh, little queen. One day you humans will learn what a waste of energy hope is."

"Hope ... isn't ... a waste," I choked out.

"And why is that?" Valdis crooned, his breath warm on my cheek. I flinched.

He loosened his fingers a small amount. I inhaled as much air as I could and spat, "Hope got me this far. And even if I fail, *they* won't, because *they* have hope. If I believe in anything, I believe in them."

Valdis tossed his head back and laughed.

A burst of golden light splashed over the battlefield. Valdis's jaw snapped shut as the Risen around Jyn were blasted backward, feral aggression twisting Jyn's expression. I didn't stop to ponder that he had used his magic. Instead, I took advantage of the distraction and thrust my blade into Valdis's torso. He flicked me a bored glance, waving his hand. My blade vanished into the crowds of armored men and women. The wound at his side healed instantly.

Then Jyn was on him and I was tossed to the ground as the Titan tried to defend himself from the rapid-moving daggers. I pulled my bow free, shooting Risen as they neared. When they were too close, I ripped the dagger from my boots and sliced as quickly as I could. Hot liquid splattered onto my leathers, my skin, caught in the braid that swung across my shoulder. I grimaced, then paused.

Blood.

I reached for one of the Risen I had cut down already, jaw clenched as I tried to pull magic from his blood. But the Risen weren't alive anymore, not truly, and the life force that lingered was tainted. I jerked my hand back. I could use the humans. The Elves, the Dwarves, the Titans. I could recharge my magic and heal more people.

A burst of heat warmed my back and I pivoted in time to see Meryn light Valdis's cloak on fire. He disengaged from Jyn, loosening the fabric and tossing it to the ground before spinning to meet Meryn. Another wall of flame rose between them and singed his skin. His magic rose to combat hers.

Jyn bolted to my side, barely dodging a wave of fire that threatened to consume Valdis. He yanked me away as the two Titans grew into larger forms, easily the size of the trees but not quite fully transformed. Our armies fled from them; the Risen that lingered were crushed beneath Meryn's boots. And still, I hesitated.

"She's fine, let's go," Jyn insisted, pulling harder. There was a desperation in his voice that sent my pulse racing. We dodged Risen, slaying a few in our retreat. I thrust my blade through the stomach of one, splattering blood as I ripped it free only to grab another reanimated being by the hair to slit her throat. Jyn winced at the expression on my face, but the more we fought the angrier I grew.

I couldn't help everyone at once. I couldn't save Camion, if I couldn't get to him. I couldn't leave Jyn. And, with a short glance over my shoulder at the growing Titans, I fought to restrain the flickering need to intervene between Meryn and Valdis.

"Princess, please, we have to help Camion."

The words snapped me to attention. The urgency. Jyn knew something I didn't.

He barreled into a Risen, shoving him roughly out of the way with his shoulder. That was when I saw what he already knew: Camion was struggling. His strength was waning against Cybele, especially with her newly boosted powers. She was dominating him, only his sword between her blade and his throat. Camion's arms shook as he pushed against her, the back of his helm pressed deep into the dirt.

Where were the other Titans?

Jyn dropped my arm. He was on Cybele before I could unshoulder my bow again. I scrambled across the gap, hurrying to tug Camion to his feet. He wobbled unsteadily and I grabbed his hand, pausing long enough to focus. My magic blazed to life, my scar alight with familiar pain.

"Are you hurt?" he asked, frowning. I shook my head, but his fingers lifted to my hairline, then quickly drew back. Blood. They were covered in sticky crimson. "Are you sure?"

I waved him off, pushing more magic into him until the wounds I could see had healed; and then I still offered more, gave all I could to make sure he was whole. Then I heard Jyn's angry shout. My attention switched to him.

Sweat poured down his brow. His daggers met Cybele's combat axes in angry clashes of steel, the blades chipping with each furious blow. She matched even his Elven speed without hesitation, her face also covered in sweat and blood. I lifted my hands, visualized her down, incapacitated, unable to fight Jyn . . .

Dark, seeping magic swirled from around my fingertips instead, the same I had seen before when anger had seared my mind and closed my senses. But instead of pouring from me, it was smothering me, snuffing my magic like it was a candle to be blown out with a soft breath.

I glanced to the side, to Camion who was wrapped in dark glittering tendrils of his own. My gaze jerked to the yellow eyes that studied me with intense interest.

"You're the little queen they're all so worried about?" A tight-lipped smile spread over Thanatos's face. "Why, you're nothing at all."

Chapter 32

"Let me go," I growled.

Dark magic swirled up my neck and curled around my face. Weight pressed down on my mouth. Thanatos clucked his tongue, stepping around me to where Camion fought magical restraints of his own. Thin, pale fingers reached for him, ribbons of obsidian magic coiling around Camion's mouth before he could dare utter a word.

Thanatos smirked and gripped his chin. "I've heard of your resilience. I'll enjoy adding you to my ranks."

Camion thrashed harder. The Titan laughed: a cruel, wicked sound that died to the chorus of battle. Then a flash of gold barreled into his side and knocked his thin frame to the ground.

"Release them," Jyn snarled in his face, digging a dagger into Thanatos's throat. "Now."

Thanatos's smirk spread into a grin. Cybele cackled with amusement, then Jyn was moving, lifted and thrown from Thanatos.

"Hasn't anyone ever told you not to toy with your prey?" Thanatos crooned, pulling himself to his feet. His dark magic swirled for Jyn but rebounded off the golden aura surrounding my friend. Thanatos dismissed his ally with a glance and Cybele winked before striding after Jyn.

A wall of flame burst to life. The dark magic recoiled and Camion and I slammed to the ground, rocks biting into my knees on impact. I hurried for my blade, and nearly stumbled at the authority in Meryn's voice.

"Leave the humans alone, Thanatos, or I'll burn you all to ash."

"I think you're all used up, *Nahara*." Thanatos turned his attention to his new competitor. "I can't believe my father hasn't already finished you off."

"Your father is a bit preoccupied." Meryn smirked as she gestured to where Valdis fought Izoryian, Andáerhyn, and two other Elves I didn't recognize. Not far off, Juris and Caru were fighting through a horde of Risen to reach Valdis as well.

Thanatos frowned. "I suppose I can't be surprised when he left his son to rot beneath a lake as long as he did. He hasn't exactly proven himself to be efficient." His yellow eyes narrowed on Meryn. "No matter. I'll resolve his failure."

Meryn ignited, a living mass of orange and yellow flame that spat fireballs at the Titan in front of her. Thanatos lunged for her and the edge of his cloak caught fire, sending dark clouds into the air.

I crawled the distance to Camion and reached out for him. My fingers brushed the raised lines on his arms, the scars. The rage inside me surfaced again. I closed my eyes, focused more magic into him even as he tried to pull away.

"Tyli don't," he said, tugging harder. "Don't expend your energy on me."

"We have to help Jyn." I coughed; the smoke burned my lungs.

Jyn had Cybele pinned. The moment Camion looked up, Jyn lost his bearings and Cybele gained the upper hand. Back and forth, they continued. Jyn couldn't gain ground on the Titan, but she couldn't seem to keep him down for long either.

I broke into a run as Cybele lunged for Jyn once more, the sharp blade of her axe aimed at his throat. My bow slid from my shoulder. I waited only half a second before I loosed an arrow that pierced Cybele's arm. She screeched in anger, ripping a different axe from her belt and throwing it in my direction.

Camion jumped to my side and threw his arm out, his sword between us. I didn't even have time to process his sudden presence. The hilt of his blade took most of the hit, but the axe sliced open the side of his thumb. Red burst to the surface. Jyn took the distraction to gain another advantage, yanking the second axe away from Cybele. Rage filled her expression and she gripped Jyn's throat with her hands. I grabbed Camion's arm, healing the cut as I shouldered the bow and drew a dagger from my boot. I caught Camion's eye. His throat bobbed, then he nodded and we moved.

Cybele froze, a flicker of doubt crossing her expression for the first time. I swung for her stomach, Camion for her throat. She rolled away, stumbling to her feet with a roar that shook the earth. My head jerked back and forth as I exchanged glances with Camion and Jyn.

Then we started sprinting. Cybele slammed her fist into the

dirt and sent cracks shivering through the ground under our feet. I raced for Garrod, who teetered on the edge of a deep line, then stretched my magic toward him. Purple and blue spun around him, pulling him back, steadying him. He gave me a grateful wave, then darted off to aid a group of his men overwhelmed by the Risen nearby. Farther off, Andimir grappled for Lucian, saving him from a fall into the widening chasm. My heart stuck in my throat until they were both solidly on the ground again.

Camion grabbed the back of my leathers. "Jyn," he said, urgency in the name. My attention shifted immediately.

Jyn was struggling with Cybele again. She had chased him, pushing him backward toward the massive gashes through the earth.

On the other side of the rift, Thanatos had taken long strides backward, his magic locked with Meryn's, the flames around her body incinerating any Risen foolish enough to step too close. My gaze darted back to Cybele.

Camion was already there, slamming into the Titan. I raced after him. She grabbed a fistful of dirt, throwing it into Camion's face, laughing maniacally when he recoiled. Her axe moved, landing solidly in his arm, and glee lit her eyes.

"Remind you of our time together?" she crooned. Her eyes flitted to where I stood, shocked. "Don't worry. I warmed him up for you."

My jaw clenched. Magic dove to my fingertips. I lifted my palms.

Bright blue flames raced across Cybele's skin. She stumbled backward, tumbling over her own feet, the most uncoordinated I had seen her. A growl rumbled from her throat. Then she moved and the earth trembled beneath her feet, raising over the chasm. I didn't dare follow. Sure enough, as soon as she reached the far side, the bridge crumbled behind her. With a wicked smirk, she raced back into the fray, killing any of our people who stepped too close.

I swore under my breath, in time with Camion. I looked up to catch his eyes, but he wasn't looking at me. Instead, his gaze was locked onto Thanatos—and Izoryian. I scanned the field for Meryn. A flash of flame burst to life beside a slightly larger Valdis, but Meryn was nowhere near us.

Jyn froze at my side as we watched, helpless, as Thanatos lifted Izoryian up and threw him into the massive crack in the earth.

No.

Not helpless.

I pulled up my magic, panting at the effort, the scar at my side burning in protest. But blue and purple magic swirled around, dipping into the crack and surrounding Izoryian, lifting him into the air and setting him back on his feet behind Thanatos.

The Titan's confidence almost bit him. But Cybele moved before the Elf could and the two tangled together. Camion and Jyn left my sides, to fend off a pack of Risen that had noticed our stationary position. I couldn't seem to tear my eyes away as the two Titans backed Izoryian toward the splintered ground. Panic rose in my chest. I unslung my bow and aimed for Cybele's heart. Thanatos batted the bolt away before it got anywhere near its target.

Then he looked at me.

And smiled.

He lifted a hand, a smirk spreading slowly across his lips. Humans around us began to fall: choking, gasping, boils springing to their skin, coughs filling the battlefield. Nearly a quarter of our remaining human and Dwarvish fighters succumbed. Even a handful of Elves went pale and started to claw at their throats.

"We can play, little queen," Thanatos called out cheerfully. Izoryian glanced my way for half a second and shook his head in warning.

That was all the Titan needed.

Thanatos grabbed him by the throat, lifting him high above the chasm. I didn't realize I was screaming until Camion and Jyn returned. Until the latter laid his hand on my arm and the former gripped my hand.

"Is there nothing you can do?" Camion asked us both.

Jyn lifted his hands, focused for a moment, then shook his head. "I don't know how to use it. Not really."

I sent a tendril of magic toward the pair of Titans, but Thanatos blew the sparkling power away as though it were nothing more than a cloud in the way of his moonlight.

"I'll catch him," I said, "I'll—"

A sickening crunch hit my ears.

Thanatos had tightened his grip, squeezed until . . . until . . .

My stomach heaved as Izoryian fell.

It wouldn't matter if I caught him now.

Cybele's shriek of delight reached my ear. Rage simmered through me. I wiped my mouth, then sent another arrow, and another, and another. Thanatos swiped them away as though they were flies on the diseased he left choking and pleading for air around the field.

And Izoryian . . .

Snuffed so easily. Right in front of my eyes. I stared at the spot where he had fallen for several seconds before Jyn's grip on my arm tightened.

"We mourn him later," he said. "We have to move. If Thanatos uses that trick again, we're in trouble."

I knew he was right. My heart didn't care.

But I still followed them north, toward an area where the ground hadn't been split open. I healed as we went, but Jyn yanked me away from any of those falling to disease. We weren't sure how the illness spread—magically, or the same as any normal plague would. All we knew was that the fallen didn't get back up, and they had only been infected for minutes.

Thanatos had to be taking some sick joy in this. If he wasn't, he was undercharged. I wasn't sure which. We couldn't afford to take any chances.

A drumbeat caught my ear. Shrill laughter filled the air, followed by a tiny storm cloud that blasted lightning around the source.

"I hope that's not who I think it is," Jyn whispered.

Another look and we bolted forward, following the surge of movement that raced for the new arrival. I couldn't make out much: a flash of white-blonde hair and a slender, leather-clad form.

Jyn groaned. "Draven."

"We need—"

My words fell off as a clap of thunder boomed through the sky and an arc of lightning scattered around the field. More of our people fell. I tried to do the math. The odds weren't in our favor. Especially when a new wave of Risen scrambled through the storm; Risen that were mounted on Marawolves and Kotsani, beasts that snarled and snapped and leapt around our people.

Jyn let out a low string of swears. Marawolves were bad enough, but none of us had forgotten the venomous Kotsani from our venture to find the Imber Scepter. The canine like animals, with wolfish faces and feline claws, twisted horns and shimmering runes tracing through their fur, were acting like vicious pets beneath their Risen riders. Sharp teeth nipped at anyone who got too near.

"Lucian," Camion said quickly.

He was gone before I could question him. Jyn and I tried to follow but Andáerhyn stumbled from nearby, nearly taking Jyn and I down as he tried to steady himself.

"We need to retreat," Andáerhyn panted. "We're losing everything too fast. Fighters. Morale. Stamina. We can't take these Titans with the numbers we have left."

"I know," Jyn muttered. I was surprised at the revelation, but he just shook his head. "I don't know what we do from here, Princess." He watched Camion, fighting side by side with the prince. Phelix wasn't far from them, his sword swings beginning to lag. "Maybe this was never our fight."

"So, what do you suggest?" I asked, noting the hysterical shrill to my voice. "That we just give up? That we quit? That we die, here and now, and the last year of our lives was all for nothing?"

"We always knew we might have been chasing the stars," Jyn said softly.

A Risen dove for me and I slammed my blade into his throat. "It's not a possibility, Jyn. I refuse."

Andáerhyn shook his head. "I don't see winning this, Natylia.

We should retreat. Buy your people time to try to flee. Get your family out. We need rest. But we don't have the people to run relief."

"Let your people say their goodbyes," Jyn said, twisting his daggers behind him and skewering a pair of Risen that tried to flank him.

"We're not losing this!" I screamed.

A loud roar echoed across the field, nearly cutting me off. The woosh of wing beats nearly silenced the combat below, a shadow wide and sharp in their wake.

I shielded my eyes from the setting sun with my hands.

"Dragon," I whispered.

The dragon from Thastrag, the Dwarven ruins. Meryn's dragon. He landed among the scattering Risen. Black scales glinted in the sun, his bright orange belly glowing with fire as he snapped at the Risen that rushed for Meryn.

A horn sounded and we raced forward again, our jaws falling wide.

Reinforcements. We hadn't thought there were any.

"Oh good, help. We needed that," Aurial said in my ear. I jumped, swinging my sword, but she caught the blade and grinned. "Good reflexes. Save them for *those*."

She pointed at a group of Risen that had tried to flee the new arrivals but, instead, ran straight for us. A familiar-looking form stepped forward, huge and bulky in shimmering black armor. He made quick work of them, before Aurial said, "I don't know who that one is but I'm glad that dragon brought capable reinforcements."

I studied the man for a moment, racking my brain to remember why he looked so familiar. Then it clicked. Fel. He and his band of followers had given us information about the catacombs in Thrais, when we were in Lytalian. And now they were here, an immense fighting force, cutting through Risen with all the strength of a fresh combatant.

A force of Numyra, a fighting race from the east, followed the Titans forward, bloodlust and excitement bright in their orange-toned eyes even from this distance. The lines collided and three more Titans melted into the midst while an angry force of Numyra dove into the fray.

"Spread the word. With reinforcements we need to give people time to rest."

"You need time to rest," Jyn said. I frowned but he added, "If you don't, you'll keep using your magic until you pass out or die. You won't be any good to us then. Just take a nap."

"I can use blood to restore my magic."

"Blood can't replace a few hours of sleep. Come on."

"And you?"

"I'll come too. I promise." He looked around. "But first we need to spread the word."

Meryn was already running toward us. Andáerhyn and Aurial broke off, running for the major leaders. The ones who were left, anyway. Losing Izoryian . . .

"Don't look so sad. This isn't over yet," Meryn said. Her brow dripped with sweat, her hazel eyes bright. She looked mostly unscathed, but for some cuts that ran the lengths of her arms. "We still have time. But we should probably rest while the reinforcements are fresh."

"We started sending word around already."

She nodded her approval and cast a look at the dark sky. "I can't believe we've been fighting all day."

"I can't believe it's still not over."

Meryn looped her arm through mine. "Don't worry. One way or another, it'll all be over soon enough."

"That's not reassuring," I said with a frown.

"Unfortunately, I know."

Chapter 33

"I know what I have to do," Meryn said quietly.

I jumped. The silence in the massive tent was so tense I could wade through it. All eyes turned her direction.

"What *you* have to do?" I frowned. "That sounds . . . ominous."

Her gaze dropped to the floor and my stomach flipped uncomfortably. "Meryn?"

"I need help." Her eyes slid to Andáerhyn, Garrod, Camion, then mine. "We need to replicate the Stave."

"Absolutely not," Phelix said.

"Are you mad?" Audri agreed.

Andimir frowned, tugging at his hair. "I don't know that I like this."

I lifted a hand, waiting until the others fell silent to say, "We can't possibly get their life essences. You know that."

"I have two." She held up the blue and white stones from Eurybia and Boreas. "I need two more."

I rubbed at my temples. "How do we get Cybele's?"

"Don't worry about that." Meryn smirked. "I have that taken care of. My question is who do you think you can kill? Valdis . . . or Thanatos?"

"Valdis," Lucian growled without hesitation.

"He's too powerful," Jyn said. "All the souls he stole from Lytalian, all the souls he's likely taken from the field . . . We can't kill him. Not easily, and certainly not with so many dead, wounded, or exhausted."

"Marinus, Ushriya, and Juris stayed out there to help the reinforcements so we could rest," Meryn said quietly. "Don't underestimate your allies."

"What do you mean *you* can kill?" I asked Meryn softly, ignoring the men's debate. I didn't like the way she averted her eyes at the question.

Andimir caught my train of thought. "Meryn? Answer her."

"If we can replicate the Stave, using these dead life essences and that of two living Titans, I can wipe their remains from the world. Thanatos, Valdis, they could never raise the other Titans as powerful Risen, and the Titan whose essence was in the core would be completely destroyed." She glanced around at the specific people she had studied before. "I need people who can forge them. I need Elven, arcane magic." She looked to me. "I need blood."

"Why hers?" Camion asked. "Mine was what was used to forge it in the first place."

"You misunderstand, Camion . . ." Meryn gently corrected. "I was . . . I need *your* blood. But the cost . . . if I fail . . ."

"It would be a death sentence," I said, understanding. "The Titans would know. You would have another target on your back, for the rest of your life." I frowned. "We're not going to kill them all for this?"

"No. I need the last two to be alive, or there will be no one left to power this Stave. It would be little more than a conduit, and I'm going to need a boost."

"If we do, I die, if we don't, I die," Camion said. "I don't see a lot of choice in this."

My frown deepened. "You know I don't accept that as the only solution."

"That's the worst-case scenario. That's *if* we fail," Meryn said. "Because if we fail, they will never stop hunting you. They would kill everyone in this room just to be sure they got the right blood to unforge the Stave again. And I wouldn't be able to help you. We only have one shot at this."

"At what, exactly?" Andáerhyn pressed, brows drawn together. "You're being cryptic."

"The Dwarves built a failsafe into the first Stave. In case the pieces were ever found and reconnected," Meryn started.

Garrod's eyes widened. "You can't mean—"

Meryn nodded. "A Titan can offer their powers to overload the Stave. One Titan, connected to the centermost, and in this case, living life essence."

"Why didn't we do that before, if that's all it would have taken?" Andimir asked.

My heart ached. I choked out, "Because the sacrifice would kill the Titan involved. No Titan would sacrifice their life if there was another choice." I glanced around. Caru and Aurial nodded their heads, confirming my thoughts. "Meryn you can't."

"I can," she said quietly. "I am your best shot at having this succeed."

"Why you?" Jyn demanded. He began pacing, glaring angrily at the other Titans. "Why aren't any of you willing?"

"Even after a day of using my powers, I still have more than both of them combined," Meryn said. Aurial and Caru nodded, but guilt lined their eyes. "It's not a slight on their abilities. It's how I've always been. It's the curse and blessing of carrying souls."

"Who will release souls into reincarnation then?" Jyn asked. I heard the desperation in his voice and reached out to grip his arm. He paused at the touch, as though he had forgotten there were others in the room.

"My powers will pass to another. A younger Titan, likely, a child. Or someone capable of carrying the magic until the proper Titan is born."

"You can't leave everyone in limbo waiting for a Titan or someone worthy of carrying your powers to be born," Jyn argued.

"That's not how it works," Meryn said gently. "If the next one worthy was, say, an unborn human? My powers would pass to the mother, then immediately to the child on birth."

"Why would your powers pass to a human?" Garrod asked. "That doesn't follow."

"Because Elven children are rare and Dwarven children even more so. But to my knowledge, there are no young Titan children in the world at this time." She glanced up at Aurial and Caru.

"Not that I'm aware of," Caru said.

Meryn continued. "Humans reproduce at a higher rate. If my powers don't immediately go to a young Titan, the odds favor them ending up with a human."

"A human? Any human could have the powers of Nahara?" Jyn asked. "You don't realize how utterly insane that is. You can't do this."

"Jyn." Meryn stared at him—unflinching yet pleading. He met her eyes fiercely, until tears surfaced and he had to blink them away. "Trust me. I don't want to do this anymore than you want me to, but . . . it's the right thing to do."

"I don't agree to this." My voice hitched. Camion reached for my hand, looping his fingers through mine before I added, "No. There has to be another way."

"I can set the mock Stave off. I can drain my powers. And, if I'm successful, it will end this war for you. Thanatos won't stand nearly as high a chance without his father at his side. I won't be leaving you an easy fight. But you can do this. You can kill him. And I can make sure they don't use Risen Titans against you."

"Meryn—" Andimir began.

She lifted a hand. "My mind is made up. We don't have time to debate this. Jyn was right. Valdis is a formidable foe. At his height, his powers nearly matched mine. And he's been stealing souls all these years I've been in hiding. He's stronger than he should be." Her eyes skated around the room. "I will do this for you. My dragon can help me take Valdis's life essence. He's already been working on Cybele's, with Marinus. But the Stave will have to be ready when we do. We will have minutes, at most, before he comes for his life essence."

"We don't have the materials," Andáerhyn reasoned. "There's no time. We need another way."

A small smile tilted Meryn's lips and she reached behind her.

When she turned again, her hands were full of the broken shards of the Stave of Thanatos.

"We have what we need," she said. "I just need you all to help."

"And if we refuse?" Garrod asked. His tone wasn't convincing.

"Then we all die. And eventually, your people too.

"Grim," Andimir murmured.

"But what about Sylvr?" I tried again.

"Sylvr and I have said our goodbyes. She knew this was a possibility. I haven't left her with nothing."

"But—"

"Let me do this," she pleaded. "Please. I know the cost. But I know what I'll be saving. We've never been against one for the many." Her eyes landed on mine.

"But it's you," I said, voice breaking. "I can't . . . I . . ."

She crossed the tent. Camion released my hand only for Meryn to scoop them up, squeezing gently. A curl sprang free of her tie, dangling down her cheek. "In all my life I've never known a queen to act so selflessly for a people who mistreated her so much. And I've never met anyone as loyal, as self-sacrificing, as *passionate*, as you. The world needs you. I had my time. I want you to enjoy yours. You're so young Natylia. So young." Her gaze flicked to Camion, then back. "Make beautiful babies with this handsome soon-to-be-husband of yours. Or don't, and spend your lives enjoying each other. I don't care. But I do care if you live. Because you *deserve* that much."

"Meryn—" I choked out.

"I have memories for hundreds of years now. And never in my life have I ever found such joy as I've had these last decades with you." My eyes burned and she added, "Take this offer, Natylia, from a friend who knows I'll see you in the next life. Live this one first. I can give you happiness. You gave me mine."

Tears rolled down my cheeks. I wanted to argue. I wanted to fight back, to shut her down with logic, to fight her rational. But she was right. And there was a hole growing in my heart already.

***

We set to work. I tried not to think as I did what she asked, helping Andáerhyn and Jyn piece the wood together. Garrod and Camion forged each Scepter again, each piece meticulously fitted to the Stave that we needed them to be. In between the sounds of our work, the night air was filled with the sounds of screeching, moaning. Dying. The voracious cackling of Draven in the distance and the thundering cracks of her lightning striking again and again.

Meryn left for a short period, long enough to claim the green stone that Marinus brought to her. Cybele was in a rage, but we had time. Not much, but time. If we pulled this off, her rage wouldn't matter. The detonation would kill her too.

I would hold the Stave while Meryn stole Valdis's life essence. Camion would shove it inside. I would fuse them with magic. Then Meryn . . .

Andáerhyn could have helped with this part. Jyn. I had silenced them both with a glare. If Meryn was going to do this, I was going to be there.

The field was eerily quiet when we crept out, despite the Risen and Numyra, Titans, Elves, and Dwarves that still battled furiously. Far off in the distance, sparks of magic and thunder showed where Ushryia and Draven still fought; the latter wouldn't be able to get to Valdis in time to be of help. Meryn, Camion, Jyn, Andimir, and I moved through the shadows, our group reunited.

One final journey.

I didn't try to stop the tears that flowed down my cheeks now. I wiped them away and kept moving. And when we spotted Valdis, Andimir and Aurial sent Fetian and Kotori to retrieve the life essence. They clawed at Valdis's chest, ripping him apart, while Andáerhyn subtly worked enough magic to hold him in place. Flickers of onyx caught in the moonlight between Fetian's claws and then he was airborne, flying for his master as Kotori tried to distract the furious Titan.

We didn't have long.

"Hurry," Meryn whispered as Camion wedged the wood apart, fitting the stone inside. "He can only buy us so much time. I won't let him die for this, if he doesn't have to."

Meryn's dragon swooped in unsummoned to aid the owl. He bought us minutes, but the roar of pain he released sent a new wave of fear through my stomach.

Enemies scrambled to Valdis's rallying cry. Risen from every race, Thanatos, Draven, they all came scrambling from the fields to chase the disturbance away from their master. I concentrated furiously on the Stave in my hands, ignoring the men who moved to block my magic from sight.

Another minute passed, and both the owl and dragon took flight, pumping their wings desperately to get away from the spitting Titan. Magic chased them, but Kotori dodged and the dark power bounced off the dragon's scales. Valdis paused, all the flurry of the previous minutes gone in a swift second.

"Where are you, Nahara?" Valdis cooed. But there was an edge to his voice, a carefully restrained fury. "It doesn't matter, you know. One stone won't do you any good."

The Stave fused into place. Meryn met my eyes. "I love you." Glancing around, she added, "I love you all."

Before I could open my mouth to utter even a syllable, she was gone, striding past me onto the field, the Stave tucked behind her back.

"Looking for this?" she asked, her voice filled with all the confidence and grandiose of a performer on a stage. "Because I might have what you need."

Valdis eyed her. She whipped the Stave from behind her back and his jaw dropped open. "What? How?"

"Because no force in this world, in any world, is stronger than love." Meryn glanced over her shoulder, the slight quirk of her lips bright in the camp's fire lights. Then she grinned, spinning to face Valdis. "And because damn, I'm good."

Meryn ignited.

The dragon soared above her in the sky, a cry of agony ripping from his throat. He knew. Somehow, he knew. The blaze around her ignited everything close by. I almost shielded my eyes, so intense was the heat, but I couldn't look away. I wouldn't miss her last moments. Not with what she was doing for us, what she was sacrificing.

Flames filled the night sky, flickering, bright, oranges, and yellows. A fire the size of our city. Risen fell, destroyed in the heat. They raced for her, then collapsed, their tether to this life shattered.

Valdis sprinted away, as though distance could save him. But with one final blast, Meryn's light filled the night sky. And as her ashes fell, Valdis crumpled and disappeared into the earth.

Chapter 34

Part of my world shattered in front of my eyes and I couldn't stop it. What she had done . . . what she had sacrificed . . .

Andáerhyn's horn broke through the chaos and our armies surged forward to confront Thanatos and Draven. Our one chance. A final stand against the last major players that threatened our people. Our lands.

I knew the importance.

And I was shattered.

My knees hit the earth before I registered the fall. The pain in my chest left me gasping for air. Lightning flashed across the sky but abruptly went dark. Draven must have fallen. Screams reached my ears, and the pain, the aching pressure, was replaced by something else.

Something toxic.

A deep, dark, uncontrollable anger.

Anger that smothered and drowned my grief. I pulled my

blade free, brushing off the hands that reached to comfort me. I didn't know whose—I didn't care.

We had fought and suffered and struggled. We had felt pain, hunger, exhaustion. More than one of us had nearly lost our lives. Too many of us did.

For this?

For our sacrifices to not matter in the end?

I didn't accept that.

Purpose ignited my veins and pushed me to my feet. My father. My mother. Izoryian. Meryn. Countless others I hadn't had the chance to identify yet. All pawns to the games of these Titans.

Meryn's sacrifice left me one job to do, and I wasn't going to fail her.

I had never felt particularly brave or strong. My skill with a sword was easily matched. But as I strode across the field, watching my people fall, determination flooded my veins.

Enough.

I lifted my sword and swung, not giving Thanatos a chance to fully register the attack. My blade shimmered with my magic—Myrdin's magic. A fitting final stand. The point of my blade nicked his skin before the Titan spun, his eyes flashing with anger.

"You've taken them all," Thanatos growled. "But if you think that will stop me, you're a fool."

He lifted his hand. A quarter of our people fell—coughing, gasping, tearing at the red patches that began to swell along their skin.

"Enough!" I screamed, thrusting my blade forward.

Thanatos dodged to the side, long pale fingers grappling for the charm at my throat; the one protecting me from the diseases he cast. I backed up a step, nearly stumbling into the people behind me. I caught a glimpse of golden light and I was steady. Thanatos's jaw flexed.

"Fight me," I screeched. I didn't recognize my own voice, or the venom coursing through my blood. "Right here, right now. One on one. Fight me."

"Call off your dogs, then." Thanatos's lip curled. "Humans are weak. I'll show you enough mercy to make your death only mildly agonizing."

He waved his hand and rose, doubling in height in seconds, a wicked grin spreading across his lips. I gritted my teeth, hiding the fear that coursed through me. How was I supposed to take him out like this?

But then, I hadn't expected to kill him. I glanced around at the remaining armies, the leaders, swarming around us. Ready to attack the moment I gave a signal. They would take care of Thanatos when I couldn't.

All I had to do was wear him down.

"Too bad Nahara was too weak to finish the job," he crooned. "She left you to me. So cruel."

His arms spread wide. Dark, curling magic flecked with silver spread from his palms, falling like fog across the ground. The effects were almost immediate. Humans dropped to the ground, clutching their chests while gasping for air. Disease moved through them, casting the Dwarves and Numyra to their knees before spreading through the Elves, who looked unsettled at the boils erupting across their skin. Even the mighty Fel's knees buckled, and he toppled over to lay still on the ground. The only ones who remained untouched were those of us Ushriya had gifted pendants. And even I felt a tickle rising up the back of my throat.

"Leave them and face me," I yelled.

Thanatos laughed. "You are but a flea, human."

"And fleas are persistent," I snarled under my breath. I took a deep, focusing breath and threw my sword to the ground. Thanatos chuckled, assuming my surrender, but instead I closed my eyes and concentrated.

My magic was mere dregs in the bottom of my soul, but I pulled up everything I had left, no source of blood near enough to recharge me. It didn't matter. I would sacrifice every drop of my life energy for this, to save as many as I could. I opened my eyes as the blue and purple swirls engulfed me, then speared into the darkness on all sides. My scar seared in agony; the draw of healing was too much. I had given so much of myself all day . . .

Hazel eyes flashed in my mind and I kept pushing. Meryn had given more. I wouldn't let her sacrifice be for nothing.

I looked around, at the armies who fought to keep the lingering enemies away, risking themselves against the Kotsani and Marawolves, and saw the suffering they endured. Thanatos would draw out their deaths and make each one excruciating. They didn't deserve this. None of us did.

So, I pushed my magic out in billowing waves, hoping that a strain of Myrdin's power could resist the evil pouring from the Titan in front of me. My knees began to wobble. Humans began to lose the fight, slowly fading and falling to the ground. Unmoving. My heartbeat thundered in my ears, that voice in my mind screaming that I was too late. That this was a lost cause, a lost fight.

My heart wouldn't accept that, though. I drained my magic until my legs gave out and hard dirt bit into my shins. I kept going. Warmth pressed into my side and I spared a glance at Camion, who looped an arm around my waist and offered me his hand.

A hand whose palm had been slit open.

I met his eyes as I realized what he was offering. The sacrifice he was willing to risk. If I couldn't control the magic draw, I could kill him. I could kill us both.

"Take it, Tyli. I trust you," he whispered in my ear. I hesitated, even as his fingers locked with mine. "We always knew we would end this together. One way or another."

"I love you," I murmured, tightening my grip.

Magic poured from our clasped hands, stronger now, young and powerful and so utterly fragile. Human. But it wasn't enough. Even as our magic shoved into the darkness, I saw that we were barely breaking through. A minute passed and Jyn claimed my other hand, his blood running down my forearm.

"Together."

"Together," I agreed, and tears filled my eyes.

Familiar golden warmth flooded my system, more powerful than it had been when I had used it before. His power revitalized the dregs of my own magic and boosted the offering Camion gave. Our magic surged forward, a mass of shimmering gold twisting into the purple and blue. The pain in my side dulled a bit, soothed by the new sources of magic.

Around us, the dark magic started to splinter. Thanatos's confidence faltered. His magic thinned, then fell off, suffocated by the magic pouring from our hands.

Thanatos's foot lifted, then slammed into the ground in front of me. The earth shook and I almost lost my grip on the two who only tightened their grips on me. But we held, unwavering, glaring up at him. Thanatos frowned.

Camion and Jyn remained steady, pulling me to my feet, offering support when I wavered. Andimir, Lucian, and Phelix stepped in front of us, their swords brandished. Roused to action by Andáerhyn, the ranks fell in around us—stumbling, shambling, sore and tired from the disease still pulling them down—but they came.

Elves. Humans. Dwarves. Numyra. Titans.

Suffering together. Fighting together. Willing to die together to stop this, to end the tyrant Titan who would kill us all and inhabit the world himself, if we allowed him to.

And when that very Titan turned and tried to cast a new wave of darkness over the crowd, it was Celestyna who stopped him.

Who rose to his height and plunged a blade through his chest, even as tears streamed down her cheeks. A conflict she had never wanted to enter, but that she had ended.

Thanatos's face lit with betrayal, then fell blank, his body crumbling to the ground in a heap as she removed the blade and released his life essence.

She stared at the stone on her palm, her expression twisted with sadness, and said, "It's over."

Chapter 35

A wave of collapse swept over the field. Men and women dropped where they stood, exhaustion, injuries, and illness weighing them down. I released Jyn and Camion, then fell into Camion's waiting embrace.

I sobbed, then. I cried until the tears ran dry and my chest ached from the effort of breathing. But when the tears stopped, when I couldn't find any more inside and my heart throbbed in a hollow, empty way, I pulled myself from Camion's arms and lifted the helm from his brow. And I kissed him.

Our people needed healing. He needed to bandage his hand. I was dangerously teetering a line between needing sleep and my body claiming it. But for one moment, one singular moment, I indulged in the reassurance that we were both alive.

Alive.

I pulled back, only for Camion to swipe a stray tear from my cheek. He looped his arm around my waist and I leaned heavily into him before I reached for Jyn, tightly gripping his hand as I surveyed the field.

Our losses were great. Most of the Dwarves were down. I didn't know how many lived, but too many were unmoving across the field. The Numyra were split. Some looked disappointed the fighting was over. A majority of the Elves were fine, even now healing from the diseases that lingered on their skin. But dotted across the field, golden auras began fading into the red sunrise.

Humans suffered the most losses. Not only in my own people and those of Kalum who had come to aid us, but also the Risen that lay scattered between them. Innocents, turned against friends and family by tyrants.

I glanced at Andimir, whose gaze scanned the field, and noticed the tears that pooled in his eyes. I slipped from Camion and Jyn and moved for him, wrapping my arms tightly around his waist.

"I'm sorry we couldn't save them all," I murmured.

His tears spilled over as he shook his head. "We did all we could. It doesn't ease the guilt."

I nodded and squeezed him even tighter. "I know. I don't think any of us will be rid of *that* for a long time."

When I stepped away, his pain was still written across his face. I wished I could wipe it all away.

"We saved some. We could have lost all." Jyn laid a hand on Andimir's shoulder and, for a moment, their eyes met. Then Jyn pulled him into a tight embrace, and Andimir's quiet restraint failed.

Audri and Phelix joined us then, holding up a limping Lucian.

"We'll do ceremonies. Burials, proper burials, for everyone,"

I said quietly. "I'll set aside a piece of territory, claim it as burial land, to be protected and preserved as such. We will honor these people."

"I know my people would be honored to be buried with our allies," Phelix said.

Audri smiled. "They would be honored to be buried with our friends."

"We'll be better allies and friends going forward," Lucian said, offering his hand to Phelix. "And I will make up for the mistakes of not only myself, but my father. Even if I'm not entirely sure how at the moment."

I moved to stand in front of the prince and eyed him for a moment. Then I wrapped my arms around his waist, hugging him tightly. I felt him jump in surprise, then he freed himself from Phelix and squeezed me back.

"You've done a lot, Lucian. I don't think you should beat yourself up too hard."

"That means . . . a lot," he admitted, voice cracking.

"I'm sorry about the loss of your mother," I offered softly. "And your father."

Lucian dipped his head. "I suspected as much. I don't think I've had a chance for it to sink in, though."

"As someone who knows exactly what you're feeling, know that I'm here if ever you need to talk. Or simply need a friend," I said, pulling away. Jyn glanced in my direction as I spoke, but he didn't open his mouth, so I added, "Andáerhyn will need to take care of the Elves. We need to find Garrod too. The Dwarves sustained the greatest losses out of the number they sent. I want to give them personal thanks, and if the Dwarves and Elves wish to be honored here, I don't want to ignore any customs and cause offense."

"It would be hard for you to cause offense," Andáerhyn said.

I spun at his voice, a wellspring of emotions in my chest. Not sure where to start, I blurted, "I'm sorry. About Izoryian."

"Me too. He was a good man. But he knew what he signed up for. There was always the chance of death."

"Still," I said, "I'm grateful. I don't know that we can repay you, but this battle would have gone very differently without your people."

"You owe us nothing." He looked to the field, shaking his head. "As Izoryian said in Eythera . . . this fight was always meant to be ours. We should have taken care of the Titans years ago instead of locking them away."

"All Titans?" Aurial asked, a small smirk tilting her lips.

"No," Andáerhyn said with a grin. "Not all."

She nudged Andáerhyn's arm. Caru moved to her side. He was covered in evidence of the battle; scars and burns the most prominent of them. Not far behind, and supported by Marinus and Ushriya, Juris walked with a heavy limp, a lightning shaped pattern of dark scarring branched across his torso and arms.

Andáerhyn shifted, gingerly avoiding putting weight on his left side, and I eyed him warily. "Are you hurt?"

"I'll heal."

"I could help."

"You shouldn't, Princess," Jyn interjected. "He'll heal fine. You nearly killed yourself."

The thought pushed my carefully buried thoughts of Meryn to the forefront. Splinters of pain tore at my chest, but my leathers were smooth under my palm. My ribs tried to shove themselves through anyway, the pressure so intense I couldn't breathe.

"Tyli?"

Camion's hand was warm against my cheek. I almost leaned into the touch. But a thought occurred to me and I shoved the rising emotions down. I brushed my fingers across Camion's wrist before trekking across the remnants of the Titan camp. For a moment, I struggled to find the exact spot I needed. The field was a mess of blood and sick and death. Cybele's remains were ribbons, shredded to pieces by Meryn's dragon and left to rot. But I ignored it all, instead focusing on a patch of charred grass that led me on.

A pile of ash glittered under the slowly rising sun. I didn't know for sure what was Meryn, what was the wood from the Stave, and what was remnants from the shattered Titan life essences. I didn't care.

Footsteps sounded behind me, gentle on the grass, and I glanced up. Jyn met my eyes, then realization clicked into place.

"I'm on it," he said.

He was gone in a flash. I knelt down, carefully pushing aside some of the ash. I knew what I hoped to find and I wasn't disappointed. A glittering red and purple stone caught the sun, shimmering with light.

Meryn's life essence.

Or Nahara's, I supposed, as I picked up the dragon opal and let it rest on my palm.

Andáerhyn appeared behind me. "What will you do with it?"

"Give it to Sylvr, maybe. That seems appropriate." I studied the stone. "No other Titans can use this, right?"

"No," Caru said, leaving Aurial's side to kneel beside me. "Our life essences are generated on an individual basis. More like souls for us, than stones. But when our souls are released for reincarnation, the stones become little more than decoration."

"We need to find the person who inherited Nahara's powers." I glanced around the field. "They're going to have to help us."

"And what of the souls that Valdis took? That he used?" Andimir asked.

Caru waved at the air. "They're here. All around us. I can feel their emotions still. Nahara released them, all of them, when she burned his body. You'll know who inherited her powers soon enough. They'll know, and they won't be able to stay away from this large a harvest."

"The power can't be . . . corrupted?" Andimir's expression was wary.

"No," Marinus said. "Nahara has the purest soul of any of us. That's the reason she could help souls cross over, and that's why it's always the young that her soul waits in until she's reincarnated."

"Then Meryn will return?" The hopeful tone in Andimir's voice broke my heart all over again.

"No," Caru winced. "Not as you know her, anyway. She will be Nahara. She will be able to wield her powers when she is of age. But . . . she will have no memory of you. Of this. She will make a new life. And depending on how she is reincarnated, it could be a human life."

"Or an Elven one," Andáerhyn offered. I wasn't sure I liked the smidge of excitement in his expression, but Caru nodded.

"So, we need to find this person who's holding her powers for her," I said. "Or Titan. We'll need to ask for their help."

"I might be able to help with that."

I spun. "Annalea? You should be resting, not . . ." Protectiveness flared through me. She shouldn't see the disease riddled, combat mangled corpses . . . What if she caught what these bodies carried? I winced. "You should go back to the palace."

"Nat"—Annalea stepped closer—"I think you should see this."

Before she moved, Jyn had her arm. He held out a pair of gloves and a strip of fabric. I had no idea where he had found them. Maybe he saw Annalea coming.

"Just in case the disease is infectious," he explained. Then he turned to me, offering over a small silver jewelry box.

"How did you get this?"

"Sylvr gave it to me before the fighting started. I kept it back at the tents. Why?"

"It's Meryn's," I said. The knot returned to my throat. "It . . . she . . ."

Camion's hand fell to my back, running a soothing path the length of my spine. I took a long breath. "Sylvr knew Meryn would . . ."

"She suspected." Jyn said. "I can—" His words fell off as he stared at the box, then he gestured to the small pile of ash.

I nodded. "Please."

Annalea had tied the strip of fabric over her mouth and nose, and pulled the gloves up to her elbows. Gently, she leaned over one of the Risen, holding her palm only inches above the deceased's chest. For a moment, nothing happened. Then a soft swirl of white light lifted from the body to rise toward her hand where it shattered and melted into the morning air.

My eyes widened. "You—?"

She nodded. "Sylvr explained everything. Or, she explained her suspicions while we waited. She wasn't sure but . . . she had a hunch I might be more susceptible because of who Nahara was to you."

My brows pulled together, then my eyes shot wide again. "The baby."

Annalea nodded. Audri looked between the two of us curiously, then rounded on my sister. "Baby?"

My sister put her hand to her stomach and offered a small smile. "I'm not far along."

The excited smile Audri offered her in return spread a welcome warmth through my chest.

"You're far enough along that your baby was considered a viable host," Aurial said.

Annalea winced. "That's . . . an unsettling way to phrase it."

Aurial smiled at her. "Maybe so. But it's a high honor for a human to carry a Titan's powers until she is reincarnated into a proper form. Your little one must have a very beautiful soul."

"This means . . . you'll have to release all the souls?" My certainty wavered as I considered my sister's face, seeing the innocence that was still there. Maybe it was simply the way I perceived her, young and immature. I had mistaken the two for so long, I never realized there was a difference. I was barely mature enough to be comparing.

"It's going to be a long few days," Annalea said softly, scanning the field. When she caught sight of the concern in my eyes, she added, "Don't worry. I'm up for the task."

"I'm sure you are," I said. I leaned heavily into Camion's side and rested my head against his shoulder. "It's strange though."

Jyn fell into place on my other side. "What is?"

"We've spent months running around. Now we have all the time in the world."

Chapter 36

"We need at least one member from every race."
"That might not be possible," Andáerhyn threw out. "You might find negotiations with the Numyra difficult."

"But we need to try," I said again. "Our last Council went down too easily. If we have representation from every race, maybe we can prevent this from happening again."

Lucian frowned. "And what of Valeria? She may well be the last of the Vampyr."

"Regardless, Valeria escaped during the Titan assault." I frowned. "We needed our best in the front, and she slipped past her assigned guard with ease."

"She's gone?" Audri asked. "That seems unsafe."

"We're going to search for her soon," Andáerhyn said. "She killed Devlyn on her way out."

Lucian's eyes widened. "How? Why?"

"She's a Vampyr and she probably felt like he betrayed Valdis.

She doesn't need much more reason than that." Andáerhyn shivered. "Don't ask for the details, you don't want them."

Jyn shrugged. "Regardless, I think our victory may hold her at bay from considering another attack."

"But that isn't something we should leave to chance," Phelix said.

I agreed, but only nodded. I let their words roll over me as my eyes roamed over the Council Room we sat in, discussing the future of our world. The room was unchanged, but *I* felt so different, even though we hadn't been in here that long ago. Maybe that was the grief talking—I didn't know. But I felt Meryn's absence keenly, and looking around, I knew I wasn't the only one.

Only a handful of days had passed since the battle ended. A few Risen had managed to survive Valdis's death, our only guess being that they had some Titan blood that helped them stay alive. Regardless, they were rounded up and executed. The only comfort any of us received from the process was from Annalea, who had released their souls immediately. At least in death, and in their next lives, they would be free of the vile beings they had been turned into.

Some small decisions had been made, even though we hadn't formed an official Council yet. Wulfric would retain his seat; we had been surprised to find he and Helyna sitting on the steps of the palace the morning of the battle's end. Apparently Aurial's owl had done his job well. When Helyna received Aurial's message, she tracked down the Titans we needed as well as recruited the Numyra—and all on her own. We couldn't be more grateful to the two of them. Without the second wave, loss had been a probability. I didn't like to think about it.

Lucian was to be instated as King of Wydus. He would send regular reports to Audri and Phelix, as well as myself and Camion, detailing reconstruction efforts, which included weeding out anyone who still sympathized with Drask's cause and, thus, might try to lead an uprising. If Lucian failed to report, a full and immediate investigation would be launched. For his safety, as well as ours.

Audri nudged my arm, breaking me from my thoughts. "We need to find time to crown your king." She smirked when Camion's face paled.

"You need to find time to *marry* your king," Aurial added.

Fetian cawed from Andimir's shoulder, as though he could sense the tension that filled the room—Sylvr was present. Talk of marriage, of futures . . . I frowned, trying to get a read on how she felt even though she stared determinedly at Ailuros, who was curled up on her lap. Meryn's felie had clung to Sylvr's side since . . .

I couldn't quite bring myself to think the words yet. Not without pain, at the least.

Sylvr's eyes were still red and swollen. I didn't know what consolation to offer. I felt her pain, acutely, and I didn't know how to cope with it myself. All I knew with certainty was that if I didn't focus on the monumental tasks in front of me, I might crumble.

I swallowed back the knot in my throat. "We haven't really discussed the matter, with everything going on."

"You could marry quietly," Andimir said. "Privately. Then announce his status at the masquerade. Simple as that."

"You run the risk of angering people at the break in tradition," Audri warned. With the battle over, Phelix was content to sit back and let his wife take the reins again, evidenced by how silently he listened to those around him instead of contributing.

"We've broken them already," I said. "Why not one more? Besides . . . my people have always been angry at me. Perhaps now, they'll give us some slack. We did just save them all."

Nerves tugged at my stomach, though, in contrast to my words. Nerves I didn't want to speak. Camion and I had talked about marriage in hushed, hurried tones. The ring sat heavy on my finger. With the pressure off, did he still want to marry me? And so soon?

As though reading my thoughts, Camion squeezed my hand. "If I'm marrying you, I'm happy. You know that. Honestly, I'm honored that you trust me with all the rest."

"You care, Camion," Audri interjected gently. "You'll be a good king, with a more than capable queen to guide you."

His cheeks flushed at the compliment. "I know you're right about that last bit . . . I hope you're right about the rest."

"She is." I offered him a small smile. "We can discuss this more later."

Audri offered a mock-pout, then said, "Once he's been officially declared your king, we can begin drafting treaties between the kingdoms and races. If that's agreeable?"

She looked to Lucian. He nodded, then added, "From here forward, Wydus will be a land of peace, not ill-intentioned opportunity."

"I look forward to it," Audri said, offering him her hand.

"You'll need a new High Priestess," Helyna offered quietly.

"True." I found her bright blue eyes. My chest tightened at

the sadness there. So much sadness lingered over us these days. "Do we have any potential candidates?"

"Any of the surviving priestesses, really. With . . . everything that happened—" Helyna paused long enough to clear her throat, shooting a wary glance at Sylvr. "It would be simple enough to choose one of the eldest, or most well-trained women."

"You can't still mean to worship Nahara?" Jyn's brow scrunched together.

I shrugged. "I don't really know what will happen. But one way or another, we'll need someone to lead our people toward their faith, new or old. Maybe that will mean worshiping no one, or the earth itself."

Soft murmurs built again. Debates over the religions, over the Council, over potential priestesses. I kneaded my fingertips into my temples, sighing heavily. "With all this decided, I want lists of potential Council members by tomorrow afternoon. Is that doable?" When all parties nodded, I stood. "Then I'm going to rest, if you'll excuse me."

The room filled with words of agreement and well wishes. Camion offered a clipped bow to the room before following me out. I looped my arm through his but paused in the foyer.

"Tyli?"

I stared at the room. So much was unchanged. Time passed, and yet this room stood still, the same way the Council Room had. The art, the rugs, the foundations . . . all untouched, as though the last several months of my life had never happened. My stomach turned into uneasy knots.

"I feel like nothing's changed," I murmured. "But everything's changed. I'm not sure how to be okay, but I know I have to be."

"I'll help you, if I can."

"You have healing of your own to do," I reminded him softly. "You've more than earned that much."

"So have you."

I leaned my head against his arm, inhaling the soft scent of lavender and woodsmoke. A small smile tilted my lips as I said, "Together, my love. We'll get through this together."

***

Behind the palace, tucked into the forest, was a small clearing with a beautiful pond filled by a soft waterfall. The canopy of trees was parted above, the sky a mural of stars. Camion had kissed me here, the very first time. We thought it was an appropriate place to marry, to finalize our vows to one another. There weren't many of us in attendance: my sister and Raul, Jyn, Andimir, Audri and Phelix, Lucian, Andáerhyn and Sylvr, Aurial and Caru. The other Titans had departed days before, refusing anything I offered for their assistance. Juris wore a self-satisfied grin while pointing to the lightning marks on his chest every time I had attempted to offer a gift of thanks. He had accomplished his reward.

So, we stood, tucked into the forest, waiting for our newly appointed High Priestess to arrive. She was young and beautiful, but well trained, and her patience with the citizens of Thrais had been unwavering. Her appointment had won me some favor with my people, as if saving their lives hadn't been enough. Regardless, we had heard words of thanks when we went to ask her to lead the temple—instead of words of scorn.

Andimir stood to Camion's right, Jyn to my left. We both knew I had asked Meryn. I had cried most of the morning over her absence tonight. But I had Jyn, a fact for which I was eternally grateful. I remembered the pain when I thought he was gone acutely. He meant no less to me, was no consolation prize. I was glad for him, and even more so that he didn't mind breaking tradition to stand with me.

A bottle hung from the tree behind us, a little vial of starlight that lit our path back to the palace as Camion had requested what seemed so long ago. Beside us, decked in a dress to match the moon, was the new High Priestess. She looked to Camion, then me, a soft smile on her lips.

"Are you ready?"

I paused. Studied him for a long moment.

Once, I had thought that Camion was the most handsome man I had ever laid eyes on. And once, I had been too scared that I might feel something for him to let him know. But now . . . now handsome wasn't the right word. That was too superficial, too shallow for the depths of this man. I wasn't sure a word existed, in any tongue, that could explain why I loved him so much. He was perfectly imperfect, a balance to my flaws, an enhancement to my strengths.

And I had never wanted anyone so much in my life.

Camion nodded, rustling the collar of his white cotton shirt. He had kept the collar loose, the waist tucked into his breeches. Casual, but somehow he still made it look elegant. I nodded slowly, casting a shy glance over my own dress—white silk, with an overlay of white tulle that was edged in purple floral embroideries. The gown was long and simple, with the corset loose and a top that clung around my shoulders in the front but fell into a deep, skin-baring vee down my spine.

Simple, elegant, and more than enough for our private wedding.

"All right," the High Priestess said. "Let's begin."

She went through her ceremonial chants. Many of the gestures she made reminded me of my coronation, and nervous butterflies fluttered through my stomach.

So much had changed since then. So many lives had been lost.

Camion squeezed my hand. I must have been showing my thoughts because he offered up an understanding half smile.

"If you're ready, we'll begin the vows," the High Priestess said cheerfully. "Both of you are to repeat after me."

We nodded, saying in unison,

"As long as there are stars in the midnight sky,
As long as the dawn follows the night.
Through ill and good fortune,
Through long days ahead,
Forever in love,
Now shall we be wed."

"And with that, I declare you married." The priestess smiled. She dipped into a low, graceful curtsy, backing away slowly as she went.

I met Camion's eyes, trying to read the emotions I saw there. Joy, a small hint of excitement . . . and at the forefront, soft against the other emotions laid bare, I saw reflected back to me the love and adoration that swelled within my own heart.

I didn't know what lay ahead for us. I wasn't sure where our future would go. But we had each other. And when he lifted his hands to cup my cheeks and pulled me into a kiss that swept me off my feet, I knew that was enough.

Chapter 37

With the new treaties in place, and Araenna in better diplomatic standing than it possibly ever had been, I surveyed the masquerade from my throne. Music filled the night air, soft melodies that calmed and soothed and paced the dancers spinning around the floor. And for once, I felt like I was in the right place, at the right time.

Even if the dress I wore was too big, layered, and a shade of green that I wasn't so sure about. Annalea's choice.

Since Thrais had missed the Autumn Solstice and the day of my birth, the decision had been made to decorate the halls in the decor that would have been used for those celebrations. The colors were brighter, cheerier. We needed that.

Camion and I had hosted a formal dinner early in the night, in a room filled with candles and moss and branches laden with orange and red beading. The ballroom had been similarly decorated, after I had ordered the Titan mural removed and put away in storage. I couldn't bring myself to burn it, but I didn't want those evil eyes darkening the hall any longer.

Only a fortnight had passed since the battle. Funerals were still ongoing; we wanted to ensure that every single lost soul was freed, that everyone who honored us with their greatest sacrifice was given a worthy burial. But more importantly, we wanted to remind the survivors that life would continue to move forward. We would never forget the lost. I could never let go of Meryn so easily. I still couldn't quite manage to think of her without pangs of loss searing through my chest.

Everyone in town had attended, all the allies that were able. The ball had spilled over into the foyer. I didn't mind. They were happy, and I wasn't inclined to squash their joy. Garrod and Andáerhyn were currently drinking their weight in wine, shipped in from Dalbran over the past week, Aurial cheering them on with riotous yells. Phelix stood with his and Audri's daughter, Scarlet, whom they had sent for the moment the battle ended. The palace was so happy, so teeming with life . . . tonight was about celebration, and happiness, and I needed to find mine. I took a steadying breath and looked to my right, where Jyn stood, stoically watching the dancers around us.

"Dance with me."

Jyn's eyebrow lifted. "What?"

"Dance with me."

Jyn shifted uncomfortably. "I don't think I should—"

"Oh stop," I teased. "You've done your job. And I've proven I can take care of myself. Relax. Dance with me."

"What about Camion?"

I nodded to where he currently danced with Audri. By the way her lips were moving, I knew she was chattering his ear off.

The thought made me smile.

"I have time." I smirked. "Come on."

Jyn groaned, then sighed. "For you. And only you."

He took my hand, leading me out onto the floor and looping his hand around my waist. I grinned, delighted, when he was surprisingly good, matching each twirl and dip with the grace of a well-trained dancer. When I tilted my head, he narrowed his eyes.

"I didn't know you could dance so well," I explained.

"I was trained. Even if I'm not very fond of it."

"Andimir likes to dance." My response was another heavy sigh, but his eyes flicked to where the pirate was dancing with Sylvr. "You should have some fun tonight."

Jyn rolled his eyes at that. "I am having fun. See?"

I lifted a shoulder. My grin faded a bit as I said, "I never got to thank you."

"For?"

"For everything. For being my friend, my guard, my companion . . . for putting up with me all this time."

"You know this hasn't really been a job for me in a very long time."

"I know," I said. "But regardless. Thank you for being in my life."

"It's my honor, Princess."

"Are you keeping the magic?"

He glanced down at the golden aura. "I don't know. Eáryn gave me special permissions because we stopped the Titans. I wouldn't be held to the laws of Eythera, and I could return later. I could guard your family forever . . ." Jyn's eyes filled with sadness.

"But I don't know that I want to outlive you by centuries. I don't know if I can watch your family line go on for years and not have you . . ."

His words fell off. I pulled him from the floor, so we wouldn't be in the way of other dancers, and then I yanked him into a tight hug.

"Do what feels best for you. I love you. Powers or no."

"I know. And I love you, Princess."

"Aw, are we sharing love?" Arms wrapped around Jyn and I, the scent of roses and sea added to Jyn's coconut and hazelnut. Andimir laughed too close to my ear. "I love you both. I hope you know that."

"I'm glad things went as they did," I admitted, slipping free. "I'm glad you're back in my life."

Andimir winked. "Of course, you are."

"Dance with me?" Lucian asked, stepping to my side. I nodded, looking at Jyn and Andimir.

"I'm sure you two will be just fine. Dancing. Together." When Jyn's eyebrows shot up, I laughed, really laughed—and realized that, even though happiness had become so hard to find, it was still there. Inside me all along.

Huh.

"Enjoying yourself?" I asked Lucian, falling into step.

"I am, but . . . I wanted to let you know I'll be leaving in the morning."

I frowned. "So soon?"

"Yeah. You deserve time with your family." His eyes darted around the room, then he added, "And I need some time to process everything I've been through. And what it means to be

King."

"And half-Titan. How are you adjusting to that? Any other signs of your powers?"

"No," he admitted. "I don't know how to explain it, but half-Titan feels like the simplest thing to accept comparatively."

"Don't be too hard on yourself, Lucian," I said quietly. "It's easy to forget who we are when we're being manipulated. Your father fed you what he wanted you to know. What he thought you needed to know to suit his purposes. That's not love. You deserved better than that. Your mother deserved better than that."

His throat bobbed. "I only wished I'd spotted him for what he was. I regret that I didn't save her."

"That's easy to think when you're looking back. Don't you ever forget that her death wasn't your fault. That's a road you shouldn't go down."

Lucian nodded. "Thank you. For being a friend, even when I didn't deserve it."

"I haven't always been so amazing either. Here's to growing up."

He laughed at that. Our conversation became lighter, and I was glad to see more of the friend I had known. Lucian was trying to do the right thing. That was a hard path even for the best people. I was proud of him.

And when our dance finished, when I stood to the side again, watching my friends and family mingle together, my heart filled with a kind of warm content I didn't know I could have. I had a new appreciation for the small things: for the way Annalea eyed the wine even as she sipped at her water, at the way Audri bounced from partner to partner, glee on her face. At the way

Phelix watched her with joy even though he didn't care to partake in the festivities as actively. At the way Sylvr stepped out of her shell, introducing herself to strangers with strained smiles and sadness in her eyes, and at the way Scarlet openly stared at one of the noblemen from Evenlea.

There was joy in these halls.

We needed that.

"Everything all right, Your Majesty?"

I started at the voice, then relented a small smile. Camion's own grin was radiant, spread across his face in a kind of joy I hadn't seen from him in such a long time. Even the partial mask he wore couldn't conceal the happiness that lit his eyes.

"Since when have you called me by my titles?" I teased.

Delight filled his expression and I knew he remembered then. Our first dance. My coronation ball. Such a different time.

"Fair enough," he said, offering his hand.

And as before, I accepted, letting him guide me to the floor. But this time there was no traitorous assassin hiding in the crowd. No looming mural, no watchful eyes of my mother.

No Drask, planning the demise of everyone in the room.

No Meryn to sweep me away to giggle about Jyn being overprotective.

"She's here in spirit," Camion said quietly, watching my face. "You know she is."

"I wonder if I'll ever see my friend again."

"After reincarnation?"

"Ever," I said with a quiet smile. "I would gladly befriend her again and again if it meant I could keep her in my life."

"I know you would." Camion freed his hand, tilting my chin

slightly so he could press a gentle kiss to my lips. "But regardless of what life we're in, we'll find each other. We'll always find each other. That's what families do."

Epilogue

Five years later . . .

"Tell Andimir hello for me," I teased.

Jyn rolled his eyes. "I don't know what makes you think I'm going to see him."

"He's been gone for almost a year. I know you better than that."

"You could come see him, you know." Jyn sighed. "He's your friend too."

"We will." I smiled at him, running a hand gently over my stomach. "Tomorrow though. I'll give you and your *fiancé* the night."

Jyn shook his head, exasperated, but his eyes had locked on my fingers, on the path they took over the gentle curve of my stomach. His expression softened. "Take care of my nephew. I'll see you in the morning."

My turn to roll my eyes. "Niece!" I called after his retreating back.

He only lifted a hand to wave me off.

Andimir had gone to help rebuild Lytalian and to help the survivors, the few people who had fled to Mendlyn or into the Twilose Forest when the Titans arrived. Not many, but enough. So Andimir had spent nearly a year sailing and rebuilding. Tonight marked the start of his first real break, a full fortnight home with his family.

I knew Jyn missed him, even if he wouldn't say the words. He might be open with his emotions with me, but he would probably never be truly public with how he felt about Andimir. The silver band on Andimir's finger said enough—I also knew the only reason Jyn hadn't gone with him to Lytalian was his undying sense of loyalty.

That was why, even though Camion and I were happily married, in a period of peace more prosperous than the humans had ever known, he refused to leave his position as my personal guard. I had insisted he make a life for himself, though. He no longer stayed in the palace, because as Captain of the Guard he had his own quarters. My soldiers and guards were better trained then they had ever been under his guidance. And if I ever did venture from the palace, which was more infrequent these days, Jyn was faithfully at our sides. Traveling was much harder with a small one and another on the way, though.

Annalea and Raul had moved from the palace two years prior—after they wed, a much more grandiose ceremony at my sister's insistence. They, with my own niece and nephew, lived in a beautiful palace on the coast of the Corothean Bay. We saw them frequently, along with Audri, Phelix, and Scarlet, who had become regular visitors to our lands. Scarlet had even recently begun to speak of a noble from Evenlea, the one she had been eyeing at the ball.

I built a tribute to Meryn near the temple of Nahara. A statue of wood and dragon opal that I thought only she would appreciate, especially when vines grew up and around the base. Late in the evenings that dragon of hers liked to come and sit with the figure. I mostly knew because there had been days when I spent long hours there, reading, or cleaning the monument, or simply chattering to the friend I still missed so dearly. But then I had become pregnant, and those days grew few and far between. I still missed her every single day.

"She woke up looking for you."

Camion's voice shook me from my reverie. I smiled at him, watching the squirming bundle in his arms, Lethe close on his heels. Our little princess cooed up at me as I took her from her father, blinking at my face as though she had seen me a hundred times and still longed to see me a hundred more.

But little Edana Meryn Areith was special.

I didn't know who I had to thank for this small miracle on my lap. Not because she was the most beautiful creation I had ever seen—she was—or because the tiny sigh she released sent my heart fluttering—it did.

No. Something or someone in our world had a sense of humor—the Gods, the Ancients, karmic comeuppance, I wasn't sure. But despite Camion's blond hair and mine of darkest black, my lavender eyes and his of blue and green, the little girl that cooed up at us had hazel eyes the color of the forest.

And red hair, bright as flame.

The End

Acknowledgments

Oh man. I don't even know how to begin these. I can't believe that this journey, this fifteen year journey to finally publishing the story of my heart, is coming to an end. Wow. What a crazy, mixed set of emotions.

Somehow I'm simultaneously ready to leave behind these characters and not ready at all. But Nat, Cam, and crew will live in my heart for always and forever and I'm so grateful that you guys took this adventure with us. These books wouldn't be what they are without readers, and I'm forever thankful you gave them a shot. <3

But, I do have some more specific notes, too.

To Corey — For living with my crazy and tolerating my excessive work hours. For supporting me when I needed it and not rolling your eyes too hard when I commissioned yet another piece of art. And most importantly, for supporting my dream even when deadlines turned me into an absolute beast. Thank you. I love you.

To Ethan — The love and light of my life. If not for you, I don't know if I ever would have started writing again. You are forever the reason I aspire to do better—my inspiration, my world. I love you so much.

To Chris, Wayne, Matt, and Ally — You guys have been cheering me on since I was 14, in different ways. Guess what? I did the thing! <3 And I'm so grateful that all these years later I still get to call you guys my best friends. <3 I love you!

To Hannah — You were the very first person to read Imber and I remember being *so* scared . . . and now I'm so grateful that not only did you help me kick off this journey, you've stuck with me and become such a cherished friend. Love you!

To Jesikah — Girl I am eternally grateful that you took me under your wing and guided me through this industry. I love you! Even if you think your blacksmith is bigger than mine. Because really though. Have you seen my blacksmith? ;)

To Jessica U — You are amazing, and I appreciate you so much. You've kept me going, truly, on days when I was at my wits end. And I'm sorry for what I did to your beloved Meryn. I love you!

To Chelscey, Sarah, and Briana — For being not only incredible beta's but amazing friends. I'm so glad booksta brought us together because honestly, what would life be without you girls. :3 To wine and someday crashing Chelscey's bar. You're the best and I love all three of you <3

To Jenn Buckler — You've been a tireless supporter of me and my books and I am so so glad to call you a friend. I love all of our conversations—about writing and otherwise, haha!—and I can't wait to see both of our author careers soar. <3

To Joe — Who helped me bleed my precious Camion without actually killing him. Thanks for your endless knowledge, your eagerness to help, and your friendship. You're amazing!

To my street team — Allisa, Briana, Casey, Chelscey, Danielle, Grace, Heather, Jamie, Kate, Kathy, Maria, Chelci, Nadya, Nicole, Sarah, Taylor V and Taylor F, Blaire, and Marissa

. . .You guys have risen again and again to every challenge I've thrown at you. I sprang another book release on you and you guys didn't even flinch. Thank you so much for all your help. I am SO grateful for you, every single day.

To the Lit Happens ladies — To a group of writerly queens who went from total strangers trying to do NaNo to real, lasting friendships. I love you girls. I can't wait until all of your incredible books are released into the world!!!

An additional note of thanks to my beta readers — Chelscey, Hannah, Sarah, Briana, Chelci, and Heather. I couldn't have done this without you guys. Thank you, for your time and your amazing advice.

Thank you to all the Bookstagrammers who have volunteered time and again to share my covers, to hype my books, and to just generally be supportive and amazing. You know who you are and you are appreciated beyond words.

And last, but so so far from least, thank you to the readers. Thank you for giving my babies a chance. Thank you for following them this far! I hope the ending was satisfying and not too brutal. <3 I am eternally grateful for you all, because without you guys, I couldn't do this author thing. So, thank you. <3

<u>Also by Tyffany Hackett:</u>
THE GENESIS CRYSTAL SAGA

About the Author

Residing in New York's Southern Tier, Tyffany Hackett is the author of *The Thanatos Trilogy* as well as co-author of the *Genesis Crystal Saga* with Becky Moynihan.

She spends her days chasing after her rambunctious toddler and her nights trying to make the words go. In her down time you can find her killing reapers, darkspawn, or battling for the horde.

Thank you so much for reading!! If you enjoyed the book, please consider leaving a review on Amazon! They're so incredibly helpful to authors! <3

SIGN UP FOR TYFFANY'S NEWSLETTER
to be among the first to find out about Tyffany's upcoming projects!
https://www.tyffanyhackett.com/newsletter

CONNECT WITH TYFFANY:
www.TyffanyHackett.com
Instagram.com/Tyffany.H
Twitter.com/Tyffany_H

Ventus Playlist

TOP TEN SONGS

- Battlefield — *SVRCINA*

- This Is The End—
  RAIGN

- Fire in My Mind —
  Andy Black

- Chromatica I —
  Lady Gaga

- Dynasty — *MIIA*

- Into the Unknown —
  Panic! at the Disco

- Face My Fears {English} —
  Hikaru Utada

- Heroes — *Zayde Wølf*

- The Dawn will Come —
  Trevor Morris

- Mechanical Heart —
  Really Slow Motion

Bonus:
- Rescue Me —
  *Marshmellow ft
  A Day to Remember*

Full Playlist on Spotify
https://spoti.fi/2YzviCb

Made in the USA
Middletown, DE
01 July 2020